A WILD CARDS NOVEL

DEATH
DRAWS
FIVE

The Wild Cards Universe

A WILD CARDS NOVEL

DEATH DRAWS FIVE

Written by
John Jos. Miller

Edited by
George R. R. Martin

TOR

A TOM DOHERTY ASSOCIATES BOOK

New York

DEATH DRAWS FIVE

A Tor Book
Published by Tom Doherty Associates
120 Broadway
New York, NY 10271

www.tor-forge.com

Tor® is a registered trademark of Macmillan Publishing Group, LLC.

The Library of Congress Cataloging-in-Publication Data is available upon request.

ISBN 978-1-250-22723-2 (hardcover)
ISBN 978-1-250-22725-6 (ebook)

Our books may be purchased in bulk for promotional, educational, or business use. Please contact your local bookseller or the Macmillan Corporate and Premium Sales Department at 1-800-221-7945, extension 5442, or by email at MacmillanSpecialMarkets@macmillan.com.

First published in the United States by iPicturebooks

First Tor Edition: November 2021

Printed in the United States of America

0 9 8 7 6 5 4 3 2 1

In memory of Mookie,
beloved and loyal companion for almost fifteen years,
and for faithful companions everywhere

Acknowledgments

The author gratefully acknowledges his obvious debts to all Wild Card writers over the many years and many books, without whose contributions this novel would have clearly been impossible.

Thanks, guys.

Prologue

JERRY STRAUSS AND JOHN Fortune walked through the double doors that opened onto the Mirage auditorium and stopped just inside the entrance to the cavernous room. Jerry didn't like the way it was set up. He didn't like it at all. About fifteen hundred seats clustered around a T-shaped stage, the runway of which projected deep into the auditorium. John Fortune had insisted on getting as close to the action as possible, so their seats were next to the stage, about halfway down the runway on the right side

The kid looked at Jerry. "What's the matter?" he asked.

Jerry, who had chosen the appearance of Alan Ladd (circa *The Glass Key*) for this assignment, grinned at Fortune in Ladd's semi-sinister manner. "Nothing, kid," he said. "As long as the tigers don't go berserk. If you haven't noticed, our seats seem to be well within claw reach."

"Ah, jeez, Jerry—"

Jerry could see the look of disgust on the kid's face, and forestalled further complaint by holding up his hand. John Fortune had been closely protected, too closely in Jerry's opinion, all his life. His mother, the beautiful winged ace Peregrine, had watched over him nearly every second of his existence. When she wasn't able to watch over him personally, she hired men like Jerry for the task.

Jerry, who usually called himself Mr. Nobody, had almost as many names as faces. It got confusing sometimes. John Fortune knew him by his real first name, but as Lon Creighton he was Jay Ackroyd's partner in the Ackroyd and Creighton Detective Agency. Peregrine had retained the agency for nearly sixteen years to help shield her son from danger. Actually, from even the remote possibility of danger.

The irony, Jerry thought, was that John Fortune's biggest danger was his own genes, and neither Jerry nor anyone else in the world could protect him from that.

"Okay," Jerry said. "It's cool. I guess I'll have to just throw myself in front of you if a hungry tiger tries to make you his early evening snack."

John Fortune grinned as they went down the aisle to their seats.

"Not much danger of that," the kid said confidently. "Siegfried and Ralph have been performing in Vegas for more than twenty years and no one in their audience has been eaten yet."

Jerry grunted. "There's always a first time for everything," he said.

Still, the kid was right. Peregrine's paranoia was rubbing off on him. Vegas, after all, presented a carefully groomed environment that encouraged visitors to relax, have fun, and spend as much money as humanly possible. Of course, he'd done nothing but bodyguard John Fortune since they'd arrived for the premiere of Peregrine's latest documentary at the Las Vegas Film Festival. Not that he was a decadent hedonist who habitually sank into the depths of every available fleshpot, but he'd hoped to catch the All Naked Review at the Moulin Rouge, or perhaps the charms of Brandy the Topless Magician, or maybe even the Midnight Fantasy at Jokertown West. Needless to say, having the kid in tow made all of that impossible. Jerry couldn't even get in any gambling. If he was on his own he could have hit the casinos that catered to wild carders, but he couldn't drag John Fortune along to those often-dubious establishments.

The show wasn't due to start for half an hour, but the auditorium was already thronging with patrons seeking their seats as performers went through the room, warming up the crowd. Not that John Fortune needed it. Ever since they'd arrived in Vegas all he could talk about was Siegfried and Ralph. It hadn't been easy to score tickets on short notice, but Peregrine had the connections and the bucks. Too bad, Jerry thought, she didn't also have the time to accompany them to the show.

As they made their way through the press of tourists they stopped suddenly as a tall joker with the head of a bird stepped before them and looked down at them intently with unblinking eyes. He was a lanky six foot eight or nine with long thin legs, long thin arms, and a long thin beak that jutted at least a foot out of his head. His face was covered by fine, downy feathers, though his sleeveless Egyptian-style tunic (similar, Jerry thought, to that worn by Charlton Heston in *The Ten Commandments*) revealed normal human skin on his arms and legs.

Jerry pushed himself protectively between the joker and John Fortune. He hadn't guarded the kid all these years only to have him pecked to death by a skinny old bird-man.

"It is the one," the joker intoned in a deep voice, punctuated by odd clacks as his beak broke off his words, peppering his speech with oddly placed silences.

Jerry suddenly relaxed. He didn't want to be bothered by paparazzi while working on a case, so he usually chose the appearance of old-time actors, hence his current resemblance to Alan Ladd. But sometimes someone in the crowd still recognized him. Or rather, the particular face he'd chosen.

"Oh, well," he said to the bird-faced man, "I get that a lot. Of course, I'm not really—"

He fell silent when he realized that the man wasn't listening. The joker sagged awkwardly to his knees, as if suddenly overbalanced by his long beak. He bowed his head and held his hands straight out, his palms up.

"It is he blessed with the strength of Ra," the bird-man intoned. "The power of the sun is his, the fire to light the world."

Jerry realized that the joker wasn't talking about him, but John Fortune. And Jerry also suddenly realized that they weren't alone.

They'd come from all over the auditorium, moving silently and swiftly through the tourists who were mostly too busy finding their seats to pay them much attention. A handsome, broad-shouldered dwarf. A sinuous, fur-covered female feline with claws on the tips of her fingers and toes. A lean bald man with a braided chin-beard who looked like a leather-faced rock star who'd somehow survived the turbulent sixties. A man and a woman, obviously siblings, floating hand in hand five feet off the floor.

Jerry realized that they were the Living Gods, jokers, deuces, and even some rather minor aces who'd taken their names from the old Egyptian pantheon. He remembered reading that they'd been driven from Egypt by the rising tide of Islamic fundamentalism, but he couldn't imagine the bizarre fate that had brought them to Las Vegas as members of Siegfried and Ralph's performing troupe.

They gathered around Jerry and John Fortune, kneeling before the boy, reaching out beseechingly to him. John Fortune looked on in consternation, but not a little disguised delight, as they were led in murmuring prayer by the bird-headed joker, who Jerry now remembered was named Thoth after the ibis-headed god of knowledge and writing.

"How do they know me?" John Fortune asked.

Thoth rose slowly to his knees, throwing the floating brother and sister a thankful glance as they helped him stand. Thoth laid a hand on the shoulder of the man with the chin-beard, the only one of the bunch who looked older than the bird-headed joker.

"My brother Osiris, who died and came back to life able to see the future, knew you when you were in your mother's womb many years ago."

Jerry nodded. "The World Health Organization–sponsored tour to study the effects of the wild card virus around the world," he told the kid, "before you were born, back in 1986 and '87."

Jerry had read all about it in Xavier Desmond's book, which had chronicled the fateful journey that had changed so many lives—his included. The plane full of aces and jokers and reporters and politicians had also gone to Sri Lanka, where Jerry was a cast member of *King Pongo*, the giant ape movie being filmed in the island's jungles. You might say that Jerry was the biggest cast member, as he was playing the big monkey himself. Jerry was then still the mindless Great Ape, a form he'd been trapped in since the mid-1960s. During the Sri Lanka adventure Tachyon had freed him from the ape body, using his mental powers to return Jerry to normalcy.

If, Jerry reflected, you could consider his post–Great Ape life normal. Not many would.

Thoth frowned.

"Where is your *achtet?*" he suddenly asked John Fortune.

"Ac—*achtet?*" the kid asked, stumbling over the unfamiliar word. He looked at Jerry, who shrugged.

"An amulet of red stone," Thoth explained, "given to your mother for safekeeping. For you to wear when old enough, to guide you in the use of your powers."

John Fortune glanced at Jerry, who shrugged again.

"You got me on that one," Jerry said. "Maybe," he added diplomatically, "Peregrine thinks he's not ready for it. After all, he, uh, hasn't come into his powers yet."

And, Jerry thought to himself, *the odds of him ever doing so are extremely unlikely. Still, sometimes you beat the odds. Las Vegas, after all, was built on that theory. Or dream.*

Thoth conferred with Osiris in Arabic. They looked at John Fortune and nodded.

"Yes," he said. "But Osiris says that your time will come soon." The old man smiled peculiarly with his stiletto beak, but Jerry could see warmth and benediction in his eyes. "The blessings of Ra upon you and yours," Thoth said, bowing deeply. He gestured at the other members of the Living Gods, who bowed as well. "We must be off about our duties," he said.

Jerry nodded. "It was nice to meet you all," he said. "We have to go now, too." He glanced at John Fortune, catching his eye after a moment.

"Yeah. Um, nice to meet you," the kid said.

They all smiled, bowed, and, murmuring their farewells in Arabic, drifted off to various quarters of the auditorium.

"Weird," John Fortune said. "Why do you think Mom never mentioned this prediction to me, or never gave me that *achtet* thing?"

"Your mom has a busy life," Jerry said as they made their way toward the runway. "Maybe she put it away and forgot about it. Or, maybe . . ."

"Yeah," John Fortune said a few moments after Jerry had fallen silent. "Maybe she thought they were all just nuts."

"Maybe. But I've seen a lot of apparently nutty things in this world actually come true."

"The power of Ra," the kid said musingly. "What do you think that is?"

Jerry shook his head. He did that a lot around the kid.

"I don't know," he said. "But I do know that it's almost time for the show. We'd better hustle to our seats."

As Jerry had feared, they were disconcertingly close to the action, which to his taste was loud, flashy, and somewhat nonsensical. John Fortune, however, loved it.

The show was Egyptian-themed, which explained the presence of the Living Gods, although there were also snarling white tigers jumping through hoops and a chorus line of babes tricked out in metallic bikini armor and Ralph transmogrifying into a leopard and bevies of lions and Ralph getting crushed by a giant mechanical crocodile and prancing white stallions and Ralph getting spitted on a giant metal spear and almost-naked dancing muscular guys and almost-naked long-legged dancing girls and disappearing elephants and Ralph swinging ten feet above the audience on a wire and an evil queen sawn in half by a great electronic buzz saw and endless costume changes involving flowing glittery capes and rhinestoned jumpsuits and thigh-high leather boots and puffy shirts with lace. And that was just on Siegfried and Ralph.

It was all so flashy and noisy and glittery and exciting. Jerry could see why the kid was into it. The white tigers were beautiful. Their apparent ferocity contributed to their magnificence. Siegfried and Ralph, though they wore a little too much makeup and a few too many spangles for Jerry's taste, did have an authentic rapport with and love for the beasts that they put through complicated routines. The big cats actually seemed to enjoy jumping through their hoops and leaping about like furry, four-legged acrobats.

That made it all the more terrifying when disaster struck like a lightning bolt from a clear summer sky.

Ralph was kissing a seven-hundred-pound tiger on his nose when the tiger casually reached out, put his paw behind Ralph's head, and drew him in closer. His massive jaws crunched together where Ralph's neck met his shoulder. Then the tiger calmly walked back up the runway, dragging Ralph's twitching body and leaving behind a smeared trail of blood. Jerry and John Fortune were so close to the action that a spatter of Ralph's blood showered down at their feet.

John Fortune made a strange sound in his throat. Jerry tore his eyes away from the chaos on the stage and looked at the stricken expression on the kid's face. At first Jerry assumed Fortune had been frightened by the horrific tiger attack, but then he realized that it was something more. Something terribly more.

"John—" He reached for the boy, cursing, as a man rushed by, bumped him, and knocked him to the floor. Jerry's ankle twisted, the man stepped on it, and Jerry felt something give.

Shit, Jerry said to himself. He didn't think it was broken, but it hurt like sudden hell. The last thing he needed was a bad ankle as the crowd around them dissolved into crazed panic. He stood and swore again as he tried to put his weight on it. No go. He tried to ignore the awful pain. Something was wrong with John Fortune, and Jerry was afraid that he knew what that something was.

"John—" he repeated. When he took the kid in his arms, he knew for sure.

John Fortune's eyes were glassy. His breath was rapid and harsh. His skin was flushed. Jerry put a hand on the kid's forehead. He didn't have to be a doctor to know that Fortune was running a temperature.

And was radiating a pleasant, orangish-yellow glow.

His skin hadn't changed color. It was still the normal pinkish hue called "white," if actually darker than usual, as if he were blushing all over. But the kid was projecting a dim aura, almost like glowing halos around his face and hands, that was clearly visible in the dark auditorium.

"Shit," Jerry swore again.

The boy's card had turned, and he was doomed.

The wild card virus, let loose on Earth almost sixty years previously by cold-hearted Takisian scientists to test its ability to turn ordinary people into super-beings, worked after a fashion. It killed 90 percent of those it infected. Usually in horrific ways. In many cases, however, the dead were the lucky ones. Another 9 percent of the virus's living victims were twisted in body or mind, typically in terrible ways. A final 1 percent did receive some kind of ability, ranging from the ridiculously useless to the cosmically sublime. Jerry himself had turned over an ace. But he knew that the kid, who had inherited virus-tainted genes from his parents, was most likely a dead man. But only if he was lucky.

"W-w-what's happening to me?" John Fortune stuttered through clenched teeth. He was sweating visibly now. His hair was plastered to his forehead and his shirt was already soaked as water ran out of his body in rivulets. "I feel so weak."

Jerry couldn't crouch over him anymore. His ankle was killing him and his thighs were beginning to ache. He kneeled on the floor, trying to ignore the tumult around them as the audience fled, Siegfried stood frozen in horror, and the company of performers stuttered around him in their bright costumes like a flock of frightened birds. Jerry put his arms around the kid, holding him close.

No one could help John Fortune now. It was all in the hands of God, or the cosmic crapshoot, whichever was in charge of human affairs. But whatever was happening to him, Jerry wouldn't let him face it alone. He'd failed to protect the kid from this most awful danger, the danger that Peregrine had foreseen and tried so fruitlessly to prevent, but he'd stay with him and hold him and comfort him as best as he could. It was all he could do.

"Your card's turned, John," he said quietly. He felt the kid's arms tighten around him, holding him hard. He heard him gasp. The kid knew the odds of living through this as well as Jerry did. The fact that he wasn't sobbing aloud spoke volumes about his courage.

Moments passed. John Fortune's fevered body pressed tightly against him; his breath was ragged in Jerry's ear. After what seemed an eternity, John Fortune said, "You've hurt your ankle."

"How do you know that?" Jerry asked, astounded.

"I'm not sure," John Fortune said. "I can feel it. Somehow. I think . . . I think that I can fix it."

"Hold on—" Jerry began, but, almost immediately, a wave of relief washed down Jerry's throbbing leg. It settled around his ankle like a soothing puff of cool air and the pain began to fade. After a few moments Jerry sat back and then slowly stood. He put his foot down gingerly. There was no pain. No pain at all. He and John Fortune looked at each other.

"How do you feel?" he asked the boy.

John Fortune considered. "Warm. Still scared. But—" He looked at Jerry, a smile dawning on his face. "—I'm still alive. I made it."

Jerry looked at him, even more astonished than Fortune himself.

"More than that," he said. "It looks like you're an ace."

"An ace!" the boy said jubilantly. His smile was beatific. "Yeah, man, an ace!" He and Jerry grinned like idiots.

"Take me backstage," John Fortune said. "I think I can help Ralph."

They looked up. The troupe of Living Gods hovered on the edge of the stage, watching them.

Thoth raised his arms to the heavens.

"All praise to Ra," he intoned, and the others took up his chant.

Chapter One

Turin, Italy: Cattedrale di San Giovanni Battista

JOHN NIGHTHAWK HAD ALWAYS been fascinated by churches. He'd been inside hundreds during his long life, from humble whitewashed clapboards in the Deep South to magnificent cathedrals in both the United States and Europe. As far as he was concerned, the humble and the grand both had their pluses and minuses. It was hard to experience a personal, intimate relationship with God in a cathedral. They were also usually extremely drafty. On the other hand, a cheap wooden shack didn't quite capture the glory of God on high and they were also prone to falling down after a very few years. Surprisingly, though, decades of experience had taught Nighthawk that both kinds of houses of worship were relatively easy to break into.

"Cattedrale di San Giovanni," the big man standing to Nighthawk's right read from the Turin guidebook he'd taken from his hip pocket. He gestured at the structure across the plaza and then looked innocently at Nighthawk. "Isn't Giovanni Italian for John?"

"That's right," said the other big man, who was standing to Nighthawk's left.

The big man on Nighthawk's right smiled. "Is this cathedral named after you, John? You're probably old enough."

There was quiet laughter from the other big man. The woman standing between them remained stone-faced, as always.

"Don't blaspheme," she said.

Nighthawk smiled and shook his head. "This church was erected in 1491. You don't think I'm *that* old, do you?"

Speculation about Nighthawk's age was something of an ongoing joke with his team. It was impossible to pin down precisely, although he was certainly older than Usher and the others. A small Black man with very dark skin, Nighthawk was about five foot five and maybe a hundred and forty pounds. At first glance his face appeared unlined. Close observation in good light, however, revealed a fine network of wrinkles around his eyes and mouth. The lines on his forehead also deepened to legibility when his face crinkled in laughter or a frown. He could have been a hard fifty or an easygoing sixty-five. His hair was still dark but his hands had the rough, gnarled look of someone who'd done physical labor for a good portion of their life. At least, his right hand did. His left was hidden by a black kidskin glove, despite the warmth of the early summer evening.

"Anyway," Nighthawk added, "you've got the wrong John. This cathedral was dedicated to John the Baptist. And if you're done playing tourist, Usher, you can put the guidebook away so we can get down to the job."

Usher took Nighthawk's rebuke good-naturedly and stuffed the guide back into his pocket. He was a big man, six foot four or so, and strong as an ox. Nighthawk knew that Usher was also the smartest member of the team. He was Black, but light-skinned enough that there was a time when he could have passed for white, if he'd wanted to. If he could have gotten the kink out of his hair. Curtis Grubbs was the other big man. He was white, from somewhere in rural Alabama, but somewhat to Nighthawk's amusement, was Usher's sidekick and yes-man. He wasn't quite as big as Usher, but he had a touch of the wild card and was as strong as two oxen. He followed orders if you gave them slowly and in great detail. The woman, Magda, was dark of hair, dark of eye, and dark of mind. She was from some European country that hadn't been a country for very long. She spoke with a slight accent that made her voice husky and sexy. She was ruthless, quick, and dedicated. Sometimes too dedicated. She was a fanatic. She followed Nighthawk's orders because he was in charge and also because she feared him, but he never knew when she'd get a wild notion to disobey a directive she reckoned blasphemous. He had to watch her constantly. Sometimes she was more trouble than she was worth, but, again, he had to remind himself who he was working for.

They're a good team, Nighthawk thought. *Maybe a little short on brains, but that was to be expected.* He had also been offered the services of the Witnesses, but turned them down despite their potent ace powers. Their tendency to grandstand often turned them into liabilities. He'd also passed on Blood. He didn't think a joker-ace who had to be led around on a leash so he wouldn't molest stray pedestrians or passing cars would fit in on a mission where stealth was necessary.

It was past midnight, but there were still people on the street. *Damn tourists,* Nighthawk thought. It was unlikely to get much quieter, so he signaled Usher to move. The big man nodded and slipped quietly into the night. He crossed the Piazza San Giovanni, keeping to the dark side of the street, blending naturally into the shadows like a big cat or a seasoned mercenary, which he'd been before signing with the Allumbrados as an *obsequentus.* Nighthawk figured that the big man had joined the Enlightened Ones for the pay. He had neither Grubbs's naive credulousness nor Magda's vicious fanaticism.

Usher crossed the plaza in shadow, unobserved, and after ten or twelve seconds Grubbs followed him across the square. He was not as quiet or as inconspicuous as Usher, but he tried hard to emulate him. After both men had vanished in the night Magda followed at Nighthawk's nod.

She was halfway across the plaza when a burst of sudden revelation struck Nighthawk like a thunderbolt. As always, it exploded across his brain almost too fast to grasp. The figures in it were dark and grainy like in an old-time movie, and the poorly lit scene they played was open to several interpretations. But one thing was certain.

One of the team would die that night. Nighthawk couldn't be sure it wouldn't be him. Caught in the grip of awful fear, the old man looked across the plaza at the ancient cathedral, wondering if that night he would find the answer to the question that had haunted him for the last sixty years. The gloved fingers of his left hand closed around the old harmonica that he always carried, currently in his inside jacket pocket. It was his lucky piece as well as a reminder of past friends. He smiled to himself, but without humor.

"Maybe we find out tonight, Lightning," he said quietly. "Maybe finally tonight."

Las Vegas, Nevada: The Mirage

PEREGRINE TRIED TO SLAM the newspaper down on the hotel suite desk, but since it was open it only fluttered limply. Still, Jerry got the message that she wasn't happy.

"You could have been hurt!" she said angrily to John Fortune, who watched her glumly as she paced about the room. "Even killed!"

"There was no danger of that," Jerry interjected.

Peregrine paused in her pacing and turned her eyes upon him. Suddenly he was glad that she hadn't packed her titanium talons for the trip.

"You know that how?" she asked in a voice gone quietly silky. Through long experience in bodyguarding John Fortune, Jerry knew that when she used that tone she was at her most dangerous. She looked at him with the eyes of a lioness sizing up an antelope for the kill. Even though she was in her late forties, Peregrine was still one of the most beautiful women Jerry had ever seen. Tall, lean, and athletic, her stunning wings matched a still-stunning figure that had made only the slightest concession to age and gravity over the years.

"I made sure we kept far away from the tigers when we went backstage," Jerry said quietly, but his words did little to mollify the angry ace.

"Tigers!" Peregrine spat, as if he'd said mosquitoes or something equally insignificant. "I would expect you to handle tigers." Jerry's chest expanded at the unanticipated praise. Suddenly, her eyes narrowed. "Maybe," she added. She paced some more around the room, then stopped and looked at her son. He was still glum. Still handsome. Still normal looking, except for that orangish-yellowish glow that hovered around his head and the exposed skin of his hands and arms like halos. "But how do you know that simply using his power isn't dangerous? He's just a boy. I would expect him to be excited when he turned his card. But you should have known better."

"Aw, Mom," John Fortune said, "I had to go help Ralph. You should have seen him. The tiger had grabbed him by the neck and there was blood everywhere! He would've bled to death if I didn't do anything. But I healed him. Ask Jerry. He was right there all the while, making sure nobody crowded us or anything. I just held Ralph and concentrated and he healed right up. It was easy."

"No," Jerry said, shaking his head, "your mother's right. There's no telling how dangerous using your power might be—"

"Listen to him," Peregrine said.

"It's not dangerous," John Fortune said, his impatience showing in his tone. "I'm *fine*."

Peregrine put the back of her hand against his forehead. "You feel warm to me."

"Aw, Mom."

"Could just be the effects of a speeded-up metabolism," Jerry offered.

"Could be," Peregrine said. Suddenly, she enwrapped her son in her arms and wings and held him to her tightly. She closed her eyes, fighting back tears. "If you only knew how worried I've been for you, all these years."

"Aw, Mom," John Fortune said again, his head muffled against her chest. Jerry was envious. "I'm all right. I knew I would be. My card turned and now I'm an ace, just like you and my father. I mean, Fortunato."

Peregrine nodded, unable to speak for a moment as years of desperate worry seemed to squeeze out of her body. But some still remained.

"Promise me one thing," she said as she still held him tightly. "Don't use your power again until we get home and have you checked out at the Jokertown Clinic."

"But what if I have to save someone—"

She pulled away, and held him at arm's length.

"John," she said sternly, "you have your whole life ahead of you. You have years and years to save people. And listen to me. There's a big lesson you have to learn right now."

"What's that?" the kid asked.

"No matter how powerful you are, no matter how much time and effort and sweat and blood you expend," Peregrine said slowly, coming down hard on each and every word, "you can't save everyone."

The boy was silent for a long moment, as if digesting her words.

"All right," John Fortune said quietly.

"Believe me," Peregrine said.

Jerry nodded. "Believe her."

He knew. Sometimes that was the hardest thing about being an ace of all.

♠

Branson, Missouri: The Peaceable Kingdom

BILLY RAY WAS IN Loaves and Fishes, lingering over lunch and wishing he were anywhere in the world except here, when the kid tracked him down. Ray didn't particularly look like an ace, let alone a dangerous one. He was an average-sized five ten, one hundred and seventy pounds. His suit was expensive and neat, without wrinkle, spot, or blemish. Though a couple of years on the wrong side of forty, he looked younger. His green eyes were sleepy-looking. His features were bland, if a little ill-fitting. His broken-angled, rather prominent nose stood out from the rest of his face. He moved slowly, almost languidly. He was even more bored than he looked.

As the kid approached, Ray looked up from his plate piled high with beef ribs and chicken fried steak with gravy and biscuits, green beans, corn on the cob, and real scratch-made mashed potatoes, not from a box. He liked Loaves and Fishes because it was all you could eat, but lately he'd been losing interest in food as well as everything else. He knew what was wrong, but he knew also he couldn't do a damn thing about it.

"Hi, Mr. Ray," the kid said.

Ray sighed for about the billionth time and said, for about the billionth time, "I told you not to call me mister."

"Okay, Billy." Ray knew that wouldn't last long. It never did. If the kid was anything, he was respectful. Alejandro Jesús y Maria C de Baca looked like he was about fourteen years old. Slight, slim, dark-haired, dark-eyed, always smiling, always cheerful, fresh out of spook school and so goddamned respectful that he sirred waiters. It was clear to Ray that Nephi Callendar, their boss at the Secret Service, had teamed them up specifically to annoy Ray.

"Say, mi—uh, Billy, President Barnett wants to see you, right away."

Ray sighed. God, he hoped that it wasn't for another prayer session. "Did he say why?"

The kid shook his head. "Nope. I was with him when he saw something in the paper that got him real excited, and he wanted to speak to you right away."

Ray sighed again. He caught himself, realizing that he was doing entirely too much of that lately. He looked down at his lunch. He wasn't hungry now, anyway.

"You want some lunch, kid?" Ray asked his colleague.

"I already ate, sir, uh, Billy. But it'd be a shame to waste all that food. I can box it up and drop it down at the homeless shelter after our shift."

Ray nodded.

"You do that," he said. He left Loaves and Fishes and strolled through Barnett's vision of Heaven on Earth to his headquarters centrally located on the top floor of the Angels' Bower hotel. He had to cut through the part of the park called New Jerusalem to reach it. As always, the Via Dolorosa was crowded with tourists, so Ray took the back way that looped around the rides, exhibits, and concessions. He went by the twenty-foot-high statues of the Twelve, wondering, not for the first time, how they'd decided which apostle was bald, which one had a big honker, and where in the hell Judas was. He could hear the faint screams of the faithful as the Rapture took them to Heaven and then dropped down to the Pit with a stomach-flipping hundred-and-eighty-degree turn that piled on over three gs of acceleration as it fell forty stories straight down to Hell.

Roller coasters, Ray thought disgruntledly. Maybe he should take a ride. Put some excitement into his life.

It was, he had to admit, his own fault. He'd smart-assed his way here, calling his boss "Nehi" one time too many. Before the ink had dried on his orders he'd found himself, accompanied by the kid, exiled to the suburbs of Branson fucking Missouri to wet-nurse an ex-president as he whiled away the years running his crazy-ass theme park in the middle of redneck Heaven. Of course, by law every ex-president was accorded Secret Service protection, but the odds of Barnett being stalked by an assassin in the Peaceable Kingdom were about as great as him running a Pagans Get In Free weekend special.

It was a hell of a way to wrap up his career, but not entirely unexpected. Ray had ruffled too many feathers along the way, and not just by being a smart-ass. He'd played a major role in breaking the Card Shark conspiracy and saving Jerusalem—the real one, not Barnett's Disneyfied version—from getting A-bombed to hell, but it had cost him not only April Harvest, the only woman he'd ever come close to loving, but also a meaningful career in the government. As it turned out, the government had been riddled with Card Sharks, and no one was exactly pleased that Ray helped expose that little fact. Sometimes Ray wondered if they'd rooted them all out. Probably not. Probably some unexposed Sharks were still pulling strings. And that had been the problem. Ray had embarrassed the string pullers and decision makers, the powers behind the throne and the voices in charge. Publicly he was a hero. Privately he was just another wild carder who knew too much. A wild carder with a reputation for flying off the handle and running his mouth when peeved.

That explained the next seven years spent in the shitholes of the world, but at least the tedium of those years had been broken up by episodes of real excitement. Among other things, he'd helped the mujahideen against the Soviets, and when the Soviet Union went to pieces he helped the people of Afghanistan against the mujahideen. He served a tour in Peru, teaching the Shining Path the real meaning of fear. He was on the team of international aces that went into Baghdad and snatched the tin-plated dictator Saddam Hussein, catching him cowering in his gold-fixtured bathtub, after Saddam had kicked the UN weapon inspectors out of his crappy excuse for a country.

Ray hadn't minded the lack of recognition or applause. He'd spent seven years doing what he did best, kicking ass if occasionally forgetting to take down names. But now, he was rotting in paradise.

He breezed into Barnett's office. Sally Lou, Barnett's blond receptionist, looked up from her magazine. She was sleek and sexy-looking, and Ray suspected that Barnett had hired her for something other than her typing skills. She could have put some of that long-sought excitement back into his life, but it seemed to Ray that, as far as she was concerned, he was just another one of the hired help.

"The president—"

"Yeah, I know." He waved as he strode by. He paused at Barnett's door, nodding at the Secret Service guys standing to either side of it, nats in dark suits and sunglasses, for Christ's sake, knocked once, and went on in before its occupant could reply. What more could they do to him for being a smart-ass? Send him to Antarctica? Even that would be an improvement over his current situation.

"You wanted to see me?" Ray asked, stopping before the big desk and the man behind it, who was reading a newspaper spread out on its teak surface.

Barnett smiled. "Yes, I did," he said.

Leo Barnett was still a handsome man, even after serving eight years as president of the United States. He was tall and still slim even though he was pushing sixty, blond-haired and blue-eyed, and dimpled as a baby's butt. Ray couldn't help wondering how he did it. Ray had been with the Justice Department for almost twenty-five years. He'd spent a good portion of that time bodyguarding presidents and presidential candidates, and he'd noticed early on that the presidency, even just running for the office, tended to wear a man down. It put bags under his eyes, creases in his face, and dye in his hair. Not Barnett, though. He looked as wrinkle-free today as he did the day he ascended to the office. Ray wondered what his secret was.

"Have you seen the papers today, Billy?" Barnett asked, slapping the open newspaper with an immaculately manicured hand.

Ray shook his head. He didn't bother reading the news. He was more used to making it.

"It seems as if a new ace has joined our constellation of heroes."

"Is that so?" Ray asked with a modicum of interest.

"Indeed it is," Barnett said, and looked down at the paper spread out in front of him and began to read. ". . . 'Ralph Holstedt, partner and star performer in the famous Siegfried and Ralph magic act featuring white tigers and other dangerous beasts, was severely mauled during yesterday's matinee performance when a half-grown male tiger playfully grabbed him by the throat and dragged him from the stage. Fortunately for the performer, John Fortune, son of the beauteous ace Peregrine and the mysterious Fortunato, who has spent the last sixteen years in seclusion in Japan, was in attendance and for the first time publicly revealed his own ace. Fortune, who to all accounts was glowing a mysterious but pleasing shade of orange-yellow, took the performer in his arms and almost instantly healed the wound threatening the magician's life. The newly revealed ace, a good-looking boy in his mid-teens, politely refused all requests for interviews and was seen leaving in the company of a man who witnesses said bore an uncanny resemblance to 1940s actor Alan Ladd.'" Barnett looked up at Ray. "What do you think of that?"

Ray shrugged. "I think that Ralph was one lucky tiger-lover."

Barnett sat back in his chair, nodding. "Yes. But doesn't it strike you that someone else in that scenario was fairly blessed in the luck department?"

"John Fortune," Ray said. He knew what the odds of drawing an ace were as well as anybody. "Of course."

"Exactly," Barnett said, as if Ray just answered the million-dollar question.

Ray shrugged again. He didn't see the point.

"These are troubling days, Billy," Barnett said. "Some say," his voice dropped dramatically, "the End Days."

Oh shit, Ray thought. It didn't take Barnett long to drag religion into even the most mundane conversation. Ray himself wasn't much of a believer in anything. But Barnett could make almost anything sound reasonable when he was orating. After all, he'd been elected president of the United States. Twice.

"But it's 2003," Ray said. "If you're talking about the, uh, Millennium, surely that passed—"

Barnett shook his head.

"Actually it's just around the corner, my boy," Barnett said. "Timekeeping was not an exact science when the Bible was written two thousand years ago. Records were not precise. The calendar as we know it is a relatively modern invention. Anyway, you'd expect an error of a year or two to crop up over a couple of millennia, wouldn't you?"

"I suppose," Ray said, noncommittally. He still had no clue as to what in the hell this had to do with a kid saving some Vegas magician from his overgrown kitty cat.

Barnett nodded. "Of course. Hell, nobody took notes on the year when they wrote down the Bible. Nobody even cared. Besides—the signs are the important things, and all signs say that Armageddon is approaching."

"What signs? Tiger attacks in Vegas?"

Barnett frowned, the twinkle suddenly gone from his baby blue eyes.

"The prophecies, my boy. The continued existence of Israel, the nation whose existence you helped preserve, and don't think I've forgotten that, is but one of them. But let's not get bogged down in details now." Barnett opened the middle drawer in his desk. He took out an impressively thick manuscript. "Here. I wrote a book about it. Not intended for everyone of course. Wouldn't want a panic among the general populace. But give it a study, my boy. You'll see. It's all very convincing." Barnett handed the volume to Ray. It was heavy. "This is strictly for people within my organization, I guess you'd call it."

Ray looked up from the thick manuscript to Leo Barnett. "Organization?" he asked warily.

"A think tank I founded after I had the honor of serving as president of this great nation. The Millenarians. We believe that the time of the Apocalypse is at hand."

"That's a bad thing, isn't it?" Ray asked doubtfully.

"Not at all, Billy, not at all," Barnett explained. "Though many people believe that. Apocalypse means simply 'unveiling' or 'revelation.' It is the time when the truth will be revealed for all to see. When the Lord Jesus will return to this earth to usher in a thousand years of peace and prosperity for those who believe in his name."

Ray's expression was unchanged.

"Well, read my manuscript," Barnett said. "It explains everything."

"All right," Ray said as sincerely as he could.

Barnett frowned.

Apparently, Ray thought, *I don't sound quite as sincere as I think I do.*

"We need a man of your talents, Billy," Barnett said earnestly, turning up the wattage of his charm. "To guard me and, um, other figures important to the Parousia—that's the founding of Jesus' kingdom on Earth, which will usher in the thousand years of peace and prosperity of the Millennium."

"I thought you said that the End Days were approaching. Doesn't that mean, like, the end of the world?"

"It does," Barnett said seriously. "But only after the thousand-year peace of the Millennium. And only, of course, if we triumph in the upcoming conflict. We have foes, Billy. Powerful foes. Some might say satanically powerful foes."

Here we go, Ray thought. He knew this just wasn't going to be a simple little story. "I'm already guarding you," Ray pointed out. "Exactly who are these others who need guarding?"

"Christ," Barnett said.

Ray waited a beat, but Barnett added nothing to what Ray initially thought was an uncharacteristic expletive.

"Christ," Ray repeated. "You mean, *Jesus* Christ?"

"Jesus Christ," Barnett confirmed. "The Second Coming of the Son of God is upon us."

"Well," Ray asked, "where is he?"

Barnett cleared his throat. "Apparently," he said, "in Las Vegas."

"You don't mean John Fortune?"

Barnett nodded earnestly. "I do. You have to trust me on this, Billy. Years of study have led me to this conclusion. His act of healing this, uh, animal tamer, is only the final indication of his real identity."

"And you're sure of this?" Ray asked.

Barnett pursed his lips. "Sure? Well—reasonably. And we're not the only ones who think so."

"No?"

Barnett nodded. "There are others who have come to a, well, similar conclusion about the boy's importance. But they want to harm him. He has to be protected from them."

"But—"

"No, Billy." Barnett shook his head. "If you truly want to serve me—and the Lord—you must go to Vegas, get the boy, and bring him back here where we can protect him from these others."

"Who are they?" Ray asked.

"The Allumbrados," Barnett said, almost spitting as he pronounced the name. It sounded fairly sinister to Ray.

"So, you want me to go to Vegas, pick up the boy, and bring him here for safekeeping?" he recapitulated.

Barnett nodded. "Yes."

Ray suppressed a smile. "If you say the boy needs help, then that's good enough for me," he said.

Barnett beamed. "The Lord will reward you," he said.

I'm so out of here, Ray thought.

◆

New York City: Waldorf-Astoria Parking Garage

THE MIDNIGHT ANGEL LURKED in a dark alley overlooking the entrance to the Waldorf-Astoria's underground car park, a troubled expression on her face.

She didn't care for New York City. It was much too big and loud and fast. It smelled funny and sounded worse. She felt claustrophobic on its busy streets, hemmed in by the towering concrete and steel cliffs. She'd been born in Yazoo City, Mississippi, and though—contrary to her mother's advice—she'd willfully deserted the town of her birth to seek her fortune in the wider world, she still wasn't accustomed to many aspects of that world.

She also didn't much care for skulking. Skulking in shadows didn't match her sensibilities. She was much too forthright to skulk. There was no room for deception and lies in her makeup, for such were the tools of Satan. But what could she do? The Hand had sent her on a mission where subtlety was necessary. She'd told him that she was not the person for this job, as she found it difficult to blend into even familiar surroundings. At five foot eleven and a tautly muscled one forty-five, she was long-legged, wide-hipped, and big-bosomed. If things had been otherwise, she'd have borne many babies and raised them in the way of the Lord. But that life was closed to her. Her body, as suitable for childbearing as it was, was to her everlasting shame also cursed with the mark of the wild card. She carried the stain of the alien beast. Her mother had drummed into her early on that she must find another way to serve the Lord. Of course, the Angel was not following the path that her mother had mapped out for her, but her body, curse that it was, was also her blessing. God had burdened her with it, but it was a burden she bore meekly in his service.

The Hand had made her see that. She'd been with him for a year, and the Angel burned with an almost sinful pride that he trusted her so much that he'd sent her on such an important mission. To know that the Right Hand of God held her in such high regard made her little short of ecstatic. It'd be better if he didn't look at her with such fire in his eyes and lust in his heart, but she forgave him. Even though he was the Hand he was still only a man and, therefore, a weak sinner. Anyway, it was her fault. She tempted him with her body, though the Lord knew she didn't mean to.

The Angel tensed as a long black limo pulled up to the entrance of the hotel's underground parking lot. The car had Vatican diplomatic plates. It had to be the one she'd been expecting. She waited until it entered the building's dark bowels, and then followed. There was no booth attendant this late at night, only an automatic ticket dispenser. She slipped under the wooden arm that barred entrance to the urban cave stinking of oil, gas fumes, and waste, praying to the Lord for strength and cunning.

God knows she needed it. She was on the track of the Allumbrados and she knew that her quest was dangerous. The Hand had sent others to investigate them who had simply disappeared after relaying the most uncertain, though provocative, hints that the Enlightened Ones, as they styled themselves, were preparing for action.

The Hand knew that something big was imminent. He knew the general warning signs as well as the Allumbrados did, though as Papists their knowledge had to be imperfect. The Allumbrado conspiracy, however, had thrust its roots deep into the hierarchy of the Catholic Church. They could call on the vast powers and riches of that ancient institution whereas the Hand had only himself and his loyal minions, such as the Angel, to rely upon. Not that the Allumbrados had defiled everyone in the Church, of course. Most Papists were not satanic. They were just misguided.

The Angel, keeping to the darkness that enveloped the parking structure like a choking shroud, suddenly caught her breath. The limo's dome light winked on as the driver opened the door and scurried around to let out his passengers.

The first to emerge was a patrician-looking man in his late sixties, but still tall, handsome, and distinguished, with a head of thick, white hair. He wore the black, scarlet-trimmed regalia of a cardinal of the Papist church. It was, the Angel realized, just as the Hand had feared. Cardinal Romulus Contarini had come to America. He was a Dominican, of course. His sect had had an intimate connection with the Holy Office (*A very bland name for something as terrible as the Inquisition,* she thought) for a very long time. Contarini led the section of the vast and shadowy Vatican bureaucracy that dealt with theological purity. He was the highest-ranking member of the Allumbrados that the Hand's agents could uncover. Before he'd suddenly and mysteriously disappeared, the Hand's man in the Vatican had said that the cardinal was possibly headed for the United States. This was obvious confirmation of the news he'd probably given his life to deliver.

Contarini was not alone. Three men got out of the limo with him. One was short, chubby, and bearded. He looked soft and jolly, like everyone's favorite uncle. The other two had such similar facial features that they were probably brothers. But one was tall and strong looking while the other was thin, round-shouldered, and slumping. The tall, strong-looking one was possibly the most attractive man the Angel had ever seen. Her heart caught at the angelic handsomeness of his face, which was white as unflawed marble. His eyes were as blue as Heaven, his hair a golden torrent with wave and thickness to rival her own. His lips . . .

She could almost taste them in her sudden desire. They were full, sensuously curved, and red as a woman's. But his features were masculine, with a broad forehead, high cheekbones, and a strong jaw. His short-sleeved shirt exposed arms muscled like a blacksmith's.

The Angel felt herself breathing heavier and then suddenly the silent parking garage echoed with the trilling opening notes to "Ode to Joy." She had forgotten to turn off her cell phone, and it rang at the worst possible time. Her hand fell to her side pocket, grabbed the instrument, and silenced it.

Perhaps, she thought, *they didn't hear.*

The men stopped on their way to the elevator. The cardinal looked impatient, but the jolly little man gazed into the darkness where the Angel lurked, holding her breath. His cheery blue eyes suddenly focused with a startling intensity.

"Someone's out there," she heard him say in a British accented voice.

"Witness—" the cardinal said.

The two men, different, yet alike enough in features to be brothers, looked at each other. The tall, handsome one said, "Check it out," and the other, grumbling to himself under his breath, moved off toward the darkness where the Angel hid.

♥

Turin, Italy: Cattedrale di San Giovanni Battista

THE CATHEDRAL'S TWO-STORY EXTERIOR was white marble, a little worse for age and blackened by five centuries of urban pollution. The detached bell tower on the cathedral's left was constructed of darker, less noble material—simple brick—and was also some two hundred years younger. The intricate dome of the Cappella della Sacra Sindone, a few decades older than the tower, loomed behind the cathedral. Their target was in the chapel.

Nighthawk waited in the shadows until the others had crossed the almost empty piazza. Traffic was sporadic, but there were still a few pedestrians wandering about, and Nighthawk had not reached his advanced age by being reckless. He waited until Usher and Grubbs had entered the cathedral through the middle of the three doors in its front facade—Usher pausing only the briefest of moments to force the cheap padlock that tried to deny him entry—and then he crossed the dark piazza in an unhurried stride as Magda surreptitiously joined her teammates inside San Giovanni.

It was dark inside the cathedral. The interior was lit only by some still-burning votive candles and a dim night-light or two scattered like faraway stars among the massive columns of the Gothic-style nave.

"We need the stairs at the end of the presbytery," Nighthawk said in a quiet voice that a trick of acoustics turned into a reverberating whisper.

Usher thumbed on a pencil-thin flashlight and slashed it around the darkness.

"This way," he whispered in an imitation of Nighthawk, grinning at the echoing sibilance of his own words.

They followed Usher down the aisle, past the rows of empty pews to the high altar set upon a dais in the rear of the nave. Two stairways flanked the altar.

They were black marble, which contrasted vividly with the soft pastels of the cathedral's painted interior. The stairs spiraled upward into a small antechamber from where Nighthawk and his team could see inside the chapel's central room.

The Capella della Sacra Sindone was the masterpiece of the baroque architect Guarino Guarini. It was a perfectly round chamber of black marble roofed by an intricately decorated six-tiered dome that was said to enclose a bit of Heaven in its complexly ornamented cupola. Nighthawk could feel its holiness in his soul. He gazed upward, as if expecting to see cherubim and seraphim dancing like flights of fireflies through the enshrouding shadows.

An intricate baroque altar of black marble ornamented with detailed bronze friezes sat atop three marble steps under the center of the soaring dome. The altar was surrounded by what looked like golden bars, but according to the guidebook were actually only gilt wood. Four marble angels holding unlit silver lamps clustered protectively around the altar like holy guardians. A reliquary, an iron box covered in intricate silver facings and spangled with precious stones, sat atop the altar's highest point, protected by a gilded iron fence.

"There," Nighthawk said quietly, gesturing at the reliquary.

Grubbs grinned. "Like taking candy from a baby," he said.

He went up the marble dais, brushing away the gilt wood fence contemptuously, as if it wasn't even there. One of the guardian angels stood close enough to give him a boost up the altar. He clambered up to the altar's pinnacle and braced himself to get a good grip on the gilded iron bars caging the reliquary. He pulled hard and a length of grillwork broke away with a loud screech.

Nighthawk glanced around the darkened room. It was probable that the chapel had a security system of some kind, but they'd been unable to discover any details concerning it. A brotherhood called the Savoias was charged with protecting it since an anti-religious fanatic had tried to burn it down a couple of years before.

"Careful," Nighthawk hissed.

"Don't worry," Grubbs said in a too-loud voice. He reached out and lifted the reliquary effortlessly, though it must have weighed several hundred pounds. He held it over his head triumphantly. "The Mandylion is ours!" he said ecstatically, and John's revelation suddenly came true as a single shot rang out from somewhere in the shadows and struck Grubbs right in the middle of his chest.

Grubbs' expression changed only slightly, crossing that thin line from ecstatic to pained, and he slipped from his perch atop the altar, falling heavily against one of the statues that decorated the altar's middle tier like a tiny bridegroom on an overly ornate wedding cake. The reliquary slipped from his fingers, bumped the same statue, and bounced with a thunderous boom onto the marble altar, then rolled downward and crashed through the remnants of the gilt guardrail.

The reverberations from the single shot still echoed across the chapel as Magda and Usher both fired into the darkness from where the bullet came. Nighthawk moved in the shadows, black in black, and reached the dying man at the base of the altar. Grubbs was numb and confused, but he felt and clearly recognized the sharp talons of death crawling up his body as organs shut down and blood flowed like a river from the hole punched out through his back. The dying man spoke despite all his terror and confusion.

"John!"

"Hush," Nighthawk said in a soft whisper.

"John, what happened?"

"Time to sleep, boy," the old man told him. "Time to rest." He took his glove off, reached out and touched Grubbs' left cheek, and stopped his heart.

He had only a moment in which to act. Grubbs' soul was leaving his body, taking with it the energy that would have powered his life to its natural conclusion if he hadn't stopped a bullet some forty-odd years ahead of schedule. Nighthawk stripped it of that energy, leaving it weak and uncertain.

Nighthawk had no concrete knowledge, but little hope for the nature of the ultimate destination of Grubbs' soul. But Grubbs' fate was out of his hands. He had to concentrate on the situation unfolding around them, or there was little doubt that they'd all be joining Grubbs on that Hell-bound train before the night was over.

They hadn't expected an armed and trigger-happy guard. This was, after all, sacred ground. But times were different. Terrorists were ready, willing, and able to strike anytime, anywhere, and the Capella della Sacra Sindone had been attacked in the past. Clearly, Nighthawk realized, they had underestimated the strength of the Savoias' resolve and willingness to shed blood in protection of their sacred charge.

"Usher," he said in a calm but strong voice, "retrieve the reliquary. Magda—keep up the suppressive fire."

He caught a glimpse of her teeth shining in a feral smile. She was a fanatic. She had no more regard for the lives of the Savoias than if they were animals. Nighthawk did. In a strange sense, they were all part of the same brotherhood, though it was a truism that families often fought bloody battles amongst themselves.

She ripped the darkness with automatic fire as Usher scuttled forward to retrieve the reliquary. Bullets flew. They whined off marble surfaces, smashed through stained glass, and even bit through flesh here and there. Three members of the Savoias fell as Magda screamed in some Slavic tongue that Nighthawk didn't recognize. He reached out eagerly with his mind. Two were dying, dissipating their precious energy into the void. He held himself back. He couldn't get greedy and slow of thought and action. He needed his wits about him if he was to lead his team to safety. He could already feel Grubbs' energy crackling through his system like logs added to the furnace of the engine that drove his body. He smiled. He didn't feel a day over eighty. They had to get back to the Holy See where they had diplomatic immunity from the most conceivable crimes, and even from some inconceivable ones. From there they would take the Mandylion over the ocean, back to New York, where the others waited.

For a few moments it was tricky. Nighthawk didn't like blind firefights where anything could happen. But he felt no sign of a coming revelation, and again, he was right.

Usher retrieved the chest. Nighthawk and Magda laid down suppressive gunfire, and no one came out of the chapel after them. After that it was only a matter of keeping quiet. Of keeping to the darkness and avoiding the growing search. Their car was ready. They made it past the roadblocks before they could be set up.

They reached Rome at dawn and Nighthawk took the reliquary into the Vatican before the rest of the tiny city-state was even waking up. Only then could Nighthawk relax. He'd gotten the Mandylion, the actual burial cloth, the Shroud of Jesus of Nazareth, into the hands of the Allumbrados. That was the hard part. The rest, getting it to New York and the Brothers who waited there, would be easy.

The mission was practically over. It had cost the life of one of his team members and an uncounted number of Savoias, but it had been worth it. Returning Jesus Christ to the world would be worth it all.

♣

New York City: Waldorf-Astoria Parking Garage

"SAVE MY SOUL FROM evil, Lord," the Midnight Angel murmured, "and heal this warrior's heart."

She stood up, leaning over the driver's-side door of the vehicle next to her. It was an SUV, big, shiny, and new looking. She wondered at the idiocy of a city dweller buying a vehicle like this. Was it excessive pride? Envy? Of course, maybe she was guilty of immoderate judgment herself. This was a hotel parking lot, after all. Maybe the SUV's owner lived in the country somewhere and actually needed it.

She had, she suddenly recalled, little time for moralizing.

She punched through the window effortlessly, her arm protected by a leather gauntlet and a full-body, form-fitting leather jumpsuit. A burglar alarm clanged raucously as she quickly leaned in through the shattered window and slipped the transmission into neutral. She shoved the SUV, sending it skittering toward the Allumbrado, who had halted his approach when the alarm started to scream.

The Angel peered out from behind the car in the next parking slot—it was a late-model Ford of some sort, and she approved much more of its lack of ostentation and relative utility than she did of the conspicuous and consumptive SUV—and watched as the Allumbrado, suddenly frowning, made a complicated set of hand gestures as the SUV bore down on him.

He finished with his left hand clenched into a fist, held chest high. His right hand was next to it, palm open. He pushed that hand out, extending his right arm fast, like he was throwing some kind of open-handed punch at the SUV, which was now almost upon him.

A wall of force met the SUV head-on. Its front end crumpled as if it had hit an invisible fence and it rebounded backward right at the Angel as a sudden wind buffeted her, stirring her long, thick hair in its passing.

Her heart pounded with desire. She wanted nothing more than to stay and fight this man, but she knew that there was a chance, however slim, that he and his companions might overpower her and prevent her from getting her message to the Hand. She scuttled back among the parked cars as her opponent threw another force wave in her general direction, setting off numerous car alarms as the vehicles in the wave's pathway rocked as if in an earthquake.

The message was foremost in her mind as she slipped away in the darkness.

The cardinal has come. And he has brought aces with him.

But also, not so far buried, was an image of the man who accompanied the cardinal. The handsome, strong-looking one.

There, she thought, *is a proper foe.*

Or perhaps, something else entirely.

♠

Hokkaido, Japan

IT WAS TWO IN the morning, about an hour and a half before the *unsui* would strike the sounding board with his wooden mallet, waking everyone for the start of the long monastery day, but Fortunato was already awake.

He'd been having trouble sleeping lately. Not even lengthy recitation of the Heart Sutra, which by virtue of its hypnotic repetitiveness was supposed to pacify the chanter by affording him a glimpse into his true nature, could lull him to sleep. It never had, and Fortunato was beginning to suspect it never would. He was having trouble sleeping because he was beginning to suspect that he had made a mistake.

I'm sixty-two years old, Fortunato thought.

The Zendo, the hall where the monks practiced zazen and which also doubled as their sleeping quarters, was pitch-dark. It was silent but for the various rustlings, snortings, and snorings of the other fifty-some monks who slept fitfully or soundly on their tatami.

He envied them their slumber.

He realized that part of his problem was physical. After sixteen years of a fairly rigorous vegetarian diet, Fortunato was even leaner than he'd been as a pleasure-loving ace in New York City. The temple's harsh physical discipline helped keep him fit, but he'd developed arthritis a couple of years back, presumably from sleeping on a hard, cold floor on only a thin straw mat wrapped in a single blanket. It had settled in his neck and shoulders and was getting worse with every passing month. Now he was even occasionally feeling biting pain in his long, thin fingers. Pain was something to be endured as part of monastic life, as there were few drugs in the monastery's frugal medicine cabinet, except for aspirin for fevers and colds, Tiger Balm for sore muscles and joints, and Preparation H for the hemorrhoids brought on by hours and hours of sitting on a hard floor in the lotus position.

Worse yet, the brief Hokkaido summer had barely started and the season would turn again all too soon. Fortunato did not look forward to the change. In Hokkaido the winter came early and lingered long. The winter winds were razor-sharp and the snowfall was measured in feet, not inches. He had a single quilted blanket from which the mice had already been stealing stuffing. He couldn't in all good conscience blame them for taking the cotton batting to line their nests against the terrible cold.

Lately Fortunato had been beginning to suspect that this portion of his life, the ascetic self-denial of pleasure, was as much of a dead end as his earlier years spent reveling in tantric sex, drugs, and the sheer gusto of life as one of the most powerful aces in the world, a life he'd turned his back on in a quest to find his true nature in the way of a Zen monk.

Dogen, his Zen *roshi* and head of the small monastery, had told him when he'd first asked to join, "If you want to live in the world you must admit your power. If you want to feed your spirit you must leave the world."

Only, Fortunato thought as he lay staring into the indecipherable darkness, his spirit was as hungry as ever. *Have I actually progressed down the Tao this last decade and a half,* he wondered, *or become petrified, congealed in an unbreakable lump of amber closed off from the world? Is that what I really wanted?*

He wondered why.

There was a sudden disturbance in the Zendo as a fully dressed figure made his way among the sleeping monks. Fortunato recognized Dogen's secretary and chief assistant. Fortunato had disliked the man ever since he'd entered the monastery, and the feeling was mutual. He had a sour look on his face, as if he'd been up all night sucking lemons, as he nudged Fortunato with his *tabi*-covered foot.

"Wake up," he said in a voice loud enough so that those next to Fortunato stirred, grumbling in their sleep. "Dogen wants to see you."

Fortunato didn't question him, not wanting to give him the satisfaction of offering useless answers. He rose silently on stiff joints and followed him out of the room. They went wordlessly down dark and silent corridors, Fortunato wondering what Dogen wanted at such an unlikely hour. This wasn't the first time he'd been summoned to the abbot's private quarters. He'd gone there plenty of times for instruction, to receive a new koan to meditate upon, or even for conversation about his varied experiences in the outside world. He'd even been summoned into the abbot's presence once or twice for disciplinary measures.

But, Fortunato reflected, not for the latter reason for years. The last time had been after Tachyon's visit. Fortunato had gone over the wall after the little alien Fauntleroy had left and spent a week drunk in the village at the base of the mountain. But those days had passed. He couldn't even begin to guess why Dogen wanted to see him now.

Dogen nodded as his assistant led Fortunato to the open doorway of his small, austere office.

"Leave us," he said as Fortunato stared at the man sitting uncomfortably cross-legged on the mat before Dogen's low desk. The man smiled up at him like they were long-lost friends.

"Hey, Fortunato," Digger Downs said. "Long time, no see."

Fortunato looked from the star reporter of *Aces!* magazine back to Dogen, mystified.

"Indeed," he said, and entered the room, bowing to the abbot. He looked back at Downs. Downs was a small, lean, brown-haired, brown-eyed man pushing a well-preserved fifty. Fortunato hadn't seen him since he'd entered the monastery. "What are you doing here?" he asked.

"I was just in the neighborhood and thought I'd stop by," Digger said with a smile much too bright for so early in the morning.

"You were in the neighborhood at two o'clock in the morning?" Fortunato asked in disbelief.

"Well," Digger allowed, "it did take me awhile to get here from Tokyo. I left as soon as the news broke. I wanted to be the first to get your reaction, and," he added with some satisfaction, "it looks as if I am."

Fortunato sighed and closed his eyes. He had no reason to like Digger Downs. The man was, at best, an obnoxious pest. But over the years he'd tried to learn how to put such feelings away. He opened his eyes to see Dogen observing him with silent reproof. His master knew that he was letting himself get caught up in a swirl of unpleasant emotion. Yet again.

"Digger," Fortunato said patiently, "pretend that this is an isolated monastery on a secluded mountaintop in far north Japan."

"Man, I don't have to pretend," Digger said. "It was hell getting here."

"We don't get much news about the outside world."

"Excellent!" Digger beamed. "Then I can get your exclusive reaction to the news regarding your son."

"My son?" Fortunato asked. Suddenly, his stomach felt as if it had dropped out of his abdomen. He had never seen his son. The last time he'd seen Peregrine, weeks before entering the monastery, she'd been heavy with their child. Up until then he hadn't even known that she was pregnant. He'd told her that he'd be there for her and the child. And then he'd gone into the monastery. Not even Tachyon, who'd come in person begging for his help, not even the telegram announcing the death of his mother, had induced him to leave his sanctuary.

And now . . .

He looked at Digger. The man was smiling, but that didn't mean he was the bearer of good news. He cared for the story, not the implications the story might have for those caught up in it. It seemed unlikely that he'd travel all this way to impart good news . . . whatever that could possibly be.

Fortunato had a sudden premonition that had nothing to do with the powers he'd left behind so long ago, but had everything to do with being a wild carder. And the parent of one.

"Has," his voice suddenly went raspy and he swallowed hard, "has his card turned?"

Downs nodded. "Yes—and," he added quickly as he saw the expression on Fortunato's face, "don't worry. The boy lucked out. He turned over an ace."

"An ace!" Fortunato felt a sudden rush of relief underlaid with pride he quickly realized was unjustified. The boy had come unscathed through the most dangerous moment in a wild carder's life. The expression of the virus was the ultimate crapshoot against horribly stacked odds. Everything after that was just living. But the boy had had to experience it without Fortunato's help. Not, he realized, that he could have done anything but watch the boy die if he'd pulled a Black Queen. But still . . .

"Yeah," Downs continued, "and he immediately used a healing power of some sort to save the life of a Las Vegas performer who'd been mauled by a tiger."

"Tiger?" Fortunato asked, having trouble focusing on what the reporter was saying.

"It's big news," Downs said. "Flashed all over the world. I'd like to get our interview in the can, because half the media in Japan is hot on my trail. Not to mention the planeloads of reporters from other countries heading here to get your reaction to the story. But," he added triumphantly, "as usual, I've scooped them all. Lucky for me I just happened to be in Tokyo to interview the new ace Iron Chef—"

"Planeloads?" Fortunato interrupted.

Downs nodded. "Of course. Like I said, big story. Beautiful ace mother, mysterious ace father. Kid beats the odds, becoming a hero overnight—"

Fortunato looked at Dogen, who looked back calmly.

"This is a monastery," Fortunato said to Downs. "They can't swarm all over it with their camera crews, mobbing the place. Think of the disruption it would cause."

Downs shrugged. "Think you can stop them?"

"I—" Fortunato knew the answer as well as the reporter did. He looked again at Dogen. "I can't allow the entire monastery to be disrupted because of my presence. What should we do?"

"What we must," the ageless abbot said calmly.

Fortunato nodded. There was only one solution to the problem. "Then I must take the cause of disruption elsewhere. I must leave the monastery."

"Leave?" Downs asked, suddenly frowning. "You're not going to leave before I can interview you, are you?"

Fortunato looked at him. "I don't care about your interview," he said. He paused, frowning. "But I have nowhere to go."

It was true. He'd turned his back on his own country, his own society, and his own identity as the most powerful ace of his time to make this monastery his home. But the rest of Japan was as foreign as the far side of the moon.

"Go?" Downs asked. He suddenly snapped his fingers. "I've got it! Come back to America! On me. Well, on *Aces!* anyway. It'll be great." His eyes focused outward as if reading an imaginary headline. "PRODIGAL SON RETURNS. Or something like that. It'll play great with the kid becoming an ace and all!"

Fortunato frowned. It didn't exactly sound appealing. Besides, there was as little for him in America as there was in Japan. His mother was dead. His girls were all gone. There was nothing but Peregrine, married to another man these fifteen years or more. And his son . . .

He looked at Dogen, who smiled his gentle smile.

"Perhaps Mr. Downs is right. You can't deny that lately you've been restless. Perhaps it is time that you walk in the world again, to get a fresh perspective on what you've given up and what you have now."

Fortunato smiled wryly. There was no way to hide anything from Dogen. The old man knew Fortunato's mind perhaps better than the ace did himself.

"Perhaps you're right," Fortunato said.

"Right? Of course he's right," Downs said, looking from one to the other and smiling broadly. "Cripes, what a story! I can see it on the cover of *Aces!*: FORTUNATO'S RETURN TO AMERICA."

"Do you think anyone will care?" Fortunato asked thoughtfully.

"They will when I get done with it," Downs promised.

Fortunato, though, wasn't so sure.

Chapter Two

New York City: Tomlin International Airport

JOHN NIGHTHAWK WAITED PATIENTLY at the baggage carousel for his luggage to arrive. If there was one thing he'd learned over the years, it was patience. Usher stood to his right, a silent monolith. Magda, dressed in a traditional black-and-white nun's habit, a uniform that she habitually wore when they weren't on a mission, stood to his left as baggage was disgorged onto the meandering belt. They all watched for the black satchel with the faded Vatican coat of arms decal on its side.

"I miss Grubbs already," Usher complained as the bag they'd been waiting for finally appeared. He reached down and picked it up as it glided by. Toting and carrying had always been Grubbs' job.

Nighthawk said nothing. Their stop at customs was expedited by their Vatican diplomatic passports. If the customs agent was dubious about the old Black man, the bruiser who looked like a heavyweight champion, and the hard-eyed nun traveling under the auspices of the Holy See, it didn't show on his bored expression. They carried no luggage besides the diplomatic pouch, which of course went unexamined as they breezed through arrival formalities and exited Tomlin International.

A limo with Vatican diplomatic plates and two occupants was waiting for them at ground transport. The silent driver had the proper degree of unassuming servitude. The man with him was the handsome blond man Nighthawk knew only as the Witness. He was one of two Witnesses who worked for the cardinal. They were brothers. Nighthawk differentiated them in his mind as the Asshole and the Bigger Asshole. This one was the Bigger Asshole.

"Any problems?" the Bigger Asshole asked.

"We lost Grubbs," Nighthawk said.

The Witness shrugged. "I'm sure he's gone on to his proper reward. But you got the Mandylion all right? No problems with that?"

Nighthawk shook his head. "No. No problems with that." He gestured at the bag emblazoned with the Vatican crest.

"Put it in the trunk," the Witness said.

Usher did, after the driver popped it open from where he sat behind the wheel. Usher slammed the lid and came around to the limo's back door, but the Bigger Asshole shook his head.

"The help takes taxis," he said.

Usher looked at Nighthawk, who nodded briefly. The big man sauntered over to the line of taxis at the nearby cab stand, followed by a stoic Magda. The Witness looked at Nighthawk, who looked back. The Bigger Asshole pursed his lips, but said nothing as Nighthawk opened the limo's door and slid into the seat. The Witness got in, sat next to Nighthawk, and the limo pulled away from the curb.

"Is everyone else in town?" Nighthawk asked, more to pester the Bigger Asshole than because he was really interested.

"Everyone was," the Witness said briefly. "Dagon and my brother left yesterday on a mission."

"Where to?"

"Gomorrah," the Witness smiled, "to fetch the Anti-Christ to cower in chains before the throne of Our Lord." His smile turned to a frown. "Although there's talk that others will join them soon via Blood's tunnel. It seems that the Anti-Christ has his own cadre of aces."

Nighthawk was startled. Despite the fact that he and his team had been sent to fetch the Mandylion, he hadn't really believed that after all these years the cardinal's plan had finally been set into motion.

"It's starting then," Nighthawk said.

"Oh yes," the Bigger Asshole said with a broad and glittery smile that looked more malevolent than cheerful. "And nothing or no one can stop us now."

◆

Las Vegas, Nevada: The Mirage

RAY STEPPED OUT OF the heat of the early June afternoon into the sweet coolness of the Mirage's air-conditioned lobby and stopped for a moment to watch the tourists mill around while he considered his next move. All of a sudden he wasn't so sure that this trip was such a good idea.

Sure, he had traded the utter boredom of the Peaceable Kingdom for the relative excitement of Las Vegas, but now that he was here, his pulse wasn't exactly pounding. Not yet, anyway. It all seemed . . . well . . . tawdry wasn't a word he often used, but somehow it seemed appropriate. All around him middle-aged, middle-class, Midwestern tourists were avidly chasing excitement. Had he really joined their ranks?

What's wrong with me? Ray thought. *Am I actually developing some sense of values?*

He'd started to notice some unsettling things lately. He'd been getting more tired than he'd ever been before. Pain lingered. It took longer to come back from injuries. Something that would have taken only a couple of hours to heal twenty years ago now took a day, sometimes longer. Everything seemed to hurt worse.

Not that I'm old, he told himself, *but I do have a lot of mileage. Maybe the odometer is getting ready to turn over. Maybe it's even running out. Nothing ever said that I could go on forever, my powers undiminished. . . .*

Ray's uncharacteristic mood of introspection suddenly screeched to a halt as he noticed the woman approaching him from across the Mirage's lobby. For the first time in a long time, he felt his pulse start to race. At least a little.

He wasn't sure if she was beautiful, exactly. Her expression was far too gloomy, for one thing. Her features were bold rather than delicate, with a generous mouth, aquiline nose, and large eyes that looked haunted. By guilt, by melancholy, Ray couldn't tell. Her skin was milk white, almost luminous in its pale perfection, contrasting vividly with her night-black hair, which was thick and wavy and though bound in a heavy braid hanging down to the middle of her back seemed to be struggling to escape its bonds. Ray was not overly imaginative, but he could picture it blowing about her face in a gentle wind, or spilling in luxuriant waves over her pale-skinned shoulders.

She was wearing a black leather jumpsuit and black boots that came to her knees. She was built. Really built, with wide hips and large breasts confined as uneasily as her hair and long legs. Her leather jumpsuit clung tightly to her curves, as snug as a second skin.

She held an ice cream cone in one hand and a sheet of paper in the other, as well as the strap of a large duffel bag that she carried easily, without a sign of strain. She moved rapidly through the knots of tourists standing around the lobby. From time to time she looked up from the paper she was studying, but she was paying more attention to the ice cream cone than she was to her surroundings. She licked it rapidly, almost rapturously. She walked quickly.

She glanced up and their eyes suddenly met.

But it was too late.

♥

Las Vegas, Nevada: The Mirage

THE MIDNIGHT ANGEL WAS tired. She hadn't slept in over forty-eight hours, and hadn't eaten a proper meal—you couldn't count the tasteless mess they served on the plane—in much longer. The flight from New York to Las Vegas had seemingly taken forever. The plane had been packed with Vegas junketeers eager to begin their carousing. Alcohol flowed freely and annoyingly uncontrolled laughter was all too common. She hadn't been able to sleep at all.

There's no rest, the Angel thought, *for the wicked.*

She'd phoned the Hand right after her encounter with the Allumbrados in the Waldorf-Astoria's parking garage. The Hand, though not exactly pleased with her news about Contarini and his aces, had been pleased with the way she'd handled herself.

"I knew you'd come through, Angel," he'd told her. She'd smiled at his praise, puffed up with a pride that was almost sinful.

There was a thoughtful silence as the Hand pondered the information she'd relayed. The Angel could visualize his handsome face, his strong, dimpled chin, his wide brow crinkled with frown lines as he considered what to do.

"All right," he finally said decisively. "I want you to go pick up the boy. We have to move fast. It's important—vital—that you bring him to safety, so I'm sending you some help, an experienced agent named Billy Ray. He's a top-flight man. Toughest bast—er, fellow I've ever run across, but I wouldn't entirely trust him with all our plans." He paused briefly and his voice lowered to a conspiratorial whisper. "Not sound, theologically speaking. But we use what tools we must. You'll meet him in Las Vegas—"

"Vegas?" The Angel was so horrified with the thought of traveling to the American Gomorrah that she interrupted the Hand.

"That's where the boy is. Actually, it's a good thing he's not in New York, as the place seems to be crawling with Allumbrados right now. Take the first flight you can get. When you arrive at the Vegas airport check the Pan American customer-service counter. I'll fax you Ray's photo so you can recognize him. Meet him in the Mirage lobby. That's where the boy's staying with his mother and bodyguard."

"But—"

"No time for buts, honey. I know you can do this. We have to gather the boy to the safety of our bosom in the Peaceable Kingdom. I'll see you soon." He rang off before the Angel could further protest her exile to Las Vegas, but his final words of praise warmed her all through her flight across the continent.

The promised photo was in fact waiting for her when she'd arrived at the Vegas airport, along with the additional information that in a bit of fortuitous timing, Ray's flight had arrived only a few minutes before her own. He was probably on his way to the Mirage, if he hadn't reached it already.

Upon reflection, though, the Angel realized that maybe the timing wasn't so fortuitous. She'd hoped to check into the hotel and maybe catch a few hours of sleep. She definitely had to find something to eat. Her body burned calories at a prodigious rate. It seemed that she was always hungry. She ate and ate but never felt really satisfied. She worried about the sin of gluttony, but could she be considered a glutton if she never gained an ounce of weight?

It isn't really gluttony, the Angel thought, *if you need every mouthful you swallow.*

On her way to the pickup spot for the hotel's courtesy van, she stopped at an airport snack bar, looked over the menu board, and winced at the prices. They were outrageous. She had enough cash for a large soda and a few chocolate bars. Cadbury, the big ones with nuts and raisins. They were really quite nutritious.

She tried to eat slowly, but her hunger drove her to gulp down the chocolate bars quickly. Even so, a large soda without ice and three Cadbury bars failed to sate her appetite, but there was nothing to do about it but hustle off to the Mirage. Time was flying. She had to meet this Billy Ray. They had to make plans. She hoped he'd brought some money with him. Despite her careful shepherding of the funds the Hand had given at the start of her mission, she was almost stone broke.

Buzzing along on caffeine and sugar and lack of sleep, the Angel strode through the airport concourse, aware of every staring male eye, of every impure thought that must be hiding behind their bland but oh-so-obvious expressions. She retrieved her one piece of luggage, a battered old duffel bag, from the revolving carousel, and went out into the blazing Vegas afternoon where she waited impatiently for the shuttle to come along on its appointed rounds and take her and about twenty other sweating tourists to the Mirage.

Hunger still gnawed at her. To take her mind off her grumbling stomach, she studied the photo that the Hand had faxed to her. This Billy Ray didn't look like anything special. He wasn't very big. Didn't appear to be particularly muscular. Didn't even look too bright, actually. Still, there had to be something special about him if he worked for the Hand. The Hand clearly had confidence in his ability, if not his ultimate loyalty.

The thought that he had so much confidence in her warmed her heart. The

Hand was a handsome man. Even more importantly, he was a man of and for God. She had given him her complete trust when she'd joined his group. The Angel knew that her mother wouldn't have approved of her straying out into the world, but her mother was no longer with her and she had to do something with her life. At least her mother would have approved of the Angel's decision to utilize her abilities in the service of the Lord. The Angel was sure of that.

When the shuttle finally arrived at the Mirage, the Angel trooped off the bus with the rest of the tourists. She endured a suggestive glance from the driver as he handed over her duffel bag and sighed in unselfconscious pleasure as she entered the cool lobby. She glanced around. It was bigger and much more crowded than she'd ever imagined it would be. It might not be as easy to spot Billy Ray as she'd thought.

She did, however, immediately spot an ice cream stand near the lobby's far wall. Her stomach rumbled out loud. She had about three dollars left from the money the Hand had given her. She realized then of course that even if she'd wanted to get a room and rest before meeting Billy Ray, she couldn't possibly afford it. She did have enough for an ice cream cone, though. Maybe a double scoop.

The ice cream boy, tall and thin and wearing a chocolate-, strawberry-, and vanilla-spotted white suit, eyed her insouciantly as she approached.

"What can I get for you?" he asked with a leer.

"Chocolate cone," the Angel replied frostily.

"Two scoops or one?" Somehow he made his query sound like an indecent proposal.

She pulled all her money out from the right front pocket of her tight leather jumpsuit, and frowned at two sweaty singles.

"One," she said with disappointment.

"Here," the ice cream boy said grandly, adding an extra scoop to the cone. "Just for you, babe."

The Angel hesitated, but greed overcame her and she accepted the pilfered scoop of ice cream. Tonight she would pray long and hard over this, she thought.

"Thank you," she said.

"Anytime, babe," the ice cream boy called out as she drifted back into the maelstrom of the lobby. "Come see me again sometime," he added hopefully.

The Angel took a lick of her cone and shivered ecstatically as the cold chocolate melted on her tongue. She took another lick, pausing partway through as she caught a glimpse of a man who could be the one she was looking for, glanced at the photo to check, realized that he wasn't her quarry, then turned and saw that she was walking right into a man who was looking at her with an expression that could only be described as predatory.

Their eyes met and she recognized him. It was the man in the photo. The man the Hand had called Billy Ray.

And then they collided.

As the Angel bumped into him words of apology were already on her lips, but his expression suddenly turned horrified and he moved quicker than anyone she had ever seen, smooth and graceful like Fred Astaire gliding around Ginger

Rogers on the dance floor in those movies that her mother had always punished her for watching whenever she caught her. He was no longer staring at her, but rather at the ice cream cone that she clutched in her hand inches—just inches—from the jacket of his spotless, expensive-looking suit. The suit was very nice. Impeccable, really. He didn't look like he'd just gotten off a plane after a long flight. He looked like he'd just come from a glamour shoot. Except he wasn't very handsome. There wasn't anything really wrong with his features. His crooked nose was a little too long. His mouth a little too thin-lipped. His jawline somehow unfitting. They just didn't seem to all add up. It was almost like he'd had facial reconstruction surgery and had chosen randomly from a menu provided by the doctor.

His pale green eyes had transferred their gaze to her ice cream cone and its imminent impact with his faultless suit. The Angel jerked her arm back quickly and gravity did the rest.

The top scoop of chocolate shot forward in a flat trajectory and landed right where his lap would have been if he were sitting down. He looked at the soggy mass of ice cream sliding slowly down the front of his pants, then back up at the Angel.

His eyes were wild.

"Oh," the Angel said. She hunkered down and tried to wipe the mess from the front of his pants. A glob of ice cream ran down his right pant leg, leaving a rather noticeable trail. Then she realized what she was doing. All she could say was "Oh" again.

The fury disappeared from Ray's face, replaced by an expression of sudden bemusement. "If you keep that up we'll have to get a room." He grinned crookedly. "Good thing we're already in a hotel."

The Angel stood up before him. She could feel a blush infuse her features, and that made her blush all the harder.

"Not that I don't appreciate the way you introduce yourself," Ray said, "but who the hell are you, anyway?"

The Angel realized she was staring at him from a distance of only a few inches. Their eyes were on the same level. Their bodies were chest to chest, almost touching.

"The Hand sent me to meet you—"

"The Hand?" Ray interrupted.

She reached out and grabbed his arm to forestall, she was sure, another off-color comment. She had always thought it a corny cliché of romance novels, which she knew she shouldn't read but sometimes couldn't help herself, but his eyes did burn into hers. For a wild moment she thought he was going to kiss her right there, right in front of all the passersby who were glancing curiously at the scene being played out before them.

Then he said, "Let go of my arm. It's going numb."

The Angel released him, flushing again with embarrassment. Once again her cursed body had shamed her. If she had hurt this agent of the Hand. If her clumsiness had damaged him—

Billy Ray flexed his hand to get the feeling back in his fingers. He smiled at her.

"That's quite the grip you've got," he said.

The Angel backed away, confused by his lightning-quick mood swings. "We must go," she said. "We have a job to do."

"Maybe," Ray allowed. "If by 'the Hand,' you mean Leo Barnett."

The Angel started, barely suppressing her urge to clamp a hand over his mouth. She looked wildly about to see if anyone had heard him blurt out his ridiculous indiscretion. "You're not supposed to say his *name*," she informed Ray in a ferocious whisper.

"What, Barnett's?" he asked innocently.

"Shhhhh!"

"All right, all right," Ray said, laughing. "Let's go somewhere where we can talk about this job we're supposed to do together."

"Where?" the Angel asked suspiciously.

"I suppose the coffee shop would do," Ray said with a tinge of disappointment in his voice. "Although a room—"

"The coffee shop," the Angel said definitively.

"All right," Ray agreed, easily enough. "What's your name, anyway?"

"The Midnight Angel," she told him.

"Angel," Ray repeated, nodding. "Cool. It fits you."

"Not 'Angel,'" she corrected. "The Angel."

Ray frowned. "Whatever," he said as they moved off together through the lobby. "I'm not going to call you 'the.'"

♣

New York City: The Waldorf-Astoria

THOUGH IT HAD BEEN decades since he'd last seen it, the Waldorf-Astoria's lobby was much as John Nighthawk remembered. Intimate lighting caressed dark wainscoting, potted palms, marble accents, and expensive carpets, as well as a huge bronze clock that dominated the room like an art deco behemoth. Nine feet in height and two tons in weight, its marble and mahogany base was topped by a bronze Statue of Liberty that gleamed in the twilight-lit lobby as if it had just been polished. Other statues incorporated into the ornate clock included Queen Victoria, Benjamin Franklin, George Washington, Andrew Jackson, and Ulysses S. Grant. It looked like a bastard to dust.

As I know well, Nighthawk thought. He had dusted and polished it himself often enough, ages ago in another lifetime before the Takisian virus had changed him and all the world.

The woman he'd been sent to meet was in a dark corner of the lobby, wraithlike in a vintage dress that made it look as if she'd been waiting for a dinner date for the last seventy-five years or so. The only thing that ruined the effect was her oversized handbag. A small clutch purse would have gone much better with her black beaded dress and pert hat crowned by a single egret feather. Her ensemble brought back memories of the 1920s to Nighthawk. Some of them were fond.

Up close, she looked impossibly young in the uncertain light. Her brown eyes were as large and innocent as a doe's. Her long, wavy hair cascaded down to the middle of her back like a golden waterfall. Nighthawk knew her real name, her background, and her ace abilities. But he called her the name she preferred, the name she'd taken from the bit of antique jewelry she wore on a black silk ribbon choker around her slender, elegant neck.

"Miss Cameo?" he asked.

"Cameo will do," she replied.

Nighthawk nodded. "Mr. Contarini sent me to escort you to his tower suite," he said. Contarini hadn't resorted to a fictitious name for this business, but he wanted Cameo kept in the dark about his relationship with the Church. Nighthawk paused, glancing around their corner of the lobby. "I thought that you were going to bring a bodyguard with you?" he asked.

"That's right," the young ace said. "I did."

"Where is he?"

Cameo held out her handbag. Nighthawk took it from her and looked inside. Among the usual trove of feminine paraphernalia was a battered old fedora.

"A hat?" Nighthawk said.

Cameo nodded. "How perceptive of you."

He handed the purse back to her. He knew all about Cameo and her hat. He had researched her thoroughly before entering in negotiations with her on the behalf of the cardinal. However, he didn't think it prudent to let her know that he knew.

"Don't sass your elders, missy," he said briefly. "If you'll come this way."

Cameo accepted his rebuke in silence. They went to the elevator bank and took one nearly to the top of the Waldorf's Tower block, the suite on the forty-first floor where Contarini always stayed when he was in New York City. Nighthawk led her to the apartment, opened the door with his key, and took her through the anteroom, as well as a couple of sitting rooms and living rooms, to arrive at last in a spacious library.

Glassed-in ceiling-to-floor bookcases covered two adjacent walls. Most of the glossy black bookshelves now housed vintage bric-a-brac, though some books and folios were still on the shelves. A comfortable-looking sofa and matching love seat ranged against the two other walls. The rest of the furniture consisted of a black wood desk that matched the bookshelves, and scattered leather chairs and floor lamps. The ancient reliquary that Grubbs had given his life to obtain was on a low coffee table in front of the sofa. The cardinal waited on the sofa with an aura of impatience clinging to him like a wet swimsuit. He was incognito, wearing a six-thousand-dollar Armani suit with suave elegance. Usher stood silently at one end of the sofa. Magda, looking as disapproving as always, at the other.

Contarini didn't bother to rise as Nighthawk and Cameo entered the room.

"I am Romulus Contarini," he announced in his deep actor's voice. His English was colored by a slight Italian accent that only made it sound more lyrical than English usually does. His handsome lips were pursed as he gazed at Cameo, as if he didn't approve of her obvious youth, or perhaps of her, herself, in general. Nighthawk knew that the cardinal didn't like wild carders, though he was not averse to using them to further his schemes.

Cameo nodded. "Mr. Contarini. Nice to finally see you face-to-face after so many chats on the telephone."

She glanced at Usher and Magda, but Contarini didn't bother to introduce them.

"Nice to see you," he said, coming down slightly on the last word. "I'm glad that you weren't foolish enough to take the down payment we had deposited in your account and . . ." He paused, as if groping for a word.

Cameo's eyebrows rose. "And abscond with it?"

Contarini inclined his silver-haired head.

"Are we not both businesspeople, Mr. Contarini?" Cameo asked. "We both have reputations to maintain. I trusted you enough to come to this—" Cameo paused for a moment as she glanced around the sumptuously furnished room. "—elegant but rather private meeting place to channel an unknown object for a fee of two hundred thousand dollars. If I trusted you enough to accept your offer, surely you trusted me enough to fulfill my part of the bargain."

Contarini grunted inelegantly as Nighthawk suppressed a smile. He thought he was going to like Cameo just fine. After she finished her business with Contarini, he had something else for her to do, something that was as important to him as this rigmarole was to the cardinal.

The cardinal turned to Usher, and nodded at the reliquary. "Open it."

The big man bent over the old box. They had looked inside it just once before while they were on the road to Rome, only to make sure that they hadn't been tricked into stealing a decoy. They hadn't.

The cardinal leaned over and removed a rectangular length of stained linen, folded upon itself several times. His fingers caressed it as he lifted it from the box; his lips murmured ancient Latin prayers. He held it to his chest for a moment, his eyes lifted to Heaven.

Nighthawk glanced at the others. Cameo was watching the cardinal, uncertain, frowning. Usher stood as relaxed as always, instantly ready to run, to leap across the room, to dive to the floor, to do whatever the next second might call for. Magda's eyes were riveted on the Mandylion, as if wishing she were the one caressing it. A sheen of sweat covered her forehead. Her lips were clenched in passionate desire that was almost lustful.

Contarini took a deep breath, as if he were wallowing in the scent of the cloth that had once covered the dead, bleeding body of Jesus Christ, and then suddenly held it out to Cameo.

"Take this. Sit there."

Cameo looked from the Shroud to Contarini's face to Nighthawk.

"Is that the Shroud of Turin?" she asked, wide-eyed.

Nighthawk only nodded.

Cameo wet her lips. "Where . . . how . . ." Her voice ran down.

"Don't ask, missy," Nighthawk said softly. "Just take it. Or walk away."

Contarini thrust it again toward her. "Take it," he said commandingly, "and call Our Lord and Savior."

Cameo hesitated for a moment. Any sane person would, Nighthawk thought, and then she took the Shroud from Contarini and sank into the luxurious old armchair he'd indicated. She took a deep breath and held it. For a moment her eyes were unfocused, and then her expression changed utterly and it was clear to Nighthawk that someone else was looking out of her eyes at them. Nighthawk felt his heart skip a beat, then hurry as if to catch up. He swayed on his feet, caught in the grip of powerful emotion, torn by fear and hope intermingled, as he had been on that day in 1946 when he lay dying in a hospital bed as the Takisian virus came raining down out of the sky and touched him with the glory of God on high, turning him into something more than human but perhaps somewhat less than angelic.

"I say," Cameo said in an uncertain voice. "Wha—what's happening?"

Contarini fell down on his knees, muttering wildly in Italian, his head bowed as if he were afraid to look upon his Lord revealed. Magda stared as if she'd been gaffed, her cheeks puffed out in astonished ecstasy. Only Usher, Nighthawk saw, observed unperturbed, still ready for anything.

"My Lord!" the cardinal finally said, holding out his hands beseechingly.

The person looking out through Cameo's eyes focused on him.

"My Lord?" she repeated. "What's this all about?" She looked around. "Why am I here in my apartment again? I died, didn't I?"

Nighthawk had the sudden realization that something had gone terribly wrong.

Contarini frowned. "Died—yes, and risen as before. But—your apartment! I don't understand. What do you mean? Who are you?"

"Who am I?" Cameo repeated, more in indignation than as an actual question. "Who are you, sir, and what are you doing in my apartment? I—what's that voice in my head saying? I . . . I'm a woman!" she exclaimed, holding her hands out, examining them in what Nighthawk thought was half shock, half delight. Her hands went down to her thighs, gripping them, hard. "I've got both of my legs!"

Suddenly, Nighthawk knew. "Mr. Porter," he said quietly.

Cameo looked at him. "You know me? What am I doing here? Am I alive, *again*? What—the voice in my head! It's all so confusing!"

"What's happened?" Contarini demanded in a shrill voice, just on the edge of losing control.

"Apparently," Nighthawk said, immersed in memories of long ago when he'd worked in this hotel and known quite well the man who had lived for many years in this very suite, "Cameo has channeled the spirit of someone we hadn't intended."

"If not the spirit of Our Lord Jesus Christ," Contarini demanded, "then whose is it? For God's sake, whose?"

Nighthawk cleared his throat. "Apparently," he said, "it's Cole Porter."

Contarini's eyes looked as if they were going to bug out of his head. Magda observed the proceedings with a baffled expression that was quickly sliding toward unimaginable fury while Usher tried unsuccessfully to smother a snort of uncontainable laughter.

♠

Las Vegas: The Mirage Auditorium

THE OVERNIGHT TRANSFORMATION OF John Fortune from anonymous teenager to wild card ace who'd saved the life of a popular Vegas entertainer was big news. The fact that Peregrine hadn't allowed any interviews had only heightened the frenzy. It got to the point where neither John Fortune nor Peregrine, nor even Jerry, could leave the hotel suite without being besieged by reporters and stalked by hordes of gawkers. Jerry had quickly realized that the only way to break the siege was to give the public at least something of what they wanted.

"Give 'em an interview," he'd told Peregrine. "Break the story and the pressure will go away, like the water through the dam in *Frankenstein Meets the Wolf Man*."

Peregrine had looked askance at his metaphor, but ultimately agreed with the substance of his argument.

"All right. Arrange something," she'd said, holding up a hand as Jerry nodded. "But make sure it's not exploitative. I don't want my son treated like a media freak."

"In *this* town?"

"Do the best you can," was Peregrine's final order.

He did, and as he stood in the wings looking out upon the Mirage's stage, the very place where it had started, it looked as if things might work out after all.

He'd approached the Mirage publicity people with a complete concept. Have a local media personality interview John Fortune and his mother live on the very stage where his card had so recently and dramatically turned. Siegfried and a very grateful Ralph would take part in the program. Have a few tigers prowl about. Small, cute ones. *Not* the one that had attacked Ralph. The Living Gods would hover in the background as Siegfried and Ralph described the horrific events of that terrible night the show had gone all wrong, praise John Fortune for his fortitude and quick thinking, explain to everyone that the audience had been very safe indeed, present John with a lifetime pass to the Siegfried and Ralph revue as the kid says a few blushing words, and then smiles, hugs, and handshakes all around.

The Mirage publicity people liked the concept. Peregrine, when Jerry described it to her, liked the concept, especially the idea of using a local celeb—if she wasn't going to exploit her son on national television, neither was Barbara Walters—who ultimately turned out to be Kitty O'Leary from Channel Seven KASH Eyewitness Evening News.

It all came together nicely, Jerry thought, observing from the wings. The auditorium was packed with an eager audience. Peregrine looked beautiful on the comfy sofa, which was part of the temporary set arranged on the stage. They opened the program with Peregrine and the extremely photogenic Kitty O'Leary chatting about how difficult it was being a mother in modern times, especially when you had to worry about the wild card virus as well as drugs, alcohol, and unprotected teen sex.

Jerry suddenly felt a restless presence at his side and looked at a nervously smiling John Fortune who had joined him in his vantage spot in the wings.

"Hey, you look great in makeup," Jerry cracked, trying to break the tension a little for the clearly agitated kid.

"Thanks a load," John Fortune said with heavy teenage sarcasm. He took a deep breath. "I'm not so sure about this television stuff. What if I say something stupid?"

"Then you'll join the ranks of everyone else who's ever been on TV," Jerry said. He punched the kid in the shoulder in a comradely manner. "Be cool. You wanted to be an ace."

"Yeah," John Fortune agreed. "It's so much better than the alternative."

"The point is," Jerry said, "when you're a star, you have to take the sour with the sweet."

Of course, Jerry thought, *I'm so utterly anonymous that I constantly change my face and I call myself Mr. Nobody. Who am I to preach to the kid? But then—nobody ever said that you have to live what you preach.*

"But I'm not a star," John Fortune muttered.

Jerry suddenly knew what to say. "You're not a star now, kid, but after you go out on that stage, you'll come back one!"

John Fortune suddenly smiled again. "You think so?"

"I know so," Jerry said, thinking, *Thank God for 42nd Street.*

Sudden applause welled up from the audience.

"Cue," whispered one of the backstage flunkies, making a shooing motion in John Fortune's direction.

"You've got the genes, you've got the talent," Jerry said. "Go knock 'em dead."

John Fortune nodded silent thanks and stepped out onto the stage, a fixed grin plastered on his face. The Living Gods had already appeared, presenting a colorful background chorus as the kid made his way onto the set. Jerry could see Siegfried and Ralph, with, yes, a pair of leashed tigers, waiting for their entrance cue in the other wing.

Better the kid than me, Jerry thought, remembering with little fondness his pitiful career as the shape-changing comedian known as the Projectionist. Still, there was no sense dwelling on his own past. He smiled as he realized that the long-running drama he'd been a peripheral participant in over the last sixteen years was finally coming to an end. And a happy end at that. John Fortune wouldn't need a bodyguard anymore. He'd cheated the odds and won a well-deserved chance at life. Sure, "ace" wasn't the safest occupation, but Jerry didn't know any that went around with a coterie of bodyguards. Even Peregrine wouldn't make him do that. With her son having cleared the biggest hurdle in his life she was sure to back off and give him some room to breathe.

"You Creighton?"

Jerry turned. His eyes went wide in surprise as he recognized the speaker. "Billy Ray?"

Ray glanced at his companion, a smoking babe in a leather jumpsuit with a body like a young Sophia Loren and a frown on her handsome face. Ray's expression suddenly matched hers.

"Do I know you?" Ray asked.

"Uh. No. No, I don't think so," Jerry said. *Too many faces, too many identities,* he thought. It was getting difficult to keep straight who and what each of his many guises was supposed to know.

Of course, he and Ray had crossed paths before, when Jerry had been wearing another face. The last time . . . the last time had been during the Battle of the Rox, when he and Ray had been part of a government team sent in to smash Bloat's joker rebellion. It was a long story without a good ending, and he didn't care to dwell on it.

Ray was still frowning. "You look familiar."

"I got that type of face," Jerry said in his best Alan Ladd imitation. "I recognized you, of course. Who wouldn't?"

"Oh, well." Ray's frown vanished. He glanced at his partner, visibly preening. Her frown deepened a fraction.

"How'd you know me?" Jerry asked before Ray had too much of a chance to think about his previous reply.

Ray gestured over his shoulder. "Guy back there told me you're the kid's bodyguard."

Jerry nodded. "That's right."

"This is Angel," Ray said, indicating his partner. She looked at Jerry sourly as he glanced at her. He decided not to voice any of the half dozen or so puns on her name that had immediately popped up in his brain.

"She's new," Ray added, as if that explained everything.

"What's the government want with the boy?" Jerry asked.

"Well—" Angel began.

"You see—" Ray said.

And suddenly all hell broke out on the stage.

◆

New York City: Tomlin International Airport

WHEN YOU RETURN HOME after a sixteen-year absence and no one is there to greet you and there is no place for you to go, have you really come home after all?

The question ran through Fortunato's mind in an endlessly repetitive loop like a not very difficult koan as he and Downs flew across the Pacific. There was little else to occupy him. He watched a thread of drool gather at the corner of Downs' mouth as the reporter slept soundly in the first-class seat next to him. Watching spittle drip down Downs' chin was preferable, he soon discovered, to watching the movies available on the individual screens set into each of the admittedly comfortable seats.

The technological advances that Fortunato had missed out on while at the monastery were amazing, but unfortunately could do nothing about the quality of the movies they delivered. He watched about twenty minutes as some idiot named Jim Carrey cavorted like a fool as he played an ace with godlike powers. The best thing he could use his abilities for were turning his piece of crap car into a high-powered sports job and add a few inches to the circumference of his girlfriend's already quite suitable breasts.

It would have been laughable if it wasn't so unhysterically bathetic.

Downs awoke right before they landed in LA for the transcontinental leg of their seemingly unending journey. Unfortunately, his company proved little better than Jim Carrey's.

The hours finally caught up with Fortunato and he fell asleep before they crossed the Midwest. He dreamed he was an ace again. All the women he'd once known—Caroline, Veronica, Peregrine, and many of the rest—paraded before him. He used his powers to increase their breast size to mammoth proportions.

They all thanked him profusely before they left him alone and feeling utterly isolated. He awoke sweating as they landed at Tomlin International.

"Welcome home, Fortunato," Downs said with a grin as the plane taxied to the gate.

But Fortunato felt nothing, nothing but empty.

♥

Las Vegas: The Mirage Auditorium

A HIDEOUS STACCATO ROAR shattered the air like a hammer striking multiple metallic gongs in precise rhythmic succession. The Angel had no idea what caused the awful sound. She looked out on the stage horrified as one of the Living Gods floating above the stage crashed, bleeding, onto Kitty O'Leary's desk. The blonde anchorwoman sat frozen in her chair with a stunned expression on her face as the Living God writhed and bled all over her.

Siegfried and Ralph, accompanied by a pair of leashed tigers, had just been introduced to the audience. They stopped before O'Leary's desk. Their cats roared in sudden fear, adding to the growing commotion.

John Fortune and Peregrine sat on a sofa adjacent to the desk. The boy looked out into the darkness of the auditorium with a puzzled expression. Peregrine jumped to her feet, wings widespread, her face that of a bird of prey. She stepped in front of her son as another blast exploded out of the dark auditorium's depths.

The Angel suddenly realized that a hail of bullets were screeching stageward, striking Peregrine and stitching a bloody line across her chest and hurling her back against her son as he sat stunned on the sofa. The sofa tipped over, spilling both backward. Kitty O'Leary, her pert anchorwoman's face spattered by a fine spray of Peregrine's blood, started to scream in mindless terror, her piercing shrieks louder than tiger roars or gun blasts. The Living God fell off O'Leary's desk and tried to crawl away. O'Leary's screams were echoed by some audience members as a third wave of bullets hammered the air.

"Jesus fucking Christ!" Ray blasphemed.

The Angel was too stunned to reprimand him. Ray moved before she could even gather her wits. She looked wildly at Creighton, but he was only a couple of steps behind Ray as they ran out onto the stage. Ray leaped crazily into the darkness beyond the lights while Creighton headed for the shocking tableau at center stage.

The Angel was completely unused to such chaos. *What to do?* she thought desperately. *What to do?* Her heart pounding with wild uncertainty, she followed Ray into the dark and saw men with guns running down the aisles. They seemed to be everywhere. The Angel couldn't be sure how many there were. Ray didn't seem to care.

She couldn't tell what had happened to the first one, the one in the lead. He was already jackknifing backward, flopping oddly like a broken doll as he flew through the air. Ray had his gun. He turned to glare at the Angel as she landed next to him on the auditorium floor and, despite the fact that her heart was as a lion's in the service of her Lord, she flinched at the expression on his face. It was like when she'd dropped the ice cream on his suit, only horribly, terribly more so. It was worse in that now, underneath it all, he was smiling.

"Can you use this?" he asked her. She shook her head curtly. She'd never fired a gun in her life. She didn't like them. She didn't need them. "Then fuck it," he said, smashing the rifle's stock to pieces against the floor and beaning another assassin with the barrel as somewhere a tiger roared and people screamed as the audience tried to surge out of the auditorium, unconsciously hindering the gunmen from gaining the stage.

"On the frigging floor!" someone shouted after letting loose another wild burst of gunfire. "Get on the frigging floor or we'll frigging shoot you all!"

Anger suddenly burned through the Angel's breast, making her forget all her bewilderment and uncertainty. Whoever these men were, they were threatening the lives of innocents, and this she could not allow.

She lifted her arms to Heaven. "Save my soul from evil, Lord," she prayed, willing it to come to her in her time of need, "and heal this warrior's heart."

And it did.

The fiery sword appeared in her hands. With a four-foot blade licked by flames from its plain cross hilt to its blunt tip, it was a weapon that could be wielded only by an ace stronger than most nats. The flames burning up and down its length lit the Angel's face with an almost hellish glow as she glanced swiftly about. It was difficult to see what exactly was happening, but Ray was spinning like a dervish and the gunmen were retreating before him. Some were out of his reach, and one of those was aiming at the figures clustered at center stage. She lunged, swinging her sword, and the fiery blade chopped through the gun's barrel like a glowing knife through butter. The gunman turned to stare at her, and the Angel was gratified by the expression that she saw on his face. He slunk away. She turned to look for another victim, and she saw him: the blond-haired man she'd seen in the Waldorf-Astoria's parking garage, strong and tall and as beautiful as an angel. He came toward her slowly, smiling confidently. Smugly. *He has reason to be smug,* the Angel thought. He was the most handsome man she'd ever seen.

He was big, towering five or six inches over her and outweighing her by at least a hundred pounds. He wore track warm-ups and a short-sleeved shirt that clung to his broad shoulders and massive chest like silk. Perhaps it was. His arms were muscular, but not grotesque. *Just pleasing,* the Angel thought. His face was handsome without being pretty, with a strong jaw and high but not delicate cheekbones. His nose was hawklike, his eyes bluer than seemed possible. His hair was a thick blond mane that swept in loose coils to his shoulders. His coiffure might have looked dainty on some men, but he was masculine enough to carry it off.

"I am the Witness," he said to the Angel. "I tell you now. Turn away from the path of unrighteousness, or I will be forced to teach you a lesson."

"Lesson?" the Angel asked. She released her grip on her sword's hilt and the weapon vanished. This Witness was unarmed and she had never used her blade against an unarmed man. She smiled to herself. For all his muscles, he had never faced the Angel's God-given strength before.

"Yes." His white, even teeth flashed in a dazzling smile. "It is called 'the kiss.'"

Suddenly she realized that he was close enough to grab her and pull her to him. His grip was strong enough to damage an ordinary woman, but the Angel was not ordinary. As he wrapped his arms around her she could feel heat radiating off his body in palpable waves. She could smell the scent of him. He wound his right hand in her thick hair and pulled her head back, exposing the strong column of her throat. He bent over her and brought his lips down on hers.

The Angel couldn't believe the sensations that swept over her body. She wanted him more than anything she'd ever wanted in her life. More than the Hand's approval. More than Heaven itself. She closed her eyes, feeling hot and cold, weak and strong all at once. She wanted to possess him thoroughly and eternally. Her desire flushed her strength from her body as his tongue penetrated her mouth. She had experienced that only once before in her life and her mother had caught her and the boy and had beaten them both with a broom handle. Eventually the boy was able to run away home, but she couldn't. She was home.

"Angel!" A voice spoke her name from far away, warningly.

She opened her eyes and his face was upon hers, so close that she could barely focus on it. He was smiling. But it wasn't in joy or with need or even in lust. It was the smile of a conqueror reveling in his superior strength. In his imposition of his will upon another.

The Angel was suddenly horrified. As much as she could never admit it to herself, she had longed for an embrace such as this. Her need was so great as to approach desperation. This man could have been the answer to all her dreams. He was as handsome as she could ever imagine a man to be. His strength matched hers. It had seemed that his desire matched hers as well, but she now realized that they desired two totally different things.

She needed love. If it couldn't be spiritual, she realized now openly and to her shame, at least it could be physical. Her mother had not succeeded in beating that sin out of her. She had only driven it deep into her soul where it had finally blossomed with undeniable lust.

But the Witness needed only to conquer. To take. To impose his will and then immediately discard. She saw it on his face and read it in his sneering expression and forced embrace. No matter how great her need, the Angel could not countenance this. But did she, she desperately wondered, really have a choice?

She twisted her neck. Her lips slipped away from his, and the Witness looked down at her and laughed, which only confirmed her worst fears. She pushed against him, but he was the strongest man she'd ever encountered. There was no doubt that he was an ace himself. One of her arms was trapped between their chests. The other was pinned against her side by his encircling arm. She could find no leverage to help her break free. He knew this as well, and laughed at her again.

"The kiss," he said, "is only the first lesson I'm going to teach you, slut." Desperately she brought up her knee, trying to smash his groin, but it struck his massive thigh and rebounded. "Every time you strike me," he said in a curiously tender voice, "I'll strike you twice. Then I'll take you, whether you're conscious or not."

The Angel clenched her teeth and hit at him again and again with her knee, but he only laughed. She writhed in his grasp like an animal caught in a trap. She'd gnaw her own leg off to escape him, but there was no such easy remedy to her awful situation. She'd been in his embrace for only seconds, but it seemed like an eternity.

"Christ, Witness, score on your own time. Right now we've got a bloody job to do."

The Witness looked up, frowning. It was the jolly little chubby man whom the Angel had also seen in the Waldorf's underground garage. He frowned himself a little, and suddenly he didn't seem so jolly.

"Ah, Dagon," the Witness said sulkily, then when the jolly little man's expression turned even less jolly, he quickly released the Angel. He looked back at her scowling ferociously. "All right. But I'm not done with you, slut. I'll see you again, and then I'll give you what you deserve for tempting a Godly man."

"Butcher Dagon." It was the voice that had called out moments before, warning the Angel when she'd been in the Witness's grasp. Now she recognized it. The three of them turned to see Billy Ray brushing futilely at the bloodstains that had utterly ruined his impeccable suit. "What brings you to these parts?"

The little man was looking jolly again, like everyone's favorite uncle. He smiled. "You recognize me?"

"Sure," Ray said. "I've seen your picture in the paper a few times. Usually above the caption 'Crazed Killer Strikes.'"

Dagon laughed. It was a jolly sound, but out of place in the auditorium's chaotic atmosphere filled with wailing and crying and screaming. "I don't recognize you, but I think I can identify you by the way you went through our spearcarriers. Billy Ray, isn't it?"

Ray nodded.

"So," Dagon said thoughtfully, "somehow the government has become involved. Interesting. Still, you are outnumbered and outgunned."

"Yet, we're kicking your asses."

Billy Ray grinned a mad grin, and Butcher Dagon shook his head and changed.

The thing facing Billy no longer looked chubby or jolly or even remotely human. It stood upright on two thick legs. It had arms encased in slablike muscle, a bullet head set directly on broad shoulders, and a prehensile tail as long as its body. Dagon's clothes had vanished along with his human form, either destroyed during his instantaneous transformation or somehow absorbed into his new, thickly pelted body. The Angel couldn't tell which. She had little experience with shape-shifters.

Dagon's new body had brindled black and brown fur covering it from head to toe; beady, wild-looking eyes; a long snout full of sharp, gleaming teeth; and keen-looking claws sprouting from his finger and toe tips. His tail whipped back and forth like an angry snake and copious amounts of saliva drooled from his wicked jaws.

"Je-sus," Ray said emphatically, and Dagon charged.

They collided like smashing meteors, and the ensuing battle was so fast, so frantic, that the Angel could barely discern who was who most of the time and was certainly unsure which one had the upper hand. They tore at each other like enraged wolverines on amphetamines for twelve or fourteen seconds and then broke as suddenly as Dagon had attacked.

The transformed ace leaped back six or eight feet and the combatants stood staring at each other, panting and bloody. It was hard for the Angel to say who was worse off. Ray was down to his shoes and underwear and a few shreds of clothing. He was bleeding from too many places to count. While some of the shallow bites and scratches healed right before the Angel's astonished eyes, a big flap of skin and flesh hung on Ray's muscled chest and his upper right arm bled profusely from where Dagon had mangled it with his jaws.

Dagon didn't look much better. One eye was swollen shut and his right arm was dangling uselessly, the shaft of his broken forearm sticking out jaggedly through his torn flesh. The Angel realized that at least some of the blood dripping from Dagon's slavering jaws was his own, not Ray's, as the hairy ace spit out some broken fangs.

Ray smiled crazily, and at that moment the Angel wasn't sure which of the two combatants she feared the most.

"Round two?" Ray asked.

Dagon said something. The Angel couldn't understand his words, either because of his injuries or perhaps his transformed vocal cords. But whatever he said was angry and vicious.

They hurled themselves at each other again. Ray managed to grab Dagon's broken arm. He yanked at it and the transformed ace screamed in a disturbingly inhuman, high-pitched whine. The crazed smile was now fixed on Ray's face like a horror mask as they strove breast to breast, Dagon's tail whipping around as if it had a mind of its own. It finally struck Ray's neck, clung, and wrapped around, pulling tight. The Angel could see it sink into Ray's flesh like a garrote. Ray clenched his teeth and the tendons and muscles in his neck jumped out like granite ridges.

Dagon tried to rake Ray's stomach with a clawed foot, but the angle between them was wrong. Ray whipped his head back and forth, but Dagon's tail was tight as a constrictor around his neck. Ray's face started to turn red, the veins bulging out on his neck and forehead. Ray grabbed Dagon's tail with both hands and Dagon howled with what sounded to the Angel like fiendish glee.

Ray looked horrible. His face was turning even darker. He frantically tried to pry the strangling tail from around his neck, but it was stronger than nylon rope. The Angel started to go to them, but the Witness, who had also been watching with an approving smile on his handsome face, blocked her path and shook his head.

The Angel clenched her fists as Ray stopped prying at Dagon's tail, grabbed it with both hands, and brought it up to his mouth. He lowered his head and bit down, hard, grinding his teeth like a starving dog trying to crush a bone for its marrow.

Dagon screamed again and tried to pull away. Ray continued to gnaw at his opponent's tail while yanking at it with all his strength. It suddenly parted with an audible snap and Ray catapulted backward, past the Witness. The Angel caught him, staggered, and went to the floor with him on top.

Dagon hopped about like his feet were on fire. His tail whipped like a decapitated snake, spattering gobs of stinking ichor all over. The Angel helped Ray pull the coil of tail away from his throat as Ray gasped greedily for air.

Dagon frothed at the mouth, wildly screaming words that were mostly unintelligible, but which seemed to contain the phrase "Kill you, fucker," in various combinations throughout. The Angel blushed.

Ray rose to his feet, staggering unsteadily, as if drunk. "Watch out," he muttered to the Angel, pushing her aside. "The weasel's coming back for more."

The Angel couldn't believe that Ray had strength left in reserve. He met Dagon in mid-charge, and before they could collide Ray launched himself feetfirst, face up and back parallel to the floor, as if he were a soccer player attempting a bicycle kick and Dagon's genitalia were the ball.

Dagon screamed as Ray connected. The force of Ray's kick propelled him right at the Angel, who wound up and hit him with everything she had on the point of his jaw.

Pain jumped through her hand, ran up her arm, and jangled through her shoulder. Her hand went numb, which was actually something of a relief, as Dagon changed direction again. He flew back toward Ray, hit the floor, rolled at Ray's feet, and lay there bleeding.

Ray looked at the Angel crazily. "Hey, we're a team," he said, and his smile suddenly turned to an even more frightening frown. "But let me tell you something. The next time you pull that blazing pigsticker out of the sky, I want you to gut that fucking blond asshole before you put it away again. All right?"

The Angel smiled feebly and nodded.

"Where is that scumbag, anyway?" Ray asked, looking all around.

Before either of them could spot the Witness, every light in the auditorium suddenly cut out. The room turned pitch-black. Ray swore, blundering about in the dark. The Angel stood where she was, counting a slow twenty before the lights on the stage went back on. A handful of seconds went by before the Angel and Ray realized that John Fortune was missing, as were the Witness and some of the gunmen who had still been conscious when the lights went off.

The taste of failure was a bitter gall in the Angel's mouth.

Chapter Three

Las Vegas, Nevada: The Mirage Auditorium

JERRY HAD BEEN IN tough situations in the past where lives were on the line, but this was almost overwhelmingly desperate. If Ray hadn't charged onto the stage he might have hesitated for a long time, but when the government ace had leaped into action something in Jerry made him follow Ray into the heart of danger.

It certainly wasn't his brain. If he'd thought about it at all, he'd have run away from the flying bullets. Whatever it was that made him accompany Ray was something deeper in his makeup. His heart. Perhaps his gut. His reaction was more instinctive than rational. Jerry would have sighed to himself if he'd had the time. He'd always considered himself a smart guy, and this was just crazy.

Ray executed a sharp right and hurled himself into the offstage darkness. Sudden sounds of fists hitting flesh and bone, the cracking of those bones, and screams of pain quickly followed. Jerry didn't follow Ray. Realizing that people on the stage needed help, Jerry passed by Siegfried and Ralph, who were petrified by fear but otherwise unharmed, and headed for Kitty O'Leary's desk, where the hysterical anchorwoman was covered in blood.

"Get your tigers out of here before something terrible happens," he said to the entertainers as he went by. "Again."

They glanced at each other and then took his advice and ran, their leashed cats roaring wildly as they bounded after them. Jerry dropped down to one knee when he reached O'Leary's desk and checked the body propped up against it. It was the male half of the pair of floating Living Gods. Jerry didn't know his name. Blood pumped sluggishly from a series of horrific puncture wounds in his torso. As Jerry grabbed his wrist to feel for a pulse, the injured man suddenly focused his large, beautiful eyes on Jerry's face, and said something in Arabic. Jerry looked on helplessly as he vomited a gout of blood and died.

Jerry stood, suppressing a sigh. He didn't have time for pity. He examined O'Leary quickly for wounds and discovered that none of the blood splashed on her chest and face seemed to be hers.

"Shut up," he said, and "get down."

She just kept screaming, so he grabbed her shoulders and shook her. When that didn't catch her attention, he slapped her, adrenaline making his open-palmed blow a little harder than he'd intended. She shut her mouth and looked at him in amazement. Anger flared in her eyes. Jerry was suddenly glad that he looked like tough-guy Alan Ladd. It made it all the easier to act the part.

"I said, shut up," he repeated, putting his hand on the top of her head, "and get the hell down."

He shoved hard enough to push her to the floor and she crawled under the stage furniture. That was the safest place for her. He turned away, hoping she'd stay put. He couldn't waste any more time on her.

More sounds of gunfire and terror came from the auditorium. Ray, and Angel, Jerry supposed, were keeping the bad guys off the stage. At least for the moment. Jerry went swiftly to the overturned sofa where Peregrine huddled over the bloody, unmoving body of her son. He vaulted over the divan and went down to one knee beside her. Her teeth were clenched. She was panting like a hyperventilating dog, or a woman trying to give birth.

"He's all right," she gasped out. "Not hurt. Hit his head when the sofa went over. Just knocked out. Be . . . all . . . right . . ."

Her voice started to fade. Jerry took her arm and half lifted her off the boy, wincing at what he saw. A line of slugs stitched sideways across Peregrine's body from her loins, across her abdomen and chest, to her right wing where feathers had been shot away and delicate bones shattered.

"Christ," he said in a low voice.

It didn't look good. He stripped his off shirt, ripped it to rags, and applied pressure bandages as best he could to what seemed to be Peregrine's worst wounds. Her only response was to moan feebly. There wasn't anything else he could do for her, and he realized that Peregrine didn't have much time left if she didn't receive immediate medical attention. He turned his attention to John Fortune, thinking that Peregrine really needed his newfound ace abilities. But the kid was still out cold.

What a time to get knocked senseless, Jerry thought. He tried to revive the boy, but the best he could get from him was an unintelligible groan. He could feel a knot on the back of the kid's skull the size of a golf ball. He must have really slammed his head hard on the floor when the sofa had tipped over on them.

Jerry felt as useless as Rock Hudson in the opening scenes of one of his screwball comedies. He didn't want to mess around with the kid, in case he had a real head injury. And Peregrine needed expert attention, fast. Someone would have to help. Angel, he thought. Or Ray . . .

Jerry stood and went swiftly to the edge of the stage, shielded his eyes from the light, and looked out just in time to see Ray go mano a mano with a chubby little guy who looked like someone's favorite older uncle until the guy suddenly turned into something that wasn't so avuncular. Jerry recognized the transformed man. He was the British killer ace called Butcher Dagon.

Eerily, it seemed as if the world had stopped to watch their breathtaking exhibition of violence. He saw Angel, some stiff who was much too good-looking for his own good, and even a few of the goons with guns as well as some of the crazy-scared onlookers pause to take a breath as Ray and Dagon tore at each other like gladiators from another, much more savage age.

For a moment John Fortune was forgotten. Even Peregrine slipped from his mind until the epic battle ended with the brilliant one-two punch of Angel and Ray coldcocking the British ace.

Jerry saw the handsome guy climb onto the stage. Some of the surviving gunmen followed him. Fortunately, none were near Jerry. He knew that he had only a few moments in which to make the right move. Peregrine was now beyond any help he could give her. There was only the kid, his sacred charge, to consider. He suddenly knew what to do.

He ripped off his clothes and the lights went out as he took on mass.

The auditorium fell into utter darkness. It was all very much like that night back in '65 when he'd turned into the Big Ape and sucked enough energy out of his surroundings to start a chain reaction that blacked out New York City and ultimately most of the Eastern Seaboard.

Energy to mass, as the equation went. This time around, he needed a lot less mass, so he siphoned off a lot less energy. Enough, probably, to blow most of the electric circuits in the auditorium, maybe in all of the Mirage. He welcomed the darkness. It made his task easier.

Jerry knew that he had to work fast. He added pounds of flab to his transformed frame. He didn't have time to get his features exactly right, so he puffed them up into a pulpy mess. His hands were already bloody, so he smeared them on his face and torso, blurring more detail. He groaned realistically and threw himself down, huddling on his side, his hands over his still-changing face. Someone kneeled next to him.

"Dagon?" an unfamiliar voice asked.

Jerry squinted upward.

"Wh—who?" he quavered.

"It's the Witness," said the handsome guy in a voice decidedly lacking pity. He leaned closer. "I'm surprised you're already conscious. Man, you got your ass kicked." The Witness looked up. "Juan—Sam—let the others grab the kid. Come over here and give Dagon a hand," he said with open contempt. "And for God's sake, get something to cover him up with. He's fat and bloody and naked. Come on. Move. Move!"

The last was a general order shouted to everyone as the two men Witness singled out came to Jerry's side.

"Here you are," one of them said, slipping a cloak around Jerry with surprisingly gentle hands. "Up you go. Come on, before that asshole Ray finds us hanging around here on the stage."

Jerry moaned convincingly. They hustled him away, right behind another pair of gunmen who were dragging a limp John Fortune into the wings.

"What about the others?" one of the men supporting Jerry asked as they passed Witness, who was waiting impatiently.

"They knew what they were getting into," he said shortly. "Let's get the hell out of here."

Jerry kept his face burrowed in the cloak as best he could. He was sure he hadn't copied Dagon's features perfectly, but the bruising and swelling and blood that he'd smeared on his face seemed to be an adequate disguise.

The kidnappers, with Jerry and John Fortune in tow, burst out into the sunny parking lot where a van was waiting for them. The two thugs hustled Jerry into the back with six or seven other gunmen, as well as John Fortune, who was only now starting to come around.

The Witness hustled to the front of the van. Its engine was already racing and it started to move before he could slam the passenger-side door shut. They pulled away from the Mirage quickly and immediately headed for the side streets off the Strip.

Jerry couldn't see out of the van's windows. He didn't know this part of Vegas—no tourist did—and he was immediately lost. The muscles joked and kidded with macho toughness now that the fight was over, except for the one who cradled his broken arm and endlessly cursed Ray.

They drove for perhaps twenty minutes. Jerry's mind raced in high gear the entire time, but he was unable to construct a workable plan to escape from the gang. John Fortune groaned awake halfway through the trip. One of the gunmen told him to sit down and shut up, and the kid wisely took his advice. Jerry tried to catch his eye, but Fortune wouldn't look at him.

Finally they stopped before an abandoned, boarded-up 7-Eleven. The asphalt parking lot shimmered in the summer heat, drooping weeds poking up through aimless cracks in its surface like dying flowers on the floor of Hell.

"Let's go, let's go," Witness ordered.

This guy clearly, Jerry thought, lacked patience. Mystified, Jerry allowed himself to be half-dragged to the convenience store's front door, which proved to be unlocked. Three men were waiting inside. One had a gun, another held a leash, and the third one wore it.

This last unfortunate was obviously a joker. His body was twisted so that his legs were thick hindquarters, his arms scrawny forelegs. His face had a vaguely canine look, with a snout underslung by a long jaw, no chin, and drooping ears that could have belonged to a hound dog. His skin was unfurred, but sallow, blotchy, and unhealthy-looking. His expression was not intelligent.

"Let's go, Blood," his handler said.

The joker looked at him, snuffling eagerly.

"Home, boy. Let's go home. There's a nice steak waiting for you. Nice and raw and dripping."

Blood drooled, grinning idiotically, and walked on four limbs toward the store's back wall, and then into a tunnel that suddenly appeared the instant before his nose would have touched the wall. They all followed him. Jerry was totally mystified, wondering what the hell was going on.

It was cool and quiet on the other side of the tunnel, which opened into a small room built of naked stone. The room had no windows to the outside and was lit by a single unreachable bulb dangling from a naked fixture in the ceiling. The only door leading out of it was iron, with a tiny barred window. The small chamber smelled of ancient sickness that seemed to have soaked into the very stones of its walls and floor. Jerry didn't know where they were, but suddenly he was afraid.

Blood howled for his meat.

♣

New York City: The Waldorf-Astoria

JOHN NIGHTHAWK WATCHED CONTARINI stare at Cameo as if she'd just hooked a quarter from the collection plate, or done something equally unforgivable. Usher and Magda looked on with interest. Usher's expression seemed mild.

He really had no dog in this fight. Nighthawk knew that he was along just for the paycheck. But Magda's expression was hurt compounded with fury.

If there's trouble, Nighthawk thought, *it'll come from her.*

Magda looked at Cameo as if she'd expected the Second Coming to occur right before her eyes and instead had been given a third-rate vaudeville act. (Which, Nighthawk realized, was pretty much close to what had happened.) The nun looked from the transformed Cameo to Nighthawk to Contarini, searching for a clue as how to react. Cameo posed no immediate threat to the cardinal or anyone else. But, obviously, things hadn't gone right. The Shroud should have produced Jesus Christ. Instead they'd gotten . . . someone else. It was clear that Magda had no idea who Cole Porter was, but Contarini, whom Nighthawk knew was a well-educated sophisticate, quickly showed that he labored under no such handicap.

"I don't understand." The cardinal's voice sounded like cracking ice on a frozen lake in the Italian Alps. "What . . . where is Our Lord? Why do we have this, this degenerate writer of, of degenerate popular songs instead of Our Lord?"

Nighthawk, who knew a little about music, couldn't agree with Contarini's assessment of Porter's talents and was also more than a little amused that the cardinal's fury had made him almost tongue-tied. More importantly, he had an explanation regarding Porter's unexpected appearance.

"It seems," Nighthawk said quietly, "that we may have been a little impetuous in insisting that Cameo do her reading here instead of her usual room in Club Dead Nicholas."

Everyone, even Cameo channeling Porter, looked at him with interest.

"What do you mean?" the cardinal asked.

Nighthawk shrugged. "It's obvious, isn't it? Look around. This is Porter's apartment. When he was in New York he lived in the Waldorf-Astoria since when?"

"Nineteen thirty-four," Porter said. "Though I did move once, from another room in the hotel to this very apartment. It's so much more spacious than my old flat."

"Did you bring your furniture with you?" Nighthawk asked.

"Some," Porter allowed.

"Like the chair you're sitting on?"

"Yes," Porter said. "It's a very comfortable reading chair. Naturally, I brought it along for my library."

Nighthawk looked at Contarini and spread his hands in a silent, there-you-have-it gesture.

"Are you saying," the cardinal said in his low, dangerous voice, "that somehow the spirit, the soul, of this, this sodomite jingle writer—as expressed in his chair—somehow *overcame* the potency of Our Lord Savior's soul—as expressed in his Shroud?"

"No," Nighthawk suggested quietly. "I'm saying that the scientists and skeptics have been right all along."

"*Che?*" Contarini's anger made him slip into his native language.

"Like the scientists and skeptics have said all along, maybe this isn't really the burial cloth of Jesus. Maybe it's a fake."

For a moment Nighthawk thought that the cardinal was going to have a stroke. The churchman's face turned white, then a dangerous-looking red. Veins stood out on his forehead and he swayed on the sofa as if tossed by unfelt winds. Finally he steadied himself and stared at Nighthawk like a malignant demon or a righteous angel. Nighthawk couldn't decide which.

"It isn't," he hissed. "It is real. It is the burial cloth of My Lord and Savior. My faith tells me so."

"This is all so fascinating," Porter said, eyeing them closely, "but what does it all have to do with me?"

Nighthawk shook his head. "Nothing," he said, and thought silently to himself, *And everything.* Nighthawk knew that he had to end this farce soon. Magda was picking up on the cardinal's distress. There was no telling how she'd react if the cardinal made a hasty, unfortunate decision.

And if she reacted badly, his chance to learn what he'd hoped to learn when he'd accepted this mission would probably vanish. It was clear, whatever the cardinal's faith told him, that the Shroud was a fake, but this little comedy had shown Nighthawk one thing: the undeniable durability of the soul. There *was* life after death. The soul did transcend the death of the body. What had been a matter of uncertain faith had suddenly become a matter of certain fact.

He had so many questions he wanted to ask Porter, but he couldn't ask them now. Not in front of the cardinal. He hated to see the revenant go, but Porter had to go back to wherever he'd come from before the situation blew up in their faces. There'd be other opportunities to get answers to his questions. Now, for the benefit of all involved, Nighthawk knew that he had to end this scene as quickly and quietly as possible.

"Mr. Porter," he said in polite tones, "would you come here for a moment? There's something I'd like you to see."

Porter looked at him from across the room. "I'd love to, but you see—" He interrupted himself, laughing. "Of course. I have legs that work now. One forgets after doing without for so long." He glanced down at Cameo's limbs. "Such slender, pretty ones, too. I would have been quite the popular chap in the old days. But, no, of course, I suppose it wouldn't have been the same."

He stood with a sigh, and Cameo swayed as her body broke contact with the chair. She reached out as if to steady herself against the chair's arm, then snatched her hand away before touching it. She looked from Nighthawk to Contarini, ignoring the two who stood behind her like door guards in a medieval hall.

"It didn't go as you expected." It was a statement, not a question.

Contarini stared at her, frowning. "No. It didn't. Not at all."

Nighthawk didn't like his expression, or the inflection of his voice. It didn't take a revelation to realize what the cardinal was contemplating. The only question was how far the cardinal dared to go.

"Nighthawk." The churchman snapped the ace's name without looking at him, his terrifying gaze reserved solely for Cameo. "Take this . . . take our . . . visitor . . . out of my sight."

Nighthawk suddenly relaxed. Whichever way Contarini wanted to go, he, Nighthawk, would actually be in control of Cameo's destiny. And he'd find a way to work things out.

Nighthawk went to her side. "Come with me," he said quietly.

She looked at him, made a move to her handbag. Nighthawk shook his head briefly, almost imperceptibly, but she noticed. She looked at him for what seemed a long time, and then she finally nodded.

"Take her to St. Dympna's," Contarini said in detached, almost uncaring tones. He gestured vaguely. "Usher and Magda will accompany you."

"I don't need—" Nighthawk began, but Contarini interrupted him with a lion's roar.

"Don't tell me what you need or don't need!" he shouted. "I tell you what to do. You obey. *Capisce?*"

Nighthawk bowed silently. Usher moved as quietly as a jungle cat on a deep pile carpet, and before Cameo had a chance to react, he grabbed her handbag away from her. She made a single convulsive motion toward snatching it back, but Usher just shook his head and held it out of her reach.

"Uh-uh," he said. He looked inside, and frowned. He reached in and took out a battered old fedora that had definitely seen better days. "What's this?" he asked, bemused. "I thought you were lugging a hand cannon around with you, and it's just an old hat?"

"Don't let her touch it," Nighthawk said warningly.

"Whatever you say, boss," Usher agreed.

Cameo glared at Nighthawk, who offered her the slightest of shrugs.

Nighthawk glanced at Contarini. The cardinal stared with eyes wide open at nothing at all but the scene of loss and devastation playing in his head. Nighthawk could almost feel sorry for him, if he didn't dislike the stiff-necked old bastard so much. Magda, taking her cue from her beloved leader, wore a lost-soul expression that also would have been touching if Nighthawk hadn't known her better. She looked as if she wanted to comfort Contarini but was stopped by the fact that human emotions were so foreign to her that she just didn't know how to do it. Only Usher looked cool and composed, and openly wondering as he observed the byplay between Nighthawk and Cameo.

Nighthawk could do nothing now. He could only get the girl away from Contarini as quickly as possible. And then see what he could do about St. Dympna's.

"Come with us," he said quietly, and for once something went right. She nodded and followed him without a word, Magda and Usher bracing her like prison guards on death row. Nighthawk looked back as they left the library to see Contarini still staring fix-eyed at nothing.

Christ's supposed Shroud was tossed carelessly over Cole Porter's unoccupied reading chair.

Las Vegas, Nevada: The Mirage

THE BLOOD HAD BEEN the hardest thing. That, and the screaming. The Angel couldn't decide which was worse. She also didn't like the memory of the Witness's lips grinding against hers, but she was a warrior for the Lord and she could deal with wounds and indignities. It was the suffering of the innocents that bothered her so.

She'd fought for the Hand before, but never in a battle this intense. It wasn't so much her and Ray fighting the Allumbrados. The fighting had been fine. Thrilling, even. Except when it came to the Witness. The Angel knew that she hadn't acquitted herself well with him. But she realized she shouldn't dwell on that. Or on the blood. Or on the screaming, especially of the innocent tourists caught in the indiscriminate firing. Of Kitty O'Leary, screeching like a maniac behind her desk. Of Peregrine and the bloody sheet wrapped around her as they took her off on a gurney. She shouldn't dwell on all that, she knew, because it was part of the Lord's plan. But the blood—

"Hey."

The Angel's eyes focused and she realized that Ray was standing before her. "You okay?"

His once immaculate suit was torn into rags. His body didn't look much better. His face was battered and bloody. A vivid purple welt like a scar from a noose colored an arc around his neck. A flap of skin and meat hung down from his upper chest, exposing the muscle underneath, as well as a glimmer of bone. He was still bleeding from half a dozen body wounds and he held his side as if he had broken or at least rearranged ribs.

But he'd proved himself more competent than she thought he'd be. He'd handled himself quite well and his fighting technique had been, well, a revelation. He was faster than she was, if not stronger. And, she had to admit, much more deadly, with a killer instinct that at times was frightening.

"Yes," she finally lied. The next sentence came out unbidden from her mouth. "Tell me something."

Ray brushed at his cheek, smearing a trail of clotting blood. "Sure." He waited a moment, frowned, and then asked into the silence between them, "What is it?"

The Angel forced herself to focus. "Do you ever get used to the blood?"

"The blood?" She could see that he was puzzled. It was almost as if she'd asked him if he ever got used to the air he breathed, or the food he ate. "If blood bothers you, you're in the wrong line of work, ba—uh, Angel. The people we deal with bleed all the time." He grinned, and it was not comforting. "Better them than us, but we have to bleed too, sometimes. It's the nature of the job."

She nodded. She believed his words, but she wasn't sure that she understood them. She'd have to pray over it and seek the Lord's guidance.

"What do we do now?"

"Now?" The word came out of Ray as a long sigh. "Now we wait for the paper pushers to show up and start asking stupid questions."

The Angel looked around the auditorium. It was quieter now than during the attack, but almost as chaotic, though the chaos had a controlled feel to it, as the men and women in EMT uniforms worked to alleviate the pain and suffering that surrounded them.

It wasn't long before a florid-faced man with a dark rumpled suit and short rumpled haircut that screamed COP approached, looking as if he'd rather have a gun than a notebook in his hand as he faced them.

"Now just who the hell are you two?" he asked unpleasantly. "Witnesses said you two played a major part in the fight—"

"Somebody had to protect the citizens while you were out chugging donuts," Ray said.

"Just a minute—"

"I'm going to reach into the back pocket of my pants," Ray said, "and get my ID." He frowned. It was not a pleasant sight. "If the pocket's still attached to my ass." Fortunately it was, and the ID wallet was still in it. He took it out and showed it to the cop. "I'm Agent Billy Ray. Secret Service. This is Agent Angel."

"You—" the Angel started to say, but he froze her with a look.

That doesn't, she thought as the cop frowned at Ray's ID, *happen very often.*

The cop looked up. It was hard to say if the realization that the Feds were on the case made him more or less truculent. "Ray. Yeah, I guess I heard of you. Well," he said gruffly, "you'll have to come down to the station and make a statement."

"Certainly, officer." The Angel was amazed at the sudden courtesy in Ray's manner and tone. "Do you mind if I stop bleeding first? Maybe change out of my rags? Get my broken ribs bound up?"

The cop's florid features grew redder. "No," he said shortly.

"Excellent, officer." Ray took the Angel by her upper right arm and moved off. She went with him without a murmur. "We'll stop by as soon as possible. Perhaps tomorrow morning. Whatever the doctor says."

The cop opened his mouth to say something, then seemed to think better of it. He waved them on.

"You didn't have to lie," the Angel said when they were out of his hearing.

"Lie?" Ray asked innocently.

"I'm not a Secret Service agent."

"Did I say you were a Secret Service agent?" Ray shook his head. "No."

"You said—"

"I said 'Agent Angel,'" Ray quoted himself. "And didn't you tell me yourself that you're an agent of the Lord?"

"I—" the Angel paused. "Maybe. I—I probably said 'instrument of the Lord.'"

Ray shrugged. "Agent, instrument. Let's not get technical. Now, be quiet for a moment."

They'd reached the exit, which was blocked by uniformed cops. The Angel didn't even listen to Ray's explanation as he showed them his identification. Something about clearance levels and need-to-know and having to report back to the chief immediately as to what had happened. She was suddenly so tired that she really didn't know how he'd managed it. The sleepless hours, the exhausting travel, the mentally and physically draining combat had finally caught up with her. Suddenly they were outside the auditorium.

People stared at them as they went through the lobby, but the Angel for once hardly noticed, let alone cared. She could hear the buzz of conversation. They were already whispering about the "mayhem at the Mirage," as she and Ray went to the elevator bank. Unsurprisingly, no one else got on the elevator with them as they went up to the connecting rooms that Ray had rented earlier.

Ray looked at her judiciously in the hallway outside their rooms as he handed her the electronic key for her half of the suite. She took it from him and managed to insert it into the lock on the third try. She opened the door and stumbled into the room.

"You'd better get some rest—" Ray began, and she closed the door in his face.

She thought about taking a shower, but barely managed to peel off her torn and bloodied fighting suit and slip off her sweat-soaked underwear before collapsing onto the cool, welcoming bed.

If she dreamed, she didn't remember.

◆

New York City: Jokertown

FORTUNATO DITCHED DIGGER DOWNS at Tomlin International as soon as they cleared customs and reached ground transport outside the terminal. He'd had enough of the man's company on the long flights across the Pacific and over the country. He needed some time to himself, some time to think about his return to a land he'd left behind sixteen years ago along with a life he had no desire to renew.

Before getting into the cab waiting in line at ground transport, he took a few hundred in expense money from Downs, as well as a cell phone so they could keep in touch. Fortunato marveled at the slim piece of equipment before he slipped it into the pocket of his robe. Portable phones had gotten a lot smaller since the last time he'd used one, but Fortunato was sure that they wouldn't be the only marvel to meet his eyes.

The cabby glanced up into the mirror as he pulled away from the curb. He had a turban and a long, thick beard, and he wore white robes. He spoke barely understandable English.

"Where to, Mack?"

It was, Fortunato reflected, good to back in the good old U.S.A. And that was the question. Where to?

"Manhattan," Fortunato said. Who in New York, he pondered, did he still have ties to?

Peregrine. He had no idea where she lived or what her phone number was. Besides, she was still in Vegas with the boy. His mother was dead. Miranda . . . Veronica . . . the last he'd heard from her had been a telegram telling him of Ichiko's death. He'd ignored it. He could hardly drop in on her now, even if he knew where to find her. There were others, but time had not been good to his friends, allies, or even his foes.

Xavier Desmond, the onetime unofficial mayor of Jokertown and one of the best clients Fortunato had when he ran his string of geishas, had been dead more than fifteen years. Cancer had taken him soon after that memorable around-the-world trip on the *Busted Flush,* right after Fortunato had taken up the monastic life.

Chrysalis, purveyor of fine drink and even better information, had followed Des into death not long after. Her Crystal Palace had burned to the ground.

The amiable Hiram Worchester, one of the aces Fortunato had been closest to back in the day, had gone down for her murder. Though not a lot of news had reached Fortunato while he'd been isolated in the monastery, that had, and it had shocked him. He understood that Hiram had retired from public life. Even his fabulous restaurant, where Fortunato had first met the unbelievably beautiful Peregrine and had commenced his final battle with the Astronomer, was no more.

Yeoman, whom he'd traveled with to the gut of the Swarm . . . there had been a bond between them born of mutual respect and shared danger. But as far as Fortunato knew there hadn't been an Ace of Spades killing for a long time. He had no idea what had happened to his onetime comrade. They hadn't exactly been swapping Christmas cards the last decade and a half.

Even Tachyon, the whiny little space wimp, was gone. He'd run back to Takis when the going had gotten tough. First he'd come to the monastery begging for help. Then he'd gone back to his own planet, trapped in a woman's body, like . . . like a man running to a monastery on a distant and remote island, cutting himself off entirely from his old life. Cutting himself off from family, friends, lovers, comrades, and enemies. Cutting himself off from everything.

Christ, Fortunato thought, *is that what it's come down to? Unflattering self-comparison to that little alien Fauntleroy?*

Fortunato stared out of the taxi window, knowing that he had to get out of the awful, self-pitying, introspective mood into which he'd fallen. It wasn't doing him, or anyone else, any good. He had—

"Stop," he said suddenly, and the cabby took him for his word. He yanked the taxi's wheel hard right and they squealed to a halt against the curb. The cabby thrust his head out the window and screamed words at the driver of the car behind them, who had swerved and barely missed sideswiping the cab, and was now going down the street with his hand sticking out the driver's-side window, middle finger extended.

"Amateur!" the cabby screamed as his final insult. He caught Fortunato's eye in the rearview mirror. "Your destination, Mack?"

Fortunato nodded. Even if this wasn't his destination, he realized he'd better get the hell out of that cab if he wanted to live through the first day of his return to New York.

"Yes, this'll do." He got out of the cab and nearly did a double take when he saw the fare. He counted off a couple of bills and added a ten. "Here you go."

The cabby didn't seem overly excited by a ten-dollar tip. Times *had* changed.

"Thanks, Mack," he said, and roared off to his next adventure, almost clipping a passing Caddy as he pulled away from the curb.

Fortunato looked around. He should have been surprised to find himself in the heart of Jokertown, but he wasn't. It was almost as if he'd been magically drawn to there. As if he were a pigeon that'd returned, almost unconsciously, to home territory. He smiled to himself. Jokertown hadn't changed much. It was just as dirty as it had been in his day. Just as crowded. Just as damned funky.

He put out a hand to touch the curbside glass-and-plastic phone booth that was plastered with handbills advertising the next rave at the Freak Zone (THE HOTTEST NEW JOKER HANG! NATS WITH MASKS WELCOME!). Pedestrians with too many or too few limbs, with fur, with feathers, with skin like leather, with skin like silk, with extra mouths, noses, ears, or eyes, passed him by without a glance. To the jokers he was nothing, just a tall, skinny Black guy. Maybe a nat, maybe a hidden joker. Maybe strung out, maybe grossed out. It was all the same to them. They had their own problems.

He used to be Fortunato. Tachyon had once called him the most powerful ace of all. Once, they all would have known who he was.

He didn't know where it came from, but sudden anger churned his gut as if he'd ingested a five-star curry. He knew it wouldn't go away, so instead he focused on it to the exclusion of all else, building a pyre that burned hotter and hotter until he could incinerate all the frustrations of the last day.

The last day? he asked himself. *How about the last sixteen years?*

"Hey, old man, what you doing?"

The voice was young, careless, and uncaring. It tore Fortunato from his standing meditation back to the dirty, noisy present of the Jokertown street. He focused his eyes on a group of kids standing around him. There were half a dozen of them. They weren't threatening, but Fortunato had the sense that they could be, in a heartbeat. All the pedestrians around them had suddenly faded from the scene. Their innate urban-dweller senses perceived imminent danger and they either crossed the street or turned and retraced their steps when they saw the knot of juveniles surrounding the lone man.

The kids were all jokers. Some, like the slag-faced hulking giant who stood behind the speaker, were severely marked. Others, like the speaker himself, whose only visible abnormality was a rather attractive pair of feathery antennae that sprouted where his eyebrows should have been, were only touched by what was still regarded as the taint of the wild card, even after all these years.

Fortunato looked at them tolerantly. They were his people. He could have been one of them, if he hadn't been inhumanly lucky in the cosmic crapshoot. Their expressions, as they looked back at him, ranged from totally blank to utterly hostile.

"I'm just standing here," Fortunato said, finally answering the spokesman's question.

The spokesman snorted. "You on our corner, man."

Fortunato's eyebrows rose. This was the old game that had been played on the streets for generations. He himself had played it, before he'd gone on to bigger games.

"Your corner?" he asked.

"Yah," the kid replied. "We're the Jokka Bruddas, dig, and like I spoke, you taking up space on our corner. You owe us, man."

"Owe you?" The anger in Fortunato's gut flared at the gangbanger's insouciance. "I owned this corner, this street, and all those around it before you were born, boy. You'd best believe that."

There was no fear in the boy's eyes. "Yeah? Who are you supposed to be, old man?"

"I'm Fortunato," he said.

There was a moment's silence as they all stared at him, then the kid started to laugh and all his followers joined in. "Fortunato!" He shook his head. "You ain't nothing but a crazy old man. Fortunato, he dead, old man. Been dead many a year. Everybody knows."

"Knows what?" Fortunato said through clenched teeth, his gut roiling as the anger threatened to explode all bonds.

"He died years ago, before I was born. He flew up into the sky and fought the Devil. They fought all night, throwing lightning and thunder at each other. My daddy told me. He saw it. Fortunato was strong, but the Devil, he stronger. Fortunato fell from the sky like a stone and burned all up and the Devil took his soul to Hell because he was a pimp and a whore runner."

"They weren't whores," Fortunato ground out, "they were geishas."

The boy shrugged. "You Fortunato? Go ahead, hit me with a lightning bolt. Fly. They said you could even stop time. Go ahead, old man. Do it. You better have more'n your mouth because we're going to cap your ass and take everything you have."

Fortunato's anger called on the power, but nothing responded. He had shut it away for too long. He had turned his back on it, and now when he needed it, it wouldn't respond. And Fortunato knew, suddenly and desperately, that he really needed it. The giant whose face was a lava field of pitted sores grinned horrifically and stepped forward. Fortunato tensed.

"Are you all right, my son?" a deep, concerned voice asked. Suddenly, all around them was the smell of the sea.

They all turned to see a man in priest's robes who was not as tall as Fortunato, and more than twice as wide. His skin was a shiny, glabrous gray. His round face had nictating membranes over his eyes instead of normal lids, and a fall of short, constantly twitching tentacles where his nose should have been. His hands, folded over his comfortable paunch, were large, with long attenuated fingers that twitched bonelessly. Vestigial suckers lined his palms. He smelled like the ocean on a pleasant summer day.

"Father Squid," Fortunato said.

"My son," the priest of the Church of Jesus Christ, Joker, acknowledged with a bow and a smile, "or should I call you 'my brother'?"

"Whatever you call me, Father, it's good to see you."

Though not a touchy-feely person, Fortunato accepted the priest's embrace gratefully. Held against his broad chest, the smell reminded Fortunato of boyhood summer days spent at the beach. They hugged for a long moment, then Fortunato backed away.

Father Squid looked at him critically. "You look tired, my son."

"I've been on a long journey."

Father Squid nodded. "I'm glad to be here to welcome you home." He gestured benevolently at the bangers standing all around them. "I'm glad that some of my flock has already welcomed you." There was shuffling of feet and almost inaudible murmurs. "But it might be best if you were to come down the street to my church and rest for a while. We can catch up on the happenings of the last fifteen years."

That suddenly sounded like a good idea. Father Squid was a well-known, well-beloved figure about Jokertown. Or, Fortunato thought, at least he was the last time he knew anything about Jokertown. But something the joker priest said wasn't right. Fortunato frowned as he glanced at the street sign on the corner.

"We're across Jokertown from Our Lady of Perpetual Misery," Fortunato said. For a moment he wondered if his mind was going. If he was starting to forget details of his previous life. "Aren't we?"

Father Squid smiled behind his fall of nasal tentacles. "The *old* Lady of Perpetual Misery," he explained, "burned down almost a decade ago. We moved our premises here after the fire to a desanctified Roman Catholic church in an abandoned parish." He leaned forward to speak in a low voice. The odor of the ocean wafted from his ample form. "Frankly, the insurance money didn't go as far as we thought it would, and the real estate in this part of Jokertown is cheaper."

Fortunato glanced at the Jokka Bruddas still standing around, some shuffling their feet, some glaring, and nodded.

"Right," Father Squid said, smiling again. "This way." He paused for a moment and glanced at the youths, taking them all in with his kindly but penetrating gaze. "I haven't seen you boys at confession lately. Or, come to think about it, even Mass. I hope you'll be there this Sunday."

"Ah, Father," said their spokesman.

Father Squid's gaze turned somewhat less kindly. "Carlos."

The joker hung his head. "Yes, Father."

The priest looked at the giant with the terrible face. "Ricky, you make sure Carlos makes it to Mass, won't you."

"I will, Father," the giant said in a curiously high, sweet voice, the words of an angel issuing from a hellhound's mouth.

"All right," Father Squid said with a nod. "We'll see you boys soon."

Carlos mumbled something as they walked away. To Fortunato it sounded like a slurred threat, but he ignored their words and their unblinking glares as he went off down the street with the amiable joker priest.

♥

New York City: To St. Dympna's

ON THE WAY DOWN from the Tower, Cameo said to Nighthawk, "I don't think I like the sound of St. Dympna's." She paused momentarily. "Whatever it is."

Nighthawk shook his head. "You shouldn't," he said. "It's a charity hospital for crazy folks. It's been shut down for years, but the Church still holds the deed and Contarini uses it as his sort of unofficial headquarters. It's where the *obsequenti* have their barracks and Blood his kennel."

Cameo frowned. "That doesn't sound good."

"It's an awful place," Nighthawk agreed.

The elevator came to a stop and Nighthawk politely waited for her to exit, holding the door for her and then following her into the lobby with Usher and Magda still at her side. He paused for a moment to look around. Whenever he stood in the Waldorf-Astoria's lobby, it made him feel as if seventy years had fallen off the age of the Earth. And off him.

She gazed at him.

"So," she said, "you're not taking me there. Right?"

Nighthawk looked around the lobby. So many memories. There was a maid he'd loved, lived with, and lost to a younger man who'd been a flashier dresser and had better prospects. She was young then, when he was old, but now she'd be ancient, if she'd somehow managed to survive. Nighthawk suppressed an introspective sigh. The past had been weighing heavily on him lately. He had to rid himself of it, one way or the other.

He looked at Cameo, wishing he'd gotten some really useful ace ability, like telepathy. But that, he thought, would have just made things too easy. "I have no choice," his voice said. His eyes pled, *Trust me. Just trust me for a little while longer.*

"What if I scream?" Cameo asked conversationally.

"I wouldn't recommend that," Usher said.

Magda just smiled.

It was the nun's smile, Nighthawk thought, that decided her. For now. Her gaze withdrew. Her eyes became hooded. It wasn't exactly as if she lost all interest in her surroundings, but she acted as if she were preoccupied with something else more important, as if she were conversing with unseen spectres.

Maybe, Nighthawk thought, she was.

Usher went to the parking garage while Nighthawk, Cameo, and Magda waited on the street. It was late, and almost quiet. Cameo looked at Nighthawk, ignoring the silent nun.

"Can't I go and find some place to hide until this is all over?" she asked. "Whatever this is."

Nighthawk nodded approvingly. "That would be the thing to do." He paused, frowning. "Unfortunately, this will only be over, one, if Contarini dies, or, two, when Jesus Christ again walks this earth. I ain't saying which is more likely. At this point, I don't know."

"Contarini is that determined?"

"He's a fanatic. Fanatics are usually fairly determined."

"And you're not?" Cameo asked him. "A fanatic, I mean?"

Nighthawk laughed. "Not like Contarini. I have faith, but I'm not blinded by it. I have . . . questions. That's why I took this job. I'd done some work for Contarini's Allumbrados in the past—"

A big black Mercedes pulled up to the curb, Usher behind the wheel. Nighthawk opened the rear passenger-side door and gestured for Cameo to enter. She got in gracefully and slid across the seat. Magda started to follow her, but Nighthawk took her forearm with his gloved left hand and shook his head.

"In the front," he said, "with Usher."

She stared at his gloved hand on her arm, then looked up at Nighthawk as if she were going to dispute his order, but dropped her gaze after a few moments. She pulled her arm away and got into the front passenger seat, obviously perturbed.

Nighthawk got in the back and toggled the dark glass panel into place between front and rear seats. Magda twisted backward to glare at them as the panel slid into place. Usher pulled away from the curb, melding easily with the light stream of traffic.

"She doesn't like you," Cameo observed.

"No," Nighthawk said. "But, even better, she fears me."

Cameo looked him over coolly. "Why?"

Nighthawk smiled. "Pray you never find out, missy."

She seemed to consider this for a moment, then nodded.

"All right," she said. "You mentioned 'Allumbrados,' what does that mean? Who exactly are they?"

"It means 'the Enlightened Ones.' They're an ancient brotherhood within the Church. Cardinal Contarini is their current leader, but they've been around since medieval times. Some say back to the time of the Inquisition, to which they had tight ties."

"Contarini's a cardinal?" she repeated, half to herself, as if not totally surprised. "I'm not totally surprised," she said. "The stink of sanctimony clings to him like cheap aftershave."

Nighthawk smiled. That was a pretty fair assessment.

"But these Allumbrados, what exactly do they believe in?"

"They believe in the Millennium," Nighthawk said. "They believe that Jesus Christ will return to the Earth. That after casting Satan and his minions into the pit He'll establish a Kingdom of Peace and reign for a thousand years. Then He'll fight the Devil one last time, and in this final confrontation will be victorious. Then the world will end and the righteous will go to Heaven to spend eternity praising God."

"Literally?"

"Oh, yes. They believe this to be the preordained fate of the universe. They believe that they can help this process along and hasten the coming of Parousia."

"Parousia?"

"Sorry," Nighthawk said. "You hang around these people enough and you forget how to talk like ordinary folk. Parousia is just a fancy word for Jesus' Kingdom on Earth."

"So, they hired you to help them?"

"I got them the Shroud, didn't I?" Nighthawk asked with some indignation. "I found you to channel Jesus' spirit so the cardinal could discover how exactly they could help bring about Jesus' return. Is it my fault you got Cole Porter instead?"

Cameo had to fight back a smile. "No."

"Anyway," Nighthawk said, "that's only part of the plan."

"The other part being?"

"The other part being destroying the Anti-Christ, who Contarini believes has already appeared on Earth, as Scripture has predicted."

"That's crazy," Cameo said. "Just who is this supposed Anti-Christ, anyway?"

"The spawn of the Whore of Babylon and Satan himself."

Cameo shook her head. "I'm still in the dark."

Nighthawk sat silently as Usher drove with quiet, sure skill through the empty streets. The Mercedes windows were all blacked out so Cameo could have no clue where they were going. That was part of the reason why he had activated the barrier between the front and back seats. He also didn't want Usher or Magda to hear their conversation. He slouched back on his seat.

"The Whore of Babylon is a famous television star and documentary film producer who has dared to oppose the Church on pretty much every social issue imaginable. Abortion rights. Ordaining women for the priesthood. Homosexuality. Even the doctrine of papal infallibility which, it turns out, was invented in the nineteenth century. Plus, she's a wild carder."

"Peregrine?" Cameo hazarded.

Nighthawk nodded. "That's right, missy. Now, Satan himself: He's also a wild carder. He deals in sex, drugs, and violence. Or at least used to. He's Black—"

"Fortunato! But," Cameo said, "he's been in that monastery in Japan, what, it seems like forever now."

"Doesn't matter," Nighthawk said. "If he doesn't come out when things start happening, Contarini will send someone after him. And," Nighthawk added significantly, "things have definitely started to happen."

"And the Anti-Christ," Cameo said thoughtfully. "Their son, John Fortune."

Nighthawk nodded again. "You got that right. The only known offspring from the union of two aces. That's important to Contarini. Wild carders are equivalent to demons in his theology. He believes we're all damned from birth. That we'll all suffer the agonies of Hell for eternity."

"Yet you work for him," Cameo said with an edge of disgust in her voice.

Nighthawk shook his head. "I don't work for him. I take his money. There's a difference."

"A vague one," Cameo said.

"No. An important one. I told you before—I took this job for a reason."

"The money?" she asked.

Nighthawk shook his head silently. His gaze turned inward, as if he were reliving memories of old, unforgettable, unpleasant events.

"No. I took this job because I wanted to see if you were the real thing, or just some kind of fake."

"It wasn't my fault that I got Cole Porter either—" Cameo began, but Nighthawk interrupted her.

"No, I believe you. You've convinced me that you can channel the dead."

"Then what do you want?"

"Your trust, for now." He frowned. "We're probably all right, here, now. If we're being taped, we're both dead if the cardinal ever hears this conversation—"

Cameo snorted. "I thought you weren't afraid of the cardinal."

"I've lived a long time, missy," Nighthawk said, "and I didn't do it by being stupid. Of course I'm afraid of the cardinal. If you had any sense, you'd be too. I can't afford to openly oppose him. I'm one old man. He has the Allumbrados. Aces. Money. More thugs with guns than I could kill in a year."

"All right," Cameo said in a small voice. "I believe you."

"You better," he said. "St. Dympna's now, is not a nice place. It will be hard for you there. But you'll only have to endure it for maybe a day, no more, then I'll get you out. Trust me."

"Why should I?"

"Because," Nighthawk said softly. "I swear on the honor of my immortal soul."

They looked at each other for a long time, and then Cameo finally nodded.

"All right," she said in the voice of a little girl.

"Thank you," Nighthawk said.

She nodded again, and they rode the rest of the way to St. Dympna's in silence.

Jokertown: Rectory, Our Lady of Perpetual Misery

FATHER SQUID'S RECTORY WAS suffused with the peace of the monastery. Fortunato felt that he'd found an oasis of tranquility after nearly two days of travel and reimmersion in the strangeness of Jokertown. It was a small room in a small cottage attached to a church that had been abandoned by the Catholic diocese sometime in the 1960s after they'd pulled out of Jokertown without regard for the souls of their vastly changed parishioners. Somehow it felt very much like home.

After enjoying a glass of mellow, surprisingly tasty wine in the rectory, Father Squid took Fortunato on a quick tour of his church, which after several years of reconstruction still wasn't quite up to snuff.

"We're doing the best we can," Father Squid said as if reading Fortunato's thoughts. He gestured at the scaffolds half-holding up one of the interior walls, the flooring that was partly warped plywood, the mismatched pews that must have come from half a dozen other forgotten churches. "But money is tight. And I hesitate to spend it all on building projects when so much has to be done for the parish poor. Meals for the elderly, or those incapable of taking care of themselves. Money for heating oil in the winter. A small camp we send joker children to in the summer, so they might know what sunshine and forests and clean lake water feels like." The priest shook his head ponderously. "Never enough time. Never enough money."

Fortunato nodded. He felt ashamed. He would have felt worse if he'd let himself dwell on it. Here he'd spent sixteen years gazing at his own navel, while this fat old joker was out in the real world, trying to make a difference. He looked around the church's interior. It was nowhere as nice as the old Our Lady of Perpetual Misery. Fortunato particularly missed the icons that had been part of the old church. The old representations had been genuine works of art. Their replacements . . .

Fortunato frowned as he looked at them closely.

"I know," Father Squid said, sadly. "We lost much that night Our Lady of Perpetual Misery burned to the ground. Many parishioners. But also some things nearly as irreplaceable as human beings." He gestured at the mosaic upon the walls. The two-headed male/female joker crucified on the DNA helix; the handsome, golden-auraed demon juggling his thirty pieces of silver; the two-faced scientist in his lab coat dispensing pain with one hand and relief with the other; the thin Black man with curling ram horns and a bulging forehead hurling thunderbolts as he floated in the air. Another part of him bulged inhumanly large in his pants. "Crude as they are, these will have to do until a joker artist with more ability comes along."

Fortunato stared at the mural. The thin Black man with curling ram horns and a bulging forehead hurling thunderbolts looked familiar. "That's me," he said, half fascinated, half horrified.

Father Squid smiled. At least, his facial tentacles twitched. "It's what your legend has become, my son."

"And that is?" Fortunato asked, still unable to take his eyes off the mural.

Father Squid shrugged broad shoulders. "Like most things in Jokertown, theology is two-faced. You've become the fertility god who showers both fecundity and destruction upon his people. Pregnant jokers pray to you that their children be normal. Or at least not hideous. On the other hand, you've become a cult figure to certain of those with a destructive bent. Youth gangs in particular."

"The Jokka Bruddas," Fortunato said.

Father Squid nodded. "Among others. I deal with them frequently. Their clubhouse, as they call it, is an abandoned apartment building just across the street—"

"Excuse me," Fortunato said, as his cell phone went off. He fumbled with it for a moment, unfamiliar as he was with the controls, but finally got it working. "Yes?"

"Fortunato?" a familiar, frenzied voice asked. "Digger," it said, before Fortunato could reply. "Have you heard the news?"

"News?" Fortunato looked at Father Squid. Father Squid shrugged. He shrugged back.

"There was some kind of dustup in Vegas. Your son's been kidnapped."

"Kidnapped?" he heard himself repeating stupidly.

"Yeah, and Peregrine, she . . . she was hurt. Apparently she's been flown back to New York and is at the Jokertown Clinic—"

"This must have happened hours ago! Why didn't you find out about it until now?"

"I was busy, all right?" Digger said defensively.

"Busy doing what?" Fortunato asked.

"Writing up your story at my apartment—then my girlfriend came by and one thing led to another, and I just turned on the TV—"

Fortunato caught himself about to swear, then shut his mouth. He took a deep breath and ran through the Heart Sutra a couple of times. He didn't feel any calmer when he was finished, but he realized that it was all water under the bridge and there was no use crying over it.

"All right," he said. He checked with the map of Jokertown that was still etched into the furrows of his brain. "I'm going to the Jokertown Clinic—"

"I'll meet you there—"

"If you want."

"I'm on the way. Keep the channel open and I'll fill you in on the details."

"All right," Fortunato said. He turned to Father Squid. "I have to go," he said.

The priest nodded ponderously. "God go with you, my son."

Fortunato nodded as he ran out of the church, Digger still yammering in his ear.

♠

Las Vegas: Urgent Care Center

RAY MADE SURE THAT he was still bleeding a little when he checked himself into the emergency clinic. Experience had taught him that nothing proclaimed emergency like spurting blood. It was a sure way to jump right to the head of the line.

After Angel had slammed her door in his face, he'd figured he had nothing better to do, so he decided to tie up some loose ends. He didn't really feel like going down to the cop shop and lying his ass off to the locals, so, first things first, he went to his own room and changed into a set of old sweats. He left what remained of his suit in a pile on the bathroom floor, went down to the cab stand, and had the taxi take him to the nearest emergency clinic.

He paid off the cabby, stripped off his short-sleeved tee, and dropped it in a garbage can as he approached the clinic, then walked into the front door holding the flap of torn skin and meat up against his upper chest. The receptionist took one look at him and had an orderly escort him to an empty waiting room. Once there he twiddled his thumbs, waiting as usual for the doctor to finish his sandwich or counting his Medicaid kickbacks, or whatever it was that occupied his time when he could actually be seeing patients.

The tiny room was sterile and uninteresting. Ray looked at the poster of the little kitten dangling from a branch with the words HANG IN THERE emblazoned with bold yellow letters, and pursed his lips. All in all, it was better than being shot in the ass and having to sit in a cave in Afghanistan while awaiting medical treatment, but not by much.

Well, he told himself, *you asked for it.*

Speaking of asking for it, he reminded himself that he had some other unpleasant tasks to perform. Ignoring the sign that said PLEASE TURN OFF CELL PHONES AS A COURTESY TO THE DOCTORS AND STAFF, he took his cell phone out and dialed Barnett's number.

There was a click after the third ring and a sexy and bored voice said, "Peaceable Kingdom, President Leo Barnett's Office."

"Hello, Sally Lou," Ray said. "Let me talk to the big guy."

"You mean President Barnett?"

It was their little joke. He always called Barnett "the big guy" and she pretended that she didn't know whom he meant. But Ray wasn't really in the mood to drag this out for too long. "I don't mean the Pope."

She must have heard something in the tone of his voice, for there was a click, a buzz, and then Barnett's smooth voice was on the line, with more than a hint of distress in it. "Billy, my boy, what in the name of Melchizedek is going on there in Vegas, boy? I'm hearing strange tales. Strange tales indeed—"

"Yeah, well, you should have actually been here." Ray gave a concise report on the day's activities, and then listened to a long silence on the other end of the line.

"Disturbing," Barnett finally said.

There was no way to deny it. "Yes, sir," Ray said. "You know that those Allumbrados have aces working for them as well as assholes with guns."

Barnett sighed. "So I've heard."

"One of them is Butcher Dagon."

"Have those damned Papists no sense of morality?" Barnett asked, outraged.

"Well, Angel and I laid him out like a slab of cold meat. The local cops currently have him on ice, but I wouldn't trust them to hold a lost dog let alone a bad guy the caliber of Dagon."

"Forget Dagon," Barnett said flatly. "We've got to find Je—the boy before those murderous bastards kill him. Do you know where they've taken him?"

"No," Ray said, "but I've got an idea or two—"

There was a soft knock on the door, and it suddenly opened. A young female doctor looked in. She was Asian, probably Korean, with big dark eyes and long, straight, glossy black hair.

"—Got to run," Ray interrupted himself, and shut down his cell. He smiled at the doctor, who paused, frowning, in the doorway. "Bet you've never stitched up an ace before," he said with a bright smile.

◆

New York City: St. Dympna's Home for the Mentally Deficient and Criminally Inclined

JERRY QUICKLY REALIZED THAT they'd been transported to a hellhole that would make Bedlam look like a day at Disney World.

"Home sweet home," the big blond guy said, looking around disgustedly. He said it as if he didn't really mean it. "You know," he continued confidingly to Jerry, "I've got to say that this really sucks. The cardinal gets to lord it up over at the Waldorf, while we have to scrounge around here in a building barely fit to be Blood's kennel."

Jerry grunted noncommittally as the blond guy, as if emphasizing his displeasure, aimed a kick at Blood's ribs as his handler dragged him by on his leash. The kick landed solidly. Blood howled like a kicked dog while the blond guy sneered his satisfaction.

"You shouldn't oughta do that, Witness," the keeper said. "Blood ain't done nothing wrong. You treat him like that, you confuse him, and then he's hard to handle."

"He's disgusting," Witness said. "Get him out of my sight."

Grumbling, the handler pulled Blood away, tugging hard at his leash and saying in an aggrieved voice, "Come on, boy, *come on*," while Witness looked on, grinning. Jerry felt sick to his stomach.

Witness turned to him, his face suddenly wearing an expression of concern that didn't quite look authentic. "How you doing, Dagon? You look pretty well beat. I guess that Ray is one tough customer."

Jerry, trying to speak as little as possible, only nodded.

"I tell you what," Witness said. "Why don't you stay here and rest awhile? Get some medical attention. I'll have some of the boys help you up to the infirmary. They'll take care of you there."

Although his words were sympathetic, his voice had an underlying tone that Jerry interpreted as meaning, *Look out, I'm going to screw you now.*

"Don't worry about reporting to the cardinal. I'll go into Manhattan and do it. Though," he gripped his left shoulder and swung it experimentally while grimacing, "I could probably use some medical attention myself. I think I pulled something here."

Jerry kept a look of elation off Dagon's face. At least he knew where they were, that somehow they'd been transported back to Manhattan. That would make things easier, if they could only get out of St. Dympna's, whatever the hell this place was. Jerry nodded and made groaning noises in what he hoped sounded like an acquiescent tone.

Witness brightened perceptibly, smiling like he'd just put one over. Apparently he was eager to get to this cardinal and report. Maybe to tell him his particular version of events. Maybe to take all the credit for it. That was fine with Jerry.

Witness barely restrained himself from rubbing his hands together with glee. He turned to the men who'd been holding a silent, sullen John Fortune by his arms. "Take the brat to the oubliette," Witness ordered.

That doesn't sound good, Jerry thought.

"You others help Dagon." Jerry winced realistically as they put their arms around his waist. "Careful, dolts! Can't you see that he's injured?"

The thugs murmured apologies that Jerry accepted with a feeble nod. Witness nodded, and with a final farewell bustled off, planning whatever stab-in-the-back move he clearly intended.

This, Jerry thought, *was not a subtle guy. Probably more muscles than brains.*

As they shuffled off together, Jerry stopped, turned, and looked at John Fortune. "Be seeing you, kid," he said.

He said it as quickly and quietly as he could and still be sure that John Fortune heard him. He really didn't have a firm grasp of Dagon's voice, and he was a bad mimic anyway, as his utter failure as the Projectionist proved, so he just used his regular voice and hoped no one was really paying attention.

John Fortune glanced wildly back over his shoulder as two thugs hustled him down the hall, and their eyes met. For the first time since their capture, Jerry saw hope on the kid's face. Jerry risked a single nod as he was shuffled off in the other direction. John Fortune had understood. He'd recognized Jerry's voice, or perhaps he'd just recognized one of Jerry's favorite taglines.

He knew that his shape-shifting bodyguard was still on the job.

♥

New York City: The Jokertown Clinic

THE DOCTOR HAD A white coat, a stethoscope, and the hindquarters of a horse. *Palomino,* Fortunato thought. *Very handsome.*

His front end was good-looking, too, with a blondish, Californian-surfer-dude cast to it, but underlaid with an uncommon strength and thoughtfulness. Fortunato thought that this was a man who had seen a lot, been through a lot, and had paid a price for all the knowledge he'd won from life.

"Bradley!" Digger said, glad-handing the joker doctor. Fortunato had met the reporter on the clinic steps, and Digger had commanded him to "Leave everything to me."

Considering the state that he was in, Fortunato thought that was a good idea. Digger seemed to know the place as well as the people in charge, and it took him only moments to get them up to Finn's office.

"Good to have you back from Takis," Digger said to the doctor with what seemed to be a fair amount of sincerity in his voice. "That must have been some exciting trip. You'll have to tell me all about it."

Finn seemed more weary than welcoming, but he returned the reporter's handshake readily enough. "It was, and maybe I will," Finn said. He glanced inquisitively at Fortunato, who'd been silent since they'd been led into his cramped office by a legless joker in a nurse's uniform. "Right now, I'm kind of busy."

"Of course," Digger said. "You always are."

"Too many patients, too little time," Finn said.

"Right. Actually, we're here to see one of them."

Finn questioned him with a raised eyebrow.

"Peregrine," Digger said.

The doctor looked at them both. Fortunato returned his gaze steadily, his heart beating unaccountably fast, afraid that Finn would turn them away, afraid that he wouldn't. "She's in no condition to be badgered, Digger," Finn said flatly.

"No, you misunderstand," Digger said soothingly. He looked at Fortunato. "You two have never met?" he asked.

Fortunato shook his head. "No. I haven't had the pleasure."

Digger smiled his customary knowing smirk. "Dr. Bradley Finn," he said, "this is Fortunato. He's recently returned to New York from Japan."

Fortunato could see that Finn was impressed by the mention of his name. Despite having tried to drown his ego for the last decade and a half, he was more than a little pleased that it still did carry weight.

"Fortunato." Bradley moved around from behind his desk, his bootied hooves clicking hollowly on the carpeted floor. He held out a hand. "It's very nice to meet you. I've read so much about you. Sorry I didn't recognize you."

"I've been away for a long time," Fortunato said.

"Well, nice to have you back."

"Not really," Fortunato said. He released Finn's hand. "I wish the circumstances of my return were different."

"Of course." The centaur looked thoughtful. "You want to see Peregrine, I understand, but she was severely wounded—"

"I want to know what happened," Fortunato said. Even to himself his voice sounded dry. Curiously devoid of emotion. But it wasn't missing, only constrained. He had to dam them all up. He was afraid what would happen if he gave into the feelings burning through his brain.

"She was ambushed while being interviewed about her son's, er, your son's, I should say, card turning."

"Why?" Fortunato asked.

"No one seems to know. Maybe it was a plot to kidnap the boy. He was missing after all the furor died down. But there's been no ransom demand. They left a score of wounded bystanders. Half a dozen dead." Finn shook his head at the mystifying cruelty of it all.

Fortunato's heart started to race again, but he managed to control his voice. "And Peregrine?" he asked.

"She took more than half a dozen bullets, suffering massive internal injuries and severe wing damage. Frankly, it was fortunate that her husband had immediately arranged her transportation to the clinic. I doubt that they could have dealt with the vagaries of her wild card metabolism in Vegas."

"She's going to be all right, though?" Digger asked.

Finn shook his head. "Too early to tell. But she's got a chance." Finn gestured, encompassing the extent of his tiny office. "We may not look like much, but the Jokertown Clinic is state of the art when it comes to the treatment of wild carders, even for those suffering from such mundane things as bullet wounds. Even without Tachyon, we've got the most knowledgeable doctors in the world. That said, we just don't know yet about Peregrine. She suffered damage to her internal organs. Part of her liver was pulped. Lost one of her kidneys. The delicate bone structure of one wing was smashed. There's a serious question as to whether she'll ever fly again."

Finn's calm recital of Peregrine's injuries made Fortunato feel as if he'd been shot himself. The sickness that burned in his gut because of the deaths of all the people he'd lost over the years came back. It had been gone when he'd been in Japan, but now it was back.

"Can I see her?" he asked.

Finn looked at him thoughtfully. "She's resting. Maybe sleeping. Her husband's with her. Just got back into town himself." He clip-clopped over to his desk and activated the intercom. "Jesse," he said, "check and see if Peregrine's awake." They waited in silence for a few moments until the nurse replied affirmatively. "Okay. Come to my office and escort mister, uh, this gentleman to her room, would you?"

While they waited for the nurse, Finn lectured Fortunato about not tiring her out. Fortunato only half-listened. He was thinking about Peregrine. About the night they had made love and made their son, and Peregrine had supplied Fortunato with enough energy to defeat the murderous Astronomer in combat high in the skies over Manhattan. The next morning Fortunato had left for Japan. He'd seen her only once after that, some months later when she'd come to Japan on the World Health Organization–sponsored tour. Occasionally he'd seen her photo in some magazine or newspaper. He'd never seen their son.

The nurse's face looked relatively human but for the brightly patterned scales that covered it in lieu of normal skin. Her arms were oddly sinuous, almost boneless, and she had too many fingers. She looked at Fortunato curiously, but was professional enough to simply say, "This way, sir."

As Fortunato followed her out of Finn's office he could hear the ever-optimistic Digger Downs say, "Now, Dr. Finn, about this spaceship you took back to Earth, I heard that you stopped at many planets along the way—" He heard Finn sigh as if he realized he couldn't escape Downs' relentless interrogation, and then they were out of earshot.

The corridor was clean, quiet, and dimly lit. It smelled like a hospital. Not even the burning pungency of strong antiseptic could wipe out the odors of fear and pain and death and, somewhere underneath it all, hope. The nurse opened the door to Peregrine's private room, one of the few in the clinic, and shut it softly after Fortunato slipped quietly inside.

The room was darker than the hallway outside, and Fortunato's hypersensitive senses rebelled against the hurt and pain he could discern, not all of which emanated from the bandaged form on the bed attached to a raft of tubes and machines monitoring her heart, lungs, and brain.

A man sat in a chair by the side of the bed. He looked up as Fortunato entered, fear and pain in his eyes. He looked ordinary enough, fairly handsome with blond hair and a darker beard. He nodded at Fortunato and stood.

"I'm Josh McCoy."

Fortunato nodded. He had never seen the man, but he knew the name. "I know. I'm—"

"Fortunato," McCoy said. "I know."

Fortunato moved to the foot of the bed. "How's she doing?"

"Sleeping, now. Trying to get some strength back . . ." McCoy's voice trailed off as he looked at Peregrine's quiescent form.

Somehow, seeing her lying there made Fortunato feel inadequate and inept. Like somehow he'd failed her. "I'm sorry I wasn't with her," he said, surprising himself as he realized the truth of his statement.

"Not your fault," McCoy said. "I just wish I'd been there myself."

Fortunato shrugged. "Probably nothing you could have done, except get hurt. Or killed, maybe."

McCoy looked at him. "But at least I would have been with her. For her."

Fortunato frowned. He shouldn't have to defend himself, he thought, or the decisions he'd made about his life. Not to this man. Not to any man. He was about to reply to McCoy's veiled accusation when the sounds of movement under crisp sheets came to his ears, and both of the men turned to look at Peregrine.

She'd opened her eyes. They were drugged with pain and morphine, but it seemed she recognized them both. She held up a hand taped to a board with tubes running up to an intravenous drip that Finn had ratcheted up in potency to work with Peregrine's souped-up metabolism. McCoy sat down in the chair next to her bed and took her hand and put it against his cheek.

"How you doing, darling?" he asked in a low voice.

A ghost of a smile passed over Peregrine's drawn and tired face, where, Fortunato thought, her beauty waited patiently to reveal itself, like the sun eclipsed by dark shadows. "Been better," she whispered. Her eyes wandered across the room and took in Fortunato.

"You're here," she said.

"I'm here." There didn't seem to be anything else to say.

She glanced back at McCoy. "John?" she asked.

"He's—he's missing, but okay, as far as we know."

Peregrine made a supreme effort and nodded. She looked again at Fortunato. "What's this all about?"

That helpless feeling crawled around like a snake, biting Fortunato in the gut. "I don't know," he said. "What's it ever all about? Some nut probably. Some fucking nut. You take care of one. Another takes his place. There's no shortage of nuts—" Fortunato caught himself. He took a deep breath.

"I've never asked you for anything," Peregrine whispered in words so low and slow that Fortunato could barely hear her. "But find him. Find him and bring him back safe."

The snake coiled in Fortunato's gut and clamped down on his intestines with its sharp fangs. He was being sucked into it all again, after almost sixteen years away. But how could he say no to his son's mother? How could he not go find his son?

McCoy released Peregrine's hand and stood up. "I'm coming with you."

Fortunato shook his head. "No."

McCoy's fear and pain turned to sudden anger. "Don't tell me no! You made him—I raised him. I changed his diapers. I helped him learn how to walk and talk. I helped him to grow into a good kid. Where were you all that time, you, you big hero?" McCoy's voice rose with his anger. "*Where were you?*"

"Josh . . ." Peregrine said, reaching out to him.

Fortunato shook his head. "I just . . . I just don't want to see anyone else get hurt."

"He's right, Josh," Peregrine said in her soft, pained voice. "He's made for this."

I was, Fortunato thought. *But that was a long time ago. Now, I just don't know . . .*

There didn't seem to be anything else to say. Fortunato took his leave, but they had already seemed to have forgotten him. McCoy sat next to her, his head against the mattress by her side. Her hand rested on it, so weak it was barely able to stir the strands of his hair. McCoy had earned that place by her side through sixteen years of ceaseless loyalty. Fortunato had tossed it aside.

He left the room, went down the corridor and took a side staircase down to the lobby. He didn't want to see Finn again. He sure as hell didn't want to see Downs. He didn't really want to be alone either, but he didn't have much of a choice with that.

He looked out at the street. It was fairly quiet this time of night, but there were still occasional cars, a taxi or two, trucks off on their delivery rounds. Pedestrians went by singly or in groups, without a glance his way. No one knew who he was. Why should they?

His son was out there. He didn't have a clue where. He didn't have a clue as to who took him or why they took him or what his condition was. In the old days he might have gone to Chrysalis. She knew everything that happened in this city, and most things of import that happened in the world of wild carders. But she was dead. Once, he might have gone out of his body and searched for clues himself, but those days, like his powers, were gone. He had thrown them away, just like he'd tossed Peregrine aside. And for what?

"Hey, old man."

The voice that startled Fortunato out of his reverie was that of Carlos, spokesman for the Jokka Bruddas. He was accompanied by the behemoth with the pustule-ridden face whom Father Squid had called Ricky.

"Where's the rest of the crowd?" Fortunato asked.

Carlos shrugged. "Don' worry about them. It's your skinny old ass that's in trouble."

If Fortunato hadn't recently been hammered by the double emotional blows of Peregrine's wounding and his son's kidnapping, he would have been amused. Now he was just angry at these kids for wasting his time.

"What are you talking about?" he asked.

Carlos shrugged again. "Don' get snappy with me, dog, when I'm doin' you a favor. Father Squid sent us to get you. He didn't say what the problem was, but he said to get you and bring your ass back to the church *andale,* baby."

Fortunato couldn't imagine what the priest wanted, but knew that it must be important. "All right, let's go."

He started down the street, but Carlos grabbed his sleeve.

"This way, *esse.* We got a drive waiting."

Following Carlos down the street, he turned left into the alley running alongside a wing of the clinic, and suddenly thought, *Where's Ricky?* He turned around to see the hulk behind him, grinning like a melting wax dummy as his fist descended in a blur.

Fortunato's last thought was, *Christ, I am getting too old,* and darkness dropped on him like a falling cliff.

Chapter Four

Las Vegas: The Mirage

THE ANGEL MOANED SOFTLY as the Witness's clenched fist opened and caressed her cheek, down along her jawline. She had always been sensitive there. But she didn't want him to touch her. Did she?

He stared dreamily into her eyes and said, "Knock, knock. Time to hit the road, Angel."

She woke up, startled and confused. Billy Ray was standing in the open doorway between their connecting rooms. She realized that she must have left it unlocked when she'd collapsed into bed . . . how long ago, exactly?

She sat up, pulling the sheet up to her shoulders.

"What time is it?" she mumbled.

"Ten thirty-two," Ray announced crisply.

"I—it was already later than that—"

"In the A.M., sweet cheeks."

She blinked at the realization that she'd slept so late, and blinked again when she realized that she was naked under the sheet, and Ray was staring at her.

The government ace, dressed in another impeccable suit, looked like he'd just rolled out of bed fresh from an untroubled night's sleep. The bruises had disappeared from his face and all his visible cuts had healed. He came into her room moving apparently without pain, though the Angel noted he moved gingerly when he sat down on the room's other bed. Any other man she'd ever known would still be in a hospital. He smiled at her as he sat down, with none of the wild ferocity she'd seen when he was in the midst of battle. He had seemed to like the fighting. More than that, he'd reveled in it—

"What's the matter?" Ray asked, his grin still in place.

"Oh." The Angel forced herself to focus. "Nothing. What's the plan?"

"The plan? We can discuss it in the car." He stood and stretched like a sleek and self-satisfied cat. "You still look pretty beat, but we have things we have to do. Although," he said with a thoughtful look, "if you want to catch a few more winks—"

The Angel sat up, wrapping the sheet around herself almost angrily.

"You don't have to coddle me," she said.

"No, but I'd like to," Ray said with a leer. She just looked at him, and he shrugged. "Go take a shower. It'll wake you up."

That, the Angel thought, was a good idea.

"I could soap your back—" Ray offered as she stood with the sheet firmly wrapped around her. She stepped over the sweaty pile of clothes she'd discarded by the side of the bed, grabbed her duffel bag, and headed for the bathroom. She slammed the bathroom door and, finally thinking clearly, locked it. "Anyway,"

Ray called out through the door, "you can grab some more zzzs in the car if you're still tired."

Car? the Angel thought. She turned the shower to cold and stepped under it. The icy torrent took her breath away and made her heart beat faster. For a moment she thought that it would be fun to have someone to soap her back. Maybe her front as well. Her hands slid over her flat abdomen, skirting the eight-inch scar that crawled over it like an ugly snake, and the touch of it against her fingers banished all impure thoughts. She turned off the water. She dried herself, all but her hair, letting that hang down her back in an unmanageable curly mass. She took her spare underwear and black jumpsuit out of the duffel bag and dressed. When she came back into the bedroom, Ray was lying on the extra bed, legs straight out and crossed at the ankles, hands behind his head, watching some weird movie with masked wrestlers on the Spanish station. He glanced up at her.

"What?" the Angel asked, though she knew the look on his face meant that there was lust in his heart.

"Nothing," Ray said. "That was fast. All right. Let's go."

"Where exactly are we going? If you don't mind telling me?"

"Not at all." Ray grinned. When he smiled like that he looked years younger, and just about as dangerous as a pussycat. "We're going to take a trip outside of town and drop in on the Living Gods. One of them, Osiris, is a precog, and may have some insight as to what the hell is going to happen next. Maybe even where they took the kid."

The Angel dropped her duffel bag on her bed, thinking that somehow Ray had managed to wrest all control of this mission out of her hands. She didn't like that. Also, she was hungry. "Well . . ."

"What?" Ray asked as her voice trailed off.

"Do we have time for breakfast?"

Ray made a show of checking his watch. "It'd be more like brunch, but, sure, why not?"

That's something, at least, the Angel thought.

They paused in the corridor as they left the room, the Angel making sure her door was really locked. She didn't trust those credit card–like keys.

"I hope he wasn't the one who got greased," Ray said.

She looked at him as they went down the hotel corridor. "Greased? You mean one of them was killed?"

"So the cops told me yesterday when I went down to the station."

"Why didn't you tell me you finally reported to the police?" the Angel asked. "Or bring me along?"

Ray shrugged. "What, let them bother you, too? It was bad enough that I had to deal with them."

"Did you tell them about the Hand?" the Angel asked anxiously.

He just looked at her. "You think that I was going to tell them that we're here in Vegas to rescue Jesus Christ from a bunch of crazed Catholic cultists?"

The Angel breathed a sigh of relief. She hadn't believed Ray capable of such subtlety. It was good to see that he had unexpected depths. "What about the Living Gods?" she asked as they made their way through the lobby to the coffee shop. Too bad, the Angel thought, they didn't have a buffet.

"Like I said. One of them bought it during the attack on the Mirage. The cops didn't know which one. Funny thing, the body's already been released. Some kind of religious mumbo-jumbo." He put his hands out as the Angel glared at him. "Not that I have anything against religious mum—ah, religion."

A shame, the Angel thought, ruminating on the Living Gods. They were pagans, but in their own way they were innocents.

They seated themselves in the coffee shop and the Angel ordered the he-man breakfast from the menu: pancakes, three eggs (sunny-side up), hash browns, ham, bacon, and sausage, with toast on the side. Ray, saying he'd eaten earlier, only had coffee.

She watched him watch her as she ate. She thought of ordering another side of ham, or maybe grits, but Ray's scrutiny was making her feel self-conscious. She didn't want him to think she was a glutton. Besides, she was all too conscious of the fact that she had no money to pay for the food she was consuming.

Ray didn't seem to mind, though. He cheerfully slapped down his credit card and then added a way-too-generous tip that brought a smile to the attractive young waitress serving them. The Angel didn't like that. She didn't think it was proper for young women to use their physical attributes to gull susceptible men into giving them money. And if there was one thing she knew about Ray, it was that he was susceptible.

They exited the Mirage through the lobby and a valet brought a car up to them as they waited at the curb. The Angel looked it over disapprovingly. She didn't know what model or year it was, but it was big, shiny, and expensive. "At least it's not an SUV," she muttered as she got into the front seat.

"What?" Ray asked.

"Nothing."

Ray was a fast, yet precise and careful, driver. He didn't speed. Excessively. He didn't change lanes. Excessively. He drove like he fought. Quickly, instinctually, and seemingly effortlessly. The car responded to his touch like a trained beast. It seemed to purr as it glided down the Strip. Its seats were comfortable. The soft whisper of the dual climate control fanned her like sensual tropic breezes.

She ached only slightly from yesterday's battle, and was still hungry despite her large breakfast. The batteries that drove the awesome engine of her body were still not entirely recharged. She was still tired, more than she realized. Somewhere after Ray hit the highway beyond the city limits, lulled by her comfortable surroundings and the smooth glide of the road beneath their feet, the Angel fell asleep.

She dreamed her interrupted dream again, and thought it true. She and the Witness faced each other, only this time there was love in his eyes, not contempt. They were fully dressed, and then they were naked as the day they'd been born, and the Angel felt no guilt about it. Well, not much anyway.

Any trace of guilt vanished when he touched her. His hands were gentle on her face, caressing her cheek, slipping softly to her throat. It was amazing that such a large and strong-looking hand could be so gentle as it trickled down the column of her neck as lightly as the wings of a dove. It went lower and she shivered at the touch of his hand on her right breast. Cupping it gently. Whispering over her stiffening nipple.

She closed her eyes and their lips met in a soft yet increasingly demanding kiss. The Angel's breath started to come faster. Her eyes opened and she was shocked to see that she was no longer in the Witness's arms, but was being embraced by Jonah, the only boy she'd ever kissed, ten years ago.

That meant . . . that meant . . .

Suddenly her mother burst onto the back porch, screaming at them, saying vile dirty things. She swung a broomstick at them, snapping it across the Angel's shoulders. The Angel started to cry. Jonah bounded up from the back porch swing and lit out like the hounds of Hell were on his trail, and they may well have been. The Angel put her arms over her face and contracted into a ball as her mother screamed at her, waving the broken stick ferociously.

Only, as she opened her eyes again, it wasn't her mother standing over her. It was Billy Ray. And it wasn't a stick he was waving.

The Porsche suddenly swerved and the Angel awoke, startled. She reached out, not sure where she was, and, caught in a spasm of sudden terror, grabbed the door handle and ripped it off.

Ray glanced sideways at her.

"Insurance isn't going to cover that," he said with a frown as she stared at the door handle in her hand. "Sorry I woke you. I had to swerve to miss a turtle in the road."

"Tortoise," the Angel corrected. It was better to babble nonsense than think about the meaning of her dream.

"What?"

"They don't have turtles in the desert. They have tortoises."

"Oh. Well. That's good to know." Ray drove on while the Angel looked at the door handle in her hand.

"Hang on," Ray warned her. "I'm going to turn again. Don't get all scared and rip the door off this time."

"Sorry," the Angel said in a small voice.

"Jeez," Ray said, looking stolidly out the windshield. "Lighten up. I'm just kidding. Wreck the whole frigging car if you want. I put it on Barnett's card." He took a sudden turn, swinging onto a dirt road that meandered seemingly off to nowhere. "But wait until we get back to Vegas, okay? I don't feel like legging it back through the desert."

He glanced at her. She smiled back, briefly, but said nothing. *He must think I'm a hysterical fool,* the Angel told herself. *And he'd be right.*

The dirt road curved like a snake through the desert, leading finally to the mouth of a small canyon set into a meandering line of hills that provided the only topological relief in sight. Ray drove carefully, but they still jounced roughly, Ray swearing at every pothole and washout he hit. He didn't blaspheme, though, so the Angel cut him some slack.

"I hope that was the right turnoff," Ray muttered. "These hicks don't mark their roads very clearly—yeah, there it is, ahead."

It was a ranch, a hacienda of some kind that looked old to the Angel's eye, but she was no architecture expert. She couldn't even see the main house at first, because the grounds were surrounded by an adobe wall that had definitely seen better days. The Angel imagined that it had been built to keep marauding Native

Americans out, but now it couldn't keep out a herd of marauding cows. Though it was still twelve or fourteen feet high in some places, most of it had fallen to nearly ground level. Repairs were in progress, but although tools and ladders and mud bricks were all over the place, no one was actually currently working.

The gate stood wide open, the cross arm barely hanging by a single hinge. The wooden sign over the entrance was mostly in Arabic, with the English words THE OASIS—WELCOME neatly lettered below.

"Do you think we should just drive in?" the Angel asked.

Ray shrugged. "We've come all this way," he said, and carefully pulled onto the looping dirt driveway that was bounded by a border of whitewashed stones. He stopped after the first curve and they stared out the windshield and then looked at each other. "I'll be damned," Ray said.

"Don't blaspheme," the Angel said automatically.

Suddenly, they were in paradise. It was as green as Ireland inside the walls of the old ranchero, with plants and flowers of every type and description abloom in vivid color. The grass looked like putting greens. Rows of corn, mostly hidden behind the main building, grew as tall as an elephant's eye. Tomato vines thick enough to swing on climbed groaning trellises, green beans hung on netting draped between the vines, and squash the size of pumpkins and pumpkins like boulders were scattered among them. A pond of rather larger proportions than you'd expect to see in a desert was tucked into one corner of the grounds, surrounded by reeds and cattails. Lilies and lotus of every conceivable color covered its surface, providing shelter for the exotic waterfowl diving for aquatic bugs along its margins.

"These Living Gods are some gardeners," Ray understated as he edged the car forward. He went slowly, careful not to squash any of the fancy-feathered chickens pecking among the driveway gravel. The birds squawked indignantly at the car's approach, loud enough to alert those inside the hacienda. By the time Ray and the Angel had parked and gone up to the front door, a tall, bird-beaked joker opened it. He looked sad, the Angel thought, though it was difficult to read the expression on his odd features.

"Hello, Thoth," Ray said.

"Mr. Ray. Miss . . . ?"

"This is Angel," Ray said, and somehow the Angel suppressed the urge to correct him. "She's my partner. Listen, I know this is a difficult time—"

The bird-beaked joker stepped aside and opened the door wide. "Come in," he said.

The interior of the old house was cool despite the desert heat. Its floors were tile, the walls adobe brick. There was little furniture in the rooms they went through, but a riot of colorful rugs covered the floors and walls. Thoth led them out the rear entrance, where he stopped and turned to them. They stood on the threshold of the backyard, where the other Living Gods were picking flowers from among the riot of blooms that grew there, or just standing talking or sitting silently, comforting each other as best they could.

"We are preparing our brother Sheb for burial," he explained in a sadly ominous voice punctuated by the weird clacking of his long beak. He gestured toward a square, blank-walled shed in the back. In the far reaches of the enclosed yard, out beyond that square shed, the Angel could see two of them digging a grave in the soft sand of the desert floor.

"You're not," the Angel heard herself blurt out, "mummifying him?"

Ray glanced at her with pursed lips and a frown, but Thoth didn't seem to mind. "No, Miss Angel," he said. "I'm afraid that we are a much simpler people than our ancestors were. We have neither the time nor the money to do the job properly, but—"

He fell silent for a moment as one of his comrades came from the shed. Brown and thin and weathered as an old stick, the old man carried four small jars made from white stone. He looked at Thoth, nodded, and took the jars to a woman who had obviously recently been weeping. On a small table before her were a number of small humanlike figurines, no more than six inches high, made of clay or stone.

"—we do the best we can for our brother. He goes west with his vitals safe in their canopic jars, his ushabti to provide for him in the land of the dead, and our prayers for Anubis to aid him during the time of judgment."

It didn't sound all too different to the Angel than a Christian burial. Except that part about the canopic jars. And the ushabti figures. And, actually, Anubis. She felt bad that the poor man would be condemned to Hell because he was a pagan. Anyway, it was all the Allumbrados' fault. It was something else that they had to pay for.

"That's all he could ask," Ray said.

The Angel stared at him, surprised at his unexpected compassion, as Thoth nodded his bird head. The other Living God—blasphemous as that thought was—gave the jars to the mourning woman and then joined them. He looked normal, if undernourished and over-tanned by years of exposure to a harsh sun.

"This is my brother, Osiris. He speaks little English, but there is something he would tell you."

Ray nodded. "His fame is great. I dared to come and interrupt your grief with the hope that he might have news of the boy."

Osiris spoke rapid Arabic. Ray nodded. The Angel could scarcely believe that he knew what the man was saying.

"*Alf shukr*," Ray said. "A thousand thanks for all. Our sorrow for your loss is great."

"Our strength is spent," Thoth said. "We are now all old, or weak. We only wish to pass the remainder of our lives peacefully among the oasis we have created in this desert, which reminds us so much of the home we have lost. We can aid you no more."

"You've done enough," Ray said.

Thoth shook his head. "We wish we could do more. But we have two favors to ask of you."

"Name them," Ray said, stepping on the Angel's foot when she started to interrupt.

"Save the boy. Save the beloved of Ra," Thoth said. "He is the great light who will illume the world."

"We will," Ray said. "And the other thing?"

"Avenge our brother," said Osiris in heavily accented English.

Ray smiled. It was not the simple grin the Angel had seen earlier. It was not a reassuring sight to the Angel's eyes. "That," Ray said, "I can promise."

Osiris grinned back, while Thoth grimaced like a vulture.

"No need to disturb you further," Ray said. "We can see ourselves out." He made a gesture of farewell to the old men, who bowed as Ray grabbed the Angel's hand and hustled her back into the house.

"What did he tell you?" the Angel demanded.

"Where the kid is," Ray said, smiling.

"How'd he know?"

Ray shrugged. "He's a prophet. He sees things."

"He's a pagan!" the Angel said.

Ray shrugged again. "So?"

They went through the house. The Angel shut the front door carefully behind them. "So where is he?" she asked, her concern and aggravation growing.

"Now?" Ray asked.

"OF COURSE NOW."

Ray grinned. She felt like punching him. "Osiris isn't sure. He thinks somewhere in New York City. Some kind of jail, or hospital, or something."

"That's helpful," the Angel said as they slid into the front seats of the car.

Ray twisted around and looked at the Angel. "But soon," he said with a smile that had a tinge of crazy, "he's going to camp."

"Camp?" she repeated as Ray started the car, gunned the engine, and then took off at a sedate pace up the driveway, and the rutted desert road beyond.

♣

New York City: St. Dympna's Home for the Mentally Deficient and Criminally Inclined

SINCE HE HAD THE rank accorded an ace and was also a *perfecti* in the Allumbrados, Nighthawk had a private room set aside for his use in St. Dympna's, though he rarely took advantage of that dubious perk.

The place made his skin crawl. Back in the mid-nineteenth century up through the latter part of the twentieth, when St. Dympna's was a going concern run by a nursing order of the Church, it had housed hundreds of patients within its grim stone walls. Most were kept in the large dormitory-like rooms on the first floor, segregated by sex, if not always by mental malady. The private rooms on the second floor had been reserved for more affluent patients, while the third floor was for the staff. No one ever said much about the basement and what went on in there, not even now.

Officially, St. Dympna's had closed sometime in the 1970s and stood empty for more than two decades before coming to Contarini's attention. Interested in strengthening his power base, the cardinal had secretly activated the decrepit pile of stones for use as a training station for *credenti*, the lowest rank of the brotherhood. The basement rooms also made a fine storage place for those who angered or inconvenienced the cardinal.

Cameo currently occupied one of those basement rooms. Or, perhaps more accurately, cells. Nighthawk had hoped to spirit her away almost immediately upon their arrival, but the old horror pit was alive with unexpected activity. Usually staffed by a few sleepy *credenti* and some new recruits in the dormitory-like rooms on the first floor, now it was swarming with gunmen babbling about the day's events in Vegas.

No *obsequenti* were present, but Nighthawk had learned from a couple of *credenti* that Butcher Dagon and the Witness had actually succeeded in their mission of capturing the Anti-Christ and had brought him back, bound, from Las Vegas. The Witness had gone to the Waldorf to report to the cardinal (At least Contarini would be somewhat mollified, Nighthawk thought, by the success of the second prong of his master plan.) and Dagon was in the third-floor infirmary, along with several injured *credenti,* recovering from wounds sustained in the boy's snatch and grab.

The purported Anti-Christ now occupied a cell in the oubliette, probably next to Cameo, under close guard. Security was at an unprecedented peak. The old asylum hadn't been as tightly locked down since '57 when an ace-powered psychopath had escaped the oubliette and slaughtered thirty-seven patients in the dormitory before being overpowered by a mysterious patient from the second floor who'd been catatonic for almost a decade, before suddenly waking and stopping the carnage by seemingly draining the psychopath's mind. The cryptic ace/patient had then escaped St. Dympna's in a manner unknown to the rumormongers who delighted in telling such horror stories about the history of the old sanitarium.

Nighthawk could well imagine the torments a sensitive like Cameo was suffering while being locked in a cell that had housed generations of drooling psychotics, but there was nothing he could do except bed down in his tiny room on the third floor, wait awhile, and hope that something would break for the better in the coming hours.

He needed the rest, anyway. He wasn't as young as he once was, though he was younger than he used to be.

♠

Las Vegas: The Mirage

IT WAS LATE AFTERNOON by the time Ray and Angel got back to Vegas and had dinner at an all-you-can-eat buffet. At first he tried to keep up with her, plate for plate, but gave it up after the fourth helping. She could eat like a bastard. It was a good thing, he thought, that she was so frigging active, otherwise she'd look like a balloon.

After dinner they'd gone down to the police station and tried to get an interview with Dagon, but the local donut chokers went coy on them. They wanted an order from Ray's superior, and since Ray didn't particularly want them to know who his current superior actually was, they left the station saying they'd come back. But they didn't.

They didn't know where the kid would be for at least a day, so the only constructive thing Ray could think of was to try to get Angel into the sack, but it would have been easier to break into maximum security to interview Dagon.

Ray lay in his bed in the Mirage alone, trying hard not to think of Angel on the other side of the connecting door. It had been a long, not very productive couple of days. Sure, he'd gotten to kick some ass, but those frigging Allumbrados had managed to get away with the kid, Peregrine was lying in a hospital somewhere with tubes stuck into her arms, and as yet he hadn't even managed to get a chuckle out of Angel, let alone a civil word.

That Witness, though . . .

Ray added his name to the list of jerks whose asses he'd like to kick. He didn't like the way Angel had looked at him when they'd first come face-to-face. He especially didn't like the way the pretty boy had treated her. It's one thing to best someone in combat. It's another thing to humiliate them. Ray hated bullies, and it was clear that this Witness was one.

But maybe Angel had learned a lesson. She'd done okay after initially putting herself in a hole by letting the Witness get the upper hand. Ray had thought about stepping in to even things up a bit, but he knew how he'd feel if someone did that to him. It wouldn't make him happy.

And speaking of being not happy, Ray thought. He leaned over to the phone, suppressing a groan as his still-unknit ribs scraped against each other, and got an outside line. He dialed a number he knew well, and it was picked up on the second ring.

"President Leo Barnett's office."

"Alejandro?" Ray asked. Of course it was the kid. Who else would answer in that irritatingly perky manner? "Gimme Barnett."

There was a brief silence. "Uh, sorry, mis—uh, Billy. No can do. He's in closed conference with Sally Lou."

Ray was about to ask, *At this time of night?* but instead grinned sourly at the phone. "Is that what they're calling it now?" he asked.

"Huh?"

"Never mind," Ray said. "Listen, you been following events here?"

"Yes, sir," the kid said. "President Barnett's not real happy."

"Yeah, well, I've smiled more in my life," Ray said. "What's the latest news?"

"There's not much in the way of recent developments. It's not general knowledge, but we found out that Peregrine's husband had her flown out of Vegas on a medevac Lear, back to New York. Thought they could do a better job for her at the Jokertown Clinic than in the Vegas hospital. John Fortune's still missing. So's his bodyguard."

"His bodyguard's a shape-shifter," Ray informed the kid. At least, it seemed likely from the info he'd gleaned from Osiris's tale. "So I figure he impersonated Butcher Dagon—who's in a Vegas lockup—and took off with the kid." Ray frowned into the phone. He had to keep his kids straight.

"Well, that's something," his kid said. "What happened to Dagon?"

"I kicked his hairy ass," Ray said. "Angel helped," he added, to be fair.

"Boy, she's something," the kid said.

"You got that. Listen. Tell Barnett that me and Angel are taking the first flight tomorrow morning to Tomlin."

"How come?" the kid asked.

"We have a line on Fortune," Ray said. "Something that weird old fart Osiris told me. He's not sure where Fortune is right now. He thinks he may be in New

York City—which at least narrows it down a little. But soon the kid—Fortune,
that is—is gonna show up in some summer camp in a whistle-stop called New
Hampton, just north of the city. Angel and I will be there to meet him."

"Okay," the kid said. "You got it, Billy. Gee, I wish I could be with you and the
Angel doing something useful instead of sitting around here in the office while
President Barnett takes meetings."

Ray shook his head. "No you don't, kid," he said. "I've got a bad feeling about
this one. Besides, I'm not really sure we could use your talents. Yet."

"Ah, it'll all work out fine, Billy. You'll see."

"Yeah."

"But you and the Angel be careful, okay?"

"Yeah."

"Say hello to the Angel for me?"

"Yeah."

"Good ni—"

"Good night, kid," Ray said, and hung up. He still had things to do, and he
didn't want to spend twenty minutes getting off the phone. He called the airport
and got reservations for two on the first plane in the morning headed east. It was
an early flight, which didn't leave much time for sleep. He sighed, called the desk
for a five o'clock wake-up call for him and Angel both, and settled back down
on the bed. He wasted most of the night thinking about Angel in the room next
to his, while his body went about the business of repairing itself, muscle, bone,
sinew, and nerve.

It was quite used to that, by now.

◆

New York City: St. Dympna's Home for the Mentally Deficient and Criminally Inclined

IT WAS STILL SOME hours before dawn when Nighthawk heard a soft knock
on his door. Years of strenuous living had taught him how to awake instantly
and fully.

"Yes," he said, sitting up in bed.

"Phone call for you, Mr. Nighthawk," a respectful voice said softly.

"I'll be right with you."

He was wearing his shorts and T-shirt in lieu of pajamas, so he took a moment to put on pants, shirt, shoes, and jacket and run a brush through his hair.
Nighthawk always figured that since he could meet his end at any second, he
should always be well dressed when he went out in public. If he was going to end
up in Hell, he certainly wanted to look his best. And if he was going to Heaven,
he was sure it would be expected. When he opened the door to the corridor an
unfamiliar face awaited. Nighthawk figured that he was a recently recruited *credenti*. The new recruits always got stuck with the jobs nobody else wanted, like
nighttime security.

"Yes?" Nighthawk asked.

"It's Usher. He's calling from the Waldorf and wants to talk to a *perfecti*."

"All right." He followed the *credenti* to the office where a couple of Allumbrados were hanging out, supposedly guarding the building but, Nighthawk suspected, were actually bullshitting and eating donuts. At least, the open, mostly empty donut boxes and half-filled coffee cups near every hand led him to suspect that that was the case. The three of them, including the message boy they'd sent to get Nighthawk, watched with interest as he took a seat behind the old-fashioned desk.

"Usher," Nighthawk said into the telephone.

"John," the big man said with surprise. "Good thing you're still there."

"I didn't feel like coming back into the city after getting Cameo settled."

"Yeah." Since Usher and Magda were acting as Contarini's private bodyguards, they'd returned to the Waldorf right away after escorting Cameo and Nighthawk through St. Dympna's wrought-iron gates. "Listen. We may have a problem."

"What else is new," Nighthawk said, sorting through the leftover donuts on the desktop. "Ah. Raspberry filled." He took a bite and chewed softly.

"No time for snacks," Usher said. "We've discovered that Butcher Dagon apparently isn't really Butcher Dagon."

"Really?" Nighthawk said. He looked pointedly at the coffee cup that one of the *credenti* held until the recruit scrambled to his feet and got Nighthawk one for himself.

"Who is he, then?"

"We're not sure," Usher said. "It seems the real article is in a Vegas jail cell."

"Interesting," Nighthawk said. "I'd better check it out."

"We can be there in half an hour."

"You'd better. I don't have much confidence in the local talent."

Suddenly the three *credenti* were looking everywhere in the room but at Nighthawk.

"Okay, John. We're on the way."

"Who's we?"

"Me and Magda and the Witness."

"Which one?"

"The big one."

"All right," Nighthawk said. He hung up the phone and stared thoughtfully into space for a moment while he finished his coffee and donut. The Bigger Asshole. He'd better, he decided, move fast.

"What is it?" one of the *credenti* asked. Nighthawk looked at him steadily until he added, "Sir?"

"Possible security breach," Nighthawk said, rising from behind the desk.

"Want us to come with you, sir?"

Nighthawk shook his head. If they saw what he was planning to do, he'd have to kill them all, and Nighthawk just wasn't that bloodthirsty.

"No. Give me the keys to the infirmary." One of them took a ring of keys off his belt and handed the proper one to Nighthawk, who nodded his thanks and crossed the room in his soft, measured tread. He stopped at the door and added, "If I'm not back in twenty minutes, come after me." He thought twenty minutes should give him plenty of time, if things went well. If they didn't . . . it probably wouldn't matter. "In the meantime, finish your donuts."

He closed the office door softly behind him and went down the corridor lit dimly by infrequent night-lights. *It's just like the cardinal,* Nighthawk thought, *to be stingy with the electricity. You'd think he was paying the bills personally.*

The infirmary was a three-room suite with an entrance off the corridor. The key fit the outer door, but, surprisingly, Nighthawk discovered that it was already unlocked. He opened it quietly and slipped into the reception area, which was dark and silent. A closed supply room was attached to the reception area. The infirmary itself, where the sick or injured were bedded, opened off the reception room, and by order was also locked at night when there was no nurse or doctor in attendance. Contarini had a loyal medical staff on call, but they only spent the night if a patient was in danger. In this case, Nighthawk understood that they'd transported a badly wounded *credenti* to a friendly hospital where there'd be no questions about how he'd gotten hurt.

Nighthawk stopped before the infirmary door. It was ajar. He listened intently, but heard only the random rustling movements of sleeping men. Moving as quietly as approaching death, he took the glove off his left hand and then slowly opened the door wide enough for him to look inside. There were four beds. Three were occupied by injured men, now sleeping, none of whom looked like Butcher Dagon. The fourth, with disturbed bedclothes, was empty. Nighthawk glanced at the inside of the door and frowned. A smear of blood on the lock plate was still dripping sluggishly to the floor. He touched the stain gingerly, then rubbed his fingertips together. The blood was still relatively fresh.

He checked the outer door and discovered that it, too, had a bloodied lock plate.

"Curious," Nighthawk said quietly to himself, wiping the blood off his fingers on a tissue he took from the box on the reception desk.

He moved like a ghost into the dimly lit corridor, swiftly and silently, and went down the stairway that led to the floors below.

♥

New York City: Jokertown

IT MUST HAVE BEEN *a tough day at the monastery,* Fortunato thought as he awoke and tried to sit up. *I hurt all over.* He paused, frowning. *And my tatami smells like someone's pissed on it.*

He opened his eyes, suddenly remembering a fist the size of a small boulder crashing into his face. He sat up, groaning, and looked around. He was no longer in the alley. It was dark and he couldn't tell exactly where he was, but it didn't look good and it smelled worse.

After a moment his eyes adjusted to the gloom, and he realized that he was in an abandoned building. Probably not in an interior room because light was filtering through holes in the walls and down through the floors above. It was artificial light, and it wasn't abundant. The building was apparently located in an area with few functioning streetlights.

Fortunato wasn't entirely unfamiliar with buildings that looked like they'd gone through the Blitz and then been taken over by clans of cave-dwelling troglodytes who weren't picky about personal sanitation or garbage disposal. When he was a kid he'd often played in similar ruins. Sometimes he and his friends would stumble across drunks and jokers while exploring derelict structures, but such creatures were usually more scared of him than he was of them. Though there had been exceptions.

He swiveled onto his hands and knees, grimacing in disgust at the urine, blood, and come stains on the mattress the Jokka Bruddas had dropped him on. *At least,* he thought, *they didn't just dump me on broken glass and nail-studded debris.* But he wasn't in the mood to be particularly forgiving toward the thugs who'd ambushed, then kidnapped him. He was in the mood to hit back. Hard.

He pushed himself to his feet, swaying as a wave of nausea threatened to overwhelm him.

Concussion, damn it, he thought.

He clenched his teeth and staggered like a drunk, sending bits of building debris and a couple of empty liquor bottles skittering across the floor, eventually colliding with a wall mostly reduced to naked studs. The few wall panels that remained were covered with gang graffiti.

Not much has changed since I was a kid, Fortunato thought. *This must be the Bruddas hangout. The center of their turf.* The desire to get even with the joker punks was suddenly quenched by the realization that he was in danger. Potentially fatal danger. *Got to get out of here.*

He pushed away from the wall and stood straight, scowling darkly at nothing. He suddenly realized that he was thinking like the old Fortunato, not the Fortunato who had spent fifteen years trying to learn how to cloak himself in serenity. *Worry about that later. Worry now about getting your ass out of here before those punks show up and finish you.*

"Well look who's awake," a voice said from behind him. "That crazy old Fortunato."

Too late, he told himself grimly.

Carlos and his gang of tormentors came from somewhere inside the abandoned structure where probably the rooms were intact and the garbage less ubiquitous. Their numbers had been augmented by an extra eight or ten other jokers. Fortunato squinted at them blearily. Some of the newcomers were possibly female.

Ricky, the giant, stooped low so he could get through the doorway into Fortunato's room. His high voice squeaked something that Fortunato's still-dazed brain couldn't quite make out. Most of the others laughed.

"Careful, Ricky," Carlos said in mock fear. "He's Fortunato! He's a mean old ace. Why, my dad told me that he can fly. He can throw lightning with his hands. Watch out, *hermano.* All you can do is hit him. Like you done before."

The girl (at least Fortunato assumed it was a girl) clinging to his arm tittered, and repeated, "Hit him, hit him, hit him!"

The rest of the Bruddas took up the chant. Ricky smiled as he approached, bowing at the waist so his face was almost level with Fortunato's. Fortunato stood as straight as he could, even though his head whirled with vertigo and he felt like puking. He moved fast and was almost on target. His fist struck the joker in the cheek, and stuck there.

Ricky's flesh was coated with a layer of slime with the consistency of thick mucilage. Fortunato pulled, and the joker's skin stretched a good half foot until it was taut, but he couldn't yank his fist free. Ricky laughed. He grabbed Fortunato around the waist with his titan-sized hands and lifted him high, smashing him against what was left of the room's ceiling.

Fortunato grunted, absorbing the blow as best he could, though nausea-tinged pain washed through his system like a tidal wave.

"Don't break him, Ricky," Carlos said. "Let us play with 'im, too. We wanna teach the old bastard a lesson. Let us show him who's the power in J-town now."

His fellow gangbangers howled as Ricky tossed him contemptuously to the floor. Fortunato felt glass shards rip his clothes and score the flesh beneath as he skidded half a score of feet to right in front of the Bruddas. He looked up, groaning in pain. All he saw was a sea of horrific faces surrounding him. He knew they were eager for his blood.

"You know what's funny, old man?" Carlos asked with a mocking smile. He reached into his back pocket and took out a rolled-up magazine, an old issue of *Aces!* Digger, no doubt, Fortunato thought, would be pleased. The joker finally found the page he was looking for, opened the magazine, and held it out for Fortunato to see. Fortunato squinted at it, but he couldn't quite make out the photo. "You *are* Fortunato." Carlos looked back and forth from the photo in the magazine to Fortunato, lying in the debris at his feet. "At least, you look like the old motherfucker. Well, whatever."

Carlos tossed the magazine over his shoulder, where it landed on the floor with the other, less savory garbage.

"It don' matter," he said, explaining the situation to Fortunato. "We win, in any case. If you are Fortunato, we beat you until you nice and tender, then we cut you, we cook you, and we eat you." Carlos smiled. "I get your liver. I hope you not a drinking man, because I like them nice and tender. It's, like, a sacrament. Body and blood, man. Body and blood. If you not, if you just a crazy old man, we still get a nice meal. See, fucker, any way, we win."

He drew a knife from a sheath he carried in the small of his back. It wasn't a fighting knife. It was a filleting knife.

Fortunato tried to stand as they closed around him. He couldn't rise. His head hurt like a beaten gong. His insides felt wrong where Ricky had squeezed him. All he could do was roll over on his stomach, pull his knees in, and cover his head with his arms as the blows started to fall. Some of the jokers kicked him, some beat him with boards and pipes and other handy weapons. He quickly lost track of what was happening as he drowned in an ocean of sudden pain.

I'm Fortunato, he screamed silently. *I'm Fortunato. It can't end like this.* Blood thundering in his ears, agony washed across him like a tidal wave. He screamed, "Help me, someone help me."

As total blackness claimed him, he couldn't even be sure that he had spoken aloud.

New York City: St. Dympna's Home for the Mentally Deficient and Criminally Inclined

JERRY STOOD BEFORE THE locked door, twisting his forefinger like a key in a lock. There was a click as the lock sprung, and he extricated his finger from the keyhole. A couple of inches of bone, shaped like a key, protruded from the tip of his bloody forefinger. *A skeleton key,* Jerry thought.

He rarely had the opportunity to use this aspect of his shape-shifting powers. Even though it kind of hurt when he extruded the bone through the meat of his fingertip, it pleased him when he had the chance to exercise this particular talent. As far as he knew, it was unique in the wild card world. He turned and waved a silent goodbye to his erstwhile companions. Their presence had been something of a pain in the butt, as he had to wait until he was sure they were all asleep before he made his escape, but they had also helped him in their own way. First, one of them had supplied Jerry's current outfit. Jerry had waited until he was sure that they were all asleep before rummaging through their clothes to find something that fit, but it was better making his escape in sweaty and blood-stained fatigues than in a hospital gown with his ass sticking out.

Second, they were all more severely wounded than Jerry was pretending to be, so he was able to wave most of the medical attention away from himself, insisting that the nurse check them out before turning to him. It would have been pretty embarrassing if they'd discovered that Jerry wasn't really injured at all. In fact, one of his companions had been so badly hurt that they'd taken him to a real hospital. The medics hadn't yet returned to the infirmary, which made Jerry's escape all the easier.

He crossed the dark reception room and listened carefully, his ear against the door, but there was no sound in the corridor outside. He inserted his finger in the lock plate of the door to the corridor, hoping that he wouldn't have to grow another key. It took time to mold the bone around the intricacies of a lock, and he wasn't sure how much time he had before a guard might show up. He wasn't sure if the corridors were guarded at all, but even if they weren't there was always the chance of running into someone going to the kitchen for a snack. The last thing he wanted to do was raise an alarm. He was one against how many he couldn't even begin to guess. He could only trust to the efficacy of his Dagon impersonation, and to lessen the chance of someone penetrating it, move quietly and stealthily. Jerry was good at that, but he had a feeling he would need more than skill to spring John Fortune. He would need luck as well, and that was something he hadn't been blessed with.

It could be worse, he thought. *I could really be hurt as bad as Dagon had seemed to be.*

The corridor was quiet and dimly lit by infrequent night-lights. Following the way he'd originally come, he found the staircase, and, as they did on the way up, bypassed whatever was on the second and first floors and went directly to the basement.

That area of the rambling old building was not quite as well appointed as the rest of the structure. The walls were rough-dressed stone blocks. The floors were actually flagstone. The basement reminded Jerry uncomfortably of every dungeon he'd seen in every medieval epic ever filmed. The rooms leading off the main corridor were dungeon-like cells with stout oaken doors that had tiny iron-barred windows set into them. All that was missing was the fat, hairy-stomached turnkey with a hunchback and a black hood.

Jerry stopped to look down a corridor lit even more dimly than those on the floor above. His nose suddenly crinkled in disgust. "What's that smell?" he asked himself quietly.

It was dampness compounded by a rank animal odor that was teasingly familiar. Jerry cat-footed by the first cell, heard an odd sound, and stopped and looked in through the tiny window set in the cell door. In the dim light he could discern a twisted shape, human turned animal. He realized that this was also the source of the peculiar smell, as waves of it streamed through the window, gagging him.

It was the joker they'd led around by a leash, the one they called Blood. He was sleeping curled up in a pile of straw in one corner of the stone-floored room. Something about the very sight of the creature made Jerry shiver.

Then he woke up and looked right at Jerry. His lips curled back from his protruding teeth in a silent snarl.

Jerry froze. He didn't want the joker to raise a ruckus and alert whatever guards may be lurking around the dungeon. He smiled. "Good boy," he said lowly, in as kindly a tone as he could muster. "Good do—good fellow."

Blood cocked his head in an inquisitive manner, and got up from the pile of hay, stretching luxuriously. He went to a corner of the cell, lifted his leg, and urinated on a pile of newspaper spread out evidently for that purpose while Jerry kept his feelings of disgust off his face. There was no telling how smart this creature was, and he didn't want the thing pissed at him. Blood stretched again and ambled over to the door, looking up with what Jerry took to be a hopeful expression.

"What do you want?" Jerry looked around for something to placate the joker, and noticed a large can of Spam sitting on the floor near the cell door. He picked it up and held it up to the window for Blood to see. Blood started to drool.

"Quiet now!" Jerry ordered as the joker showed signs of growing excitement. Somehow Jerry was certain that opening the can would be beyond the joker's capabilities, so he detached the key and cranked the lid open himself. He slid the slab of glistening meat by-product from the can and tossed it through the barred window. Blood caught the slab in his mouth and capered back to his pile of hay where he carefully arranged himself and started to bolt it down as Jerry wiped his hand on his pants, fighting the queasy feeling in the pit of his stomach.

"I've got to get out of this place," he told himself.

He went on down the corridor, glancing into every cell he passed, fighting the impulse to call out loud to John Fortune. Most of the cells were empty. A few were occupied by men who were either sleeping or gazed at Jerry with dull, lifeless eyes that seemed to be without a spark of intelligence. He moved past these rapidly, afraid that they might say something, might make a plea that he couldn't answer.

He arrived at the next-to-last cell in the row. He still had the entire other side of the corridor to check, but he was getting fearful that something had gone wrong, that they'd already taken John Fortune somewhere, that they'd done something awful to him and he'd never get the kid back. When he looked in the cell he saw in the dim light a slim, youthful body standing half hidden in the darkness, and hope again flared to life.

"John," he whispered urgently, and the body moved, quick as a cat, running silently to grip the bars of the window set in the thick door, and he knew right away from the shape of it, from the long, flowing hair, that this was not John Fortune.

"Who are you?" she cried. "Did Nighthawk send you?"

"Nighthawk?" Jerry asked, confused.

It was a young woman. She was beautiful, but her face was screwed up so tightly that he knew she was barely clinging to this side of sanity. Her familiarity gnawed at him until he realized that she was Cameo, a somewhat well-known ace who would have been much better known if she'd actively sought out publicity.

"What are you doing here?" Jerry asked in a low voice.

"Nighthawk brought me here," she said in a quick whisper, almost more to herself than Jerry. "The cardinal made him. He said he was going to free me soon, but he hasn't come. I can't—I can't take this place much longer. This place is mad, insane with death and misery. It drips from the walls, running in puddles up to my knees—"

"All right," Jerry said in low, soothing tones, "all right." Her voice was rising, almost hysterically. He tried to shush her, but it was already too late.

"Quiet out there!"

The command came from inside what looked to be a larger room at the end of the corridor, perhaps the office, or the hangout, or whatever you wanted to call it, of the freak show's keeper. Jerry could hear someone moving around, probably in response to Cameo's growing frenzy.

"Can't sleep with you yelling like a crazy woman! You make me come out there and I'll give you something to yell about!"

"All right," Jerry said. "I'll get you out of here."

"My hat," Cameo demanded. "Get my hat!"

"All right," he repeated again, helplessly making placating gestures. "Just be quiet for a minute."

"My hat," she repeated insistently.

Jerry nodded vigorously, striding toward the guard room to discover the modern-day equivalent of a medieval torturer manning the dungeon as he practically bumped into a large, fat, and unshaven man coming out of the room with a snarl on a face that could have only been improved if it had been wiped clean and redone. The man started and blinked dumbly for a few moments as he stared at Jerry. He was wearing a dirty undershirt, dirty jeans, scuffed shoes, and, of all things, a battered fedora.

"Bu-Bu-Butcher Da-Da-Dagon," he stuttered with a degree of fright that was almost comical. "Wha-wha-wha are you do-doing he-he-here?"

Jerry kept his smile to himself. At least his disguise was working. He had no idea what Dagon's voice was like, so he modeled his British accent on Roger Moore.

"I've come for Cameo," he said. He remembered something that she'd said, and inspiration struck him. "The cardinal wants her."

The dungeon-keeper bobbed his head in mute and complete agreement. He turned and led the way back into his office. There wasn't much to it. A wooden table with a scarred surface that looked like someone had been playing mumblety-peg on it. A few wooden chairs that looked scarcely capable of supporting the guard's bulk. A large handbag teetered on one corner of the table with a pile of junk spread out before it.

"This her stuff?" Jerry asked.

"Uh-huh," the jail keeper replied.

Clearly someone had dumped out her oversized purse and searched through the accumulated mass of feminine paraphernalia. There was a lot of stuff, most of which Jerry didn't care to examine too closely. For a moment he was worried, because the all-important hat she'd demanded wasn't present. Jerry turned and looked at the turnkey, frowning.

"Where's the hat?" he asked as flatly as he could, discovering that it was hard to be menacing and yet sound like Roger Moore.

"Uhhh." It seemed to be the guard's favorite word. Sheepishly, he removed the battered fedora that was perched jauntily on his head, exposing a forehead that couldn't have contained a teaspoon full of brains. He held it out apologetically to Jerry.

Jerry had expected some kind of female-type hat, but if this was the one from the bag, this was the one she must have been talking about. He swept all of Cameo's other paraphernalia into the purse, figuring there might be some other vital bit of equipment she needed. He took the hat from the guard as he swept out of the room, paused in the doorway to take a key ring that was hanging from a spike hammered into the wall. The keys were iron, appropriately massive for the old cells. Jerry had thought he'd be able to do his skeleton key trick to open up the cell doors, but judging by the size of the keys in his hand, he'd have to stick two or three fingers into the massive lock plate to be able to duplicate the key, and he didn't think that would have worked too well.

He paused and turned to the guard. "Stay here. I don't want to disturb your rest any further."

He hoped that he'd managed an appropriately sinister turn of voice and the jailer would obey. He didn't want the man peering over his shoulder while he went through the cells freeing not only John Fortune and Cameo, but all the prisoners.

He went back out into the corridor, and his heart caught in his throat as he saw a dark figure. For a moment he panicked, and then he realized that the man seemed to have more of a waiting than a lurking attitude, and he didn't seem very menacing at all. He was a small, older-looking, very dark-skinned Black man neatly dressed in a dark suit with a faint pinstripe, white shirt, and polished black shoes that would have been very stylish fifty, sixty years ago. It looked, in fact, like something Bogart would have worn in *Casablanca*. The old man carried it off very well. He looked sharp, in the parlance of an earlier generation. Except for the black glove that he wore on his left hand. *What's up with that?* Jerry wondered.

"You shouldn't be prowling around the oubliette alone, Dagon," the old man said in a sweet, soft voice that revealed his Deep South roots. There was, however, a peculiar emphasis on the word *Dagon* that Jerry didn't like.

"Just checking things out," Jerry said, trying to sound like Dagon but suspecting already that he was wasting his effort.

The old man nodded. "Perhaps we should introduce ourselves," he said formally. "My name is John Nighthawk. I am in the employ of Cardinal Romulus Contarini, whose hospitality you are currently enjoying at Saint Dympna's Home for the Mentally Deficient and Criminally Inclined. And you are?"

"Butcher Dagon?" Jerry asked, trying but failing to keep an interrogatory tone out of his voice. He knew now that his cover was blown, but at least he wasn't being confronted by a pumped-up muscle-head like Witness or a stone killer like Dagon. He figured that he should be able to handle this old man, though he realized that appearances in the wild card world could be utterly deceiving.

John Nighthawk shook his head. "Time to put all the bullshit aside, son. I'm afraid that Butcher Dagon is currently a guest of the state of Nevada, city of Las Vegas. I'm afraid also that if we want to get out of here, we don't have much time. A team of heavily armed mercenaries backed by aces is going to show up in a very few minutes. It'd be better if none of us were here to answer their questions."

Jerry sighed. Once again, it seemed as if nothing were really as it seemed. He was getting tired of playing this game. "What do you want?" Jerry asked.

"I want Cameo," Nighthawk said. "I want to get her out of here. Since you came here with John Fortune, I assume you want him, and you also want out. I have no objection to that."

"Just what do you people want with him?" Jerry asked. "Who the hell are you, anyway?"

Nighthawk shook his head. "There's no time for long explanations. Let me just say that Contarini is the head of an order known as the Allumbrados, which means 'the Enlightened Ones.' They believe that John Fortune is the Anti-Christ—"

"What?" Jerry couldn't believe his ears.

Nighthawk held up a forestalling hand, the gloved one. "We can talk about this or we can get the hell out of here."

Jerry nodded. "All right. Let's get the hell out." He and John Fortune could ditch this crazy old coot as soon as they hit the fresh air. "Cameo's this way."

He led the way to her cell where she was still clinging to the bars, her eyes just this side of crazy.

"Nighthawk!" she hissed. "You promised—"

"I know," the old man said placatingly. "I'm here now. Let's just get out of here, and you can chew me out as much as you want."

That seemed to mollify her a little, but when she saw that Jerry had her bag, she thrust her thin arm through the barred window. "Gimme!" she demanded.

Jerry could see that the bag wouldn't fit through the bars, so he just handed her the hat. She snatched it from him and pulled it through the narrow opening, further squeezing it out of shape. She clapped it on her head without bothering to smooth it back into form.

"Open the door," she said.

"Working on it," Jerry said. Fortunately there were only half a dozen or so oversized keys on the ring. He dropped her bag with the rest of her stuff by the door and started trying keys. The third one worked on Cameo's door. As soon as he heard the lock click he pushed against the massive door, opening it slightly. He turned, looking down the corridor, and he moved on to a cell just a few doors down and across the way where he saw hands glowing a faint, pleasant yellow-orange gripping the bars.

"Jerry!" John Fortune called out in his excitement, perhaps too loudly.

"John, I'm here." He went to the window and looked in at the kid clinging to the bars, a lost, scared look on his face.

"Jeez, I'm glad to see you," John Fortune said. He fell silent, looking worried. "Voices in the corridor just woke me up. It really is you, isn't it, Jerry?"

"It's me all right. We'll get you out of there in a second."

He tried one key. It didn't work. He put a second in the lock and failed to turn the tumblers. He rattled a third key as a voice said, "Step away from that door. We've got you covered."

Jerry looked over his shoulder to see two men standing in the mouth of the corridor. *Damn it,* he thought. *Nighthawk!*

They both had guns. Rifles. In the darkness Jerry couldn't be sure what kind. They did have him covered. "I said," the one on the right reiterated, "step away from the door."

Jerry complied, swearing to himself under his breath. He'd been so damn close!

The two men were so focused on Jerry that they didn't see the door to Cameo's cell swing open silently. They didn't see Cameo herself, witchfire dancing like fireflies around and between her hands as she held them up. They didn't see her until it was too late.

Sparks crackled between her hands like a Jacob's ladder in the lab set in the old Frankenstein movies and then balls of electricity shot from her pointing fingers, striking the barrels of the men's rifles, running up the metal, and dancing over their bodies like a sparkling aurora borealis. The men themselves danced a brief jitterbug, and when the sparks faded they fell silently to the floor. The air suddenly smelled of hot metal and burned flesh. In his kennel, Blood howled hopefully.

"Jesus," John Fortune said in his cell.

Jerry agreed. He turned back to the door and fumbled through the rest of the keys before he was able to open it. It finally swung wide and John Fortune came out. "Am I glad to see you," he said, hugging Jerry.

"Me too," Jerry said, holding him tight for a brief second. "We've got to move."

"That's right," a voice said from a pool of blackness where no light touched an area of the corridor. John Nighthawk stepped out into visibility, putting his glove back on his left hand.

"Jesus Christ," Jerry said, "are you goddamned invisible?"

Nighthawk shook his head. "That's not one of my powers."

"Why were you hiding there?" Jerry asked as Cameo joined them in the corridor. She still wore the hat. Jerry didn't care to look into her eyes.

"I had a vision while you were opening the door to the boy's cell."

"A vision," Jerry asked.

"That *is* one of my powers." He turned to look at John Fortune, and frowned. "He is very powerful. Much more powerful than even you know. But he is not the Anti-Christ."

"What?" John Fortune asked.

"You will take him out of the city," Nighthawk said to Jerry. "I saw that. Others will follow. Some will be your enemies. Some will be friends. Some will be strangers. Some will help you."

"Could you be any more specific?" Jerry asked.

Nighthawk shrugged. "That is the nature of visions," he said. "They're always open to interpretation. All I know is that you will go north, out of the city, to a place of forests and fields and happy children—"

"Hey!" Jerry said suddenly.

"You know this place?" Nighthawk asked.

Jerry nodded. "I think I do." He paused, and looked from Nighthawk to Cameo, who still looked a lot scarier than a beautiful, ethereal blonde had any right to look. "What about you two?"

"Our paths have crossed yours only briefly. We have other things to settle. But—" Nighthawk paused, frowning. "I don't think I'm done with you all yet. I don't . . ."

"We've got to go," Cameo prompted as his voice ran down.

Nighthawk shook himself, as if trying to escape unpleasant memories of future events.

"Yes, we do. But first—the other cells—"

Jerry nodded. Anything to cover their tracks, anything to spread confusion, would be a good thing. It took only moments to free the other prisoners. There were five of them. A couple of them weren't in very good shape, but their fellow escapees helped them up and out of their cells. Jerry was expecting trouble from the jailer in his little guardroom, but he'd heard the commotion in the corridor. He probably smelled the stench of burned flesh. For once his pea-sized brain processed the information correctly, and he decided to stay safe and snug in his little room.

The escapees went by the bodies of the two men at the foot of the stairs. John Fortune paused for a moment, looking at them, at their burned skin and the smoke still rising off their cooling corpses. Jerry was glad that the light was dim.

"Should—should I try to help them?" the kid asked Jerry.

Jerry shook his head. "Remember what your mother said. You can't help everybody. Some people are beyond your help. Some people don't deserve it." He glanced down at the bodies. "I'd say these guys fit into both those categories."

John Fortune nodded and they went swiftly up the stairs hearing lonesome, hopeful keening coming from Blood's cell.

♠　♥　♦　♣

Chapter Five

New York: Heading North on Route 17

JERRY AND JOHN FORTUNE crossed the Hudson at Tarrytown just as dawn was breaking in a car they'd taken from the parking lot at St. Dympna's. It was a dark, late-model Mercedes. Not flashy, but nicely appointed with a comfortable, smooth ride and a powerful engine. Once they'd gotten safely away from the asylum, Jerry took the precaution of stopping to switch plates with a car parked on a dark, quiet street.

Cameo, of all people, had proved surprisingly adept at hot-wiring cars, utilizing some innocuous-looking tool she'd taken out of her capacious handbag. Even Nighthawk had looked surprised as she quickly started two cars, one for her and Nighthawk, the other for Jerry and John Fortune.

They had to leave the other freed prisoners to fend for themselves. Some had gone into the parking lot with them and scattered into the night. Some had opted to stay in the asylum walls, committing mischief that Jerry was afraid to contemplate.

Jerry last saw Nighthawk and Cameo get into a Cadillac Seville as he and John Fortune had roared out of the parking lot. He still had no idea who the hell Nighthawk really was and what the hell he was really up to. At that point, Jerry didn't care. He'd rescued the kid, and they were heading off to safety. Jerry didn't know if he could trust the old man, but he could conceive of no possible scenario in which Nighthawk would help them flee, only to connive at their recapture. That just made no sense. And using the camp as a sanctuary was a great idea. Once there they could take the time for a deep breath, and a long, refreshing sleep. Jerry could call the office for reinforcements. And they'd be safe. No one would ever find them because although it was located only seventy miles or so north of the city, that part of New York was essentially one big empty space.

Jerry had been there a couple of times when they were getting the camp up and running. It was a favorite charity funded to a large degree by him and Ackroyd, and administered by Father Squid and a committee drawn mainly from his parish. Located on a couple dozen acres set in the middle of nowhere that were owned by a friend of the joker priest, Camp Xavier Desmond was a year-round retreat, the purpose of which was to get poor joker and nat kids out of the city so they could hang out together and learn about each other. It was open all summer and on weekends when school was in session, just to give kids a breath of fresh air, to show them what a tree looked like and maybe help them realize that nats and jokers weren't so different after all.

Once they'd crossed over the Hudson River on the Tappan Zee Bridge, Jerry avoided the Palisades Parkway feeder road, sticking to the thoroughfare leading to old Route 17. He could have taken the 87, also known as the Thruway, which was wider, straighter, and faster. But he didn't want wide, straight, and fast. He wanted narrow, crooked, and obscure, and old 17 was that in spades.

The little traffic there was on 17 consisted of commuters heading south to New York City. Virtually nobody was traveling on his side of the road. He kept to the speed limit and drove conservatively, glancing every now and then at John Fortune, who had conked out in the front seat next to him well before they'd crossed the Hudson. The boy had been through a lot, and this was probably the first time he'd felt safe enough to get a good rest. Jerry himself was going on the last dregs of adrenaline his body had left. He couldn't remember the last time he'd slept, and food was nearly a forgotten concept. He could have stopped at one of the diners that catered to travelers on the old road, but he had no wallet, no ID, no money. Doggedly, he drove on.

Wanting real obscurity, he turned west on 17A as soon as possible, entering the empty big space on the road map. As always, he found it kind of hard to believe that there was so much nothing so close to New York City. A confirmed city boy, the nearness of so much unused land always bothered him. More than once he found himself thinking that what these open fields needed was a couple of good apartment complexes to fill them up, but intellectually he realized that these open spaces were not really wasted. The rich soil was burgeoning with crops of all kinds—corn, tomatoes, lettuce, onions, celery, and other vegetables that would eventually make themselves useful at one salad bar or another. He was just not used to seeing them in the wild.

It was slow going, and even slower once he reached the sleepy hamlet of Florida with its one traffic light. He turned from 17A onto the network of county roads that spread through the rural landscape like capillaries meandering off from larger blood vessels. The traffic was now at a minimum, mainly locals headed for their jobs at metropolises like Middletown and Goshen, places where the population didn't exceed that of a decent-sized apartment complex.

Half relieved to find the place again, he pulled into Camp Xavier Desmond just as it was waking up to face another beautiful summer day. He was still wearing Butcher Dagon's face and body, not thinking it prudent to take the time to transform in the middle of their escape, but was still easily able to establish his bona fides with the camp superintendent while keeping John under wraps in the car. It was before office hours at Ackroyd and Creighton, but he called to check in and leave a message, saying where they were and that they were all right. He got the kid settled into an empty guest cabin, had a big, satisfying breakfast, and went to the cabin himself and crashed.

He slept well and deeply, knowing that he'd earned every moment of the rest he took.

Las Vegas: Airport

THEY HAD TO RUSH through breakfast to catch their early morning flight. The Angel wasn't happy about that. All she wanted was to get her money's worth (*Well,* she reminded herself, *the Hand's money's worth.*), but there was also the fact that they were going to be on the plane for a good part of the day and plane food was notoriously bad. And scanty.

Breakfast unfortunately turned out to be the high point of the day, which went downhill really fast.

The Angel and Ray boarded the plane half an hour before takeoff. The flight was already full. Ray grumbled endlessly about the fact that they'd gotten stuck in the main cabin because they'd had to buy their tickets at the last second. He was, the Angel thought, acting like a spoiled child. Their seats were perfectly adequate.

They had two seats in a row in the cabin's central section. Ray offered her the aisle seat, but she declined. That was her first mistake. Her second was being nice to the man who sat down next to her, smiling at him when he first plopped down. He was young, and rather handsome with lean, dark good looks. Almost Mediterranean, with thick, wavy hair and dark puppy-dog eyes. She was somewhat suspicious of him at first, but she told herself not to stereotype. Not every Italian-looking man was an Allumbrado.

She had her first qualm when she smelled the liquor wafting off him in waves, the smell of which was undisguised by his rather potent hair tonic, skin lotion, and cologne. It was an uneasy combination of odors to experience so early in the morning and it didn't help any when their takeoff was delayed for unspecified reasons and the air-conditioning was turned off as they sat on the runway and waited. And waited. And waited.

The passenger sitting next to the Angel wanted to while away the time drinking, but the flight attendant refused him alcohol. He then turned his attention to the Angel and she finally realized that he was hitting on her when she felt his hand on her upper thigh.

"Take your hand off me," she said in a cold voice.

He only smiled back at her. Ray, who had been focused in on his own little world, turned his head and frowned as she spoke. "You want to take it down a notch, Jack?" he asked.

"Please, Billy—" the Angel began, but the drunk interrupted her.

"I'm not poaching your private preserve, am I?" he asked Ray.

Ray frowned. "No, but—"

"Hey," the drunk interrupted again, "she's free, white, and twenty-one, ain't she?"

Ray's expression went cold. "How'd you like to be drunk, dead, and thirty-five, dork?"

"Billy!"

"You threatening me?" the drunk asked belligerently.

Ray laughed in his face. The drunk turned red, stood, and drew his fist back. The Angel caught it in her palm as he tried to punch Ray.

"Stop it!" she ordered.

The drunk tried to pull free. She twisted his wrist a little harder than she'd intended, and heard something snap. He screamed, "You broke my fucking arm, you fucking bitch!"

Then his face turned puce and he gagged.

"No," the Angel said. "Oh, no."

He threw up in her lap.

Ray was out of his seat and standing in the aisle before the spatter could hit him. "Son of a—" he started to say when a swarm of flight attendants descended on them. Some of them tried to placate Ray, some tried to help the Angel, and a couple others led the still-retching drunk away.

"I saw it all," one of the stewardesses said. "It wasn't your fault. Not at all. But I'm afraid you'll have to leave the plane so we can clean . . . this . . . all . . . up."

The Angel saw Ray muttering to himself, barely under control.

"My name is Billy Ray. I'm with the Secret Service. This is my associate. We have to get to New York as soon as possible—"

"I sympathize," the stewardess said. "But surely you can't expect to travel in this condition."

Ray took a deep breath as if to calm himself, then screwed up his face when he got a good whiff of the Angel.

"No," he said woodenly. "Of course not."

"I'm sorry," the Angel said. She grimaced at the vomit-covered front of her pants and blouse, holding her arms out from her body in dismay. "I didn't mean—"

"No one's blaming you," Ray said. He glared at the stewardess. "Are they?"

"No, certainly not, sir. We all saw that she was simply protecting herself from an obnoxious drunk."

"That's right," chimed in an interested passenger. "We all saw it."

The captain came down the aisle, frowning. "What's going on here?" he asked. "Trouble?"

"No, sir," the Angel said in a meek voice. "No trouble at all."

But of course they had to deplane. She had to clean up, using one of the airport shower facilities to wash off the vomit that had soaked her to the skin. Ray had to buy her another outfit, because all the clothes she had in the world had finally taken off for New York City. Then the cops came and she had to tell the story. Then more cops came and they had to tell the story again. Then they had to tell it one more time, officially, for their statement. Ray's status helped, but he didn't want to push it because he didn't want the locals to look at them too deeply. It was afternoon by the time they'd cut their way through the red tape and had the satisfaction of seeing the obnoxious drunk hauled off to the pokey with his arm in a sling.

They were saying their goodbyes to the airport cops, who, the Angel thought, were ogling her all too avidly in the tight jeans and formfitting T-shirt that said I LOST IT IN VEGAS that Ray had purchased for her. Fortunately she'd been able to salvage her bra. Without it she would have been too much of a spectacle to be endured. She should have made Ray go back to the airport stores and find something a little more appropriate for her to wear. She supposed it wasn't his fault. She was difficult to fit at the best of times, and the clothing selection in an airport mall was not exactly extensive.

They were leaving the security office when one of the cops who'd just answered a ringing phone yelled out for them to stop.

"Hey, Mr. Ray," he called, "it's headquarters."

Ray stopped with a sigh and a put-upon expression on his face. He had something, the Angel decided, of a martyr's complex.

"They need your help."

He looked slightly mollified. "Sure," he said, glancing at the Angel. She looked away, rolling her eyes. "What about?"

"It's Butcher Dagon." The Angel had a sudden bad feeling that was quickly confirmed. "He's escaped."

Ray shrugged. "That's your—"

The Angel laid a hand on his arm. "We can't let him run loose. Think of the innocents!"

"In Vegas?" Ray asked.

"You know what I mean," she replied.

Ray sighed again. His expression was clouded, but the Angel knew that she had him half-convinced.

"I'll go on ahead. I can handle things at the New York end. You take care of Butcher Dagon." She added what she realized would be the clincher: "Only you can handle him."

Ray paused to consider. "Well. Yeah. All right."

The Angel paused as well. She really hated to do this, but she had no choice. "One other thing."

"Yeah?"

"I don't have any money. I'll need the credit card."

Ray's expression turned pained, but he nodded, somewhat regretfully, the Angel thought, and handed it over.

"Take good care of it," Ray thought and added, with only the slightest hesitation, "and yourself."

It was, the Angel thought, rather sweet of him to be concerned.

◆

New York City: St. Dympna's Parking Lot

"LET'S GO," CAMEO SAID flatly. She took off her old, battered hat and climbed into the driver's seat of the Cadillac Seville she'd hot-wired moments before.

Nighthawk gave a final wave to whoever the fellow was who looked like Butcher Dagon as he and the boy peeled out of St. Dympna's parking lot. He looked at Cameo. She looked back. She seemed different, somehow.

"I'm driving," Cameo said.

Nighthawk shrugged. It was all the same to him. He went around the car, got into the passenger's side, and had just settled down when Cameo gunned it. They hit a pothole, bounced, and roared out of the lot, jouncing about like Mexican jumping beans. Nighthawk grabbed the dashboard and watched Cameo. She had a tight smile on her face. Her eyes, her whole expression, were harder, somehow tougher. As if she were a different person.

Maybe, Nighthawk thought, she was.

"You all right, missy?" he asked.

"No thanks to you," she replied shortly. The inflection of her voice was different. Her words were as hard as her expression. Nighthawk wondered who he was dealing with now.

"You're not Cameo, are you?"

She snorted. "We're all Cameo, honey."

Nighthawk nodded. "If you say so."

"Where are we headed?"

"I've got some places around town," Nighthawk said. He thought for a moment. "How about Staten Island?"

"Staten Island?" Cameo asked. "It stinks. It's the sticks."

"It's quiet. It's out of sight. We'll be able to rest and talk some."

"Talk?" Cameo asked. "About what?"

"About a job I want you to do for me."

Cameo glanced at him as she skidded around a corner practically on two wheels.

"You've got nerve," she said.

Nighthawk nodded. "That I do, missy. That I do."

♥

New York City: Jokertown

FROM FAR AWAY, FROM under a league of water or perhaps a thousand yards of cotton batting, Fortunato heard someone call his name. But he couldn't answer. He was wrapped in a cloak of weakness, a cocoon that isolated him almost completely from the world.

And all of his senses told him one thing: pain. Horrific, mind-numbing, soul-eating pain that should have killed him but ironically was helping him cling to the edge of life. Pain, and from somewhere far away, insignificant insect-like vibrations that touched the edge of his consciousness.

"Father! Father Squid! Jesus Christ, come here, quick!"

There was a momentary cessation of vibration, then the whole floor quivered as if something very heavy was approaching very quickly. Then there was peace again.

"Is he still alive, Father?"

Pressure on his face, gentle, as if tendrils of a willow tree were blown across his features by a soft wind that smelled faintly of the sea.

"He is."

Fortunato was still hiding too deep in his consciousness to understand the surprise in the voice.

"It's a miracle, Father."

"I don't know about that. That mental cry for help must have penetrated nearly every corner of Jokertown. Only a powerful ace could have done it. Only a powerful ace could survive a beating like this."

"Then the old Fortunato's back?"

"I don't know about that either, but if we don't get him some help fast, we'll never find out."

"It took a long time to find a single man hidden in a falling-down building, even if he was just across the street from Our Lady."

"We did the best we could for him, now it's out of our hands. Call 911. Tell them to get here quick. I'm afraid to move him ourselves."

There were shuffling vibrations of comings and goings along the floor.

"But, good God, Father, what happened to these others? It looks like they've been torn to pieces by wild beasts. There's Carlos . . . that has to be part of that big guy . . . they're all from that gang."

The smell of the sea receded. The floor creaked as massive weight shifted upon it.

"Maybe you're right. Maybe the old Fortunato *is* back. And the Bruddas bit off a little more than they could chew. . . ."

There was an eternity of silence. Then the pain that he thought was ultimate agony exploded into agony multiplied exponentially as gentle angel wings lifted him up and brought him to mercifully peaceful, painless Heaven.

New Hampton: Camp Xavier Desmond

JERRY WAS STILL TIRED when he woke up midafternoon. He was still tired, but he knew that he had to get going. He and John Fortune were safe for now, but they weren't out of the woods yet. *Literally,* he thought, as he surveyed the forest outside the cabin window. John Fortune was still sleeping in the next bunk. The poor kid had been through hell, Jerry thought, and he didn't have the heart to wake him up. On the other hand, he didn't want the boy to awaken, find him gone, and start wandering about the grounds looking for him. Even at Camp Xavier Desmond—or, as the kids called it, C-X-Dez—a new kid who glowed would attract an unwelcome amount of attention and cause unwanted speculation.

He left a note telling John that he was not to leave the bunk under any circumstances—unless it caught fire or was hit by a meteor—and went off to the administrative office to find a phone. He dialed the office and was pleased when a sultry voice said, "Ackroyd and Creighton. How may I help you?" in a sexy, French-accented contralto.

"Hello, Ezili—"

"Jerry!" the receptionist interrupted before he could say another word. "Are you still at the camp? Are you really all right?"

Jerry was touched by the authentic concern in her voice. He'd known Ezili for years, during most of which they'd had an on-again, off-again love affair, which unfortunately had recently been mostly off again. Jerry didn't know if Ezili—who was named after the least forgiving aspect of her native Haiti's love goddess—had been touched by the wild card and given a minor ace, or was merely very, very good at her favorite activity, which was sex. He didn't love her, really, but he had feelings for her which he wasn't at all sure were reciprocated. As hot as she was in bed, she was cool out of it. It was nice to hear the concern in her voice.

"We're okay. Got the message I left on the tape?"

"Oui—"

It was his turn to interrupt. "All right. We're still at the camp. We're still all right. We still don't have a clue as to what the hell is going on. We could probably use some reinforcements, in case the bad guys show up again. I can't imagine how they could trace us here . . . but . . ."

"*Oui.* I understand."

"Is Jay there?"

Jay was Jay Ackroyd, senior partner of Ackroyd and Creighton. Though he looked more like a low-level bookie than an ace detective, Jay Ackroyd, both an ace and a detective, was one of the finest PIs in the city. In fact, as Jay liked to say since his return from Takis, he was one of the finest PIs on two planets. No one else could put that on their Yellow Pages ad.

"*Non,*" Ezili said, "he is still in Jersey on that Giant Rat of Passaic case. He hopes to be done with it today."

"Who's on call?"

Ackroyd and Creighton employed investigators of all types—nat, joker, deuce, and ace. What Jerry wanted was a boatload of aces streaming up Route 17 as soon as possible.

"Elmo Schaeffer," Ezili said, as if reading his mind, "Sascha Starfin, and Peter Pann are the only aces."

Jerry thought it over. It was a mixed bag. Elmo was a dwarf, stronger than any nat. Sascha was a blind telepath. Pann had his tinks. Not the strongest lineup in the world, but they all had their uses and Jerry was in no position to be picky.

"All right," he said decisively. "Send them up."

"I will," Ezili said. "They will be there as soon as possible."

"Great," Jerry said. His stomach suddenly rumbled, and he realized that he was hungry again. "Listen, Ezili, I've got to go. Tell them to get here ASAP."

"*Oui,*" she said. "And Jerry."

"Yeah?"

"Be careful, *mon cherie.* I have a feeling that much bad may still come out of this."

"Yeah," Jerry said. "Me too. But at least now we're prepared."

I hope, anyway, Jerry said as he hung up the phone. *I hope.*

Staten Island: Nighthawk's Nest

NIGHTHAWK'S HIDEAWAY WAS ON a quiet little Staten Island street that could have been in just about any American small town. Cameo parked the car in the detached garage. Nighthawk unlocked the front door and then opened windows to clear out the stale air. He was the only one who had access to the house, and it had been some time since he'd been there. Now that someone else knew about it, he'd sell it at his first opportunity. It was too bad, because he liked the place. It was nice and small, private and quiet, yet close to Manhattan. But that was all right. Plenty of houses fit the same bill.

He came back to the living room. Cameo was stretched out on the comfortable old sofa, eyes closed as if asleep. But as soon as he entered the room her eyes flew open, and there was something in them that told him that the old Cameo, the first Cameo he'd met, was looking out at him.

"Back, are we?" he asked pleasantly.

Cameo just nodded.

"Would you like some tea, missy?"

"That would be nice."

"Have to use lemon and sugar."

"That's all right."

He got a couple of mugs out of the kitchen cabinet as he brewed the tea. It was organic Earl Grey, one of his favorites. His real favorite was gunpowder, but that was best served with cream, and Nighthawk couldn't keep perishables in his bolt-holes. They could have stopped for supplies, but somehow that wasn't the first consideration on his mind when they were running for cover. Too bad. Donuts would have been nice, too.

He brought a tray with mugs, a teapot, sugar, and lemon juice into his small living room. The furniture was cheap, but comfy. There were few personal touches about the room, or the whole house for that matter, but Nighthawk didn't really accumulate material possessions. He knew too well what happened to them over time. For one reason or another, few seemed to last for very long.

"Here you go."

He set the tray on the coffee table and took the comfy chair set at right angles to the sofa that Cameo had collapsed on. She looked awful. Beyond tired. Beyond frightened. He watched her as she poured a cup, added lots of sugar but no lemon. Her hands shook as they conveyed the cup to her lips. She took a little sip.

"I'm sorry about St. Dympna's. But things have a way of working out for the best. I think we're safe here, for now. I don't think there's a chance in hell that the cardinal will be able to find us here."

Cameo shook her head, as if trying to clear it. "We're safe? For now?"

Nighthawk nodded, sipping at his own cup. It was time, he thought, to get down to what he really wanted from her.

"How old do you think I am, missy?"

"Umm." Cameo hesitated, as if not really caring. "Maybe . . . sixty?"

Nighthawk chuckled to himself, shaking his head. "Nope. Not even close." He looked at her, his dark eyes haunted by years gone by and the deeds done in them. "Next year I'll be a hundred and fifty-one. If me and the world make it to next year."

"A hundred . . ." That caught her attention. She stared at him, her voice trailing off in astonishment.

"Why not?" Nighthawk asked. "The world has changed considerably since the wild card virus came down on Manhattan in 1946. People fly without machines. They leap tall buildings in a single bound. Why, some even can channel spirits through objects they'd used in their lifetimes. Is it so impossible to believe a man could live a hundred and fifty years?"

"How do you do it?" she asked.

"I've never told my story to a living soul," Nighthawk said. He sipped tea thoughtfully. "Perhaps it's time I did. I was born in Mississippi in 1852, on a plantation. My people were slaves, and so was I. Pa was a field hand. Ma worked in the big house. I was a field hand like Pa. Then came the Civil War. Pa lived through that, but Ma wasn't so lucky. She died in the Yankee raid when they burned the big house. After the war, Pa stayed on as a sharecropper. It was the only life he knew, but I knew I had to leave. Slave or sharecropper, it was no life for me. I went north in '68. Never saw my pa again. Never knew what happened to him." Nighthawk paused, as if reliving the years and the events that were marked so deeply in his memory. "No sense in telling you about the next seventy-five years or so. I lived. Sometimes good, sometimes hard. I never had formal schooling, but I taught myself a lot of what I needed to know, or joined up with others who could teach me. Only problem was, I got old.

"I come from good stock. My pa was a strong man, as was his before him, and his before him. So was my ma's family. I made it to 1946, but barely." He looked Cameo in the eye. "You know what happened then."

She nodded.

"I was dying in a charity hospital full of sad old cases like me. Full of old men and women worn down by age, young men and women worn down by drink. By injury. By disease. Just by life. When the virus came it was like nothing you could imagine. Like Hell, I guess. We must have been hit by a good dose of it, 'cause most everyone on the ward caught it all at the same time. The docs just ran away. Those that could, that is. They left us all to die, and most of us did. I saw people just melt away to puddles. Saw them turn hard like rocks, screaming for breath. Saw them turn all funny like they was inside out, and flop and twist before they huddled down on their dirty sheets to die. A couple just walked away changed some, but still living. One just rose out of his bed and flew out through a window. Never saw him again."

Nighthawk fell silent. He couldn't help the sudden tears that traced twisting paths down his cheeks, but neither was he ashamed of them. He wiped them away with his thumbs.

"What about you?" Cameo asked quietly.

"Me?"

"Yes. What happened to you?"

Nighthawk sighed. "I was a dying old man. I was frightened. I didn't want to die. I felt sure that I would go to Hell for some of the things I'd done over the years. I surely didn't want to turn into a pile of goo, or grow extra legs, or turn inside out. I just kind of reached out, crying for help. I needed strength to live. I took it from the man in the bed next to me. Old Robert Nash."

"Took it?"

"Drained it right away from him. Took it right out of his body, and old Robert died looking at me, knowing what I did. I felt bad because we were friends. We talked all the time. He played music on his mouth harp. He was a blues man, nicknamed Lightning. When I knew I killed him I was even more scared. I reached out and took more from others. I felt stronger. More powerful. In the end, I didn't even know what I was doing. How many I killed. I just know that I walked out of that hospital when I'd been days, maybe hours from death. Walked away with a spring in my step, black hair on my head, and juice in my lemon, if you know what I mean. It was like I was fifty years younger."

"You turned over an ace," Cameo said. "You tapped into their life force. Somehow converted it for your own use."

"Which I've been doing ever since," Nighthawk admitted. "But usually carefully, taking the energy mostly from those about to die a violent death, drawn to them by my other power—visions, unclear and uncertain, of the future."

Cameo pursed her lips. "Awesome," she said.

Nighthawk nodded. "Yes. So you see. I have to find the answer to my question. You can tell me."

"Your question?"

His eyes were pleading, even tortured. "Have I been stealing their souls? Have I been using them up, condemning them to limbo, or worse?"

They looked at each other in silence for a long moment before Cameo spoke. "How can I know that?" she asked quietly.

Nighthawk reached into his jacket pocket and held up an old mouth organ. "I took it from Robert's bedside before I left the hospital," he said. "I've carried it with me for almost fifty-seven years."

Cameo stared into space, fingering the jewelry around her neck, and her eyes changed again. As did her voice when she spoke. "What's in it for me?" she asked.

Nighthawk smiled. "Fair enough," he said. He got out of his comfy chair and moved it aside as Cameo looked on curiously. There were seams in the carpet under the chair. Nighthawk removed a square of carpet and flipped up the trapdoor that was revealed underneath. He took a metal box from the small cavity under the flooring. From the metal box he took half a dozen bundles of hundred-dollar bills and put them on the coffee table. They were thick bundles. "How about," Nighthawk asked, "sixty thousand dollars?"

Cameo laughed out loud, uproariously. "Don't you trust banks?" she asked.

"They keep inconvenient hours," Nighthawk said.

Cameo grew quiet. She looked serious. "I think I should get out of town for a while."

"That'd be real smart," Nighthawk said, but he said it flatly, without emotion or hope.

"For that," she said thoughtfully, "I'll need money."

Nighthawk's face suddenly shone. "We best be careful," he said. "If Contarini catches us we'll both be consigned to the pits of St. Dympna's."

"I'll leave it up to you," Cameo said, "to keep us out of there."

Nighthawk nodded. He gave the old mouth organ a last loving glance and put it away in his jacket pocket. "Yes, ma'am," he said. "If there's one thing I've learned in a hundred and fifty years, it's caution."

Cameo laughed again. "I see. That's why you cross men like Contarini. Don't they ever go after you?"

Nighthawk smiled. "Not more'n once," he said.

◆

Las Vegas

THE CELL IN THE city lockup was totally wrecked. Its bars were broken and steel door burst asunder like a herd of buffalo had run through cardboard toilet paper rolls. The bodies had been removed from the corridor, but bloodstains still splattered the floor and halfway up the walls to the ceiling. Ray had seen worse, but not often.

"How many cops were killed?" Ray asked.

"Seven," Captain Martinez said through clenched teeth.

Ray looked up at the sharpness of the tone in her voice. "Hey, don't blame me. I warned you."

She sighed. Her dark, short hair was plastered to her skull with sweat that ran in runnels down her full cheeks. Her eyes were big, soft, and brown. They were not cop eyes. She herself was big, soft, and brown. She looked as if she were out of her depth. Ray actually felt somewhat sorry for her. Clearly she was not used to dealing with killer aces.

"You got any aces on the roll call?" Ray asked.

"Quite a few," she said. "Mostly telepaths and a few precogs who work out of bunco. Assigned mostly to casino duty trying to keep scumbag wild carders from robbing the casinos blind."

Ray just looked at her.

"Sorry," she said after a moment, her eyes avoiding his.

"That's all right," Ray said flatly. "I've dealt with a few scumbag wild carders in my day. A few scumbag nats, too. I suggest you take your best telepaths and precogs off keeping the casinos safe from losing a couple of bucks to rogue gamblers and put them on scouring the city to keep your citizens safe from a homicidal maniac."

"Of course." Martinez turned to a group of horrified-looking assistants who were clustered around her. "You heard the man."

One of them nodded and ran off.

Ray looked into the cell. Butcher Dagon's one-piece orange jumpsuit lay shredded among the twisted metal that had been his bunk. Fortunately, he hadn't had a roommate, or else what was left of him would have been lying on the floor in pieces as well.

"Were all the bodies fully dressed?" he asked.

"What?" the captain asked.

Ray looked at her coldly. "I'm beginning to think that you're out of your depth here, Captain. Dagon loses his clothes when he transforms into his fighting form. I was wondering if he'd managed to dress after waltzing out of your cell here, or if we're still dealing with a naked homicidal maniac. If that's the case, he should be a little easier to spot, and we're going to need all the help we can get with this one."

Martinez looked at another one of her assistants, a tall, thin man with a prominent Adam's apple that bobbed nervously every time he swallowed.

"Well." Swallow. "I don't know." Swallow. "Some of the bodies." Long swallow. "Were pretty . . . damaged." Swallow.

"Find out," Martinez said between clenched teeth.

He nodded, swallowing, and ran off as well.

Ray shook his head. "Not much we can do until he's spotted."

Martinez nodded. "I was afraid you were going to say that. I was hoping . . ."

Ray shrugged as her voice trailed off.

"I'm a fighter," he said. "Not a finder. Our best hope is the telepaths and precogs. Our second best is the ordinary citizen. If this burg has any ordinary citizens. You've got to put the word out, publicize his escape like hell. Let everyone know he's dangerous. Someone has to have seen the hairy little bastard."

Martinez frowned. "That'll only cause a panic. Plus, we'll look bad."

"You'll look worse," Ray pointed out, "as the body count mounts. Now you've got a cop killer running around. The citizens are sympathetic. But when—not *if*, but *when*—Dagon adds a couple of ordinary citizens to his score, all Hell will break out. You've got to let the public know what's going on."

Martinez nodded reluctantly.

"Put me in a room with him," Ray promised, "and I'll take care of him. Until then, I've got to be patient and wait. Just like you."

Martinez nodded again.

Ray had the feeling that this was going to be a long, difficult wait.

♥

Staten Island: Nighthawk's Nest

CAMEO SPREAD THE COMFORTER that Nighthawk had given her upon the living room sofa. It was new, right out of its plastic wrapping. She settled down on it and closed her eyes for a moment, then looked at Nighthawk.

"Ready?" she asked.

He nodded from the adjacent love seat. He reached into his inside jacket pocket and took out the harmonica, turning it over in his hands for a moment. Then he tossed it to her.

Cameo caught it deftly and studied it herself. She put it to her lips and blew a tentative note that came out like a *blaaaattt!* from a whoopee cushion. She paused, then ran a simple scale, smiled, and a song came spilling out of it that Nighthawk hadn't heard in a long time. It was Robert Johnson's "Drunken-Hearted Man," and before it ended Nighthawk was laughing and crying and clapping his hands in time all at once. He recognized the style in which it was played, and there was no doubt at all in his mind that it was Lightning Robert Nash blowing like he did back in '46 when they were both dying together in that charity hospital.

Cameo took the harmonica from her lips and smiled. "You looking good for such an old fart, Nighthawk. Too damn good."

Choked up with emotion, Nighthawk couldn't answer for a moment. "I . . . I got a disease that day. You remember."

"Hard to forget the day I died, old boy."

Nighthawk nodded. "I've never forgotten either. This disease went way deep into me, deeper than my flesh, deeper than my bone. It changed me. It gave me powers, Lightning. I can take other people's essence. I can take it from them and use it myself."

Lightning Robert whistled through Cameo's lips. "That sounds mighty powerful, John."

Nighthawk nodded solemnly. "It is. I've tried to use it righteously over the years . . . but that first day . . . when it first came over me . . . I didn't know how to control it." He looked down, unable to look his old friend in Cameo's eyes. "I took too much from you, Lightning. And I killed you. I've been living all these years afraid that I stole your soul—or part of it—to keep me alive. You, and others, that day."

Lightning looked at him. "You may have took something from me, John, but it wasn't my soul." He laughed. "I seem to still have that. I sure do."

"I'm glad of that, Lightning."

"Maybe you killed me." Cameo's head shook. "I don't know. I do know I was old and dying, anyway. The cancer was eating me alive. I hurt. Man, how I hurt. If you were able to take the pain away and by the way send me home, well, John, we was friends. I wouldn't begrudge you that."

"Thank you, Lightning."

"My pleasure, John." He looked around. "Where am I, anyway?"

"You're in the body of a young lady named Cameo. She was able to call you back by holding your harmonica."

Lightning looked down at it, held in her small white hands. "You live in a strange world, John Nighthawk."

Nighthawk laughed. "You don't know the half of it, Lightning. I'm a hundred and fifty years old now. In my time men have walked on the moon and visited the planets of another star. Men can fly. They can read your mind. They can turn invisible and disappear. They can do most anything except bring peace to the world."

Lightning shook his head. "Then I'm glad I'm where I am and you're here. You was always one for stirring things up, John. I was the quiet one."

They sat in silence for a moment like old friends who hadn't seen each other in decades enjoying an unexpected meeting.

Then Nighthawk asked, "What's it like, Lightning, where you're at now?"

Lightning looked at him and smiled. "I can't rightly say, John. It's like I don't know anything past the time my heart stopped beating, but there's dreams, like, I can almost remember. Dreams of a place that feels like home."

"Is that all you can say?"

"That's all I can say."

Nighthawk nodded. It was enough. He knew now that he hadn't destroyed his friend's soul all those years ago. If he had, Cameo would never have been able to call it back from wherever it was now.

"You got to get back right away?" Nighthawk asked.

Lightning Robert Nash considered. "I can sit awhile. Play some tunes."

"That'd be nice," Nighthawk said.

"You know this one," Lightning said, and put the mouth organ to his lips and started to blow "Sweet Home Chicago."

John Nighthawk clapped his hands and sung in a sweet baritone that age had not dulled.

Those who heard them faintly through the walls of Nighthawk's small house were mesmerized by the music. It sounded like nothing they'd ever heard before, as if it were being played by spirits, or perhaps angels.

Las Vegas

RAY SPENT THE AFTERNOON with a special flying SWAT squad investigating Butcher Dagon's progress through Las Vegas, which was marked by a tidal wave of unsubstantiated rumor and a smaller trail of very substantiated bodies spread across the city in no discernible pattern.

The SWAT team guys were all right, but Ray would have felt better if they'd had at least some other wild carders in the field who had some useful powers. It turned out, however, that the Las Vegas PD was not exactly on the cutting edge when it came to hiring non-nats. Not that the telepaths pulled off casino patrol by Captain Martinez didn't have their uses.

The command center that Martinez set up to deal with the Dagon situation got over five hundred tips in the first four hours, thanks mainly to Ray's suggestion to publicize the killer ace's escape as widely as possible. It was hard to separate the few clearly authentic sightings from cases of mistaken identity from the ravings of the lunatic fringe, but the telepaths helped. They were able to immediately discredit the obvious loonies and attention-seekers, but plenty of dead ends were left that had to be investigated.

The widespread publicity also led to a series of unfortunate gaffes. Six portly tourists were mistaken for Dagon and arrested before they could be vetted and cleared by the telepaths. Two other innocents were assaulted by irate vigilante bands, one in a cheap dive off the Strip, the other in a gay bar that was having teddy-bear day. Fortunately, neither were seriously injured.

Ray and the SWAT guys, backed up by experienced homicide detectives, investigated four bodies that were found with Dagon's MO—excessively brutal violence—literally stamped all over them, but by the time the bodies had been discovered the crime scenes were cold. There were no witnesses, no clues as to Dagon's current whereabouts.

Around sunset a fifth body was found behind an abandoned 7-Eleven in a poorer section of the city. It had been stuffed between the back seat and the floor of a vehicle that had been left in the alley behind the deserted building, the keys still in the ignition.

"What's bothering me," Ray said to the SWAT team commander, "is, what is Dagon thinking? There doesn't seem to be a pattern to his activities. Yeah, he's out of jail, he's on the run, but what's he trying to accomplish here? What's his ultimate goal in all this wandering around?"

"Maybe he's changing his hiding spots," the SWAT guy said. "But he can't stay hidden forever, especially if he keeps littering the city with bodies. He must have some kind of goal in mind—maybe he's trying to reach a safe house. Maybe someplace where he can connect with his gang again."

Ray nodded. He looked thoughtfully at the back of the 7-Eleven. It was boarded up and graffitied to hell and back. "You may be right," he said, strolling toward the structure.

He tried the rear door. It was unlocked. He looked at the SWAT lieutenant, who stared back, and then silently waved his arms to his men to gain their attention. Ray opened the door slowly, and from inside the structure came the sound of some animal howling a long, drawn-out, lingering greeting. It sounded almost human.

"Jesus Christ," Ray said. He threw open the door and looked inside the abandoned store.

It was a dusty and dirty confusion of toppled shelves, of empty refrigerated drink banks, of merchandise racks tossed in untidy piles. And on the far wall was a door. It wasn't a normal door. It was just a black semicircle imposed upon a wall that once held shelves laden with motor oil and pet food and pork rinds. A couple of men were walking right through the blackness, disappearing as if they'd been cut in half, but seemingly unconcerned by what should be a discomfiting experience.

They looked back at Ray as he came through the door, and one of them shouted, "Jesus Christ! It's that Ray fucker!" before he plunged further onward and disappeared.

A disconcertingly human-looking dog, or maybe a disconcertingly canine-looking human, was standing next to the gateway. He was held by another man on a leash, and he was fawning over Butcher Dagon, who was in his human form. Dagon looked less jolly than usual. His clothes were tattered and blood-stained, and he was pushing disgustedly at what Ray now realized was a particularly unfortunate-looking joker, saying, "Down, Blood, down."

He, too, turned to look at Ray. He didn't look happy at Ray's sudden appearance.

"Your ass is mine, Dagon," Ray said happily. "Again."

"Move it," the man holding Blood's leash said as Ray charged across the room, dodging empty merchandise racks, "you've got to go through first before Blood can close the gate."

"Shit," Dagon said, and plunged through the blackness, Blood and his handler on his heels.

If Ray had had a clear shot across the room, he would have had him. He would have pounced on Dagon before he could disappear. As it was, he had to zigzag around and jump over half a dozen obstacles, and as he reached the far wall Blood's handler had already dragged the joker through the blackness. Blood's hindquarters were disappearing. The blackness was starting to dilate shut like the closing of a pupil in a bright flash of light.

Ray heard the SWAT team charging after him. He heard their cries of amazement. He didn't hesitate. He hurled himself, diving arms outstretched, at the shrinking pool of blackness. He went into it headfirst. The shouts from the SWAT team were cut off as if by a knife. He heard nothing. For a disconcerting moment that might have lasted hours for all he could tell, he saw nothing, neither darkness nor light. He felt nothing, neither coolness nor warmth. He wondered if this was what death was like. If this was the Big Nothing. The sensation, or lack of sensation, of a spirit plunging endlessly through limbo. He was suddenly afraid. This was something that could drive a man mad in little order. To be stuck inside his mind, feeling nothing, forever. He concentrated as hard as he could, questing outward with all his senses. Suddenly he felt a low thrumming throb, and he realized that it was a single beat of his heart, stretching out impossibly long, its reverberations filling up the universe.

Abruptly, it ended.

He fell on his face on grass and dirt. It was dark, nighttime, wherever he was. The air felt cool and soothing on his skin. His knee hurt a little from where he'd landed right on a sharp-edged pebble. He breathed a sigh of relief. He was back again, somehow, in the real universe.

He looked up at the circle of men who stared down at him with varying degrees of disbelief on their faces. Butcher Dagon. The man and his leashed joker. Three guys with guns.

All right! Ray thought joyously. And he got to work.

A quick-as-a-cat leg sweep brought down two of the men. He swarmed over them, punching and kicking, as Dagon ran off into the night. As the third jerked his rifle into line, Ray yanked it away from him and tossed it away over the small rustic building that was at their back. The man tried to run, but Ray snagged his ankle before he could take a step and pulled him down, kicking and screaming and clawing at the dirt. Ray bounced his head once off the ground and he shut up.

Ray got to his feet. The deformed joker cringed before him, huddled against the man holding his leash. "Don't hurt Blood none, mister," the handler said. "It ain't none of his fault what went on."

"What the hell is he?" Ray asked.

"He's an ace, Blood is," the man said, nodding vigorously. "He can open gates, like, to connect places that are far away from each other. Bring them next door, like. Only"—the man shrugged helplessly—"he ain't too smart. It ain't his fault we fell in with bad men."

"It's your fault, then?" Ray asked. He stepped closer to the two and Blood whimpered piteously.

"It is," the man said. "It is my fault." He put his hand out in a gesture as piteous as Blood's whimpering. "You don't know these people, mister. Yeah, I got ourselves mixed up with them. I'm trying to look out for the boy. I'm his brother." He put his hand down on his Blood's head, protectively. "I got us working for them, which was a sure enough mistake. These people are mean, mister, I mean *mean.*"

"Yeah, well, so am I."

The man nodded. "I know, mister. They're afraid of you. They truly are."

That made Ray feel at least a little better. "Well, where the hell are we, anyway?" he asked.

"Some place called New Hampton," the man said, and Ray almost did a double take at his revelation.

"The camp?" Ray asked. "The camp where John Fortune is hiding out?"

The man nodded vigorously.

"How the hell did they discover that the kid was here?"

The man shook his head. Blood, sensing that the mood of the conversation was shifting, tried to smile. "I don't know. They don't tell me shit. Just, have Blood take us here, have Blood take us there. You'd think it was easy on the fellow for all they put us through—"

"We all got problems," Ray said flatly. "Focus on mine."

"Yessir."

"The boy's here?"

"Yessir."

"They've come to get him again?"

"Yessir."

"Why, for Christ's sakes?"

"Well, that's just it. The Allumbrados think he's the Anti-Christ whom they have to bind in chains if the real Jesus Christ is to come to restore his Kingdom on Earth."

"Jesus Christ!"

"Yessir."

Ray didn't bother to explain that he was just exclaiming, not questioning. Though, in a way he was. This was no time, though, to sort through dubious theology. There'd be time for that later. Maybe.

"How many men have they got?" Ray asked.

"About twenty, counting me'n—"

"Aces?"

"Well, there's Blood—"

"I know that," Ray said impatiently.

"—and now Dagon, of course. The Younger Witness—"

"Younger Witness?" Ray repeated.

"Yeah, there's two Witnesses to Revelations. They're brothers—"

Ray nodded. "One's big and blond—"

"The other's dark and skinny."

"Right," Ray said grimly. "I've seen the blond one in action. He the younger one?"

The man nodded.

"Any more aces?"

The man shrugged. "Nighthawk and his team are supposed to be here, but the cardinal couldn't find Nighthawk. He was real peeved about that—"

A cascade of gunfire echoed through the still night, waking it up. Ray turned toward the rolling thunder of sound like a dog on point, practically quivering with eagerness. He turned back to Blood and his brother.

"All right," he said. "Stay out of this. Get out if you can. But stay out of my way. You're only getting one warning."

Blood's brother nodded. "Yessir. Thank you, sir."

"Don't thank me," Ray said, before he vanished into the night. "Just obey me."

And then he was gone.

♠

New Hampton, New York

JERRY WAS IN THE administration office drinking coffee with the boys from the agency when Sascha Starfin, the blind telepath, suddenly put his mug down. There was just an unbroken expanse of skin where his eyes should have been.

"What is it?" Jerry asked.

"Men approaching," he said. "Ten or so. They want the boy."

Damn it, Jerry swore to himself. "How the hell did they track us down so fast?"

Peter Pann, the immaculate Englishman, shook his head. "Damned if I know. But we can worry about that later. Get the boy. Vanish."

"We'll hold them," Elmo Schaeffer said. He was about four feet tall and almost as wide. He was strong, even for a wild carder, but Jerry was not sanguine. A blind telepath, a strong dwarf, and a man who could call upon tiny little fairies that he called "tinks" to do his bidding.

Somehow it just didn't seem like enough.

But Jerry didn't waste time arguing. He slipped through the back door, keeping low to the ground and moving fast into a copse of trees. From there it was a short shot to the guest cabin where John Fortune was still resting after his ordeal of the past couple of days. He made the trees and looked out back toward the admin building. A squad of armed men had converged on it. Gunfire rattled the night and Jerry worried about the men inside, all of whom he'd worked with for years, all of whom were his friends.

It was a tough business, Jerry thought, but the customer always had to come first.

And then he ran into a brick wall.

Fingers like steel cables grabbed him from behind, whirled him around. His eyes went wide with astonishment. His lips formed the word *Ray!* but before he could say anything a punch exploded like a sledgehammer in his gut and the only thing holding him up were the fingers from Ray's left hand digging like claws into his shoulder.

His lips worked frantically but no sounds, other than a wheezing grunt, came from his mouth. Ray was winding up for another blow and all Jerry could do was shake his head feebly, his eyes wide and horrified as it descended like a thunderbolt.

Somehow, at the last instant, Ray pulled it. Most of it, anyway. It still rocked Jerry's midsection and he felt like puking. He held on grimly, because he knew that the last thing he wanted to do was throw up all over Billy Ray. It might, in fact, be the last thing he would ever do.

"What's the matter, Dagon," Ray sneered. "Can't take it all of a sudden?"

Somehow Jerry sucked air into his laboring lungs. "Nuh-nuh Dag'n," he wheezed.

Ray looked at him skeptically.

"Jer-jer-ry."

Ray frowned.

Shit, Jerry thought. All those identities, all those names were really catching up to him. For a moment he couldn't remember the name that Ray knew him by. It had blown out of his brain like the air from his lungs. He forced another shuddering breath down his trachea. It hurt like hell. "Cray-ton," he managed to gasp.

Ray's eyebrows went up. "Creighton? The kid's bodyguard?"

Jerry nodded weakly.

"Jesus, man," Ray said, "it is you. That's how you managed to get away with the kid. By mimicking Dagon."

Jerry nodded again, relief in his eyes.

"Hey, man, I'm sorry."

"All right," Jerry wheezed. "Breath coming back. Can stand now."

Ray let him go and he stood bent over, his hands on his knees. Sounds of commotion came to them from the cabin.

"What's going on?"

"Cabin attacked by Dagon's men," Jerry said. "Our men trying to hold them off."

"Where's the boy?" Ray asked.

"I was going to him."

"All right," Ray said. "I'll go help them hold off Dagon's goons. Dagon himself is back, too, by the way. I saw him run off a few minutes ago. You vanish into the woods with the boy. We'll find you, eventually."

Jerry nodded.

"Can you walk?"

Jerry nodded again, and took a step, gingerly.

"All right," Ray said. "Good luck."

Jerry waved back as Ray ran toward the sounds of conflict. *All right,* Jerry thought. *All right. All I have to do is walk. And breathe.*

The first few steps were agony, but his breath soon came back and all he had to deal with were the rolling waves of nausea that threatened to overwhelm him with every step. Somehow he fought it down and made his way to the guest cabin where it was still and dark.

He entered quietly and went to John Fortune's bunk. There was no need to turn on a light, because the kid's face, arms, and hands were glowing softly like a beacon in the night as he slept fitfully.

John Fortune had had a quiet day, only getting up once to eat. Jerry didn't want him to leave the cabin, and he was glad when the kid didn't argue. It wasn't surprising that he was feeling a little down after his long ordeal. He was also running a temperature. Maybe he'd picked something up in the hellhole they'd imprisoned him in, but all in all he was in pretty good shape. He just needed a little rest. Which he wasn't going to get tonight.

Jerry checked around the cabin before waking him, finding a hooded sweatshirt for him to wear. It would be a little warm on a night like this, but he didn't want the kid shining like a lighthouse, revealing their presence to the world.

He shook John Fortune gently by the shoulder. The kid woke up immediately and only grumbled a little when Jerry told him that they had to get going.

"I don't know how they found us so fast," Jerry said, "but they did. Maybe they have some precogs or telepaths or whatever working for them. At any rate, we gotta move."

"Where are we going?" the kid asked sleepily, putting on his jeans and his shoes and pulling the sweatshirt on over his head as Jerry directed.

"For now, the woods."

"The woods?" He put the hood up over his head and drew the drawstrings tight, leaving only a bit of his face showing. It still glowed a little, but it was the best they could do. Jerry wished that he had a mask handy.

"It's our best bet. If we're lucky, Dagon's men will never find us."

"I hope someone will," John Fortune muttered as they exited the cabin and plunged into the trees behind it.

"Don't worry," Jerry said with a confidence he didn't entirely feel. "It's not like we're headed off into the Amazon or anything. I mean, we're only about an hour, hour and a half north of the city."

He glanced back as the trees closed among them, hoping to God that they were doing the right thing.

♦

Memphis

THE ANGEL SAT IN an uncomfortable chair in the Memphis airport. Soon it would close down around her and she would have to leave, find a hotel for the night, and come back in the morning.

It had not been a good day. Her flight had been diverted to Memphis due to engine trouble. By the time they'd realized that they weren't going to be able to fix it and get the plane back in the air, it was night.

Their plane had been full, and hundreds of passengers scrambled to get the few available seats on the flights headed east. If Ray had been with her, he could have conceivably used his Secret Service pull and gotten them two of the coveted seats. As it was, she just had to wait and take her turn as it came up.

She prayed it would come soon.

♥

New Hampton: The Woods

IT WAS DARK IN the forest. Damn dark. The ground was uneven. Half-buried rocks lurked everywhere. Bushes and shrubs and fallen trees all clutched at their ankles and tripped up their feet. And there were mysterious sounds. Jerry had no idea *what* was making them. He didn't think there were bears or wild-cats in these woods, but he wasn't sure. Men with guns were chasing him and John Fortune, and he was unarmed. In retrospect, Jerry thought, perhaps it would have been wiser to take the gun Pann had offered him. But he wasn't the greatest marksman in the world. Probably not good enough to stand up to Dagon and his men. Running had been the wise course, the only proper action to take. It wasn't much of a plan, but it was the best he could come up with.

"You all right, John?"

"Uh-huh."

The kid looked at him. Jerry couldn't see much in the moonless night, but he could discern a glimmer of excitement on the boy's features. To him, this was an adventure, exhilaration intruding upon what had been an otherwise terribly sheltered life. Jerry could understand that. But long experience had taught him that things that started out exciting sometimes ended in disaster, even for the good guys.

"Jerry, what happened in Vegas, anyway? How's my mom?"

They hadn't had a chance to talk over the events of the previous days. Now was as good a time as any, but Jerry didn't get into details. Actually, he didn't know Peregrine's fate anyway. He didn't want to lie to the kid, but neither did he want to depress him unnecessarily.

"So, my mom's all right, then?" John Fortune asked after Jerry told him a sanitized version of the battle at the Mirage and how he had eventually rescued him from St. Dympna's.

"Maybe—watch out!"

He grabbed John Fortune's arm, steadying him before he could trip over the fallen tree that blocked their path. They weren't following an actual trail. They were just wandering aimlessly through the trees. While that tactic might throw off pursuit for the moment, Jerry knew that it wasn't a feasible long-term strategy. He didn't know what kind of technology Dagon might have access to. Night scopes. Heat detection devices. If Dagon had anything high tech with him, or maybe some kind of ace, they were sunk. He could only hope that the attackers hadn't planned on a night hunt through thick forest.

"A road!" Jerry exclaimed as they stumbled out of the trees and onto a dirt path. "Thank God!"

"It's not much of a road," John Fortune said.

And it wasn't. It was a simple dirt lane leading deeper into the woods.

"But it's all we've got," Jerry said, "and it's got to lead somewhere."

"I'm kind of hot in this sweatshirt," the kid said.

"All the more reason to hurry. The sooner we get on down the road the sooner we find someplace we can relax. But you've got to leave that hood up for now, and keep your hands in your pockets. Otherwise you'll betray our position by glowing like a king-sized firefly."

"I understand," John Fortune said, "but I could sure use something to drink."

They went down the road. It curved in lazy swaths through the forest, but it was smoothly surfaced gravel, without potholes or ruts, well-maintained, and nice and level. At least they didn't have to worry about tripping over unseen branches anymore.

"Hey!" John Fortune said. "A light."

Jerry nodded. He had spotted it himself. It was dim, rather diffuse. As they walked up the curved road they could see that it looked like a flashlight, or something of that relative size and power, sitting on the ground. It cast its light upon a wooden sign standing before an even smaller dirt lane, perhaps a driveway, diverging from the road. As they approached Jerry could see the figure of a small garden gnome leaning against the sign, as if he were guarding the turnoff.

Jerry looked up at the sign. The small floodlight only illuminated part of it.

"'Nursery' . . ." Jerry read aloud. He and John Fortune looked at each other.

"Some kind of garden store?" the kid asked.

"Maybe."

"Maybe they have a telephone. We can call for help."

"Maybe."

"What are you folks doing out in the woods so late at night?" a tiny voice asked.

Jerry felt his heart surge up into his mouth. He grabbed John Fortune by the arm and yanked him backward, stepping in front of him. Jerry looked frantically in all directions.

"Hey!" John Fortune said, peering around him. "It's the garden gnome. It speaks."

"Of course I speak," the gnome said. "Why the hell not?"

Jerry looked down at him. What he had thought was a two-foot-high statue was a little man . . . or something resembling such. He had a fat, jolly face and a white, pointed chin-beard, and wore garden-gnome-type clothing.

"Cool," John Fortune said. "Do you live here?"

"Sure do," the gnome said. "I keep an eye on the place at night. You folks in trouble or something? I heard some gunshots earlier, but that's not too unusual around here. At least in hunting season, which this ain't."

"Uh—" Jerry began.

"You bet," John Fortune said. "Kidnappers are after me. They have guns, but we don't."

"Kidnappers!" the gnome exclaimed.

"Uh—" Jerry said.

"Yep. I'm John Fortune. I just became an ace. My mom's Peregrine, the ace. You know, she has a TV show, *Peregrine's Perch,* but she and my dad also make movies."

"I guess you do need help," the gnome said. He pressed a button on the flood-light control panel, then shut off the light.

Jerry felt as if he were drowning in darkness. "What'd you do that for?"

"No sense lighting up our location if guys with guns are looking for you."

"Good idea," John Fortune said. "Are you going to help us?"

"Sit tight," the gnome advised. "I rang for the boss. He'll be here in a minute."

"The boss—" Jerry began.

"He owns this land," the gnome said, waving airily about. "And he don't allow no hunting. Not even of kids."

They stood silent for what seemed a minute. Maybe two. "Where is he?" Jerry asked, getting impatient.

"Right here," a low, deep voice said, not six feet from Jerry's side. A light suddenly flashed in Jerry's eyes, strong enough to almost blind him. He automatically threw up a hand and turned his head aside. The light went from Jerry's face to John Fortune's, who let out a plaintive, "Hey," and blinked.

"Say," said the garden gnome, "you're not the boss."

The man with the flashlight looked down, surprised. "Shut up," he said when he saw who had spoken, "before I stomp you flat."

No doubt about it now, Jerry thought. Dagon's men had found them, damn it. Again. They were infuriatingly competent. There were actually two of them this time. The man with the flashlight and a silent companion.

"You won't be talking so big in a minute or two, fella," the gnome said.

"I said, shut up." The man raised a hand cannon with a gigantic bore, spotlighting the blinking gnome with his flashlight.

"Hey—" Jerry said. He knew the man was going to shoot. Even a glancing hit would tear the gnome to pieces.

From nowhere there was a sound in the night as if the mother of all mosquitoes buzzed past them. The tough guy with the pistol grunted, like someone had punched him in the gut. He swayed on his feet, staring at the aluminum arrow shaft planted directly in the center of his chest.

"Jesus Christ," his companion said.

The man with the flashlight looked at him. Jerry could see that the arrow had gone nearly all the way through his body. Half a foot protruded from his back and blood dripped off the razor-tipped four-bladed head.

"Son of a bitch," Dagon's man said, and he fell on his flashlight, bringing darkness again to the night as his companion wildly sprayed bullets into the trees all around them. Jerry felt a shock burn across his forehead like a blow from a red-hot poker. He fell to the ground and with a frantic last effort dragged a bewildered John Fortune down with him. He held him tightly, covering him with his own body as best he could as his consciousness faded away.

Chapter Six

New Hampton, New York

JERRY WOKE WITH THE feeling that he was being watched. Closely and relentlessly. He was in a strange but comfortable bed in an unfamiliar room. He was lying on his side, looking right at a wall so he couldn't see much of the room, but Jerry was certain that he'd never been in it before.

He turned suddenly away from the wall, and immediately regretted it. A wave of pain rushed through his head, accompanied by a swarming nausea that was even more distressing. He swallowed hard and put his hand to his forehead, which he discovered was swathed in a soft, thick bandage. He looked into the room and saw his audience, and suppressed an urge to groan aloud.

Two kids stood by his bedside staring at him. One was a boy, maybe ten. The other, a girl, was four or five years younger. Jerry wasn't sure. He hadn't had much experience with kids, other than John Fortune. The boy was tall and lean. He was blond with delicate, almost elfin features. The girl was darker and stockier, but there was a certain familial resemblance between the two that marked them as brother and sister.

The girl looked at him solemnly. "Make your face do that again," she said to Jerry.

"Do what?" Jerry was surprised that his voice sounded so weak and scratchy.

"Go all funny and wriggly," the girl said.

"Jeez, shut up, will you?" her brother interrupted. "You're not being very polite."

She made a face. "I'm telling Mom you're harassing me."

The boy rolled his eyes. "Go ahead. Tell her our, uh, guest, is awake, too."

The girl ran from the room, yelling, "Mommmmmm!!!" in a voice loud enough to make Jerry wince.

The boy seemed to notice his discomfort. "Sorry about that. She can be a real brat sometimes."

Jerry suppressed his notion to nod. "Where am I?"

"Our house," the boy said, unconsciously uninformative. "Dad brought you home last night. He found you in the woods. Said you were shot in the head, but nothing important was hit."

Shot, Jerry thought. He remembered it all, suddenly. "Did he—was anyone else with me?"

The boy shook his head.

Jerry lurched upright, doing his best to ignore the whirling as the room pirouetted around him. John Fortune, he thought, was still out in the woods. Or—maybe Butcher Dagon had gotten him! He tried to stand, but couldn't make it to his feet.

"Give me a hand, would you—" he asked, reaching out for the boy, but a voice interrupted from the doorway.

"I don't think that's a good idea, Mr. Creighton."

Jerry swiveled his head drunkenly toward the doorway. The woman standing there smiled at him. The little girl was pressed against her legs, watching Jerry as solemnly as before.

Jerry sat back weakly. "How'd you know my name?" he asked.

She smiled. It looked good on her elegantly featured face. She was tall, lean-hipped, and long-legged. Her hair was blond, her eyes a light blue, and her cheekbones, mouth, and nose exquisite. She could have been a model. She was a little old for that game now, but her features were of a classic delicacy that aged well. Her shorts and sleeveless pullover revealed that she took great care of her body. She was lean and lithely muscular, despite the two kids, who had to be hers. Somehow, she seemed familiar. Maybe she was a model and he'd seen her picture somewhere. Maybe she'd even been in the movies.

"My husband owns the land the camp is on, so we have an intimate interest in what goes on there."

Jerry almost nodded again, but caught himself in time. So, he'd finally discovered the identity of the anonymous benefactor Father Squid always talked about. Or, he would when he actually met him.

"The boy—" Jerry said, and she nodded.

"I know. He's still missing. My husband's out looking for him now. Don't worry. If anybody can find him, he will."

"I've got to get to a phone," Jerry said with some urgency. He wondered how much he should tell her. "If you know my identity, then you must know that I'm a private detective. The boy is under my care. Someone attempted to kidnap him last night."

"We pieced together as much," the woman said. "My husband . . . took care of the men who assaulted you last night. But the boy apparently slipped away while he was busy. Daniel couldn't do much in the dark, but he went out at first light to try to track him." She stopped and glanced over her shoulder, then looked back at Jerry. "I think I hear him coming in now. I hope he has good news."

I hope, Jerry thought.

"Daddy!"

The little girl transferred her grip from her mother's thighs to those of the man who appeared suddenly, silently in the doorway. He was no taller than the woman, who leaned over the child to embrace him as well. He was dark-haired and dark-eyed like the girl, and his skin was tanned from long exposure to the sun. He put one hand on the little girl's back and hugged her close, saying, "Hello, sweetie."

His hands were large and strong-looking and his arms muscled, not with the kind built by pumping iron but rather lean muscle won from hard physical labor. His face was weathered and harsh-featured, but its strong lines relaxed as he embraced his girl and leaned over her to briefly kiss his wife.

"The boy?" Jerry asked, still uncertain if he should use Fortune's real name.

The man shook his head. "Vanished in the woods. I lost his trail where he stumbled on the county road. Couldn't tell which way he went, right or left. But I've still got my people out looking for him. Don't worry. He wasn't wounded. And the men hunting you didn't get him."

"How do you know?" Jerry asked.

The man only looked at him. "I know."

Jerry cleared his throat. It didn't seem reasonable to press the point.

"I'm in your debt, mister . . . ?"

The man reached down and picked up his daughter, holding her on his hip with one arm around her waist. "Brennan," he said. "Daniel Brennan." He put his other arm around the woman's waist. "This is my wife. Jennifer Maloy Brennan."

"My mom's an ace," the little girl said.

"Jeez." The boy rolled his eyes. "Stop *telling* people that."

Jennifer Maloy Brennan smiled. "We all have our little secrets. Don't we, Mr. Creighton?"

"Uh," Jerry said.

Brennan smiled at him. In other circumstances, Jerry could see how that smile could look disturbing. Dangerous, even. He felt that somehow, someway, he should know this man.

"Would you like some breakfast, Mr. Creighton?" Jennifer Brennan asked.

"Yes, I would, thanks," Jerry said. "Mind if I change first?"

The Brennans looked at each other quizzically.

"No, not at all," Jennifer said.

"Thanks. I'll be along in a minute."

He had decided to get rid of the Dagon face. He'd had even worse luck than usual since acquiring it, and he definitely wanted to change it before running into Billy Ray again.

♣

New Hampton: Camp Xavier Desmond

RAY FELT PRETTY GOOD when he awoke, even though he'd only had a couple of hours of sleep in the guest cabin that had been turned into a command post in the effort to find John Fortune. He lay back in the bunk, thinking over the past night's events.

It had begun with promise that soon petered out into the drudgery of fruitless searching, though it had not been without its high points, especially the initial battle at the administration cabin.

Pann, Starfin, and Schaeffer had been doing their best to hold the line against the Allumbrado assault team, though they were not the ideal combat force. The blind telepath was somewhat limited in his capabilities. Elmo, though very tough when he could get his hands on someone, had to face armed Allumbrados, and Pann, though competent with a gun, couldn't get his tinks to do anything more useful than occasionally momentarily blind an opponent by blinking brightly in their vicinity.

Once Ray had arrived, however, the odds turned drastically in favor of the good guys. He single-handedly transformed what had been a moderately desperate situation into a cakewalk, going through half a score of numbnuts with guns as if they'd been a troop of Girl Scouts out for a midnight hike. Ray's only disappointment was that he didn't run into any aces while he was cleaning clocks. He knew Dagon was somewhere in the night, as supposedly was that blond jerk who'd teamed with Dagon in the Vegas assault. Witness. Ray had hoped to run into him, but never did.

As soon as all of their opponents were groaning on the ground, Ray and the others lit out for the cabin where Creighton had stashed the kid, but Sascha knew that it was empty before they even got inside. They figured that Creighton had headed for the woods with the kid in tow, and went in after them, but it was a hopeless job.

They even brought Sascha along, hoping he could pick up the scent telepathically, but gave it up after a couple of hours of trying to lead a blind man through a forest at night. Ray broke away from the others after they'd heard a couple of gunshots in the near distance, but noises like that are notoriously difficult to track, especially in hilly, heavy-forested terrain. Ray couldn't do it.

He stumbled along in the dark. It was more luck than anything else that brought him back to the camp a couple hours before dawn. The whole area was quiet and secure. The Allumbrados, aces and numbnuts both, had all disappeared. Even their casualties. Camp administrators had the kids back in their bunks, fobbing them off with a story about a botched robbery. Ray and the men from the detective agency realized their best course was to get a couple hours of sleep, get up early and call for reinforcements, and then start the search in the morning when they could actually see what they were looking for.

Ray opened his eyes wide. He suddenly smelled coffee. The dwarf came into the cabin with two mugs and handed him one when he realized that Ray was awake. Ray sat up and took a sip. He grimaced. It was awful, but he didn't care. It just felt good to be in the field again.

"Any news?" he asked.

"Creighton just showed up."

"Alone?"

Elmo shook his head. "Didn't have the kid, but he was with some guy. And a joker, a little guy covered in fur."

"Little guy?"

Elmo nodded. "About two feet shorter than me."

Ray was about to crack a joke about that being *really* little, but caught himself in time. He was working on his sensitivity, and besides, he'd fought next to the dwarf the night before, and Elmo had done more than carry his own weight. Ray only nodded.

"The guy with Creighton was a local. In fact, apparently owns a lot of land around here, including the land the camp's on. Knows it pretty good. He also has a team of these little jokers working for him, or something."

"Doing what?" Ray asked, reminding himself again to refrain from the short jokes.

Elmo shrugged shoulders that would have been massive on a six-footer. "Got me. Maybe they gather nuts and berries for him. None of 'em seem much bigger than squirrels, anyway."

Maybe, Ray thought, *short jokes are okay after all.*

"They've been out scouring the forest since dawn. They'll find the kid, if anyone can."

"We should go, too," Ray said.

"Creighton said to hang on for a bit. Ackroyd's coming up from the city with reinforcements from the agency. Between us and this Brennan guy and his gang of munchkins, we should cover the area pretty good."

Ray grunted. Ackroyd. He and the PI weren't the best of friends, but what the hell, that never stopped him from working with anyone before. "And the Allumbrados?" he asked.

Elmo shrugged again. "They may be out in the woods, but we haven't seen 'em or heard 'em. Brennan has his gang keeping an eye out for them, as well."

Ray nodded. "In the meantime, how about breakfast?"

"You read my mind. This way."

Breakfast. It made Ray think of Angel. He wondered where she was, and if she was getting enough to eat.

♠

New Hampton, New York: Onion Avenue

WHEN THE ANGEL FINALLY arrived at New Hampton she discovered that there was no there, there.

It was on the map somewhere between Goshen and Middletown and Florida, but when she got there, she couldn't find it. It was all just unmarked roads, many of them single lane, fields of lettuce, corn, pumpkins, and onions, and a few scattered houses. Even Florida, which she'd encountered when she'd gone too far down the quaintly named Pulaski Highway (which was, at least, two lanes; one going each way), had a crossroads and traffic light. New Hampton, once she'd found it, proved to be devoid of such trappings of civilization.

She finally stopped at a small store on an unmarked county road where the bucolically named Onion Avenue branched off and wandered off to nowhere in particular. The sign outside the store said KALEITA'S GROCERIES. She went in to ask for directions. At least, that was her intent, but she couldn't resist first buying an ice cream sandwich from the old-fashioned slide-top cooler that was humming like a berserk air conditioner. She paid the proprietor and took a bite out of the sandwich as he searched through the register's drawer for change. He was an old man who spoke English just like he was fresh off the boat from some old country. She wasn't sure which one.

"Kid?" the old man repeated after she finally got his attention by asking the same question three or four times. Even then it was clear that he hadn't really heard what she'd asked. "You're looking for a kid? Not many kids around here. Mostly old people. Mostly old people."

"No kids around here at all?"

"Nope," the old man said. "No kids."

The Angel frowned to herself. She was probably totally off the track. "Thanks."

"There's the kids at the camp, of course."

She stopped. "Camp?"

"Yah. The summer camp up the road."

"Road?" the Angel repeated.

"Yah. Lower Road. The road that runs by Snake Hill."

The Angel told herself not to say "Snake Hill?"

"You can't miss it," the old man said. "Turn right out of the parking lot, go up the hill, take a right at the stop sign. You can't miss it. It'll be on your left after a mile or so."

"Thanks," the Angel said, trying not to clench her teeth as she went out the door. She brushed by a guy who was waiting for her to go by so he could enter the store. The Angel looked at him suspiciously. He looked like a hippie. Like something off a 1960s album cover, with ragged, holey bell-bottoms embroidered with flowers and other designs, bushy hair, and a colorful silk scarf tied loosely around his neck. His shirt was outrageously colored and patterned, and he wore tiny little glasses with purple octagonal lenses hanging on his long, narrow nose. The Angel didn't have anything against hippies. Especially. She was just surprised to see one in this setting.

The hippie's eyes were heavy-lidded. The Angel could smell fumes coming off him. It was some sweet-smelling incense that made her eyes water. He smiled and nodded in her direction, and then caught sight of the SUV Ray had reserved at Tomlin International.

It was a 2003 Cadillac Escalade. The Angel had been distressed when she discovered that Ray had rented it, but there wasn't much she could do about it. When she first got it out of the parking lot, it felt like she was driving a tank, but she quickly realized that it had a smoother ride, a much more comfortable seat, great air-conditioning, and a killer sound system. It had a three hundred and forty-five horsepower V-8 with four-wheel antilock brakes, independent torsion bar front suspension, an AM/FM radio, cassette player, *and* in-dash six-disc CD changer with eight Bose speakers, a preprogrammed equalizer, and a Bose subwoofer. It also had OnStar Virtual Advisor with email access, which, while the Angel thought it was really excessive, she kept thinking that she should use when she was lost but wouldn't because then she'd have to admit to herself that she was lost. She realized that it sounded like something Ray would do, but still . . . The transmission was a four-speed, electronically controlled automatic, but that was all right.

"Bitchin' wheels," the hippie said.

"Thanks." She glanced at the beat-up old VW van that was parked next to it, guessing that it belonged to the hippie. If it didn't, it should have. "Your wheels are, uh, nice, too."

"Thanks, man," the hippie said. "See you around."

I doubt it, the Angel thought, but bit her tongue. There was no need to be impolite. She nodded and smiled briefly and got in the car and backed out of the lot onto the traffic-less road.

The Escalade, whatever that meant, took the small, steep hill with a smooth purr. It was nice, actually, to drive something so big, so powerful, yet so quiet and smooth. She didn't have a car herself, as she didn't have a house or much else in the way of material possessions, but she'd grown up a child of the South and had learned to drive on a succession of beat-up junkers with clunky manual transmissions that her mother briefly owned before they'd been repossessed or died within months of chugging out of the used car lot. This vehicle was quite different, and, she had to admit, actually enjoyable to drive.

A small white-framed wooden church stood on the right side of the road at the hill's crest. The Angel pulled off to the side of the undivided county road to get a better look at it. The sign board in the front said SAINT ANDREW BOBULA and listed the times for Sunday services. Pity. It was Papist, though it did remind her of the white clapboard churches her mother was always dragging her to. Not dragging her to. She went with her mother willingly because she wanted to. Because it was the correct thing to do.

She thought briefly about going in anyway to offer a quick prayer. It was her habit to attend service as often as was practical, but for the past couple of days it hadn't really been practical. She made up for it by praying more than usual. When she had the chance. She hoped that her prayers would be to good effect. No. She knew they would be, even if appearances were to the contrary. The Lord, after all, had a plan, even if she wasn't privy to it.

She went on past the church, glancing out the driver's-side window to her left where there was an entrance to a working gravel pit that had been eating away at the hillside for apparently quite some time. From her vantage point on the hill's crest, the Angel could see a steam shovel down in the depths of the pit biting big chunks of dirt and rock out of the hillside.

Even here, she thought, *in the middle of apparently peaceful country, they were destroying the land. Carving it up, chewing it to pieces, and spitting it out into dump trucks to be hauled away.* She wasn't against progress, but she could mourn the price of that progress, and what it cost the peace of the natural world.

She glided down the hill's back slope and approached the T intersection that the old storekeeper had told her about. She paused briefly at the stop sign, and read, thanks be to God, an actual road sign that said LOWER ROAD. She hung a right. A long, steep, heavily forested ridge loomed on the left. On the right the terrain was more open, sloping gently down to what looked like a small river meandering in the middle distance. She drove slowly, studying the terrain she passed. The thickly wooded ridge on the left must be what the storekeeper had called Snake Hill. It seemed to be totally undeveloped forest, fronted by open fields or meadows bordering the road.

She went a mile or more without seeing a single building, before noticing a cluster of rustic-looking dwellings standing in a big open area bordering the forest margin. A dirt driveway meandered from Lower Road to a parking lot that obviously served the buildings. She wondered if this was the long-sought-for camp. She slowed down as she approached. Her heart beat a little faster at the thought that she was perhaps only moments away from again coming face-to-face with her personal savior. With Jesus Christ himself.

A car, actually another SUV of some sort, was parked by the side of the road next to the driveway leading up to the scatter of buildings. Three men were standing next to it, talking. Two were unfamiliar. But the third . . .

She pulled the Escalade over to the side of the road and killed the engine.

The third was Billy Ray. She stared at him. The three men looked back. Ray broke off his conversation and laconically headed in her direction.

"Well," Ray said as she rolled down the driver's-side window. "Well, well, well. Look who finally showed up."

"How did you get here?" the Angel asked, astonished.

He looked irritatingly smug. "It's a long story," Ray said. "I'll tell it to you some chilly night. Right now, we don't have time for chitchat. We've sent a couple of search teams out looking for John Fortune, and we're about to head into the woods ourselves."

"Looking for him?" the Angel asked.

Ray nodded. "He was here. So were Dagon's boys. In fact, so was Dagon himself. Now they've all seemed to vanish. Creighton lost the kid in the woods somewhere. We assume that Dagon's boys are out there, too, looking for him. We've got to get him first."

The Angel felt lost. "How—Creighton? The bodyguard? He's here, too?"

"Yep," Ray said. "That's him over there. The kind of geeky-looking skinny guy. He's a shape-shifter. We all got here via Blood." He held his hand up, forestalling questions. "Don't ask. It seems that these Allumbrados have a couple tricks up their sleeves we didn't know about, including this joker-ace named Blood who can zap people transdimensionally from, say, Las Vegas to New Hampton. I got zapped here last night, right when Dagon's boys—actually, supposedly they were led by Witness, but I never saw him—hit the camp. Creighton got the kid out, but lost him in the woods, later."

"Witness?" the Angel asked, trying to keep up.

"Yeah. Your blond boyfriend from Vegas," Ray said laconically. "Remember?"

Blushing, she did. If the Angel felt lost before, now her head was swimming. "All right. Who's the other man?"

"A guy I know named Ackroyd. He's a dick."

"Must you swear so much?" the Angel asked, annoyed.

"I'm not swearing. Je—I mean, Go—uh, gosh. The guy's a dick." Ray sighed at the look on the Angel's face. "A detective. A private investigator. He's Creighton's partner. He just brought a team of ops to help find the kid." He turned and waved to them. "Hey, Popinjay," he shouted, "come over and meet Angel!" Ray looked back at her. "He hates that nickname. I use it every chance I get."

She rolled her eyes, got out of the Escalade, and stretched. She was hungry again, but this was no time to think of her stomach. John Fortune, the poor boy, was wandering somewhere around the woods. He was probably tired, and much hungrier himself. She could feel her Lord's pain as her stomach rumbled in sympathy.

Ackroyd strolled up to the Escalade, followed by his companion. Ackroyd was a small man in a rumpled suit without a tie. Creighton was also small, in less formal clothes that fit him like he'd stolen them from someone who was bigger than him. He had a bandage high on his forehead. His real face was much less handsome than the one he'd worn in Las Vegas. She wondered why he'd changed it. He was young, but there was something about him, a sadness in his eyes, that showed that much was missing in his life. She wondered if his heart was filled with Jesus. It seemed unlikely.

"Nice wheels," Ackroyd said sardonically. "Did you steal them off some geezer on a camping trip?"

Ray grinned. "What's your ride these days, Popinjay?" Ray asked, then his face took on a sudden look of dismay. "Oh, that's right. You're from 'The City.' You never learned how to drive." He looked around searchingly. "Where's the subway stop that dropped you off in this godforsaken place?"

"Yeah," Ackroyd responded. "It is pretty rural." He indicated his companion. "You know my partner, Creighton, I believe."

"Yeah," Ray said. "She met him the first time he lost the kid."

Ackroyd grinned, but there wasn't much humor in his expression. "Good to see that you're still an all-around asshole, Ray."

The Angel made a noise in her throat that was something between a derisive snort and an exasperated prayer, probably because for some obscure reason she felt somewhat compelled to defend Ray. Just a little, anyway.

"We're here to do a job," she said forcefully. "Not engage in juvenile repartee and spray testosterone around like skunks marking their territory."

Ackroyd's eyebrows went up. "Skunks mark their territory?" he asked Creighton, who only shrugged. He turned to Ray. "Who's your girlfriend?"

"I'm *not* his girlfriend," she said, aggrieved.

"This is Angel," Ray said. He stood next to her, smiling. "She's new," he added, as if that explained everything.

Ackroyd nodded. "How'd the Feds get on the case already?"

"We're not—" the Angel started to say, and Ray stepped hard on her foot. She shut her mouth and glared at him, momentarily too outraged to speak.

"—at liberty to say how we learned about it," Ray said. "Confidential sources, and all."

The Angel suddenly realized that Ray wanted to let Ackroyd and Creighton still think they worked for the government and not the Hand. She could see the wisdom in that. In fact, she should have thought of it herself. She castigated herself silently for a moment, then chipped in brightly, "That's right."

"Uh-huh," Ackroyd said. He looked at Creighton, who shrugged again.

The Angel could tell that Ackroyd was suspicious. Suspicion seemed to be in his nature. But there was really nothing he could do, except disbelieve them. He seemed a man of little faith.

"So," Ray said, "got any clues as to John Fortune's current whereabouts?"

Ackroyd smiled. "Clues? Is that what we need?" He looked at Creighton as if for confirmation. "Jeez, Ray, it's great when you Feds turn up to tell us that we need clues and all. I don't know if that information came in *Detecting for Dummies*. That's the book Creighton and I use to solve all our cases. Right, partner?"

"Knock off the horseshit, already," Ray said. "Angel is right."

"Yes," the Angel chimed in. "Our job is to find the boy. Sparring with each other isn't helping."

Ackroyd sighed. "Wisdom from the mouth of babes." He held up a hand to forestall another outburst from Ray or the Angel, or both. "But, you're right. Both of you. What do you propose?"

The Angel felt Ray's eyes on her. They were calculating. Though lust lay behind the calculation, he did seem to be focusing somewhat at least upon their job. "Well," Ray said, "there's two of us, and two of you. Why don't we split our teams?"

"Good idea," Ackroyd said. "I'll go with Angel—"

"Uh, no," Ray interrupted, shaking his head. "You and me, Popinjay. We're a team. Like the old days."

Ackroyd frowned. "Only if you knock off the 'Popinjay' crap."

"All right," Ray said.

"All right." Ackroyd turned to Creighton. "I should talk things over with your little helper from last night."

"Right." Creighton spoke for the first time. His voice, the Angel thought, was the same as before, as deep and soft as his eyes. He seemed a gentle soul, unsuited for his profession. "There are some other things we should check out. Brennan told me about another settlement up the road that John Fortune might have stumbled into last night. Or Dagon's men, for that matter."

"Right," Ackroyd said crisply. "Check it out. Be careful." He fished in his inside jacket pocket and tossed a cell phone to Creighton. Ackroyd frowned. "Too bad the kid wasn't carrying one of these. All this tramping around the countryside wouldn't be necessary. Anyway, be careful. Watch out for cows and other wild animals. And if you spot any of Dagon's men—call immediately."

"That's right," Ray said. "And we'll come kick their asses."

"Let's hope," Ackroyd said. "Come on. I'll catch you up on all our 'clues.'"

The Angel could hear the quotation marks Ackroyd's sarcastic tones put around the word as he and Ray went off down the road together. She looked at Creighton. He returned her gaze. Lust was lurking in the depths of his sad eyes. *Men,* she thought.

"The commune is down the road apiece," he said. "We can walk to it." He gestured toward the ridge with the summer camp nestled at its base. "This area is called Snake Hill. Used to be known for all the rattlesnakes around here, sixty, seventy years ago. Don't worry. They're all gone now." He frowned. "At least, supposedly most of 'em are. Anyway, their presence attracted a, a religious community, I'd guess you'd call it."

"Ophiolatrists!" the Angel hissed.

"Huh?"

"I hate ophiolatrists!" the Angel said.

◆

New York City: St. Dympna's Home for the Mentally Deficient and Criminally Inclined

THE CARDINAL WAS FURIOUS. He slammed the cell phone down on the oubliette's floor and it shattered into miscellaneous bits of plastic and unidentifiable electronics. He was in the basement of St. Dympna's with Usher, Magda, Nighthawk, and the Witness, examining the damage that the big breakout had caused when the call came from upstate. The old pile of stones was pretty much intact, though the same could not be said for the *credenti* who had been manning it. Some of the released prisoners had chosen to take revenge and they'd come out of the oubliette mad and armed with looted weaponry. Such a copious amount of blood had not been spilled in the old asylum in more than fifty years. Then came the phone call from the younger Witness relaying the news from upstate. It wasn't good.

"The reception is terrible!" The cardinal swore furiously. "How do they expect me to even hear, let alone condone their whining excuses?"

Nighthawk only shrugged. He knew better than to interrupt the cardinal in mid-rant. The Witness—the Asshole, as Nighthawk thought of him—tried to catch Nighthawk's eye, but he refused to look at him.

"How many of those morons does it take to capture one boy?" Contarini asked rhetorically. "Even if he is the Anti-Christ?" He turned his gaze directly on Nighthawk. "It took only you to capture a girl after the idiots here let her escape. Just you! How many men do they have with them?"

"Twenty-six," the Asshole answered.

Ass-kisser, Nighthawk thought. *The man would sell out his own brother to gain favor with the cardinal.*

Contarini took a deep breath, struggling to control his fury. "Can those fools do nothing right? Must I handle everything, personally?" He glanced at Nighthawk. "Cameo was not as you promised, but at least you took care of her."

Nighthawk kept silent, and only nodded, half to himself. He had taken care of her. He had given her sixty thousand dollars in cash and personally escorted her to the station where he put her on a train headed west. He had told her to go somewhere, anywhere. To get out of the city and stay out until she saw from the news that it was safe to return. She was a sensible girl. She took his advice.

She even gave him the silk choker from around her neck without hesitation when he asked for it. After he saw her off safely, he searched a couple of pawnshops until he found a cameo that was quite similar to the one that she'd worn, mounted it on her choker, stained the silk with some blood he'd gotten off a juicy beefsteak he'd purchased at a grocery store, and presented it to the cardinal as proof that he'd handled the Cameo problem.

Contarini, if not delighted, had at least been mollified.

That was all right with Nighthawk. The cardinal was never going to treat him like family. It wasn't, Nighthawk realized, so much that he was Black, though that was probably part of it. More that he was an American and, worse, a wild carder. But again, that was all right. He had gotten what he wanted out of this crazy affair. He felt better than he had in years, as if a tremendous weight had been lifted off his soul. He felt truly young again, without guilt or worry. His ultimate goal now was to extricate himself from this fiasco with a whole skin. It would not be easy. Things were not going the way Cardinal Contarini wanted, and when that happened bad things tended to happen to those around him.

"It's occurred to me," Contarini said icily, "that we can weaken the position of the Anti-Christ by destroying those close to him. I've learned that both the black-skinned Satan and his doxy, the Whore of Babylon, are patients in the Jokertown Clinic. Both have been severely wounded. Both are just clinging to life. Perhaps one of you can handle them, now." He fixed the Witness and Nighthawk with his hard stare. "Perhaps two of you. Who wants the job?"

♥

New Hampton: Snake Hill

JERRY LOOKED AT HIS newfound partner dubiously. "Ophiolatrists?" he asked. "What's that?"

"Snake worshipers," Angel said briefly, her face set in a frown that seemed habitual. She was quite good-looking, Jerry thought, despite her dourness. Her leather jumpsuit accentuated the lushness of her figure, and her gloomy expression couldn't eclipse the strong, handsome lines of her features. She wasn't really beautiful, because she lacked any hint of delicacy, but she had other qualities in sufficient quantity to more than make up for that.

They walked down the road in silence for several minutes. It was pretty obvious to Jerry that if there was going to be any conversation, he'd have to initiate it. It was in his experience pretty much always a good idea to talk to attractive women, because all good things started with talking.

"So," Jerry said, conversationally as they sauntered together down the county road, shaded by the thickly forested slope that came down to the verge, "how long have you worked for the government, Angel?"

"My name's not Angel," she said.

Jerry frowned. "Sorry. I thought Ray said—"

"I am the Midnight Angel," she informed him. "Named after the hour of my Lord's Passion in the Garden of Gethsemane."

"I . . . see," Jerry said, thinking, *Why are all the great-looking ones such nuts?*

"This must be it," she said, her full lips grimacing in distaste as they halted in front of a gated dirt road that led up into the heart of Snake Hill.

Jerry peered over her shoulder to read the hand-lettered sign nailed to the wooden gate.

PRIVATE PROPERTY
POSTED
CHURCH OF THE SERPENT REDEEMED
NO TAX COLLECTORS, POLICE OFFICERS,
OR GOVERNMENT MEN
THIS MEANS YOU!!!!!

The periods at the tips of the exclamation points were represented by slightly off-centered bullet holes punched through the wooden sign. The free-hand letters were actually well-formed and on the edge of artistic. The spelling was surprisingly literate.

"Well, none of that fits us," Jerry said. "I mean, you may work for the government, but you're not a man—"

She turned and stared at him.

"I mean obviously. Not. So . . . I guess we can go in."

Angel turned without a word and slipped the small wire loop off the gate's upright post. Jerry didn't take her utter dismissal personally. It seemed the usual face that she presented to the world. She swung the gate open and Jerry started to follow her onto the winding dirt path leading up Snake Hill when, with a laboring engine smelling of burning oil, an ancient Volkswagen minivan painted in faded psychedelic designs of exploding stars and dancing mushrooms—with a big peace sign on the front panel—pulled up to the turnoff and chugged to a stop, sounding something like a lawn mower with a bad choke.

A young man stuck his head out the driver's-side window. "Can I help you folks?"

Jerry glanced at Angel. She was looking at the newcomer with recognition and active suspicion, but didn't seem prepared to comment. He stepped toward the van, smiling, ready to take charge.

"Maybe," he said. "We're looking—whoa!"

Pungent waves bearing the scent of marijuana wafted out from the open window and hit Jerry in the face with the force of a palpable blow. Suddenly he felt as if he'd been transported into a Cheech and Chong movie. The guy in the VW could have easily been a bit player in *Up in Smoke*. He was young, maybe in his late twenties—though Jerry was well aware that the wild card virus had transformed the phrase "appearances can be deceiving" from a cliché to an ultimate truth—but his hair style, dress, and general deportment seemed four decades out of phase. Though he was Caucasian, his thick, wiry black hair was fluffed up in a bushy Afro. He had a Fu Manchu mustache and large, sharply delineated sideburns that appeared more often in movies than in real life. He wore what appeared to be a paisley tie as a cravat, and had tiny, octagonal-shaped granny glasses, tinted purple, on the tip of his long, straight nose. His purple silk shirt had long puffy sleeves and was patterned in a startling green and crimson orchid print. His ragged jeans were embroidered with, from what Jerry could see, flowers, smiley faces, and peace signs. He seemed to take no notice of the fact that Jerry, a complete stranger, could obviously detect the odor of Mary Jane wafting off him in waves approaching tidal in size and effect.

"Uh," Jerry caught himself. "Are you a member of the church?"

The living museum-piece shook his head. "No, man. But these righteous dudes are like, customers of mine."

"Customers?" Jerry asked with a raised eyebrow.

"That's right. I'm like, their grocer, man. All organic. All natural. All the best."

Jerry glanced at Angel, whose frown had deepened. *Actually,* Jerry thought, *it would do her a world of good to get stoned. It'd loosen her up a little. And if she stays around this guy long enough, she'll get high just from the contact.* He coughed discreetly. The fumes were already starting to get to him.

Angel stood beside Jerry and stared suspiciously at the newcomer. "Really?" she asked. "Exactly what do you sell?"

The hippie smiled, unfazed by her glowering frown. "Hey, I know you, man. I mean, I seen you before down at Kaleita's store driving that bitchin' Cadillac SUV, though, really, man, I don't much approve of SUVs because they're really bad for Gaea and all her children—"

"Answer the question," Angel said severely.

Beaming, he jumped out of the van. Jerry took one breath and had to turn his head away. He could feel his eyes starting to water.

"I'll show you, man. Come around and take a look at our mother's generous bounty."

Jerry shrugged at Angel, and they followed him to the van's side where he'd already slung open the door, and stood proudly, gesturing at the baskets within.

Jerry had to admit that everything looked good enough to eat, even the zucchini, but he suspected that he'd been standing a little too close for a little too long to the sixties poster child and was at least a little high from the fumes the guy emitted like some kind of tangible pheromone.

Angel just looked blankly at the baskets of red, vine-ripened tomatoes, the bundles of scallions and red onions, crates of lettuce, the cucumbers and zucchini, and open burlap bags of potatoes that still had clumps of thick, rich soil clinging to them.

"What's your name?" Jerry asked him.

"They call me Mushroom Daddy," the horticulturist said, "because I grow the most bitchin' 'shrooms in Orange County. Got a special greenhouse for them with all the glass painted black and dirt that's—"

Jerry nodded, forestalling the horticultural lecture he was sure was about to come. "I'm Creighton," he said. "This is Angel."

"Woah," Mushroom Daddy said. "Angel. Cool. Creighton. Groovy, man. What do you folks want with the snake handlers?"

"Ah, well," Jerry said, "we're looking for a kid. A kid who's been lost in the woods overnight. We hoped they may have seen or heard something."

"Heavy," Daddy said. "Why don't you hop in the ol' van and I'll give you a lift. Their commune is about a mile up the hill. They don't take too good to strangers, but seeing as you're with the Daddy, they might help you. They know just about everything that goes on around Snake Hill."

"Groovy," Jerry said.

Mushroom Daddy slammed the side door shut and slung back into the driver's seat.

Jerry smiled at Angel. "Get in," he said. "I'll close the gate."

She went around to the passenger's side and gingerly got into the van. Mushroom Daddy started it up again. With much tender encouragement and delicate manipulation of the gas pedal, the engine finally caught. Jerry closed the gate and climbed into the front seat after the van inched forward, exchanging smiles with Daddy over a stiff-featured Angel as they chugged up Snake Hill, a Canned Heat tape playing softly on the eight-track.

♣

New York City: The Jokertown Clinic

FORTUNATO WOKE TO DARKNESS and pain. It was odd because he hurt so badly yet he couldn't feel his body. He tried to lift his right arm and hold his hand in front of his eyes, but couldn't manage it. He didn't know if he was lying on a bed or perhaps the floor of the abandoned building, sitting in a chair or floating in a pool of water. Though he didn't feel wet. All he felt was pain.

Then he thought of opening his eyes. He blinked at what he saw. It was himself. He was lying in a bed, and it didn't look good. The white sheet hid most of his body, but it was clear that he'd been hurt very badly. His left arm, visible over the sheet, was bandaged from palm to biceps. A drip line ran up from his elbow to a bag of clear fluid hanging from a hook over his head. His nose was bandaged as if it'd been broken. His eyes were swollen nearly shut and horridly blackened. His entire face, in fact, was as bruised and battered as if he'd been in a fight, and lost.

Suddenly he remembered that he had. He remembered the confrontation with the Jokka Bruddas. They'd overwhelmed him almost immediately. He remembered getting a few good licks in, but it seemed pretty clear from his current state that he'd lost the fight. He looked awful.

Suddenly he wondered how he could see his entire body head to toe, including his face, and the bed he was laying on. He wondered dully if he were dead. Killed, and maybe eaten by a bunch of underage street punks. *That* would mark a glorious end to his career. The man Tachyon had once called the most powerful ace on Earth beaten to death by juvenile delinquents.

But he wasn't dead. He certainly hadn't been devoured. He was either asleep or unconscious, but he could see his chest rise and fall. The squiggles on the heart monitor over his bed seemed to be spiking in a nicely regular rhythm. He suddenly realized what was going on. He was projecting his astral form, hovering over what clearly was a hospital bed. Somehow his powers—or at least one of them—had come back to him, without the need for the tantric magic that he'd once practiced to charge his batteries. Tachyon had told him that the rituals were simply a crutch for his conscious mind, but he'd never believed him.

Maybe the space wimp had been right all along.

He couldn't tell for certain what had done it. Maybe the anger. The sheer impotence of being Fortunato and yet being unable to defend himself from some pissant street thugs, when once he'd defeated the Astronomer over the skies of New York. Maybe it had been the fear he'd felt when he'd realized that he could indeed be beaten to death by those children. Maybe it had been the realization that if that happened he couldn't help his son.

He looked down at his body. He realized that, although it might be dangerous, he had to stay out of it. His body wouldn't last long without his spirit to guide and animate it, but he had to take the chance that it would hang on at least for a while. It was likely that the liberation of his astral form had been the work of his unconscious mind. If he returned to his body, there was no guarantee that he'd be able to leave it again. And his body wasn't going anywhere for a while. It looked too broken up.

His astral form was free to travel. To prove it to himself he floated out of his private hospital room and found himself in a familiar corridor. He realized that he was back in the Jokertown Clinic. He sped along the corridor, unseen and untouched by the nurses and patients he passed, though one joker perhaps blessed with a touch of second sight seemed to watch him as he floated by. But the joker said nothing. Fortunato slipped into another of the clinic's private rooms and found himself in Peregrine's presence again.

She was sleeping. Josh McCoy was dozing in the chair by her bedside. Both looked tired and worn, Peregrine more so. Fortunato's astral body hovered above her. He felt an overwhelming desire to hold her again, but he realized that he'd forfeited that right a long time ago. He reached out and touched her cheek, his incorporeal fingers slipping through skin and the flesh beneath.

He had to find his son, but he had nothing to go on. No clue as to where the boy might be. But Peregrine . . . she probably knew the latest news of his whereabouts.

He reached out with his mind, then hesitated. Suddenly he couldn't bear the thought of going into her consciousness and discovering her most intimate, most true thoughts. He looked at the sleeping figure of Josh McCoy. He wasn't wild about this idea either. But he needed the information.

He entered McCoy's mind. It was as easy as it had always been. He had lost nothing of his power. Nothing of his control. He touched lightly, looking only for information relevant to the search for his son. He didn't want to pry deeply into McCoy's private life either.

Surprisingly, the first thing he discovered was about himself. About how he had sent out a psychic distress call when he'd been attacked by the Jokka Bruddas. How it'd taken Father Squid and his search team hours to discover his torn and battered body in the rubble of the abandoned building. How they'd found the dismembered corpses of the Bruddas among the wreckage of their headquarters.

Fortunato had no memory of killing them. It must have been his subconscious that had lashed out with the deadliness of a cornered lion turning on a pack of emboldened jackals, teaching them who was still king of the beasts.

So be it, Fortunato thought. He took no pleasure in the killing, but neither did it bother him. He killed to live. That was the way.

He delved further into McCoy's sleeping mind, seeking out information of his son.

The first thing that came up was his image. It startled him. The boy didn't look exactly like him, but the resemblance was there, in the eyes, around the mouth. It was startling to see, and breathtaking in an odd, somehow exhilarating way. It was a bit of himself. There was no denying it. He stored the image in his own mind, and went on, finally uncovering McCoy's memory of a phone call they'd gotten from a detective agency whose job it was to protect the boy.

He was safe, for now, at a camp in upstate New York at a place called New Hampton. His bodyguard was with him. They were sending along reinforcements just in case of another attempt to kidnap him.

He slipped out of McCoy's mind and looked down at the sleeping Peregrine. "Don't worry," he said. "I'll find him. I'll protect him. I promise."

She stirred and sighed. He wondered if somehow she'd heard his unhearable words.

He suddenly felt younger than he'd felt for years. He felt as if the world about him was conquerable again. Like a wraith he rose in the air, through the room's ceiling, up a floor and through Finn's office where the young doctor was laying on his specially constructed bed in a corner of the room, trying to snatch a few hours of rest, and then finally up through the clinic's roof and into the open sky above.

The sun was still in the morning quarter. From the movement of nearby tree branches he could tell that it was fairly windy, but his astral form could not feel the wind itself. It was peculiar not to feel warm or cold, tired or rested. To just be. It was, in a way, the perfect Zen state, but Fortunato couldn't waste time meditating on it. He looked around for some landmarks to orient himself. He found the way north, and headed out over the city.

He flew without sensation, moving over the land without feeling motion on his unseen body. He discovered that he could judge distance, but not time. He did notice that once he'd reached the city line and found the concrete ribbon of the Thruway leading north that the sun had moved in the sky, so time must have passed. Before long—or so, anyway, it seemed—he was gliding over the fields and farms of rural Orange County where New Hampton lay. He knew that he was barely sixty miles north of the city, but he might as well have been in another world, a world of small villages, of dairy farms set among rolling hills, of green pastures, of rich land that grew a multitude of crops, of orchards and pocket forests that had been standing since before the Revolutionary War.

He was not on intimate terms with this part of the state. Like many urbanites, he was a city boy through and through, but he was able to call to mind maps he'd seen in the past. He had also burned into his brain—more burned into his spirit, since his brain lay nearly comatose on a hospital bed far away—the image of his son.

He hoped that the boy's image would lead him to him.

He came upon the camp in a rush while quartering the countryside, thankful that his astral form could see like a hawk. He rushed down, looking for the boy, but could not find him. He dipped into the mind of one of the camp administrators and discovered what had happened the night before, events that even McCoy and Peregrine were unaware of, and fled immediately before his sudden anger could do any damage to the brain he was scanning.

Fortunato burned hot with anger, yet cold with fear. He could feel the sensations run through his astral form because they weren't physical manifestations, but mental. Fear and anger. Fear of loss. Anger at being afraid. Just what he had fled from, he realized, fifteen years ago. But he couldn't flee now. His son was out there somewhere. Alone. Afraid. Maybe hurt. He had to find him.

I probably won't be able to, Fortunato thought. There was too much territory to cover. Besides, the boy would have been spotted by now if he was moving about in the open. He was probably hiding, keeping undercover for fear of the kidnappers who had almost snatched him the night before.

If they haven't gotten him in the meantime, Fortunato thought, then did his best to dismiss the idea. If they had, he was wasting his time. But he had nothing but time, and the need to fill it with something worthwhile.

Fortunato sank down to the ground and stood in the center of the camp, a ghost among the living. No one saw him. His astral form made no noise for them to hear. They were trying to go about their business as if everything were normal, but of course it wasn't. There was still speculation as to what had happened the night before, and worries that the bad guys might attack again.

This is useless, he thought. *Too much ground to cover. Too many places for the boy to hide.* There had to be another way—

There was, Fortunato suddenly realized. If he could do it.

He rose up again into the sky and hung above the camp like an unseen spectre. He simply had to try. There was no other recourse.

He had to move his astral body through time as he had through space. It was the only way he could hope to track the movements of John Fortune, and the killers who were after him.

♠

New Hampton: The Woods

RAY BATTED ANNOYINGLY AT a flight of gnats that descended upon them as they moved from shadow to sunlight, swarming like a tiny pack of famished wolves on fresh, undefended meat. Ackroyd stood next to him in a clearing in the woods. They had already been to the house where Creighton had spent the night, but his host had already gone out to search for the kid. They'd picked up a guide, a funny little fellow by the name of Kitty Cat, and he'd gone ahead on the trail to try to scope out Yeoman's current position. That was the name Ackroyd had used when talking about their host.

"So, you know this Yeoman character?" Ray asked. He was a little irritated. It was midafternoon, and hot. It wasn't so bad among the trees, though they tended to block the cooling wind. He'd already resigned himself to the fact that he was going to ruin his suit. He was sweating so profusely that no amount of dry cleaning would get the perspiration stains out, not to mention the various blobs of dirt, muck, and otherwise unidentifiable forest debris. He wished he'd had time to change to proper fighting attire, but even if he had, his clothes were now sitting in an unclaimed suitcase somewhere at Tomlin International.

Ackroyd tried to take a deep breath without sucking in some gnats, and didn't succeed. "Jesus," he said, gagging and spitting, "we may have bugs in the city but at least they're decent-sized roaches that you can chase into a corner and step on. This is all way too, too *natural* to be healthy." He waved ineffectually at the undiminished horde of gnats and took another resigned breath. "But Yeoman— well, you couldn't say that I actually know the murderous son of a bitch, but I worked with him on some stuff, back, Jesus, was it really thirteen years ago?"

Ray shrugged as Ackroyd's mind wandered momentarily in the past. "If you mean Chrysalis's murder, yeah it was that long ago."

Ackroyd looked at him sharply. "What do you know about that?"

"I've read the dossier. If you remember, at the time I was occupied by other things."

"Oh yeah," Ackroyd said. "Mackie Messer ripped you from chest to balls on the floor of the Democratic National Convention in Atlanta. Live, on TV."

"Yeah." Recalling that still pissed Ray off. "My star turn on television. I had plenty of time to read when I was recovering in the hospital. A lot of stuff connected to that case is pretty unclear. At least officially. You were involved— somehow. So was this vigilante. This guy Yeoman, the papers called the 'Bow and Arrow Killer.'"

Ackroyd shook his head. "My main interest was catching Chrysalis's murderer."

"And Yeoman's main interest?"

"The same," Ackroyd said.

From the look on Ackroyd's face, it seemed to Ray that both men were involved in the case for personal rather than political or financial reasons. Chrysalis had been an important person about Jokertown. Ray had seen her in the flesh once or twice. Though "seen her in the flesh" was something of a misnomer, since her flesh was actually invisible. She was all bone and blood vessels and interior organs covered by ghostly muscle. Kinky. But not really his type. He liked it when they had some meat on them. And you could see it. Kind of like Angel, in fact—

Ray jerked his train of thought back to the present. "Is he an ace?" Ray asked. "The dossier wasn't clear on that point. Like the compiler wasn't sure."

"I'll tell you," Ackroyd said, "I'm not sure myself. I've seen a lot of wacky powers over the years, but being real good with a bow and arrow just doesn't seem . . . likely. And he got in plenty of situations where a little super-strength or super-speed or mind control or some damn thing would have been useful— only he never seemed to use anything like that."

"What's he like?"

Ackroyd looked at him. "I told you. He's a murderous son of a bitch. As soon put an arrow through your eye as look at you." Ackroyd paused to hawk up another gnat. "You'll like him."

Ray swallowed his retort as a little creature about two feet tall came scurrying through the grass toward them. It was Kitty Cat, the guide they'd picked up at Yeoman's house. He was completely covered with a calico pelt and had feline-irised eyes. Otherwise, he looked fairly human for a two-foot-tall joker. He was talking quietly into a cell phone as he came out of the forest into the small meadow where he'd told Ray and Ackroyd to await his return.

"Okay," he said. His voice was rather deeper than Ray would have expected from such a tiny frame. "The boss has a group of guys in his sights. He doesn't know who they are, but they're sure as hell not locals. Care to come up for a look?"

"Sure," Ackroyd said.

Kitty Cat looked uncertain. "Can you guys can make it through the woods without raising too much of a racket?"

"I majored in sneaking in detective school," Ackroyd said.

Kitty Cat nodded. "Uh-huh. Well, these guys all got automatic weapons, and they're as likely to nail my tiny little ass as they are yours if they hear something crashing through the woods. So for Christ's sake, be careful!"

"I've managed to sneak past a few trees in my day without tripping over myself," Ray said.

"Let's go then." Kitty Cat hitched up the fanny pack embroidered with HELLO KITTY that he wore slung over his shoulders like a backpack.

Ray nodded at Ackroyd, and the dick followed the joker back into the woods. Ray had to hand it to him. He was good at sneaking. They could have all been tiny little jokers for all the noise they made. It helped that they followed Kitty's trail and that he kept them away from fallen leaves and other ground debris. It was cooler inside the trees, and darker. Ray started to feel his excitement ratchet up, and he had to concentrate to keep a silly grin off his face. Now, if this Yeoman was as good as he was supposed to be, he thought, maybe he'd lead them to some real action.

He came out of nowhere, wearing camo forest fatigues and a dark, short-sleeved shirt. The skin of his face and arms were painted with stripes of green, brown, and black paint, and he was carrying a strung bow with an arrow loosely nocked to the string. He'd drifted out from behind a shield of leafy branches like smoke. No. Ray would have smelled the smoke. Like a shadow of moonlight on a dark, quiet night. Ray smiled to himself. This Yeoman *was* good.

They stopped. Ackroyd wore a disgusted, *jeez what now* expression, but he kept his silence as Yeoman faced them with a finger held to his lips. Kitty Cat vanished somewhere into the forest. Yeoman waved them on, his very posture telling them to be quiet and careful.

They crept forward, slipping through the branches from behind which Yeoman had emerged. It was a thick shrub, facing the edge of a small forest glen where five men were sprawled in various attitudes of tired discontent. They watched the men fan themselves and bitch.

"Damn it, Angelo," one said, "I thought you were bringing the water."

"Me?" Angelo, young yet vicious-looking, replied with sullen anger. "What am I, your donkey? Lincoln freed the slaves, man."

"Yeah," said a third, sprawled out with his back against a tree. His automatic rifle leaned against the tree trunk as well. "That means nobody gets to drink anything."

"*You* could have brought the water," Angelo riposted.

"All right, all right," the fourth said. He was the oldest of the group. Dark, Hispanic-looking, and very hot and very uncomfortable. Ray was happy to note that his suit was looking a lot worse for wear than Ray's own, even though the chump had *known* that they were going to be traipsing through the goddamned woods like a pack of Boy Scouts. He was also the only one of the five who wasn't armed, though he could have been packing in a shoulder holster or belt rig. "I don't want to hear any more of this shit. Yeah, we're thirsty. Yeah, we're hot. But we got to find this Fortune kid. The sooner we walk our section, the sooner we get back to the car and some cold beer. Tony, how's it looking?"

Tony was looking at what appeared to be a USGS quadrant map. Looking confused.

"Jesus, Jesús," he pronounced the second "Jesús" as "Hay-seuss," "it's hard to figure out where we are with all these trees around us."

"We're in the frigging woods, Tony. There's going to be a lot of trees."

The fifth was lying flat on his back, rifle by his side, eyes closed, panting like a horse that'd been run too hard and too long.

It was Angelo, Ray decided. He was the one to watch. He still had his hands on his rifle. He was young. He was annoyed. He'd be the one. Fortunately, he was the closest to the clump of bushes where they were hiding.

Ray, standing between Yeoman and Ackroyd, glanced at them right and left, then gestured toward the clearing. Yeoman gave him a sardonic, *be my guest* look. Ackroyd looked at him like he was crazy. Ray nodded, knowing he was foolish for relying on a man he didn't know and a man he didn't really trust, but he was getting tired himself, and mostly he wanted answers. And there were five walking, talking encyclopedias in the clearing before them. He slithered through the bushes with amazing agility, though truthfully he was more concerned with snagging his suit than making noise.

He stepped into the clearing, smiling. "I'm looking for some scumbags who're trying to kidnap a kid," he said conversationally. "Seen any around here?"

The five men looked at Ray as if he were a lunatic escaped from a nearby asylum, and when they started to move Ray was already among them. Angelo, as Ray had suspected he would be, was the first to react, and the fastest. He started to lift his gun and shift into a comfortable firing position, but that was one action too many.

Ray was on him, still smiling, as Angelo lifted his rifle, and Ray plucked it from his hand like taking candy from a baby. He threw it back over his shoulder into the woods as Angelo started to stand, muttering, "Loco motherfucker," and reaching for his backup piece snugged down in a belt holster in the small of his back. Ray took his arm and broke it just like that, still smiling, and Angelo howled as Ray swiveled in one continual motion and kicked him in the chest hard enough to lift him off his ass and propel him into a tree across the clearing. In the same motion Ray reached out and snagged the gun from the guy who was lying stretched out on the ground and tossed it into the trees alongside Angelo's.

The guy opened his eyes and sat up to see Ray standing over him, still smiling, and Ray's fist came down once and the guy went back down again, no longer interested. The one who had bitched to Angelo about the water was swinging his gun around but an arrow came from out of the bushes, shining like silver as it tore through the sunlight, and pinned him through his shoulder to the tree he'd been leaning against.

Tony looked up with his mouth hanging open, the map still spread across his knees. Then he was gone, an audible POP sounding above the wounded man's screams as air rushed in to fill the vacuum that had been Tony, his map, and a layer of the dirt he'd been sitting on.

That left Jesús, who was smart enough not to draw his weapon as Billy Ray stepped toward him. "Who are you?" Jesús asked. "What are you doing?"

"I told you, Jesús," Ray said. "We're looking for some scumbag kidnappers." Ray got close to him, so close that he stumbled back a step or two. "That just happen to fit your description."

"You a cop?"

Ray's smile broadened. "If I was a cop," he asked, "could I do this?"

He slapped him stingingly, left, right, left. Jesús stumbled back again.

"Come on out," Ray called. "I think we've got it all under control."

Yeoman and Ackroyd stepped out of the shrubbery. Ray turned his smile to them. He was genuinely happy, if somewhat disappointed in the short duration and easiness of the fight.

"You know, Ackroyd, you were right." He nodded at Yeoman. "I do like this guy. Good shooting coupled with a nice sense of timing."

Ackroyd shook his head. "You're as crazy as he is."

"Maybe," Ray said. He looked at the groaning man. "Get rid of him."

The man looked up, fear in his eyes. "No—no don't kill me—"

"Wait a minute," Yeoman said, as if knowing what was going to happen. "Let me retrieve my arrow."

He strode over to the tree, grabbed the shaft, and pulled hard as the man cringed. His victim screamed as it came out of the tree trunk and through his torn flesh. Yeoman looked at the shaft critically, wiped the blood off it on the man's shirt, and put it back in his quiver.

"Maybe I can salvage it," he said to no one in particular. He stepped aside. "Okay. Do your stuff."

The man moaned again. He looked at Ackroyd, pleading in his eyes. "No. Please. Don't hurt me no more. Please."

Ackroyd gave him a tight smile. "Sorry."

He clenched his right hand into a pistol shape, his forefinger pointing at the target, his thumb pointing straight up at the sky. There was another POP and the man was gone.

"Jesus Christ," Angelo said, panting for breath as he crouched on the ground clutching his broken arm. "What'd you do to him, man?"

"I sent him to a far better place," Ackroyd explained. He looked at Ray and Yeoman. "What do you think? Him next?" He indicated Angelo with a gesture of his cocked fist.

Ray knew that Ackroyd had probably popped his first target off to the holding pen at Rikers Island, or some other similar location. That was how his power worked. He was a projecting teleport who could send anyone, or anything small enough, any place he was familiar with. The gun that he made with his right fist was the mental crutch he leaned on to make his power function. He'd probably sent the second stooge to an emergency room somewhere.

Of course, the stooges who were still their captives didn't know that.

"Hey man," Angelo pleaded. "I'm hurt. My arm's broke and I think you broke a couple of ribs, too." He grimaced convincingly.

"Is that all?" Ray asked in disappointed tones. "I was trying to crush your spleen."

"My spleen don't feel too good either," Angelo said placatingly.

Ray shrugged. "Waste 'em."

Ackroyd turned to him. Angelo tried to scuttle away, but he moved gingerly as if he did have several broken ribs. Ackroyd popped him away without any difficulty, as he did the fourth man, who was still lying unconscious on the forest loam.

Ray, Yeoman, and Ackroyd turned to Jesús. Jesús swallowed, audibly.

"What do you guys want?" he asked.

They advanced on him. "Answers," Ray said.

◆

New Hampton: The Black Dirt

THE AFTERNOON HEAT HAD come, though in his astral form Fortunato couldn't tell if it was a delightful seventy-five or a humid ninety. His insubstantial body was beyond all such considerations. He was worried that he'd been gone so long from his physical body that he might have trouble reintegrating with it, but he thrust that worry away as best he could. Other concerns took precedence.

He drifted aloft, keeping a watchful eye on the unfolding landscape as he scudded about like an unseen cloud. After all, he could get lucky and stumble upon the boy by chance, unlikely as that was. He couldn't afford to ignore that possibility, however slim. He couldn't afford to ignore any chance, no matter how slight.

The country below him was quiet and peaceful. Houses were dispersed among acres of farmland or forest or clung together in small groups of half a dozen or so on single-lane county roads. He drifted at one point over a hillside that was being eaten away by a gravel pit, which appeared to be the only sign of industrial activity anywhere in his sight. Ironically, right across the road from the pit was a small country church, closed up and silent.

He was within a mile of the camp, but the terrain had changed. It was much more open, with tiny copses of forest stranded on isolated hills. The land generally sloped downward to form a large, open bowl, like the bottom of a waterless lake. This area was squared off into fields planted with various crops. Fortunato could see corn and tomatoes, lettuce and cucumber, and, mostly, row upon row of onions sprouting from the thick, rich soil that was blacker than his own skin. In the near distance, less than two miles away, the silver ribbon of a small river ran through this rich black dirt.

He could feel the energy trapped in the soil even from his vantage point thirty or forty feet in the sky. It was opulent, fertile earth, unlike the thin city dirt that supported the concrete and steel environment that he was much more familiar with.

Energy . . .

He dropped to the Earth like a bullet, coming to rest in a field that was planted half in cucumbers and half in onions. The soil was soft and crumbly, full of brown clods of organic material that also testified to its richness. It radiated energy it had drunk that day from the sun, and ancient, even more potent energy seemed to infest its every particle. Fortunato couldn't feel the warmth it threw off, but he could see it dissipate into the air like shimmers off a mirage. The older energy seemed an integral part of the soil. Fortunato put his face into the dirt and saw the tiny pellets of power being drawn up the roots growing in it. He could see the dirt nourish the plants as they grew to their full richness.

If this energy feeds crops planted in it, Fortunato thought, *it could feed much more as well.*

Fortunato sank through the dirt as if it were the sky. He felt no sense of claustrophobia when it closed over him and he was fully interred within it as if the field were his vast grave. He sank lower and lower. Ten feet into the soil, the energy was more abundant, more vibrant, as decades of farming had only leached away bits of it. Twenty feet down it sparked and coruscated like alien-looking sea creatures living in the ocean depths. Thirty feet down Fortunato hit bedrock and stopped.

Floating in the dirt as if it were the sky, he emptied his mind until it was a complete blank. The void of him begged to be filled.

And so it was.

Suddenly he stood on the surface of a great lake, the waves of which lapped at the slopes of what were hillsides in his own time. The land around him was lush and wild. Man had never drunk from this lake or boated upon it or polluted it with his waste and industrial runoff. It was pristine and free. The forests surrounding it were impenetrable, except for the great mammoths and other immense beasts that roamed the lake's margins and rocky beaches.

Fortunato realized that he was seeing this land as it was thousands of years ago, before the coming of man. The lake seemed as if it would go on forever. But even landscapes change with the millennia. The Earth subsided, twisted, and moved. The climate turned drier, hotter. The lake started to shrink. The forests around it, the plants that grew in it, all died. They surrendered their richness and metamorphosed into thick black dirt that accumulated over the thousands of years it took the lake to die.

But the lake hadn't really died. It had simply changed. It had transformed from a fluid state to rich black soil. The clumps of organic material in the soil were plants compressed into layers of peat, then broken up thousands of years later by man's plows.

But Fortunato was down with the energy that had lingered for millennia. For longer than man had been on this continent. In the upper levels of the black earth it had slowly been leached away by farmers for two hundred, two hundred and fifty years. Down where Fortunato lingered, it was still pristine.

And, like most energy, it was begging to be used.

He embraced it. He drank it in. It filled him fuller than the sexual energy of the tantric rituals ever did. He could feel it coursing through his astral form like lightning contained by the invisible shape of his insubstantial body. When he could drink no more of it he burst out again into the sky.

One moment he was at the bottom of the Pleistocene lake. The next he was in the sky above the camp. He willed to be there the night before, and he was. He heard the commotion and saw his son. He saw the detective protect him from the kidnappers, witnessed their flight into the woods. He followed them as they moved like actors in a tape set in fast forward, burning minutes of time in seconds, hours in minutes. He went with them as they wandered lost in the woods. He saw the detective's bravery during the brief firefight. Saw the unexpected arrows lance out of the night and thought, *My God, it's Yeoman!*, saw his son stumble back into the forest. He followed him dodging and hiding, watching as he discovered the small church and spent a fitful night there. Then he saw him cautiously go out the next day, find the store at the foot of the hill and buy some bread, cold cuts, ice cream, and soda, which he took back to the church. Fortunato could understand the agony of the boy's indecision, unsure of which hand might be raised against him, cautiously waiting for help, eventually deciding that he had to go find it himself. He went back to the store to ask to use the phone, and immediately tried to leave when he recognized that the others in the shop were enemies. They went after him. He tried to run but Fortunato knew that they would catch him, and he was in his astral form unable to touch anything upon the corporeal plane. The men were closing around his son and Fortunato knew that his only slim hope was to reach out and touch a receptive mind, to find someone who could understand his pleas and come to help the boy.

Fortunato shouted for help, but he was afraid that no one would hear.

♥

New Hampton: The Woods

JESÚS HUNG TOUGH FOR a while, but once they got him talking he wouldn't shut up. It was Jay's threat to teleport his gonads to a subway stop somewhere in the Bronx that broke him. Ray didn't think that Ackroyd could actually do it, and he was pretty sure that he wouldn't even if he could, but it was Ray's experience that macho shitbags like Jesús were quite attached and often abnormally concerned about the state and condition of their gonads. Jesús started singing like the Jokertown Boys after Jay's threat, revealing some items of interest, as well as some things that Ray already knew.

"It's not like we're committing a crime or anything," Jesús confided, splitting his attention between Jay and the razor-sharp broad-tipped arrow that Yeoman was playing with as he looked on with dark, unrelenting eyes.

"Kidnapping isn't a crime?" Yeoman asked flatly.

"Well, sure. If we were actually kidnapping someone. That would be a crime, sure. And a sin. But since we're working for the church, what we're doing can't really be a sin, can it?"

"Wait a minute," Ackroyd said. "The church?"

"Sure," Jesús said confidently. "I am an *obsequentus* in the Allumbrados. We take our orders from the cardinal. Directly."

"You want to translate, that, please?" Ackroyd said.

Jesús shrugged. "Of course. *Obsequentus*—an 'obedient' in the Order of Allumbrados, the Enlightened Ones. That's the middle rank in the Order, between *credenti* and *perfecti*," Jesús added helpfully.

"You do this full-time?" Yeoman asked in disbelief.

"Well, it's more of a part-time thing—"

"Between drug sales," Ray put in dryly. He had seen Jesús's type often enough. He recognized his probable affiliation with the Colombians like a street-savvy cop could spot a pickpocket working the crowd in Times Square on New Year's Eve.

Jesús shrugged. "Hey, a man's got to eat. But you guys, you ruined my chance. If I found the kid I would have been promoted to *perfectus*."

"Enough," Ackroyd said. "What's all this about the church? You're talking about the Catholic Church?"

"I'm not talking about crazy-ass Protestants," Jesús said. "I'm talking Mother Church. Rome. The Vatican."

"What do they want with John Fortune?" Ackroyd asked, obviously having a hard time believing all this.

"I'll tell you," Jesús said, leaning forward conspiratorially. "Then maybe you let me go."

Yeoman snorted. "Yeah. Maybe."

Jesús made gestures for them all to come closer, and Ray found himself leaning forward as if Jesús were telling ghost stories around the campfire. They all did. "John Fortune ain't no kid. He's the Anti-Christ."

"Anti-Christ?" Ackroyd repeated.

Jesús nodded. "It's true. He's the Devil."

"Jesus Christ," Yeoman said.

Jesús pointed at him. "Exactly. Jesus Christ is coming. The End Times are upon us. Jesus and Satan will battle for the fate of the Earth. Jesus will win, of course, but the Allumbrados have been doing all they can to smooth his way for him."

"Like . . . kidnapping . . . John . . . Fortune," Ackroyd said slowly. He and Yeoman exchanged glances as if this were the first time they'd ever agreed on anything.

Ray himself would think the whole thing was nuts if he hadn't Barnett's solemn assurance that John Fortune was actually Jesus Christ in his Second Coming. He wasn't sure that he believed Barnett, but at least he was on the side that was trying to rescue the boy, not the one trying to drag him in front of some inquisition. For now his seemed to be the right side in this crazy affair. For now.

Ackroyd and Yeoman looked at him, and he shrugged. Now was not the time, Ray decided, to open up. "Sounds nuts to me," he said.

"Got any more questions?" Ackroyd asked, looking from Ray to Yeoman.

"How many teams are out looking for the boy?" Yeoman asked.

"Three others, as far as I know." Jesús paused. "They're not all Allumbrados, though. Most of the guys on my team weren't, though a couple were *credenti*."

"Running short on nutcases?" Ackroyd asked.

Jesús looked very badly like he wanted to say something, but he kept his mouth shut.

"Bye-bye," Ackroyd said, pointed, and popped.

Jesús had time for one startled, betrayed look, then he vanished.

"Where'd you send him?" Ray asked.

"Where he belonged. Bellevue."

"Probably not a bad choice," Ray said innocently.

Ackroyd sighed and looked around the forest clearing. "Now what do we do?"

"Pray we find the boy," Yeoman said, "before these nutcases do."

Amen, Ray thought, but just nodded.

♣

New Hampton: The Snake Handlers' Commune

JERRY AND THE ANGEL helped three of the commune members, Josaphat, Josiah, and Jehoram, carry the bushels of produce into the kitchen. It was hard to be so close to so much tempting food, because Jerry had a bad case of the munchies from the contact high he'd gotten off Mushroom Daddy. He didn't think he could wait for dinner.

Hungry as he was, it was clear that Angel was hungrier. Ravenous, in fact. The boys left them in the capable hands of Hephzibah, an old woman who looked like an extra from *The Grapes of Wrath,* who ran the commune's kitchen. When she learned that they were both hungry she put out a supply of leftovers—cold fried chicken, home-baked bread, mashed potatoes, corn on the cob, green bean casserole, tomato and cucumber salad, and a couple of apple pies—and watched in awe as Angel packed away enough food to feed a platoon. Jerry was getting a little embarrassed by Angel's gustatory display, but the food was so good and he was so munched out that he really wasn't all that far behind her in the leftover demolition. To assuage his conscience he slipped Hephzibah a couple of twenties that Ackroyd had given him earlier to cover the cost of their generosity.

Jerry was so taken with the simply prepared, yet unbelievably fresh and tasty fare that he didn't even think of pumping Hephzibah for information on John Fortune's whereabouts. Neither did Angel. They were both surprised when the sounds of an electric guitar wafted through the air, penetrating even Jerry's dazed consciousness that was threatening to slip into a digestive torpor after he'd polished off the last of the mashed potatoes.

"That's the call to worship," Hephzibah said. "I hope you're both satisfied for now." She looked at Angel, who had glanced up disappointedly from the fragments of the apple pie she'd just devoured. "Supper will be after service. If you're still hungry."

A loud belch escaped Angel. "Excuse me. Please."

At least, Jerry thought, she had the grace to look mortified.

Hephzibah waved it away. "That's all right, honey. Long as you enjoyed everything."

Angel looked down guiltily at the empty platters and plates and pie tins, as if aware for the first time of the devastation they'd wrought. Jerry wondered if she actually enjoyed anything in life.

"It was great, all of it." He looked at Angel. "I guess we should mosey on up to the, uh, services. Right, Angel? We have to thank Uzziah"—he was the commune's leader—"for your generosity to a couple of strangers."

"Friends of Daddy are friends of ours," Hephzibah said. "Besides, the generosity you receive is equal to the generosity you give."

Jerry frowned. "Wasn't that a Beatles song?"

Hephzibah leaned forward as if revealing a great confidence. "Close. You can learn much from the lyrics of Lennon and McCartney. Almost as much as from the Book itself."

Jerry nodded. "I'll remember that."

Angel seemed sunken even deeper in a digestive stupor than Jerry. Not unlikely, Jerry thought, if this was the first time she'd experienced a marijuana high. Which was probable. First-time users usually didn't get off much, but Jerry suspected that just as the Daddy's vegetables were so tasty, his other produce, as it were, was probably as potent in its own particular way. Jerry took her by the arm and helped her step away from the table.

"See you at the service, then," he said, steering Angel out of the kitchen.

Everyone seemed to be moseying toward a whitewashed structure set on a high point a little bit apart from the scatter of other structures. It was in better shape than most of the other buildings, with a fresh coat of whitewash and a well-maintained wood frame and shingled roof. The sounds of the guitar called to them.

"Say," Jerry said. "Isn't that 'While My Guitar Gently Weeps'?"

"I wouldn't know," Angel said. "It sounds like rock and roll, and I know nothing about the Devil's music."

"Oh, lighten up for once, would you?"

"We shouldn't be doing this," Angel said. "It will be dangerous for both our bodies and our souls."

"Yeah, well, we have to check them out. We'll get a gander at their service. Ask a few questions. Maybe slip Uzziah a couple more twenties to take care of the damage you did to their larder—"

"You ate their food as well!" Angel said, stung.

Jerry sighed. She seemed to be one of those women who didn't respond well to criticism, no matter how mild. "Let's not go comparing who did what to the refrigerator, all right?" Jerry said.

Angel was reluctant, but she followed him. As they ambled up the hill to the church, Jerry noticed an oddly decorated tree standing off by itself. He wasn't sure what kind of tree it was. It had bottles of all colors, shapes, and sizes tied to its branches by strips of cloth. The bottles hung close enough together that when a wind blew they jangled softly against each other, making an odd, strangely pleasing music that could be heard even above the wailing tones of the electric guitar.

"What is that thing?" he asked, wondering.

"It's a Spirit Tree," Angel said.

"Spirit Tree?"

She nodded. "That's what I said." They stopped to look at it for a moment. "They're common down South, but then so are snake cults. I 'spect these people came up from somewhere near the Appalachians, bringing their snakes and Spirit Trees with them."

"What's it supposed to do?" Jerry asked.

Angel reached up and touched a cobalt blue bottle that had once held a stomach tonic, looking at it as if it contained the secrets of the universe. "Oh, the noise they make in the wind is supposed to scare away ghosts. Or maybe catch them if they get too close." She let go of the bottle and it swung back, tinkling softly as it glanced against one of its fellows. "Anyway, that's the foolish superstition. Come on," she said, as if suddenly galvanized. "We're missing the beginning of the service."

They went on up to the church where they found seats in one of the back pews. It was already filling up. There were maybe thirty people inside with a dozen or more still filing in. The wooden pews were skillfully handcrafted. The floor was laid wooden planks, polished and cleanly swept. The church's interior was whitewashed plaster. The walls were unadorned except for some folksy portraits of Jesus Christ, most of which concentrated on the more gruesome aspects of His life. Christ scourged. Christ crucified. Christ with the crown of thorns. Most of the images made Jerry shudder. They resembled scenes more suitable for horror movies than a church, though he wasn't really familiar with anything but the staid upper-class Protestant services he'd largely abandoned once he became an adult.

A simple plank altar stood against the rear wall. Before the altar was a wooden podium, and hanging on the wall behind it was a nicely executed wooden statue of Christ on the cross. Even from their vantage point in the back, Jerry could see the agony on Christ's face, the pain in his thin, rope-muscled body as it hung from the nails driven through his mutilated palms. It was a powerful if morbid bit of folk art. It seemed to hit Angel even harder. She stared at it from her knees on the pew's unpadded rail, her lips moving in mumbled prayer.

The band was to the left of the podium. Daddy was playing the guitar, a shiny red Fender that looked like it would be far more at home in places where they played the Devil's music that Angel so abjured. He wasn't bad. Daddy caught Jerry's eye, smiled, and briefly waved at him. Jerry waved back. *He seems like a nice enough guy,* Jerry thought. *He sure raises some great-tasting vegetables.*

The rest of the band was musically less certain. A teenaged boy sat behind a scanty drum set that consisted of a bass and a couple of snares. A couple of women beat raggedly on tambourines, and a geezer had a big pair of cymbals that he whacked together at seemingly random intervals. He did seem to be having fun, as did the rest of the congregation. They were singing the lyrics to "While My Guitar Gently Weeps."

"I told you that's what the song was," Jerry whispered to Angel, who had stopped praying, but was still kneeling on the rail, her clasped hands resting on the pew in front of them. She looked around as if she'd found herself suddenly cast into the lion's den.

Daddy, apparently leading the band, segued into a rocking version of "I Saw the Light," which the congregation took up without missing a beat.

It was hot inside the little wood structure, and crowded. The pew where Jerry and Angel sat was full, as were most in the small church. The congregation, the men dressed in worn jeans or stiff polyester pants and neatly pressed shirts buttoned up to their necks, the women in ankle-length dresses with lace collars and tiny flower prints and sensible black shoes, were singing and clapping along enthusiastically with the band when Uzziah made his entrance.

He walked quietly down the center aisle while Daddy led the congregation through one more chorus of "I Saw the Light," a worn black Bible in one hand and a long, narrow wooden box carried by a leather strap in the other. He reached the podium, put his Bible down, went to the altar, and set the wooden box upon it as the congregation's sing-along ground to a ragged but cheerful halt.

Uzziah looked out upon the congregation, a thoughtfully serious expression on his lined, darkly tanned face. "Ain't it hot in here?" he asked in a soft voice that nonetheless penetrated to every corner of the suddenly quiet church.

Somehow Jerry didn't think that he was talking about the weather.

"I *said*," Uzziah said again, "ain't it *hot* in here?"

This time a chorus of "Yes" and "Amen" burst out from the congregation. Jerry looked around out of the corner of his eyes. A growing rapture was evident on many of the faces surrounding him as Uzziah opened his Bible and read the first thing his eyes seemed to strike on the page.

"'And these signs shall follow them that believe; in my name shall they cast out Devils; they shall speak with new tongues—'"

Uzziah paused briefly and there was a sudden great intake of breath as if everyone knew what was coming next. When he spoke again his voice was raised, was exulted like the roar of a lion, though he seemed to put no more effort into these words than those that had come before.

"'—THEY SHALL TAKE UP SERPENTS—'"

Pandemonium swept through the church like a whirlwind, leaving in its wake shouting, stamping, singing, crying people as Mushroom Daddy led the ragged band through a very up-tempo version of "What a Friend We Have in Jesus." The energy and power exhibited by the tiny congregation was almost frightening. Jerry had never seen anything like it before. Everything that had previously transpired was the merest warm-up. It damn well was hot in there.

He glanced at Angel and suddenly froze at the look on her face. Her features were stiff and wooden, as if paralyzed, with her eyes bulging and her teeth clenched and showing in the dead rictus smile of her mouth. A line of spittle ran down her chin. Jerry wondered if she'd had a seizure of some kind, and then she began to speak like a meth freak who'd mixed his speed with acid. Jerry couldn't understand the rapid-fire words she spit from her mouth. He didn't even know what language they were in.

Tongues, he thought dazedly. *She's speaking in tongues.*

He looked around wildly, wondering what he should do. The others in their pew watched with interest but no special concern, as if this was not a terribly unusual occurrence. Jerry supposed that it wasn't.

One man marched up and down the aisles like a windup toy, loudly proclaiming his love for Jesus while clapping his hands almost in rhythm with the band. Others prayed or testified in loud voices. In front of the congregation, near the simple altar, Uzziah opened the long narrow box and took out a snake.

It was a thick, gray-mottled, four-foot-long serpent that he held fearlessly in his hands, its rattles buzzing with a determined noise that could be heard over the band playing, the congregation singing and praying, and Angel loudly proclaiming in tongues. Uzziah held it behind its head with his right hand and supported the rest of its thick, coiled body with his left, its face so close to his own that its flickering tongue caressed his lips with its questing touch.

Jerry suddenly felt that they should get out of there. He knew that he had to get Angel's attention. He had read somewhere that it was dangerous to try to wake sleepwalkers. He hoped that the same wasn't true of tongue-talkers.

He gripped her upper arms and tried to turn her to face him in the pew. "Angel!" Briefly he considered slapping her face, then thought better of it and tried to shake her out of her trance. "Angel! It's Jerry—" Christ! He had forgotten what name she knew him by. "Jerry Creighton!" he amended swiftly. "Snap out of it! You've got—"

Her eyes focused on his, without a hint of recognition in them. Only anger.

"Shit," Jerry said.

Angel shrugged, easily breaking his grip. He reached out to her and she grabbed his arm, pivoted, and threw him against the wall. She flung out her other arm, caught the pew's backrest, and shattered it into kindling. The people around them scattered as splinters flew among them like shrapnel. The band ground to an uncertain halt.

Apparently, Jerry thought as he crouched on the polished wooden floor, this was an unusual occurrence, even by their standards. He took a deep breath. Nothing was broken, though he'd hit the wall with the impact of a multistory fall onto concrete. Fortunately, due to his wild card power, his bones were rather flexible.

He looked up to see Angel panting and staring at him. In other circumstances it might have been arousing. But her stare was fixed and it seemed that she was panting with anger, not passion. She launched herself at him, and Jerry did the only thing he could think of to possibly ensure his survival.

He curled up on the floor in a ball, his face buried in the crook of his elbows, his hands protecting his head, his knees tight against his gut. He felt something go by him like a train in the night and there was a mighty crash as Angel smashed through the church's wall.

"Jesus Christ," Jerry whispered, as if he were praying or cursing.

"Hey, man, you all right?" a concerned voice asked.

He didn't have to turn around to realize who it was, as Mushroom Daddy's clinging aura of marijuana announced his presence.

"Yeah," Jerry said. "I guess."

"Let me help you up, man."

He gripped Daddy's offered hand and the hippie hauled him to his feet. He clung to him for a moment until his head cleared. They both watched Angel run through the settlement, then stop suddenly and reverse her field.

"She's coming back," Jerry said. He wasn't sure if that was a good thing or not.

They watched in silence for a moment, then Daddy shouted, "No she's not, man! She's stealing my van! She's stealing my frigging van, man! Man, that's so not cool!"

They watched in astonishment as Angel flung the van's driver-side door open and vaulted into the driver's seat.

"How'd she start it without the key?" Jerry wondered out loud as the engine roared to life.

"The key's in the ignition, man, where I always leave it."

Jerry looked at him.

"What?" Daddy said. "We're in the country, man! Nobody steals shit here. Everyone's, like, all honest and cool, man. Besides, before I thought about keeping it in the ignition I kept forgetting where I'd put it and then I'd have to go all the way to Middletown to have a duplicate made. Oh, man!"

He said the last in a disgusted voice as the chugging motor finally caught and Angel spun the wheel and roared down the unpaved road, kicking up a spray of dirt and gravel like a contrail in her wake.

Jerry sighed deeply. He turned around. Everyone in the congregation was staring at him, even the rattlesnake who was draped around Uzziah's shoulders like a feather boa. The snake, in fact, had possibly the friendliest expression in the whole group.

"Sorry," Jerry said with a tentative smile that no one, not even Mushroom Daddy, returned.

New Hampton: The Snake Handlers' Commune

THIS HAS BEEN AN *unsettling experience all around,* the Angel thought. She'd felt odd ever since getting out of the hippie's van, but had turned away the strangeness with vast quantities of the snake handlers' unbelievably excellent food. She felt better after eating, but now she realized that she should have resisted Creighton's notion to attend the ophiolatrists' services. She wasn't entirely unfamiliar with what went on in their places of worship. Her mother had taken her along when she'd attended several such churches during her quest for spiritual enlightenment. They had also frightened her. The loud music. The crazed testifying. Tonight, for some reason, she felt herself terribly susceptible to their call.

She prayed to the Lord for strength to remain calm. But for some reason he chose to deny her prayer. Part of her watched in horror as some strange spirit rose up in her and she heard herself confessing her sins, her wanton desires, fortunately speaking in no language of Earth. Which, when she thought about it, frightened her even more.

Then she heard the Voice.

The Angel was terrified at the sound of it in her head. She had never really experienced anything like that before. Clearly, she was in the grip of the Holy Spirit and it frightened her. She knew that she was not worthy.

"John Fortune is at Kaleita's Groceries—he's being taken by a group of armed men. Someone has to rescue him! Someone out there who can hear this—please! Help!"

The voice of the Holy Ghost was deep and masculine. It spoke to her alone. At least no one else acted as if they heard it. It spoke with great urgency, telling her that the boy was in danger, telling her that she had to reach him, fast. It was clear that if she didn't he'd fall into the hands of their enemies and the Hand's plans would come to nothing. The Millennium would be denied and Jesus Christ would not take his place as God's Regent upon the Earth. It was up to her and her alone, unworthy as she was, to rescue him.

She ran almost blindly from the church. The man called Creighton—useless as he'd been throughout this entire affair—stood in her way. She removed him. She had no time to find the door. She went through the wall.

As she ran down the hill the Spirit Tree cheered her on, the bottles tied to its branches clanking musically in the wind. She remembered the store on the county road, about two miles from where she stood. It would take her about seven or eight minutes to get there on foot, maybe less if she ignored the roads and cut cross-country.

Too long, she thought. *Too, too long. The boy's kidnappers would be gone by then and the Holy Ghost's warning would have been wasted.*

Then she remembered the van sitting before the ramshackle barn, and hope sprang into her breast. *If only,* she prayed. *If only . . .*

She ran to it, and flung open the driver's-side door so hard that it rebounded and slammed against her backside as she leaned into the cab. *Praise the Lord,* she silently prayed. *The idiot left his keys in the ignition.*

She vaulted into the seat and turned the key, gunning the gas pedal. The engine groaned like a feeble old man with a hangover. *Gently,* she told herself. *Be gentle and patient. For once . . . take your time . . .*

She eased up on the gas and the engine sputtered to life. She engaged the clutch and winced as it sounded like she ground a few pounds of the transmission into metal filings. The van bucked and humped like an unruly mustang, but slipped into gear. The Angel shot backward, scattering the chickens who'd been peacefully pecking their day's ration of feed, ground another month's worth of life out of the transmission, finally found first gear, and headed on down the road.

It was twisty and not exactly well-banked, so she couldn't get the van much over forty. She skidded through the last turn, suddenly remembering the wooden gate that stood as a barrier between the sect's private lane and Lower Road. It hadn't looked too sturdy, she thought hopefully.

It turned out that it wasn't. She crashed through it like she'd crashed through the wall of the church, braking into a power turn and skidding momentarily on the van's two right tires, her right hand flying off the steering wheel and hitting the eight-track's volume knob, blasting the Canned Heat tape up to full volume.

"Going Up the Country" wailed out her window, which she'd cranked down to reduce the smell of Mushroom Daddy's peculiar incense, which actually wasn't as bad as it had seemed at first. Fortunately there was no oncoming traffic as she slewed onto Lower Road, her heart hammering in her chest. She wasted a couple of seconds searching for the right gear as the van lurched crazily up the road, finally found the right sequence, and took it to top gear as fast as she could. It roared and clattered like a metallic behemoth that should have been extinct long ago, but it responded gamely to her urging and the Angel got it up to over seventy.

The left-hand turn off Lower Road was tricky, but she negotiated the down-shifting with only minor grinding of the gears. The last stretch of road was a long glide up a steep hill, then down again. The grocery store was on the left, at the base. Mere moments had passed since the Holy Ghost had delivered His message, but would she be in time?

The van lurched over the crest of the hill like a prancing mustang, its front tires well off the road. It hit hard and slewed sideways. The Angel bounced up off the driver's seat, bashed her head on the roof, and lost control. Her hands flew off the steering wheel, her feet off the pedals. The van spun downhill as the Angel shook her head, trying to clear the stars out of her eyes.

God is with me again, she thought as she realized that the oncoming lane was clear of traffic. She gamely fought the van for mastery, and through sheer strength managed to haul it back into the right-hand lane. But it was facing the wrong direction halfway down the steep hill and in imminent danger of stalling. She clenched her teeth and slammed it into reverse. Gravity did the rest.

The Angel looked at the mirror mounted outside the driver's-side window. Her right foot found the gas pedal again and she stomped it. The van shot backward down the hill, weaving dangerously as it approached the grocery store's rutted parking lot. Two cars, both big black boats of some unfamiliar make and model, were already in the lot. A handful of men stood around watching as two others tried to stuff a wiggling and fighting boy in the back seat of one of the cars.

It was John Fortune. She was, thanks be to God, in time.

She roared into the parking lot backward, the wheels throwing pebbles like bullets. More through luck than any sort of skill, she managed to screech into the narrow slot between her enemies' cars. She stood on the brake with both feet, hitting her head again on the van's roof and ignoring the pain as the VW slammed to a halt an inch from jumping the curb and crashing into the storefront behind it. She was out of the van before the amazed onlookers stopped flinching from the shower of pebbles thrown by its squealing tires.

"*Release the boy!*" she cried in a voice like the ringing of a great iron bell.

There was a moment of silence as everyone, John Fortune included, stood stock-still and stared at her, her chest heaving, eyes wild, hair streaming back like a Valkyrie just come down from Valhalla.

The Angel broke the silence. She growled like a she-wolf, driven to inarticulate fury by their failure to respond to her command, reached both hands high above her head while saying aloud her short prayer, and called down the fiery sword. She struck one of the cars, hitting the roof dead on center, slicing all the way through to the pavement. The blade threw off coruscating sparks that sent half the onlookers diving away, screaming and batting at the cinders burning their hands and faces and setting their clothes on fire.

She took a step forward, swinging her sword in a great arc and bringing it down again on the car's roof with all her strength, cutting through roof and side panels and neatly bisecting the vehicle. It collapsed in the parking lot with a groan of tortured metal.

"Jesus Christ!" one of the men said.

She turned and backhanded him, sending him flying over the wreckage. "Don't blaspheme!" she said and moved around the front of the van, which was still chugging in place, pointing her sword at the two men who were still holding John Fortune. "Release the boy," she repeated, this time in a voice low and hard and full of undefined menace.

They did, but only to reach for guns holstered at shoulder and belt.

The Angel moved faster than seemed humanly possible. She pulled her hands apart and the sword vanished. She slapped one of the men down before he could pull out his gun. The other drew, fired hastily, and his shot spit harmlessly over her shoulder. She closed on him before he could fire again. She grabbed his gun hand, twisted, and heard things break. Some were parts of the gun, some were parts of his hand.

He went down screaming. There were two other men at the front of the car. One had a pistol out, the other was reaching into the car's front seat for a rifle. The Angel hunched over and scooped John Fortune up with one hand. She reached with the other and snagged the bottom of the car's driver's-side rear panel, right by the tire. She grunted with effort and stood, veins pulsing in her neck and forehead, throbbing as if they were going to burst. The muscles in her legs, buttocks, back, and right arm cracking with strain, she heaved.

The car flipped up into the air.

The man reaching for the rifle was thrown to one side. The man with the pistol said, "Oh, shit." He dove aside but the car came down roof first, mostly on him. He screamed like a cockroach meeting an inescapable size twelve shoe bottom.

The Angel whirled and tossed John Fortune into the van's passenger-side seat as gently as she could, leaped into the van herself, ground a bit more of the transmission to dust, whirled out of the parking lot, and sped off down the county road, across a bridge over a little river and out into open rolling country bordered by lettuce fields and occasional farmhouses, going in the direction opposite the camp, away from the useless Creighton, from the useless Billy Ray, and from the blasphemous and scary, if generous, snake handlers. She hoped they wouldn't think too unkindly of her. She took a deep breath and for the first time took a second to turn off the Canned Heat tape. *Enough of that,* she thought.

She glanced at John Fortune, who was staring at her like she was some kind of figment from an awful dream. She calmed her breathing, ran a hand through her wild hair.

"Hello, John," she said in as calm a voice as she could manage. "How are you?"

"I-I'm all right," he said in a small voice. "Who are you?"

She smiled kindly. "I am your friend. You can call me the Midnight Angel."

He looked her over carefully. "Are you taking me to my mother?"

Here, she thought, *it gets difficult.* She could not lie to him.

"No, John." She looked back out through the windshield. It was best that he learned the full truth as soon as possible. "Have you ever been to Branson, Missouri?"

"No."

"There's a theme park there," she said, trying to put the best possible face on it. "With rides."

There was a momentary silence, and she glanced back at the boy, afraid of what she might see.

John Fortune nodded. "Cool," he said.

Chapter Seven

New York City: The Jokertown Clinic

FORTUNATO WATCHED AS THE wild-eyed woman with long black hair roared into the parking lot and proceeded to kick major ass. There was no other way to put it. He would have gladly joined her, but his insubstantiality prevented him from being anything more than an invisible cheering section as she rescued the boy from his abductors.

He watched her rattle off down the road with his son safely in the seat next to her while the still-standing kidnappers tried to roll the flipped Lincoln off their screaming compatriot. Once they succeeded the man didn't stop screaming. He was in bad shape, with crushed legs and probable internal damage. He needed a hospital, fast.

That reminded Fortunato. Even though his body was safe in a hospital bed, he was actually not in great shape. His spirit had been away from it for quite a while. While he had achieved much, his success wouldn't be quite as dramatic if his body perished because he'd left it alone for too long. It was time to go back.

The transition wasn't instantaneous, but it seemed faster than the trip out. For one thing, he knew where he was going. He didn't hesitate. He just aimed himself south and flew on the unseen, unfelt etheric winds. For another thing, he had far more energy than he'd had in years. The vigor he'd absorbed from the rich black earth was still singing through his system like high-octane fuel. He didn't know how much was in his tank, but he was determined to utilize it as best he could. He pushed himself hard, and it was a good thing that he did because he arrived at the clinic just in time.

He opened his eyes to see a frantic Dr. Finn standing over him. His hospital gown was torn open, exposing his chest, which had been smeared with some messy goo. Finn was holding two shiny metal paddles that were hooked up by thickly insulated wires to a machine that had been newly wheeled to his bedside.

"Clear!" Finn yelled, and the nurses jammed around Fortunato's bed stepped backward.

Fortunato opened his eyes and grabbed Finn's hands before he could slap the defibrillating paddles onto his chest. He was pretty sure that he didn't need an electric jolt to his heart.

"Fortunato!"

Fortunato couldn't tell if Finn had shouted in fear or relief, or both. The paddles sagged in the doctor's grip. "I'm all right, doctor," he said. "Really. I don't think I need this."

"What happened?" Finn asked. "We thought we'd lost you. The monitor showed your heartbeat slowing down over the last hour or so, until we couldn't get a reading and we thought it had stopped."

"I was gone," Fortunato said. "For a bit, anyway. Now I'm back."

Finn handed the paddles to the nurse who was hovering anxiously over his shoulder, without taking his eyes off his patient. "Gone—like on a trip? Were you astral projecting?"

Fortunato nodded.

"Then your powers have returned?" Finn asked.

Fortunato nodded again, cautiously. "It seems so. It's all so new, that I'm not sure."

"Uh . . ." Finn cleared his throat. "They're not . . . activated . . . like in the old days?"

"You mean by tantric magic and the intromission of my sperm?" Fortunato asked. "That was before your time. How'd you know about that?"

"I've read your file," Finn said. "You're an unusual patient with unusual powers and presumably unusual strengths and weaknesses. Dr. Tachyon kept extensive notes on you, as he did on many aces and jokers—"

Fortunato laughed quietly. "I hope you didn't believe all the bad stuff he said about me."

Finn smiled. "Tachyon was—is—highly opinionated."

Fortunato's laughter turned to a sigh. "I'm sure I gave him cause."

He stared at the ceiling, hardly believing that this notion had come into his head. *What am I thinking?* Fortunato thought. *I must be tired. Overwrought from the action of the past couple of days. I am getting old.*

"What's the matter?" Finn asked.

"Nothing," Fortunato said. "I'm just tired. I need some sleep."

Finn looked at him for a moment, then nodded.

"All right. Do you need anything for the pain?"

Fortunato lay back on the pillow and took stock of his body. The pain from the beating he'd suffered at the hands of the Jokka Bruddas hadn't entirely vanished, but it had receded from the forefront of his consciousness, going deep into bone and muscle where it was a dully throbbing presence. He could stand it. He shook his head.

"No," he said, surprised. "It's not too bad."

"All right," Finn said. "We'll leave you then." He stopped at the doorway after the others had streamed out of the room and looked back at Fortunato, shaking his head. "Aces! You always make the worst patients. No more gallivanting around in your astral form. You need rest. Get some."

"All right." Even if the boy was safe for the moment, Fortunato still had to be sure of his eventual rescue. But now he knew how to track him anytime he wanted to. Finn was right. Now he needed rest.

Finn switched off the overhead light as he left the room, leaving Fortunato discommoded by the annoying LED lights and rhythmic blips from the machinery and monitors connected to him. He thought that the distractions would make it difficult to sleep, but he was wrong. He closed his eyes and was out almost instantaneously.

While he slept his unconscious mind shunted energy throughout his body, repairing damage old and new, restoring tissue, strengthening ligaments, and mending tendons worn with use and age.

For the first time in years Fortunato slept, and did not dream.

◆

New Hampton: The Snake Handlers' Commune

"I'M SURE THERE'S SOME way we can fix all this," Jerry said.

Uzziah shook his head. "I've seen many things happen in this here church over the years. Many strange and awful things."

"Uh-huh," someone in the audience said.

"I've seen people possessed by the Holy Spirit fall on the floor and shake like the good Lord himself had put His icy hand on their spine."

"Amen," some in the audience called, and there were scattered echoes as others took up the cry.

"I've seen people prophecy in tongues no longer spoken in this world of woe."

The response came louder as the parishioners gathered about their preacher.

"I've seen people DRINK POISON and TAKE UP SERPENTS with no harm come to them."

The cries of the audience reverberated in the tiny church, and Jerry found himself inching backward, slowly and carefully, as he realized that this might be his best opportunity to escape.

"But NEVER. NEVER in all my days have I EVER seen someone so possessed, so consumed, so TAKEN UP by the Holy Spirit that WALLS could not hold them, TONGUES could not tell of them, PRAYER could not contain the energy that DROVE them to their worship, AMEN."

Someone rattled a tambourine and the band started playing loudly and raggedly. The service, so unexpectedly interrupted, was suddenly whole again.

The dancing and praying and testifying was back up to full speed as Jerry slipped through the hole that Angel had smashed through the wall in her inexplicable frenzy to escape. Outside, the afternoon was turning toward dusk. He had to report to Ackroyd, then they had to go after Angel and the kid and rescue them both from whatever had possessed her so unexpectedly.

Something was wrong, though. It took Jerry a moment to realize that it was the music coming from the church. There was no electric guitar. He stopped, and Mushroom Daddy, following behind, almost walked right into him.

"Hey," Daddy said, "you're not splitting, are you, man?"

Jerry started walking again. He didn't have time to waste on hippie burnouts, no matter how nice they seemed to be. "Can't talk now, uh, Daddy. Got to get after Angel."

"Groovy. That's all cool, man," Daddy said, falling in beside Jerry now that he'd been noticed. "We got to go after Angel. And my van, man. I got to get it back."

"Sure, Daddy," Jerry assured him. "We'll get it back for you. She probably had a good reason to take it. I'm sure she had. Fastest way might be to call it in to the troopers. You got the license plate and tag number somewhere?"

Jerry hoped that wouldn't be too much to ask, but by the look on Daddy's face maybe it was. "Uh, man, I don't know about that. It'd be a bummer to call the pigs in. I don't know how they could help us."

"They can find the van through the plate number," Jerry said patiently.

"Well, probably not, man, because I made 'em myself."

Jerry stopped and looked at him. "You what?"

"Yeah, made 'em myself, man. In my garage. I've always been pretty good with my hands. Saves me over thirty bucks a year, that doesn't have to go to, like, the state and the military-industrial complex."

Jerry frowned at him. "Even the yearly renewal tag?"

Daddy looked proud. "That's the easiest part, man. Color Xerox and rubber cement."

"I don't suppose you remember the numbers you put on the plate, or wrote them down or something?"

"Why would I, man? They're just numbers. They don't mean anything."

Jerry sighed. "No, I guess they don't," he said. *We can still call in the troopers,* Jerry thought. *There can't be too many thirty-year-old VW vans on the road. And she couldn't have gotten far.*

They'd reached the dirt parking lot in front of the snake handler's tumble-down barn. Then he froze as he realized there were far too many cars.

"Hello, boys," a voice said from inside one of them. "What are you two doing wandering around here?"

I know that voice, Jerry thought. *I've heard it before.* He shaded his eyes, trying to look through the glare of the sun shining off the car's windshield.

"This chick friend of his stole my van, man," Daddy chimed in helpfully. "We're looking for it."

"That's funny," the voice said. "So are we."

Jerry's hand dropped to his side. He thought for a moment of going for the gun Ackroyd had given him, which he was carrying snugged in a holster against the small of his back. But he knew that would be suicide. He'd recognized the speaker's voice; he saw the others emerging from their vehicles.

It was Witness and more armed thugs.

♥

New Hampton: The Woods

KITTY CAT RACED INTO the clearing as fast as his tiny legs could carry him.

"Trouble!" he called out. "There's trouble at the snake handlers'!"

"What is it?" Yeoman asked.

"Cauliflower called my cell. He'd gone to check out the commune because he heard a lot of noise over there. Got there too late to see all of what had happened, but saw your partner"—he nodded at Ackroyd—"and Mushroom Daddy get taken by a bunch of armed thugs."

"Mushroom Daddy?" Ackroyd asked.

Yeoman gestured. "A local character. Harmless. He lives on Onion Avenue. He has some kind of weird ace—he grows the best produce in the area." He turned back to Kitty Cat. "What's happening now?"

"Cauliflower says they're beating them up. Daddy and that Creighton guy.

Beating them up and asking them questions about the boy, but they can't answer 'em."

Ray looked at Brennan. "How far's the compound from here?"

"Cross-country, a couple of miles."

"All right," Ray said. "Let's move."

They paused, looked at Ackroyd. "Go ahead," the private investigator said, "I'll follow as best I can."

Yeoman nodded decisively. "Kitty Cat—show him the way."

"All right," the tiny joker said.

"Follow me," Yeoman said, and he and Ray took off through the woods.

They left Ackroyd behind in moments. Yeoman moved fast, Ray thought, but not superhumanly fast. He set a good pace, but Ray held himself back, necessarily following the archer down the thickly forested hillside. Minutes passed, perhaps four or five, then they burst out of the woods onto the verge of a familiar road that ran along the hillside like an asphalt ribbon.

Yeoman leaned over, breathing heavily. Ray had broken a sweat, but his breath was still normal. "Stick to the road," Yeoman told him. "You'll move faster on it than cross-country. This is Lower Road—"

"I know," Ray said. "The compound?"

"Left. Uphill all the way. You'll see a gated dirt road with a sign. You can't miss it. I'll follow as quickly as I can."

"Do that," Ray said.

He started down the road at an easy lope. Yeoman kept pace for the first ten or fifteen yards, then Ray started to pull away. He ran like an animal, just for the sheer physical enjoyment of feeling his muscles work like parts of a well-designed machine, without thought of what he would find when he came to the end of his run. Like always when fighting or exercising or screwing, Ray lived in the moment, concentrating on the play of muscle and tendon, of flesh and bone fighting against gravity, of mind and will battling the inevitable depletion of the energy that ran the machine of his body.

The road went uphill at a steady grade. Within moments he was breathing hard, gasping for the oxygen that he needed to fuel his system, but Yeoman was a hundred yards back, moving okay for a nat, but beaten badly, Ray thought, just the same. Beaten badly. He looked at the slope looming before him and sucked in a long shuddering breath between clenched teeth. This hill wouldn't beat him either.

He leaned into it, pumping his arms harder as he lengthened his stride. The captives might be undergoing unspeakable tortures now at the hands of the kidnapper gang, but that was only part of what drove Ray. Not even the major part of it.

It was the hill under his feet that pushed him on, harder and harder, his breath whistling now like a dying bird as it escaped his throat. The damned hill was trying to slow him down. Trying to beat him. Trying to clip the wings off his feet. But he wouldn't let it.

He was in a full sprint when he saw the turnoff and had to slow down so he wouldn't get tangled up while he turned onto the dirt path leading into the woods. It went uphill, again. The grade was steep, right up the face of the hill, not rising gently along its edge.

He ran on the left shoulder as the path twisted and banked through the trees.

It seemed like a long time before he saw the parking area, but it was probably only a few minutes. The lot was still a hundred yards distant as the meandering path leveled out. Between the intervening trees and the surrounding cars he couldn't quite make out what was happening. A couple of big, dark sedans were parked at haphazard angles in the open space before some run-down wooden buildings. Barns or something. At least half a dozen men were standing around, watching something that was out of his range of vision.

His head started to swim, so he slowed down a little, realizing that he was on the verge of total system collapse as his muscles burned the last of the energy available to them. Fortunately, he would arrive on the scene in seconds and speed was no longer of the essence. Now silence was.

He took long, deep breaths. He tried to make his steps lighter, as if he were gliding over the ground. As he approached he got a better view of what was happening. He didn't like what he saw.

He counted fourteen men in the parking lot. He figured this Mushroom Daddy was the hippie-looking guy being held with his arms pinned behind his back by one of the thugs. Two others held Creighton, Ackroyd's partner, while a third systematically beat him with a truncheon. Eight others stood around watching. Ray grinned. Those were odds that he could enjoy.

No one had seen or heard him yet as he came closer and closer. No one . . . no one . . . no one . . .

Someone finally spotted him and opened his mouth to yell as Ray launched himself into the air. He landed on the hood of a car, catapulted off, bounced back to the ground, and hit the Allumbrado as he went by. He pulled his punch, but only a little.

Seven left.

Two were standing next to each other. Ray went down, his leg shot out in a sweeping arc, and he cut them to the ground. Ray rolled forward once, and was on them. He grabbed one by his jacket collar and headbutted him into unconsciousness. The other tried to crawl away. Ray grabbed his belt and dragged him back, kicking and screaming. He wrapped a hand in his greasy hair, made a disgusted face, and slammed his head face-first into the packed dirt of the parking lot, smashing his nose flat and stunning him like a steer in a slaughterhouse hit between the eyes with an ax. Ray left him choking on his own blood.

Five left.

Ray scrambled to his feet and saw that he had run out of luck. The man standing six feet from him had drawn a pistol. Well out of Ray's reach, he smiled and aimed carefully as Ray launched himself. The gunman squeezed off two shots, then lost his smile as he realized that he wasn't actually well out of Ray's reach. Ray's grin turned savage as one of the shots ripped past his ear and the other tore through meat and muscle high on his right shoulder, punching a hole clean through from chest to back. Ray didn't stop. He didn't even slow down. He hit the man around the waist, like back in the days before his ace turned and he was playing six-man football in high school in Montana, only now his ace *had* turned. He was hurt and jazzed with adrenaline and pain and less conscious of his own strength. He felt the man's ribs crack as he slammed him hard against a car fender and the shooter screamed as his internal organs pulped.

Four left.

Two stood side by side, their automatics out. For the first time Ray remembered Yeoman and he wondered how long it would take the bowman to reach the battleground. The two thugs squeezed off shots that whined off the car's fender, ricocheting into the night. Ray knew he wasn't strong enough to throw a car at the shooters, so he threw the only thing he had, the body he still held. They ducked, splitting apart, and Ray went in on the heels of the dead man. More shots rang out and he felt the pain of a fiery poker drilling through his left thigh and upper right chest. He drew a deep breath, his smile a death's mask, relieved when he realized that the bullet had missed his lung. That would have been trouble. Then he was on them. He grabbed a wrist and waltzed one around so that he blocked the other's shot. He snapped his captive's forearm and the injured man dropped his gun, screaming. The other, his eyes wide with fear, tried to blast through his comrade. Ray, wearing his captive like a bulletproof vest, rushed the shooter, who fired and backpedaled as fast as he could. He clicked empty and Ray hadn't felt any more impacts. Either he was beyond feeling, or his impromptu shield had absorbed all the shots. He tossed the body away and fell on the shooter, who screamed and threw his pistol. The automatic hit Ray in the cheek, the sight slicing it and pissing Ray off even more. Ray's hand closed on the thug's flailing arm and he pulled him close and wrenched his shoulder out of its socket. The man screamed. For good measure Ray grabbed his other arm and pulled that one out of its socket as well. The Allumbrado fell to the ground still screaming, and Ray turned.

Two left.

They were standing next to each other, ten feet from Ray. The others, who were holding the hippie and Ackroyd's partner, had not moved. Two left, and one was unarmed. Ray recognized him. It was the blond asshole who had abused Angel in Vegas. Ray smiled.

But the other was holding an automatic rifle and pointing it right at Ray's chest. He realized there was no chance of dodging automatic rifle fire from the distance of ten feet. Fired from that close it could dish out more pain and destruction than he could deal with. It would certainly incapacitate him, and then it would be simple to deliver the coup de grace. Ray had never had to regenerate from a bullet between the eyes, and he didn't want to try it for the first time so late in his career. He knew his only hope was to keep them talking as long as he could. He leaned over, put his hands on his knees, and took deep breaths.

"Witness," he said, brushing futilely at the seeping bloodstains that had utterly ruined his suit, "what brings you to these parts?"

The blond man frowned. "You recognize me?"

"Sure." Ray took a deep breath to slow down his hammering heart. "I saw you in Vegas, picking on girls."

Witness laughed. It was not a jolly sound. "Yes. I remember you now. Someone told me your name. Billy Ray, isn't it?"

Ray nodded.

"So," Witness said thoughtfully, "the federal government is involved. We weren't sure, but we thought it might be when your partner made off with the boy."

"My partner?" Ray asked. Then it struck him. "Oh, Angel."

"Is that her name?" Witness said. "She's quite striking. I'll enjoy it when we meet again. Well." He thought for a moment, then he glanced at the man who'd kept Ray covered the whole time. "I don't think he can tell us anything more. Kill him."

Ray tensed, ready for a desperate jump, knowing it would be useless.

♣

New Hampton: The Snake Handlers' Commune

JERRY FELT AS IF he'd gone a couple of rounds with Marciano in his prime or maybe Jake LaMotta, like in *Raging Bull*. He grimly held on to his consciousness and just as grimly tried not to puke on his shoes as Witness's man worked him over with a sap loaded with lead pellets, stopping every now and then to ask questions about John Fortune that he couldn't answer.

The sudden appearance of Billy Ray was like the arrival of an angel on Earth. His captors stopped beating him. Ray was a blur of motion as he charged heedlessly into a fight against impossible odds, but after a moment or two Jerry had the sudden hope that perhaps the odds weren't all that impossible as Ray cut through his foes like, appropriately enough, an ace through nats.

His hope, however, was short-lived as Witness and the last of his otherwise unoccupied henchmen got the drop on Ray. Everyone was watching the drama, Jerry realized, even the thug who'd been holding him while his pal sapped him down. He went limp, sagging forward with all his weight, and his right arm broke free of his captor's grip.

"Hey!" the man exclaimed, yanking on Jerry's left arm and turning him half around.

Jerry concentrated and held his right hand out, rigid as a knife. The additional pain barely registered on his consciousness as the bones of his middle three fingers lengthened and tore through the flesh of his fingertips. He didn't have time to get fancy. He just punched out with a knife-hand and caught the man in the throat. His fingers penetrated flesh and the man gurgled, released Jerry, and grabbed his throat.

Jerry fell. His fingers slipped out of the man's throat, and blood spurted from the wound, big-time. It looked as if he'd hit the carotid artery. His tormentor collapsed, gagging and choking into the bloodstained dust at his feet. Jerry fought down a wave of nausea as arcing gobbets of blood splattered his shoes. He'd seen death close up before, but it was never easy to take. Death entailed real pain and suffering and even though these guys were assholes who hadn't thought twice about beating him to a pulp, Jerry wouldn't, couldn't, descend to their level. He still felt bad about having to kill.

But only for a moment. He had other things to worry about.

The other thug lifted his sap and took a step toward Jerry. He froze suddenly when an arrow came out of nowhere and bull's-eyed the gunman holding down Ray. The thug with the sap looked around frantically, but there was no sign of the archer.

I owe him again, Jerry thought, and he kicked the thug in the knee. There was a satisfyingly loud crack, and he went down screaming. Jerry turned toward

Mushroom Daddy with the thought of freeing him, as there was a mad scramble for the fallen rifle. Witness grabbed it.

"Hold it," he screamed, waving it from Ray to Jerry to Mushroom Daddy and the man restraining him. "Come out of the woods, you murdering bastard! Come out or they all get it! Now!"

"You even look like you're going to start shooting," a calm voice said from the forest, "and I'll put you down like a mad dog."

"I'm an ace!" Witness screamed. "A frigging ace! A fucking arrow can't take me out! I'll hang on long enough to hose down all your friends. Depend on it!"

Yeoman came into the clearing without making a sound, an arrow strung to his bow, the string pulled back to his cheek.

Witness laughed. "What we have here is the classic Mexican standoff."

"We can take him, Yeoman," Ray panted, bleeding from at least four wounds that Jerry could see.

The man holding Daddy's arms looked worried. He let the hippie go and started to move backward. Witness glanced at him. Jerry could see that his eyes were crazed with fear.

"Don't move! Any of you!"

"I'm on your side," the man said.

"I SAID NOBODY MOVE!" Witness screamed.

Mushroom Daddy looked at his captor. "That's what happens when you side with fascists. Bummer for you, man."

"Shut up," Witness shouted. "Let me think."

"Why don't you just back up, get in one of those cars, and get out of here," Jerry suggested.

"You'd like that, wouldn't you?" Witness sneered. "Then your pal could shoot me in the back."

"Why don't we put all the weapons down," Ray offered, "and go hand to hand? Me and you. Mano a mano."

"You think I'm stupid?" Witness asked. "You think I don't know that you'd all jump on me? You think—"

Spittle flew from Witness's mouth as he raged on, and Jerry was about to shout, "Look out!" when there was a strange popping noise in the air, near Witness. Jerry heard a familiar voice mutter, "Shit!"

Ackroyd was at the edge of the parking lot, carrying Kitty Cat piggyback, the joker's tiny arms entwined around his neck. Ackroyd was heaving great shuddering breaths, like he'd just run a marathon, which was close enough to the truth. His right hand was pointing toward Witness, but it was shaking with Ackroyd's effort to control his fatigue. Suddenly, simultaneously, Witness vanished as inrushing air made another *POP!* as he disappeared, and another, louder noise exploded as one of the thugs nailed Ackroyd with a slug from his automatic.

Ackroyd whirled, spilling Kitty Cat, and fell heavily over a log marking the parking lot's boundary. Jerry spied the shooter, who was kneeling and still aiming at Ackroyd. No one was near him. Jerry shouted, "NO!" as the thug started to squeeze off another shot at his helpless target, but the gun went off harmlessly into the air as Yeoman's arrow hit him squarely in the chest and knocked him right on his ass. Jerry ran toward Ackroyd. Ray reached his side first and kneeled down by him.

"Ah, Jesus," Ackroyd panted. "M-missed the bastard." He paused to take a deep breath. "Missed him with my first try."

"You okay?" Jerry asked anxiously.

"Bullet wound doesn't look too bad," Ray said. "Just a flesh wound to the thigh."

"Yeah," Ackroyd said, "but I think I broke my ankle when I fell over that damn log."

Jerry looked at Ackroyd's leg and nodded. It was an easy diagnosis to confirm. A jagged splinter of bone was sticking out through Ackroyd's sock.

Ray nodded. "It's broke, all right. Though," he added as Yeoman joined them, "could have been worse. The shooter was about to pump another slug into you before our pal here bull's-eyed him."

"Thanks," Ackroyd said through clenched teeth.

Yeoman smiled thinly. "You're welcome. I appreciate the effort that took."

Ackroyd grunted. "I'm out of my head with pain."

"Where'd you send Witness?" Jerry asked him.

"Top of the Statue of Liberty," Ackroyd said.

Jerry frowned. "That's closed for repairs, isn't it?"

Ackroyd nodded. "It's the only place I could think to send him where he couldn't shoot any innocent bystanders."

"Hope he falls down the stairs and breaks his frigging neck," Ray said.

Jerry looked up and glanced around the parking lot. It resembled a bloody war zone with wounded men lying all around. Back up the hill, a semicircle of stunned snake handlers looked on. A couple of the thugs had gotten back on their feet and were edging off into the woods.

"Freeze, you dirty rats," Jerry said in his best Cagney imitation.

And they did.

♠

New Hampton: The Snake Handlers' Commune

RAY SLUMPED WEARILY ON the ground, momentarily breathing deeply of the gathering dusk, and wondered if he could stand again without collapsing. *Better try it now,* he told himself. *It's not going to get any easier.* Somehow he pushed himself to his feet, swaying a bit until his head stopped swimming.

"You look like hell, Ray," Jerry said.

"Thanks." He took a deep breath and almost toppled over. "I'll be fine after I pass out for a while."

"Save the repartee," Yeoman said. "You need medical attention, along with Ackroyd."

"I'll be all right."

"Only if we get the bleeding stopped," Yeoman said. "You can't have much left running through your veins."

"Hey, guys," Mushroom Daddy said, "I'll go get one of the first aid kits from the snake handlers. They've got some really fine ones in case of accidents while playing with their rattlers and shit."

Yeoman looked around at the body-littered ground. "Some of these guys could use attention, too. I've seen fewer bodies on battlefields."

So have I, Ray thought. *Maybe too many battlefields. God, I'm tired. To hell with standing up.* He stretched out on the ground and was asleep before Mushroom Daddy returned with the first aid kit.

◆

Pennsylvania: Somewhere on the Road

AFTER A COUPLE OF hours the Angel figured it was time to pull over at a gas station to hit the bathroom, take on supplies, and make some phone calls. They stopped in a godforsaken coal-mining town in Pennsylvania where the slag piles glowed redly like the pits of Hell and the stench of brimstone, or something very like it, smothered the air they were trying to breathe.

The gas station, pumps, and even the parking lot were covered by a powdery gray dust that clung to everything like iron filings to a magnet. The Angel swiped her fingers across the gas pump, and they came away greasy with a fine-particled ash that was invisible in the air, but so pervasive that it had settled seemingly everywhere. She could imagine what the locals' lungs looked like, and decided that the sooner they left this area, the better.

She put the nozzle into the van's gas tank and started pumping as John Fortune came out of the bathroom.

"Now that we have a chance," he said, "I should probably call my mom to let her know that I'm okay and not to worry."

The Angel nodded. "That would be a good idea."

"Should I tell her we're going to Branson?" he asked.

"I don't know about that. We don't want the Allumbrados to discover where we're going. The fewer who know our destination, the better."

John Fortune nodded, considering. "You're probably right. So, you know who the kidnappers are? Those Allumbrados?"

"They're Papists," the Angel said.

"Papists?"

"Catholics," she explained.

"I thought they were criminals. What do the Catholics want me for?"

"They think . . ." She paused. She couldn't lie to him and couldn't think of a plausible evasion. "Well, you see, they think you're the Anti-Christ."

"The Anti-Christ?" John Fortune repeated, unbelievingly.

"The Devil," she said. "Satan."

"I know who the Anti-Christ is," he said with some annoyance. "I saw *The Omen.* But . . . why? Why do they think I'm the Devil? And what are they planning on doing with me?"

"They're bad men, John," the Angel said. "I don't know what they're planning to do," she finished lamely, and wished she hadn't lied, even if only by omission, when he nodded skeptically. She ignored his question as to why they thought he was the Anti-Christ, hoping it would just go away, and was relieved when it did. At least for now.

"Okay. Then why exactly are we going to Branson?"

Here was a question she could answer. At least partially. "You'll be safe there. There's someone there who can protect you."

"Jerry from the detective agency was protecting me—"

"And doing a fine job," the Angel said scornfully.

"Well, yeah. There's that," John Fortune admitted.

"Look," the Angel said. "I'm just an operative. The Hand—my boss in Branson has all the answers. He'll be able to tell you everything. I promise."

"Well—"

The Angel put her hand on his, feeling the warmth of his flesh. He was a handsome boy, thoughtful, it seemed, and good-natured. But either he was a consummate actor, or he really had no knowledge of who he was. She could admit no other possibility, except that maybe he was testing her. She already felt closer to him than she'd ever felt to anyone. Even her mother. She would do anything for him, sacrifice everything, to protect him.

"You must trust me," she told him, all her heart in her words. "You must never doubt me. I'll do everything in my power to keep you safe. You must believe that."

John Fortune looked at her for a long, solemn moment, then he nodded. "I believe you."

"All right," the Angel said. "I will not fail your trust."

"Cool," John Fortune said. "Let's go pay for the gas and lay in some supplies, and I'll call Mom."

"Right," the Angel said.

They picked up a couple of six-packs of Dr Pepper and Mountain Dew, candy bars, cupcakes, chips, and some sandwiches that looked reasonably fresh. The Angel paid with the Hand's credit card. She could see now why Ray had insisted on taking it with him.

Since they were in a sheltered mountain valley and their cells didn't work very well, they used the Angel's prepaid phone card to make a couple of calls. She let John Fortune call home first. He didn't realize that his mother had been badly injured in the Las Vegas battle, and she didn't have the heart to tell him about it. As she'd expected, nobody was home when he called, so he left a message on the answering machine. The Angel hoped Peregrine was still alive. She told John Fortune that she and Josh McCoy were probably out coordinating the search for him. She was sure, she added, that they'd get his message soon.

As John Fortune hauled their supplies to the van, she called the Hand. It rang several times before a bright voice answered, "President Barnett's office."

She recognized the young Secret Service agent who was always so polite and helpful.

"Hello, Alejandro," she said. "It's the Midnight Angel. Let me speak to the president."

"Angel! Where are you? Do you have John Fortune with you? All heck has broken out and President Barnett is really worried about you all."

"We're fine," the Angel assured him. "We're somewhere in Pennsylvania right now, but I'm bringing him in."

"Is Billy with you?"

"No." The Angel paused. "We had to leave him behind. Let me speak to the president."

"Well, okay. Hang on while I transfer the call."

There was static-filled silence for a moment, then Barnett's booming voice came on the line.

"Yes, Angel, is that you?"

"Yes. I have him. We're coming in."

"By plane?"

She could hear the excitement in his voice.

"No, sir. We're driving. Someone may be on our trail. At least, I'm assuming it's a possibility. We'll stick to the secondary roads, so expect us late tomorrow, probably."

"Excellent," the Hand said. "What about Ray. Is he with you?"

"No." She frowned. "I had to leave him behind."

"Oh. All right. He's a big boy. He can take care of himself. Disappointing, though. I'll have to talk to him—Sally Lou, not while I'm on the phone."

Coldness suddenly clutched the Angel's heart. *Disappointing*, the Angel thought. *Yes, very.*

"All right," the Hand said. "Good plan. Listen. Call in only if there's an emergency. The less said on the airwaves, the better, if you know what I mean."

"Yes, sir." The Angel could only imagine what was going on with the Hand and Sally Lou. Actually, she realized, she couldn't, but it had to be sinful. She heard a giggle in the background, hung up, and got out of the booth.

"Can I drive for a while?" asked John Fortune, who'd been waiting outside the phone booth with one last sack of junk food.

The Angel rummaged in the bag and picked out a package of little glazed chocolate donuts.

"Do you have a license?"

"Well . . ."

"Better not then."

They went together to the old van, the Angel marveling not only at the fact that she was traveling cross-country with her Lord and Savior, but that he was also accepting her orders so meekly and graciously. She didn't know if this was the Jesus she wanted facing Satan and his spawn in the final confrontation, but for now she was happy that he seemed so amiable and willing to go along with the program. It certainly made her job easier. She could sort out the theological implications later, when they were safe and sound in the bosom of the Hand.

♥

New York City: The Jokertown Clinic

FORTUNATO WOKE IF NOT a new man, at least feeling like one. He didn't know how long he had slept. It felt like days, but it couldn't have been. He sat up and removed the drip line from inside his right elbow and stripped the other tubes and wires from his arms and chest. He swung his feet over the side of the hospital bed and put them on the linoleum floor. Like all hospital floors everywhere, no matter what time of the year, it was cold on the bare bottoms of his feet.

He was still sitting on the side of the bed, considering this koan-like factoid, when Dr. Finn came flying into the room at a gallop, followed by a pair of nurses wheeling in the heart starter.

They all came to a skidding halt, Fortunato watching curiously as Finn leaned against the metal railing at the foot of Fortunato's bed, breathing heavily. The doctor didn't look happy.

"Jesus Christ," he said, "you scared the crap out of us. Again. Why did you disconnect your heart monitor?"

"Oh." Fortunato turned and looked at the machine hanging above the bed, which was showing a disconcerting flatline. "My apologies, doctor. I wasn't thinking. About my own condition, anyway."

Finn sighed. "Tachyon always told me that dealing with aces drove him nuts. Now I know why." His gaze suddenly narrowed. "Wait a minute. Let me look at you."

"I feel fine, doctor."

"Yeah, and you shouldn't. That's why I want to look at you." Finn clattered around the bedside and tilted Fortunato's head so that he could see the right side of his face better. "Amazing. Not only is the swelling gone, but the bruising has disappeared as well." He unwrapped the bandage around Fortunato's forehead. "The cuts and abrasions have all healed." He looked thoughtfully at Fortunato and prodded him in the abdomen with stiffened fingers. "Does this hurt?"

Fortunato shook his head. "No."

"Well, it should. Your spleen was bruised."

"Was, doctor," Fortunato said. He stood and stretched. Everything felt fine. He rotated his shoulders experimentally. Even the knots of pain that had been in his shoulder blades for months had vanished. "It seems as if my powers have—"

He never finished the sentence. The window of his private room suddenly blew inward, showering Fortunato, Finn, and the joker nurses in a storm of sharp glass shards. One of the nurses was clipped on the back of the head by the blinds' valance and fell to the floor with the blinds draped over his unconscious body. Finn reared in sudden fear, nearly slipping on the tile floor despite the little booties he wore over his hooves.

Fortunato stood, cognizant of the glass shards that littered the floor like sharp-edged diamonds, and looked out the window. A smirking figure, floating in the sky outside, spoke. "You can run and hide, spawn of the Devil, but your evil cannot escape my righteous wrath."

Fortunato grinned without humor, his lips peeling away from his gleaming white teeth. "You speak in clichés," he said. "Whoever you are." He stepped forward, elevating himself off the floor to avoid the scattered slivers of window glass. "Stupid ones, at that."

"I am the Witness to the Revelation," the Witness said. "My truth overshadows your lies, demon-bred."

"Whatever." Fortunato drifted toward the shattered window. "I'm betting you have something to do with my son's kidnapping. I'm glad you tracked me down. We have some business to attend to."

Finn, stooping over the unconscious nurse, looked up to see Fortunato, dressed in his white hospital gown, glide out of the clinic through the shattered window into the dusk. The ace waiting outside had an eager, welcoming expression bordering on the ecstatic.

Fortunato drifted out into the night, forty feet above the Jokertown street. The Witness glowed like an incandescent bulb, already attracting the attention of passersby. A crowd formed on the street below, their faces turned up to the night. People pointed, eagerly waiting for whatever weirdness was about to happen.

It was just another summer evening in Jokertown.

Fortunato wondered if any one of them remembered the last time two men had faced each other over Manhattan in wild card combat. Not the strange stories that had become part of the fabric of Jokertown life, but the real facts concerning the confrontation between him and the Astronomer in the sky over the city.

He settled into the lotus position while the Witness looked on, sneering. It was a lot more comfortable sitting on air than it was on the hard floor of the meditation hall, even if his ass was hanging out of the back of his hospital gown. But that was all right. Fortunato wasn't modest in regard to his body. He rested his forearms on his crossed legs and looked at his opponent across the street.

"Comfy?" the Witness asked.

"Yes," Fortunato replied calmly.

"Then die, Hell-spawn," the Witness said through clenched teeth. His eyes glowed green and he brought his hands down, parted them, then brought them up again in a circular motion, starting the gesture to release his spasm of destructive force.

Fortunato remembered the lesson he had learned from his battle with the Astronomer. When that combat had started he'd put up multiple layers of protective shielding that the Astronomer had burnt away with fireballs he'd pulled out of his crazed mind. When it had been time for his own offensive thrust, Fortunato had chanced all on one blow. He'd gathered nearly all the energy he possessed into a single pellet that he concentrated to a pinpoint behind his navel. When he'd released it, it had blown through the Astronomer's body like a high-powered rifle slug, but it hadn't killed him or even injured him. It had barely inconvenienced him.

He'd only defeated the Astronomer by becoming a void. By becoming a vacuum that accepted everything the Astronomer threw at him, which he'd let pass through like a meteor flashing harmlessly through the sky.

Now his sixteen years of Zen training enabled him to become that much more empty. That much more of a waiting target, expression composed, eyes closed, and utterly unhittable.

If the Witness was surprised at Fortunato's passivity, he didn't show it. He hurled a massive bolt of power at the indifferent ace. It struck Fortunato, passed through him without ruffling his white robe, and spattered on the stone wall of the Jokertown Clinic behind, punching in windows and dislodging casements from the first to the upper floor.

Sucked in by the awful vortex of power that he created, the Witness was pulled toward Fortunato like iron filings to a magnet. Fortunato opened his eyes right before they collided. He reached out and grabbed the Witness by the lapels of his cheap suit and said, "Fall."

And they did.

They plummeted thirty-five feet, Fortunato atop the screaming Witness. The spectators on the street below saw them coming and scattered. The two aces hit the ground like sacks of cement and Fortunato felt the Witness's body burst like a water balloon dropped from a three-story building.

He stood and looked at the Witness's wrecked and leaking body. The ace was either smiling or grimacing. It was all the same to Fortunato. The Witness managed to make a *come-closer* gesture with his right hand, and Fortunato kneeled down and put his ear close to his foe's bleeding mouth.

"There are two . . . Witnesses in Revelation," the ace gasped, his chest laboring to bring air into his punctured lungs. "I have . . . a brother."

Fortunato nodded serenely. It was not welcome news, but not totally unexpected. He knew that this affair was far from over. His astral form had lingered at the chaotic rescue at the country store long enough to know that the strange woman who called herself the Angel was, for whatever reason, taking the boy to Branson, Missouri. He was certain he could find them there easily enough. Just as he was sure there would be more minions of the Witness who would try to stop him. The only way to save the boy was to do what he'd done to the Astronomer's conspiracy. Take off its head. It wasn't a prospect that he relished, or even anticipated, but he was committed. There was no other way to save his son.

Fortunato stood looking down at the Witness, and watched him die. It didn't take long. When he was sure that the Witness was no longer breathing, he looked up at the crowd that had assembled around them. All kinds of people had gathered in the mob. Young, old, jokers, a few nats. White, Hispanic, Asian, and one old Black man who wore a glove on his left hand, perhaps, Fortunato thought, hiding a joker deformity.

"Tell your children," he said to them, "tell your family, your friends, your loved ones, and those evil ones you fear, that Fortunato is back from the dead."

They all watched as, clad in his white robe, he ascended silently into the heavens.

♣

New York City: The Waldorf-Astoria

THE CARDINAL HAD HAD enough of St. Dympna's, but neither could he force himself to enter the room of his Waldorf suite where the Cameo fiasco had occurred. Fortunately, the suite contained other rooms suitable for a war council, and Contarini had gathered Dagon and the Witness to hear Nighthawk's report on the attack on the Jokertown Clinic.

Everyone had already heard a garbled account of events on the television, so they were prepared for the bad news that Nighthawk brought.

"And you could do nothing about it?" the cardinal asked when he'd finished his report. Contarini used his iciest voice, which had reduced more than one bishop to helplessness over the years. Nighthawk, who had heard similar tones from the mouths of overseers and slave owners, was used to it.

He shrugged. "The Witness chose to attack him thirty feet above the ground. I wasn't in any position to help him. When they finally crashed to the sidewalk, the crowd was too thick to get through. By the time I did, Fortunato had already ascended into the heavens."

The cardinal made a bitter-lemon face at Nighthawk's choice of words. "Why did he choose that tactic?" Contarini asked quietly, almost to himself.

Because he was vain and stupid, Nighthawk thought. He said aloud, "Because he craved glory, wanting it all for himself."

Contarini fixed him with a killing stare. "We are not in this for self-glory."

Nighthawk bowed his head, mainly to hide the smile that threatened to break out. "As you say, Cardinal," he murmured.

Contarini continued to look as if he were sucking bitter lemons. "Well, no matter. We know where the Devil and his bitch are. We know that his powers have returned and that she is going nowhere for now. I'll have them watched." He steepled his fingers, tapping the tips together in rhythmic order. "We also know where their spawn is. Or at least where he's going. For now he is out of our reach."

Nighthawk turned and gestured to Usher. The big man came forward carrying an old duffel bag.

"Earlier today I sent Usher upstate to look around," Nighthawk said. "And he found a couple of interesting items."

The cardinal perked up, at least momentarily. "Such as?"

"Such as Blood and his brother, skulking in the forest, afraid to come out. Fortunately, hunger drove them into the open."

"Where are they now?" Contarini asked in a voice that showed he was eager to mete out suitable punishment.

"Usher took them to St. Dympna's, to await your pleasure."

The cardinal nodded.

"But before you punish them too severely," Nighthawk said, interrupting Contarini before he could issue any foolish orders, "consider this."

Usher passed over the old duffel bag and Nighthawk offered it to Contarini as if it contained jewels precious beyond number. The cardinal sniffed dubiously.

"Yes, an old bag of clothes."

Nighthawk nodded. "Clothes belonging to the one who calls herself the Angel."

"Barnett's whore?"

Nighthawk nodded again. The Allumbrados had been spying on Barnett and his organization for a long time. Sometimes Nighthawk thought that they knew more about what was happening in the Peaceable Kingdom than Barnett did.

The cardinal smiled. Like most of the expressions that wormed their way across his patrician features, it was sinister.

"I begin to see the possibilities," he said. "All we need is for her to stay in one place for a while for Blood to track her down."

Nighthawk nodded. "He'll have a wide area to search. We know what roads she'll probably take to Branson, but still, it will take some doing."

"Yes." Contarini thought for a while. "But this time I'm taking no chances. Nighthawk, you and your team will await her at their final destination. Just in case they try to elude my Allumbrados once again." Contarini looked at Butcher Dagon and the Witness, who had the grace to look mildly abashed. "But that's not going to happen this time, is it?"

Nighthawk watched Dagon and the Witness shake their heads vigorously, while Magda looked on stoically and Usher coughed to hide his smirk.

"And just to ensure our success," the cardinal said, "I'll attend to this personally."

♠

West Virginia: Somewhere on the Road

THE ANGEL WAS DRIVING somewhere on a dark highway in the middle of West Virginia when fatigue hit her like a brick between the eyes. She was falling asleep at the wheel despite a massive intake of caffeine and sugar. She didn't know if Jesus Christ could actually be killed in a car wreck, but she didn't want to put it to a test. She saw a sign posted for a rest stop in twelve miles, and glanced at John Fortune, who was catching a little shut-eye in the passenger seat.

"There's a rest stop up ahead, John," she told him.

"I'm okay," he said sleepily.

They'd been stopping every now and then for the Angel to hit the bathroom because of all the Dr Pepper she'd been drinking. "You may be okay, but I need a few hours of sleep. We'll rest until dawn, then push on."

John seemed to wake up a little. "Hey, I can drive while you're resting. Let me. I've almost got my license. I'm a pretty good driver."

The Angel considered the idea. A couple extra hours on the road would put them that much closer to Branson. But in the end she shook her head. *Maybe if he had his license.* Without one, they were taking too great a risk. Besides, she didn't really think she should trust someone who "almost" had his license on dark mountain highways.

"We can both use the rest," she told him.

It was comfortable in the back of the van. It smelled vaguely of rich earth, vegetables, and herbs. There was room enough for both of them to stretch out. It felt odd lying down next to the boy who was Jesus Christ, the Angel thought, but his presence was both a comfort and a reminder of her awesome responsibilities. His divinity burned warmly like the sunlike halo that glowed around his head.

As she lay down, she tracked the next day's route in her head. Branson lay in south Missouri, almost on the Arkansas border, about fifty miles east of Oklahoma. They had to traverse the rest of West Virginia, then cross Kentucky and most of Missouri. It didn't seem like much. And it wouldn't add much if she took the detour that had been on her mind the last couple of hours.

Dipping down into Mississippi wouldn't be the most direct route to Branson, but it felt somehow safer to her. Somehow less traceable. And something was calling her. She felt a strong pull to home. A need to visit her origins again. Perhaps, something quietly told her, for one last time.

It wasn't exactly a premonition. Nor a vision. Nothing that concrete. Just a calling through the dark Southern night pulling her gently, like her mother crying in the gathering dusk for her to come home to dinner.

The Midnight Angel fell asleep with her Savior snoring gently at her side, memories of her childhood dancing like lost butterflies through her dreams.

Chapter Eight

In the Air to Branson, Missouri

JERRY COLLAPSED, EXHAUSTED, INTO his seat in first class. Billy Ray occupied the seat next to him. Ray looked well-rested, but Jerry was still weak and in pain from the wounds he'd suffered back at Camp Dez. Not to mention his gunshot wound, and various bruises, scrapes, and cuts he'd suffered while making his way through the forest with John Fortune. His shape-shifting powers didn't regenerate injuries, though by the very nature of his ace his recuperative powers were superior to those of an ordinary man—not to Ray's. Despite being shot multiple times, clawed, strangled, and chewed upon over the past couple of days, the government ace looked fresh as a daisy as he sipped chilled orange juice.

"You look like hell," Ray said.

"I feel like it. Tell me, Ray, are we going to get any more government help on this deal?"

That was the major question in Jerry's mind. It had gone unasked during the war council they'd held the night before in the offices of Ackroyd and Creighton after heading back to the city. Jerry, Ackroyd, and Billy Ray had been the main participants. Josh McCoy had also sat in, and would report back to Peregrine. She was apparently out of danger, but she wouldn't get out of the hospital for days yet. Maybe weeks.

They'd briefed McCoy, bringing him up-to-date on what they knew of John Fortune's current location. Ray had confirmed that John Fortune was on the way to Branson by checking in with his office. Though he'd been less than forthcoming when it came to revealing what office he was actually currently operating out of.

They could use all the help in recovering Fortune they could get. Though free from the kidnappers, he wasn't exactly home safe. Jerry had thought McCoy had been hallucinating when he'd told them that Fortunato had turned up to help in the search, but Ackroyd had surprised Jerry by confirming McCoy's story from subsequent news coverage, even though no one seemed to know Fortunato's current whereabouts. It seemed that the legendary ace had disappeared after some strange goings-on concerning an unidentified DOA ace.

"Well," Ray said, "you know I can't really talk about those things. . . ." He gestured encouragingly, it seemed.

"Sure, sure," Jerry said. "I get you."

Plausible deniability, Jerry thought. That was all the government seemed to care about nowadays. Ray's partner, Angel, had reported, saying that she was on her way to Branson, Missouri, with the kid, but Ray couldn't explain why she was taking him there. Maybe, Ray suggested, something John Fortune had revealed to her had made the trip necessary. Jerry couldn't imagine what that possibly could be, and Ackroyd hadn't been happy with Ray's feeble nonexplanation. But they had to live with it. Another thing they had to live with that Jerry wasn't happy about was Brennan's absence.

"You're moving out of my backyard," Yeoman had said after the battle at the ophiolatrists' compound. "I was happy to help around here, but with the boy gone and the government now involved . . ." He'd looked thoughtfully at Ray and shook his head.

Ackroyd had been happy to see Yeoman sign off. Jerry hadn't been, and still wasn't. The archer had proven his worth more than once during the past couple of days. Jerry was sure that they'd be sorry that Yeoman wasn't lurking somewhere, shaft nocked to bowstring, watching their backs. But all and all, Yeoman was right. This wasn't his fight.

They decided to send Sascha to Branson immediately, to scout out the territory and make arrangements for lodging, and Jerry and Ray would follow the next day, as soon as they both had a chance to catch their breaths and rest their battered bodies. Ackroyd was out of it. He'd already disobeyed doctor's orders by checking out of the hospital. There was no way he could be an active part in the rest of the case on his damaged leg. His absence was another great loss to the team, but there was nothing they could do about it.

Once their plane took off, Ray showed that he wasn't interested in idle chit-chat. He reclined his chair, put his feet up, closed his eyes, and immediately fell asleep. He was impeccably neat, even while sleeping, though he snored.

For Jerry the hours crawled like legless elephants. He wished he were like Ray. Tough and untouchable, able to bounce back from any physical ailment, take anything in stride.

Jerry still hurt physically. His body was one big bruise, inside and out. Mentally he still felt guilty for losing John Fortune. The in-flight movie was the sucky Britney Spears remake of the tolerable *Desperately Seeking Susan*. All he had to occupy his mind were thoughts about his empty personal life. Images of Ray's partner found their way into his tired brain. Angel. She was a striking woman. He wondered what Ray knew about her, and decided that he'd pump the government agent, subtly, of course, for info about her when he woke up.

"Magazine, sir?"

The steward awoke Jerry out of his introspective haze by holding a selection of magazines before him. *Businessweek. Harper's. Esquire.* A familiar-looking photo on the magazine atop the pile caught his eye. "FORTUNATO'S INCREDIBLE RETURN TO NEW YORK," the headlines blazed. "FAMOUS ACE SEEKS UNKNOWN SON. EXCLUSIVE REPORT BY DIGGER DOWNS."

"Thanks," Jerry said. "I'll take this one."

He took the brand-new issue of *Aces!* from the pile, and settled back to read about Fortunato's return to New York, until somewhere over Kentucky when he fell asleep and dreamed an uncomfortable dream in which he and Ray walked the streets of Branson, Missouri, searching for John Fortune, and were in turn stalked by man-sized walking zucchinis.

All Jerry could think was, *Why zucchinis?*

◆

In the Air to Branson

RAY WOKE UP SOMEWHERE over Missouri. He sat carefully unmoving for a few moments, taking stock of the parts of his body that hurt, and the parts that didn't. Hurt came out ahead, about ten to one.

He sighed and slowly moved his seat to the upright and locked position. Regeneration had never been painless, but lately it was taking more and more out of him. It took longer and hurt harder. He wondered if someday it would take as long for him to heal from a wound as it took an ordinary man. He wondered if someday his face might not repair itself. If his kidneys and liver and heart might not return to full working order. If skin and flesh and muscle and bone might not knit together again into a raveled whole.

He glanced over at Creighton, twitching in his sleep like he was having some sort of delicious dream, slumbering like a baby, without a care or a worry. *God,* Ray thought, *what would it be like to be a simple PI? Catch a few criminals, catch a few zzzs.* Compared to his life, it sounded idyllic.

Creighton jerked awake a few minutes later. He glanced wildly at Ray, but seemed to calm down almost immediately when he realized where he was. For a moment it looked as if he were going to say something, but then thought better of it and remained silent. *Good,* Ray thought. *I have enough shit of my own to worry about.*

Ray sat up straight all the way down to Branson, carefully drinking his orange juice until the steward came by to collect all cups and trash. He wouldn't have minded a good stiff drink even if the alcohol interfered with his body's repair work. It was, however, his ironclad policy not to mix drinking and flying. Booze coupled with unexpected turbulence was a sure recipe for disaster.

As it turned out, this flight was as smooth as a walk in the park, as was the landing. Taxiing to the gate was interminable, even though the Branson airport wasn't exactly Tomlin International. Taxiing to the gate always annoyed Ray. He was the first to stand and rescue his carry-on from overhead storage, being careful because of course the baggage could have shifted during flight. He dragged Creighton's bag down as well, handed it to him, and headed off the plane, Creighton half jogging to keep up.

"Why are you in such a hurry?" the PI asked.

Ray wasn't sure. He was just eager to get on with it, to find John Fortune and deliver him to Barnett. To finish with this nonsense and start exploring other options. He wasn't sure just yet what they might be. Hell, he had no fucking idea. Suddenly he just wanted to finish this while his skin was relatively whole.

Was he, Ray wondered, suddenly developing a sense of caution? And if so, was that a good or bad thing?

My God, Ray thought, *not introspection, too.*

They stopped as they entered the terminal proper through the covered walkway. A big white banner with big block letters painted in red was strung up near their gate. WELCOME MAGOG, it proclaimed.

Underneath, before, and around the banner were scores of women. Women dressed in pantsuits. Women wearing sensible shoes and plain, long dresses. Women with teased hair. Women with bouffant hair. Women whose hair was like the girls' hair at Ray's senior prom back in Montana in the 1970s. All had adhesive tags on their blouses that said, HI! MY NAME IS, in big letters above a white space that had names like Lurleen and Ellen Sue carefully filled in with felt-tip markers. They were all talking and embracing and standing in knots and groups and generally clogging the flow of foot traffic. Ray and Creighton stopped, stood, and stared.

"What the hell is MAGOG?" Ray asked.

"He was like, a demon in the Bible, man," a voice said behind them. "Or maybe a giant. I forget which."

Ray and Creighton turned as one, stared, then looked at each other in wonderment.

"What the hell are you doing here?" Creighton asked.

Mushroom Daddy smiled brightly. He was freshly bathed and smelled only very, very faintly of cannabis overlaid by what must have been a gallon of Old Spice. He was probably wearing his best clothes, which, Ray thought, made him look like a Salvation Army reject only forty years out of date. He had on a purple silk shirt and a paisley tie and vest to match, and suede bell-bottoms with vertical red and orange stripes. He made Ray's eyes hurt.

"Well, man, I had to come to get my van, man. I called Jerry's office and told them all about how that chick stole my van, and they told me what flight you were taking so I decided I'd better follow you guys and see about, like, getting my van back." He looked a little hurt. "I couldn't afford to sit up in first class, though."

Ray closed his eyes. When he opened them there was a narrow, dangerous cast to them. "Creighton's office told you what flight we were on?"

"That's right, man."

Ray shifted his gaze to the PI. "Now, Ray—" Creighton protested.

"Hey, man," Mushroom Daddy interrupted, "are you a PI, too?" he asked Ray.

"No. I'm with the government," Ray said.

Daddy pulled away. "Like, the CIA, man?"

Ray laughed. "CIA? Those pussies? They're afraid of us, man."

"Oh." Daddy thought it over. "That's okay, then."

Ray and Creighton exchanged another glance, then shrugged.

"All right," Creighton said. "Well, we'll see you around . . . Daddy."

Mushroom Daddy shook his head. "Uh-uh, man. I'm sticking with you guys until I get the van back."

"I don't think—" Creighton began, but Ray took his arm.

"Excuse us a moment," he said to Daddy, and pulled Creighton away a few feet. "We can't have this brain-dead hippie stumbling along after us, sticking his nose where it doesn't belong, and probably getting it shot off. I wouldn't mind that so much, but he'd probably get us shot to Hell and back, too."

"What are we going to do with him then?" Creighton asked.

Ray stood still, thinking, his lips twitching in distaste. "Bring him along for now. We can always find some pretext to dump him later. Or maybe get his ass thrown in jail for a while."

"That wouldn't be fair," Creighton said.

"Who gives a shit about being fair?" Ray asked. "I'm talking about survival."

Creighton looked him in the eye, then glanced away. "All right. I see your point. Anyway, maybe he'll be useful. Somehow."

"Yeah," Ray said. "Like tits on a bull."

An indeterminately aged woman whose frosted blond hair was piled atop her head like a plate of onion rings glared at him like he'd farted in church or something. Creighton went off to talk to Daddy as Ray found himself under the woman's suspicious scrutiny. He tipped an imaginary hat to her and walked away. She harrumphed to herself as he joined Creighton and Daddy, thereby confirming her worst suspicions.

I know, Ray thought, *where she's headed. Along with all the rest of the kooks.*

He sighed to himself, realizing that it was his destination, too.

♥

New York City: The Jokertown Clinic

"THE *ACES!* HOTLINE HAD thirty-seven calls concerning you last night," Digger Downs told Fortunato excitedly. "Most reported that you'd come back from the dead, rising out of a manhole in front of the Jokertown Clinic to defend it against a crazed ace who was attacking it for unknown reasons. Most said that you were dressed in a white robe, had a glowing halo, and ascended back into Heaven after crushing this unknown ace with a single blow."

"Did you bring the clothes?" Fortunato asked. His monk robes had long since gone into the hospital's incinerator.

"Sure." Digger paused and handed him a couple of shopping bags. "There were a hundred and seventeen calls this morning," he went on. "You've been spotted all over the city, as far east as Massapequa on Long Island, north to the Catskills, and west to Binghamton."

Fortunato stripped off his hospital robe unselfconsciously and dressed in the underwear, jeans, socks, and pullover short-sleeved shirt that Digger had bought him. "What have I been doing in all those places?" he asked the reporter.

Digger flopped on Fortunato's unmade hospital bed and gusted a deep sigh, shaking his head. "You think of it, you did it. You stopped a mugging in Brooklyn. You made a car swerve in Monticello and miss a kitten that had wandered into the road. Your face was seen etched in the dirt of an elementary school window in the Bronx."

Fortunato glanced at him. "What?"

Digger shrugged. "Like I said, you've been a busy guy."

Fortunato sat down and put on the running shoes Digger had bought. It was the first time in ages he hadn't worn simple woven-straw sandals. He stood and walked about in a small circle, testing them. They looked garish and bulky, but felt good on his feet.

"I did none of these things," he said. "Well—I did kill that ace, but I didn't mean to. Not really." His eyes narrowed and he spoke half to himself. "There were a couple of questions I'd wanted to ask him."

"Of course you didn't," Digger said. "Mean to, I mean. What we have here is a genuine phenomenon. People want to believe in something, and it looks like you may be it. You're big news, Fortunato, and you're only going to get bigger. Maybe the next big thing. Listen, let me interview you on 'Aces! Corner' on *Entertainment Tonight*. That'll only be the first step. Within the week, you'll be on *Larry King Live*. I guarantee it."

Fortunato shook his head. "Sorry. I don't have time for this now. Maybe later, when things have settled down."

Digger looked disappointed, but after a moment of reflection, nodded. "You're right. We should let the mystery deepen. The tension build. Let the rumors swirl for a while. Maybe a few hints in the written media, then, wham! I see a special, maybe on E!."

"Will that pay for the damage done to the clinic?" Finn asked, suddenly appearing in the doorway of Fortunato's room.

Fortunato turned to him. "I'm sorry about that, doctor. I really am. Perhaps I can make it up to you someday, but right now I'm checking out. I have to get going."

Finn grabbed his arm as he went by. "I should examine you first."

Fortunato stopped. There was a time when he would have pulled away angrily if someone laid their hands on him like that. But that time had passed. "I'm fine, doctor. You know I am."

"Well, maybe," Finn said. "But the police have been asking about you. I've been telling them that you're hurt, under sedation—"

"All the more reason I have to go, before I get tied up in red tape." He put his own hand on the doctor's arm, but his touch was friendly. "I know you've done a lot for me, Finn. I appreciate that. I'll do what I can to make it up to you. But right now I have to go after my son. He's not out of danger yet."

"Well . . ." Finn let his hand fall away from Fortunato's arm. "All right. Where are you headed?"

"Branson, Missouri," Fortunato said with a look of contemplation. He turned to Digger Downs. "Coming?" he asked.

Digger jumped up from the bed. "Sure. Wouldn't miss it for the world."

Good, Fortunato thought. *Because I still don't have any money.* He realized that before long he'd have to figure out a way to make some if he was going to remain in the world. He couldn't depend on the goodwill of *Aces!* forever.

Digger joined him at the doorway and preceded Fortunato into the hallway. Fortunato paused for a moment and turned back to Finn.

"How's Peregrine doing?" he asked.

Finn shrugged. "About as well as can be expected. Maybe even a little better. But she's still got a long convalescence ahead of her."

"There is something you can do for me."

"Say goodbye for you?" Finn asked.

"How'd you know?" Fortunato said after the silence had stretched uncomfortably between them.

Finn shrugged again. "I read Tachyon's dossier on you, remember?"

Fortunato nodded. "Yeah. I guess that the space wimp did have my number."
He turned and left the hospital room. Finn watched him go in silence.

Branson, Missouri

SASCHA STARFIN WAS WAITING for them near the baggage carousel. Jerry
saw him immediately once he and Ray and Mushroom Daddy had fought their
way past the crowds of women wearing MAGOG buttons.

"Sascha!"

The ace turned his head toward them as Jerry shouted and waved. Sascha's
height was accentuated by his thinness and his long neck. His hair, receding at
the temples, was stylishly gelled so that a roguish curl fell over his broad forehead. His teeth were white and straight, his mouth expressive. It was his most
expressive feature. He had no eyes, only an unbroken expanse of skin across the
sockets that should have housed them.

"Jerry, glad you made it." He turned to Ray. "Mr. Ray. Good to see you, as
well." His eyeless face turned unerringly to Mushroom Daddy.

"Wow," Daddy said. "Spooky, man. How'd you know I was here?"

Sascha flashed a smile. "I'm telepathic, for one thing. For another, I can smell
you. I didn't know there was a cannabis-scented variety of Old Spice."

Ray broke in before Mushroom Daddy could reply. "Did you book rooms in
the hotel I mentioned?"

Sascha nodded, though he looked dubious. "Yes. The Manger, at the Peaceable
Kingdom. Isn't that a little way out of town?"

Ray shook his head. "We're not here to see Boxcar Willie. Believe me, we'll be
close to the action."

"The Manger?" Jerry said doubtfully. "What kind of hotel is that?"

Ray smiled. "It's the kind where 'There's Always a Room for You, Even If You're
Not the Savior.'"

"Wait a minute," Jerry said. "The Peaceable Kingdom. Isn't that Barnett's religious theme park?"

"Yep," Ray said, "we'll discuss it later. I've got to check some things out."

He hustled away through the automatic doors and into the afternoon beyond, where he jumped into the first taxi in line. Sascha puckered his lips in a
thoughtful moue. "Ray left precipitously, didn't he?" the eyeless ace said. "That
man has secrets."

They followed Ray outside into the warm summer afternoon on the fringe of
the Ozark Mountains. Jerry shrugged as they went up to the cab currently at the
head of the line.

"He's a spook. He probably has more secrets than a madame in a high-class
cathouse. But you're right. He's been helpful so far, but really, how far can you
trust these government types? Keep an eye on him."

Sascha grinned and made an okay sign with thumb and forefinger as Jerry
opened the cab door.

"Where to, gents?" the cabby asked as the three slid into the air-conditioned
comfort of his back seat.

"Peaceable Kingdom, the Manger," Jerry said in a resigned voice.

The cabby cleared his throat as he eyed them, especially Mushroom Daddy, in the rearview mirror. "I see that you gentlemen have, uh, sophisticated tastes. If you're interested in any of the real *thrilling* sights, stuff the tourists generally don't get to see, I'm your man. Real joker acts. Some real wild ones, if you know what I mean. Aces, too, sometimes, with powers that'll blow your mind. Totally *unregulated* gaming," he said, glancing in the mirror at Sascha, whose wild card nature was rather obvious.

"I didn't know there was any of that in town," Jerry said.

"Oh, sure," the cabby said, nearly sideswiping a white stretch limo as he snuck through a red light at the last second, shooting the limo's driver the finger and Jerry a sharklike smile. "Not in town, of course. The town is strictly for the squares. Lennon Sisters. Pat Boone. *Joseph and the Amazing Technicolor Dreamcoat.* That yodeling guy. You know, 'Una Paloma Blanca.'"

"Boxcar Willie?" Daddy asked.

"Slim Pickens?" Sascha asked.

The cabby shook his head. "Nah. That's not him. Anyway, the real action is outside of town. The roadhouses. The *exotic* attractions. Like the riverboats out on the lake."

"Riverboats on a lake?" Jerry asked.

The cabby shrugged. "Close enough for the tourists. Some places have free access to all kinds of games, even to wild carders, which I hope you don't mind me saying kind of stand out in this place."

"I don't mind," Daddy said.

"Good." The cabby nodded. "Roulette. Craps. Slots. You just got to know where to look. And know how to not get caught cheating."

"We'll keep that in mind." Jerry looked out the cab window as they passed through the town. All roads from the airport, it seemed, led through Branson. That was the point of them, after all.

Compared to Vegas, Jerry thought, Branson was kind of . . . mediocre. There was traffic, but more pickups and Winnebagos than limousines. There were lights, but fewer of them, and dimmer. There were hotels and theaters, but smaller, definitely less glittery. There were stolid brick buildings, not phantasmagorical palaces of exotic sin. The names on the marquees were more pleasingly familiar than exotic. There was, Jerry noted, a dearth of topless reviews but plenty of gospel choirs. One constant, though, was common to both tourist Meccas. There were plenty of buffets.

Branson wasn't as big as Vegas either. A trip down the Strip took less than twenty minutes, and suddenly they were out in the open country of a small peninsula jutting out into Table Rock Lake. From a distance, the Peaceable Kingdom looked pretty much like any other theme park, its skyline dominated by a high Ferris wheel, a twisting roller coaster, and some whirling, whipping, and falling-down-really-fast rides that Jerry had never really seen the point of.

The cabby pulled up in front of the Manger, which, yes, did have something of a faux Middle Eastern look about it. "Remember what I told you," he said as they decamped with their luggage. He zoomed back into the unrelenting traffic.

"Your bag, sir?" someone said. Jerry turned to see a joker in a bellhop uniform—if you could call faux Arabic robes and headgear a uniform—reaching for his suitcase. His third arm, coming right out of the center of his chest, grabbed the bag. Handy, Jerry thought, for a bellboy. The bellboy turned to Sascha and Daddy.

"I've already checked in," Sascha said.

"I'm cool, man," Daddy said to the bellboy.

"No luggage?" Jerry asked.

"Like, why should I bring clothes, man?" Daddy laughed at the self-evident absurdity of the idea. "If I need more I can always get some."

If? Jerry thought. *Good God, he's not staying in my room.*

They went through the large revolving door and the air-conditioning hit Jerry in the face like a blast of frigid wind howling down from the North Pole. The lobby was dark, cold, and crowded. The decor was hotel-lobby modern, with a twist. There was faux marble, thick carpeting, palms and other plants commonly found in that ecological niche, and comfy chairs scattered around. The twist was in the decor.

The ersatz Middle Eastern theme was continued with walls made of pseudo-adobe bricks (at least Jerry hoped that they were pseudo; it rained far too often in southern Missouri for adobe to be a viable building material) and wooden beams coming out of the walls acting as false support columns. Jerry half-expected piles of straw (or maybe fake straw) strewn around the simulated flagstone flooring. The hotel staff all wore burnooses, like they were extras from *The Ten Commandments*. Religious art and iconography was scattered all over the walls, all with a cute, if not kitschy, turn.

It was all too much to take in. To avoid having to deal with it all, Jerry went around the knots of chatting guests, many of them women wearing MAGOG-welcoming tags, and marched up to the check-in counter, followed by Sascha.

"What are all these middle-aged Midwestern types doing here?" he asked in a quiet voice as they waited behind the red velvet rope for a clerk to check him in.

"This is the Mecca of Midwest tourism," Sascha said equally quietly as the white-haired woman ahead of them turned to stare suspiciously, caught a look at Sascha's face, and immediately turned away. "But it's also MAGOG's national convention, and, luckily for us, the Manger is one of the convention hotels."

MAGOG—Mothers Against Gods Or Goddesses—was one of those grassroots organizations that had sprung up overnight after some social tragedy or another, in this case a school shooting by some doped-up losers who claimed to be pagans. Jerry wasn't sure if MAGOG had actually ever accomplished anything over the years of its existence, but they sure knew how to generate noise and publicity.

One of the check-in clerks caught Jerry's eye and gestured him up to the counter. Sascha and Mushroom Daddy followed. It went pretty much like all big-hotel check-ins, with some fumbling around with the name the reservation had actually been made under. The clerk gave him a key, and Jerry gestured over his shoulder to Mushroom Daddy.

"Better give him one, too," he said, instantly knowing that somehow, some-way, they would regret this.

♠

Kentucky: Somewhere on the Road

THE ANGEL AND JOHN Fortune were somewhere on a mountain road half-way through Kentucky, singing along to a song on the Canned Heat tape playing in the eight-track.

The Angel wasn't familiar with much in the way of popular music from the past couple of decades. Her mother had frowned on most of it and wouldn't let her play it on the radio, and they never had much money for records, though her mother had a couple that she listened to obsessively, especially if she'd been drinking. Most of the people at the churches they attended over the years considered pop music the Devil's music, and the Angel had been pretty willing to accept their opinion.

But some of the tapes that Daddy had in his van were actually pretty good. The Canned Heat one they were listening to was fun, and oddly appropriate to their current situation. She and John Fortune had listened to "On the Road Again" over and over until they knew the lyrics by heart, at least those they could understand. They just made up their own words for the ones they couldn't, and sang along with the driving beat. She suddenly realized, almost guiltily, that they were having fun. She tried to stop.

"My dear mother left me when I was quite young," they sang as the Angel negotiated a sweeping downhill curve. "She said, 'Lord have mercy upon my wicked son.'"

Appropriate. How appropriate. She could hear her life in this old song. They could have been singing about her. She glanced at John Fortune. He was smiling, enjoying the adventure that his young life had turned into. *He has a good heart,* the Angel thought, *as well as steady courage and compassion.* Yet, the passing hours that they had spent together had shown her that he seemed more of a boy than the Savior of the world. *Is it possible,* she wondered, *that he hasn't yet realized who he is?*

"I ain't got no woman to call my special friend," John Fortune sang. He smiled at her, and the Angel felt a sudden warmth on her upper right thigh. She glanced down to see his hand resting there. She could feel the heat it radiated through the leather of her jumpsuit. She looked back up at him.

"You know, Angel," he said, "you're really beautiful."

She could feel herself blushing, but worse, she could feel the curse of her body betraying her again. He was only a boy—even worse, her Savior. How sinful was she if she could tempt her Savior into carnal thought? She shook her head. "I'm just a soldier in the army of My Lord," she said, looking grimly out the windshield.

John Fortune turned as much as his seat belt allowed to face her. "I know you're older than me," he said, his expression pleading, "but not by all that much. What's a couple of years?"

"Seven," she said, concentrating on the winding road before them.

"Seven!" John Fortune said, as if she'd just proved his point. "That's nothing! Why, my mom's almost that much older than my dad. And I'm mature for my age. Everyone says so. Besides, we have so much in common—"

The Angel shook her head. "John—"

"We're aces," he pointed out reasonably. "Both of us. And, uh, we're good aces, too. We use our powers to help people—"

"John—"

"Unless . . ." John Fortune suddenly looked downcast. He frowned at her, then sighed. "You must think I'm pretty stupid to think a hottie like you doesn't have a boyfriend already."

The Angel glanced at him, her heart in her throat at the sound of his voice. "No, John, no. I don't think you're stupid at all. And . . . you're right, actually. I don't have a boyfriend."

The recuperative powers of the young put a smile on his face again. "Well, great, then. Can we go out sometime? I promise you'll have a good time."

The Angel's answer was interrupted as the van's engine suddenly coughed, sputtered, and died right there on the highway. She glanced at John Fortune and sighed. This was too much to deal with now. Too much.

"We'll see," she said, "but first we have to take care of this, this breakdown, whatever it is. Then we have to get to Branson, where you'll be safe."

John Fortune nodded confidently. "Sure. First things first. I'm willing to wait. For you. What do you think is wrong with the van?"

They were still on the long downward glide. The Angel took her foot off the brake and let gravity do all the work.

"I have no idea," she said. "But I hope there's a town at the bottom of this mountain with a service station in it."

"Sure there is," John Fortune said. He leaned forward and punched the Canned Heat tape out of the eight-track. "Let's listen to this one again."

He put *Surrealistic Pillow* in the tape machine and "Somebody to Love" blared forth.

"I like this," John Fortune said. "You know, the chick singing sounds like that one who did that old song. You know?"

The Angel shook her head.

"'They Built This City on Rock and Roll.' Think it's her?" John Fortune asked.

The Angel shook her head again.

"I have no idea," she said, guiding the van down the mountain like a toboggan down a snowless hillside.

◆

Peaceable Kingdom: The Angels' Bower

THOUGH RAY HADN'T EXACTLY lied to Creighton, he had let him and Ackroyd both make unwarranted assumptions that he didn't want to explain at this time. With Sascha on the scene, he decided he'd better split before the eyeless ace picked something awkward out of his mind. He had to report to Barnett anyway, and see exactly what the hell was going on with Angel and the kid.

Ray made his excuses and dashed off, trying to diffuse any probes from Sascha by keeping a picture of Angel foremost in his thoughts. It wasn't difficult. She had real eye appeal, even when she was being grumpy. Which was almost always. He couldn't help wondering what she'd be like in the sack. Wonder what that body looked like under all the leather. Maybe framed, for a change, with lace.

On second thought, Ray thought, *screw the lace.* He had the feeling that she was a woman who looked best naked. Or maybe wearing only a thin, slippery sheen of sweat.

"We're here, sir," the cabby said, interrupting the most pleasant thought Ray had had in months.

Ray tossed the driver a couple of twenties. He slung his bag over his shoulder, jumped out of the cab without waiting for change, and took the steps up and into the lobby. He went straight to the elevator bank and whisked himself up to the penthouse. To the tip of the great glass pyramid that was the headquarters of the huge entertainment complex Barnett had designed to separate the suckers from their money. The elevator came to a smooth stop, chimed softly, and let him out into a corridor that ended in closed double doors guarded by men in nicely tailored suits and dark sunglasses.

He went down the corridor with the jauntiness of a mastiff approaching a couple of Pekinese.

"Billy," one said, stepping aside. "President Barnett is expecting you."

He opened the door and Ray entered the antechamber where Sally Lou was playing at receptionist. She looked at Ray with the gleam of a hungry tigress in her eyes. "We heard you got shot," she said.

"I got better," Ray said briefly. He still hadn't forgiven her for her prior treatment, but if she kept on looking at him like that he figured that eventually he'd forgive her for damn near anything. Angel was on his mind, but Sally Lou was definitely in reach. "Barnett—"

"—is waiting for you," Sally Lou interrupted. "Go right in."

Ray paused for a moment. "Later?" he asked.

Sally Lou looked at him coyly. "Maybe."

Ray went by her desk to Barnett's office door. He didn't like games. It looked like Sally Lou did. He could put up with it for a while if the end result was worth it, and it looked like Sally Lou might be. In the meantime, though, there was still a kid somewhere on the loose in the wilds of America in a van with Angel at the wheel.

Leo Barnett didn't look too concerned about the still-missing John Fortune and the now-missing Angel, but then he rarely looked concerned about anything. He was on the phone when Ray came into his office, sitting behind his big desk of dark wood, cigar in hand, nodding expressively as he talked.

"I know talent is scarce right now, Sammy boy, but I tell you what—" He made some kind of face at Ray that the ace couldn't interpret and gestured broadly for him to sit in the chair before his desk. Ray did. "You find me some boys who know how to do a job and will keep their mouths shut. Sure. Sure. Of *course.*" Barnett rolled his eyes. He hung up the phone and looked at Ray, smiling but shaking his head.

"I've got to find me some good boys, Ray. Boys like you who know how to take orders and keep their traps shut. Boys who have a little extra juice, you know what I mean?" Ray nodded. "Whatever happened to that Mechanic fellow?"

"Belew?" Ray shook his head. The Mechanic had led the first operation that Ray had ever been on—the failed attempt, through no fault of their own, to extract the American hostages from Iran, way back in the Carter administration. "We haven't crossed paths in years."

"He's a stud I'd like to have on our side when the Allumbrados come to town. How about that Straight Arrow?"

"Nephi Callendar? He's a desk jockey now."

"George Battle? He was just an ordinary joe, but tough as the dickens."

"Uh." Ray didn't really want to get into much detail about Battle's fate. "I'm afraid he's dead."

"Pity." Barnett looked up to the ceiling. "Oh Lord, see me through these trying times." He looked back at Ray. "What can I do for you, son?"

Ray remembered something Barnett had just said. "The Allumbrados are coming to town?" he asked. "Contarini's outfit?"

"Of course, son. Of course. We've got the baby Jesus. They're going to come after him sure as Satan is frying souls in the Fiery Pit right this very minute."

Ray nodded. That was good. He'd like to get his hands on Butcher Dagon again. This time he'd bite the bastard's tail off at the root and strangle him with it. Still . . . "They've got a whole cadre of *credenti* and believers and shit working for them," Ray said. "Some tough-ass mercs. Some aces."

"Don't I know that? That's why I've been on the horn all day trying to beef up my forces."

"Who do you have?" Ray asked.

Barnett looked at him. "Well, there's you."

Ray nodded impatiently. "Yes."

"And Angel, of course."

Ray pursed his lips. "I don't know about her."

Barnett leaned forward, pointing his cigar at Ray. "Well, son, she got the baby Jesus. You got bubkes. Besides—" He leaned back in his chair, took a deep pull on the cigar, and blew smoke toward the heavens. "—she said the same thing about you."

"What *exactly* did she say?" Ray asked with narrowed eyes.

"Don't get your panties in a twist, son. I know she can be difficult. But if you handle her right, she'll eat right out of your hand."

Ray frowned. "Well, who else do we have?"

Barnett put his cigar in his mouth, his hands behind his head, and his feet on his desk. "Well, there's Sally Lou. But she's not much use, unless we want to screw the Allumbrados to death."

"She can do that?" Ray asked, startled. There was an ace . . . years ago. But she had disappeared.

"Don't be so damn literal," Barnett said. "Maybe she couldn't *really* screw those boys to death. But she *could* tire them out some."

"Oh," Ray said. He waited for Barnett to go on, but when he didn't Ray finally said, "That's it, then?"

"Oh, there's Alejandro. And we got boys with guns. Plenty of those. But so has the cardinal. And this battle won't be won with guns, I don't think. I've got some guys on the line who might be useful."

Ray nodded. He agreed with Barnett. It didn't seem to be shaping up in Barnett's favor, but long odds never made Ray run from a fight.

"Well, what about Angel and the boy?" he asked. "Are they okay? Are they almost here?"

Barnett sighed. "She's out there somewhere with the boy in tow. I expect she'll be reporting in sometime soon."

"She's out there *somewhere?*" Ray asked. "That's the best you can do?"

Barnett poured himself a couple of fingers from the decanter that sat on the side of his desk, added some ice, and took a long drink from his tall glass, the ice cubes tinkling merrily against its side. "You've seen her. She's a big, strong girl. She can take care of herself."

I hope so, Ray thought. *I really, really hope so.*

♥

Branson, Missouri: The Angels' Bower

"A SUITE OF OUR own," Digger Downs said. "Pretty sweet, huh?"

Fortunato looked around the spacious living area with a sofa, love seat, widescreen television, and minibar. It was somewhat more luxurious than the quarters he'd shared with fivescore monks the past sixteen years or so. The angel decor, though, was not exactly to his taste.

"Does it have to be this . . . colorful?" he asked.

"Well . . ."

The room was done in pastel shades of green, blue, and pinkish-red that, despite their muted tones, managed to be quite garish when taken together. The bathroom was black, pink, and white faux marble tiles, which were laid in swirling patterns that hurt Fortunato's eyes. He hadn't been in Digger's bedroom, but his had a round, beanbag-shaped bed that was enshrouded with gossamer-thin fabric that looked like puce-colored mosquito netting. Worse yet, there were photos and paintings, and even relics of all sorts all over the damn place.

"It's the best we could do on short notice." Digger shrugged. "The place is crowded even by their usual standards. There's some kind of big convention that's taking a lot of the rooms."

"Barnett seems to have bought himself a license to print money with this place," Fortunato said.

Digger shrugged again. "Barnum was right, but we have our own fish to fry. What's the plan?"

Fortunato roused himself. "Angel was bringing the boy here for some reason. Suppose we poke around a little and find out why?"

"All right," Digger said, sensing another intriguing story line. "Anything specific we should look for?"

Fortunato shook his head. "I don't know. You're the investigative reporter."

Fortunato looked thoughtful. "A talk with the head man himself might be in order."

"Barnett?" Digger asked. "Yeah. Go straight for the top, I always say."

"Could you swing it?" Fortunato asked.

"Maybe."

"One thing, though," Fortunato said. "I need to find some way to recharge my batteries."

"If you're looking to put hookers on the company charge card—" Digger started.

Fortunato grimaced. "It may come to that. Maybe. But I think I've moved beyond that. To something new."

"Like what?" Digger asked, plainly intrigued.

"It's all so new," Fortunato said, "that I'm still not sure about it. But I'll probably know it when I see it."

"Probably?" Digger asked.

"Hey, man," Fortunato said, "that's the best I can do."

♣

Peaceable Kingdom: The Manger

"IS THIS A NONSMOKING room?" Mushroom Daddy asked.

Jerry, Mushroom Daddy, and Sascha were in the living room of their suite trying to figure out what to do next. It was furnished in a sort of 1950-ish style that Jerry kind of liked, though the Naugahyde sofa was slippery and the orange carpet was a little bright.

Sascha looked at Daddy curiously. "No. You can light up if you want. Do you happen to have some decent cigars on you?"

Daddy shuddered. "Tobacco? Never touch the stuff, man. It's, like, a killer." He looked thoughtful. "Except of course for those groovy organic Cuban cigars that teenaged señoritas roll up on their soft, creamy thighs. Those are okay, every now and then."

Jerry frowned. "What are you talking about, then?" A sudden thought struck him. "Not—"

Daddy nodded. He reached into an inside vest pocket and pulled out a baggie packed with rich green weed.

"Jesus Christ," Jerry groaned. "You brought that with you on the plane?"

"Sure," Daddy said. "I always take some weed along when I travel. It's the best, man. Here, try some. Um, you don't happen to have a water pipe on you? I couldn't bring mine 'cause I didn't bring any luggage."

Jerry collapsed on the Naugahyde sofa. *I guess it's true,* he thought. *God does take care of drunks, little children, and idiots. Sometimes, at least.*

Sascha looked as amused as an eyeless man could. "No. I'm afraid I left my bong at home."

"Oh, that's okay, man," Daddy assured him. "I brought some rolling papers." He sat down next to Jerry on the sofa and bent over the glass and chrome coffee table in front of it and dexterously rolled a fat joint.

"Got a light, man?" he asked Jerry.

Jerry shook his head. "No. I don't smoke."

"Here," Sascha said. He tossed him a book of matches.

"Thanks, man." Daddy carefully lit the joint and took a long toke. "Want some?" he asked, offering the jay to Jerry.

Jerry closed his eyes and shook his head. *What the hell,* he asked himself. *Why not?* He accepted the joint and took a tentative pull. The smoke roiled down his throat and into his lungs. It was warm, but without harshness. Not a cough in the carload, as the old saying went. He looked at Mushroom Daddy in surprise.

"Smooth, huh?" Daddy said proudly. "It's my own. I grow it organically. Totally chemically free. Nothing in it but good old Mother Nature's goodness, man."

"Let me have a hit of that," Sascha said, crossing over to the sofa.

"Sure!" Daddy said. "You dudes can split that one while I roll another."

Jerry took another hit and passed it to Sascha. He held the smoke deep in his lungs, then let it out in a fragrant cloud. It smelled great, Jerry thought. He could already feel himself starting to relax.

Sascha took a long hit. "Not bad," he said in a choked voice as he held the smoke in his lungs for as long as possible. He finally let it out in a long *whooooosh.* "In fact, pretty good."

Daddy was rolling a second joint when someone knocked on the door, and the three looked at each other, trepidation in at least two sets of eyes.

"Sascha, you get the door," Jerry said. "Daddy, get your shit out of sight. I'll turn up the air conditioner."

There was another knock. It sounded loud and impatient. What, Jerry thought, his panic growing unaccountably, if it was the cops? They probably had some mean-ass cops in Branson. He didn't even want to think of what they'd do to someone caught smoking dope in the Peaceable Kingdom.

"Coming," Sascha called out. He went up to the door and stood before it.

"Who is it?" Jerry asked.

"I don't know," Sascha said. "I can't see."

"Well," Daddy said, "ask him."

"Who is it?" Sascha asked the door.

"It's me," a voice called out gruffly. "Billy Ray. Sascha, that you? Open the goddamned door."

"Damn it," Jerry said. "The Feds."

"Oh, man," Daddy said. "The man. Oh, man."

"Just a minute," Sascha said.

"Open the windows—" Jerry said.

"Oh, man," Daddy said. "Busted, man. Who's going to take care of all my plants if they send me to the slam?"

"Can't," Sascha said. "Hotel windows. Can't open them."

The door rattled ominously.

"Are you guys in trouble in there? I'll break the door down—"

"He will, too," Sascha said.

Jerry made a helpless gesture with his hands.

"Open it. Open it. Maybe he won't smell anything."

Sascha nodded. He took the chain off the door and threw it open. Ray stood out in the hallway, hand up and ready to pound on the door again.

"Hello, Ray," Sascha said with a smile. "Come on in, Ray."

Ray entered the room suspiciously. "What the hell is going on in here?"

"Nothing," Sascha said.

"Nothing," Jerry said.

"Nothing, man," Daddy said, trying to shove the baggy full of weed farther between the sofa cushions.

Ray stopped, sniffed the air, and frowned thunderously. "Are you guys smoking pot?"

Sascha, Jerry, and Mushroom Daddy looked at each other.

"Us, uh—" Jerry began.

"You're holding out on me, you bastards?" Ray said. "I haven't gotten high since I did some hash with a bunch of Afghani warlords. I had to smoke with them, of course. Had to put them at their ease."

"Well," Daddy said, "if you like Afghani hash, you'll love—"

"Daddy—" Jerry began.

"It's all right," Sascha said, as if suddenly remembering that he could read minds. He sank down gratefully into the love seat across the coffee table from the sofa. "He's cool."

"Of course I'm cool," Ray said, sitting down next to Daddy. "What, you think I'm a narc just because I work for the Feds?"

"Course not," Jerry said as Daddy produced the baggy of pot and an already rolled joint that he handed to Ray.

"Thanks," Ray said. He lit up and took a toke. "Of course," he said in a strangled voice, "if I was my old boss, that tight-ass Nephi Callendar—" He paused to blow smoke and take another hit. "—your asses would all be headed for the nearest federal slam, right now. Hey. Very nice."

Daddy nodded happily. "I grow it myself."

Ray looked at him. "So, what's the story, man, are you some kind of burned-out hippie, or are you an ace?"

Daddy shrugged. "I don't know. All I know is that I can grow things. They taste good, and they do good things for your body and your head."

"Maybe," Jerry suggested, "you should call yourself the Green Thumb."

Ray frowned, and then started to laugh. Within moments they were all giggling like hopeless fools. It felt good, Jerry thought. Really good. Ray handed Daddy the joint. He took a toke and passed it on to Jerry.

They sat together, smoking, talking, and laughing, for the next hour. Ray turned out to be a fount of surprisingly amusing stories about foreign and domestic diplomats. Every now and then Jerry would just say, "Green Thumb," and they'd all laugh again, though Jerry had the feeling that Mushroom Daddy didn't see anything particularly funny in the name and was maybe seriously considering it.

They finally polished off their fifth or sixth joint and Ray looked at them all seriously.

"I'm hungry," he said. "Room service, or buffet?"

They all thought about it for a moment, and then as one man said, "Buffet!"

Daddy gathered up his paraphernalia, but Ray made him leave it all in the suite. Together they descended in the elevator to wreak havoc on the first buffet that they could find.

♠

Peaceable Kingdom: Loaves and Fishes

RAY WAS RAVENOUS. HE wanted either food or women, vast quantities of either. It didn't matter which, but he wanted them now. Everyone else seemed fixated on the idea of food, so that was all right with him.

They rode the elevator to the ground floor, passing the hotel restaurants in unspoken accord. They didn't want to go sit down at a table, wait for a waiter to show up to take their drink order, come back to take their food order, go turn it into the kitchen, and then wait for the kitchen to cook it, wait for the waiter to go pick it up and bring it to their table, and after all that get only a miserly little plate of food and they were all pretty sure that a plate of rolls or a small loaf of wheat bread wouldn't hold them in check while they waited.

They hit the street with hunger rumbling in their stomachs and anticipation roiling in their brains. Their eyes focused on the building before them. LOAVES AND FISHES!!! STEAKS! CHOPS! SEAFOOD! SALAD! DESSERTS! ALL YOU CAN EAT! They looked at each other and nodded, even Sascha. They had found their Mecca.

They descended on the restaurant like a swarm of locusts, and after paying their $14.95 apiece at the door (Ray covered Mushroom Daddy with his personal credit card, bitching that Angel still had Barnett's.) they tore through the buffet line and salad bar, leaving devastation in their wake like a category-five hurricane.

Ray got himself a steak, a couple of pork chops, and a whole roast chicken. He decided to leave the carving station—turkey, ham, and lamb—for later. He piled on some mashed potatoes, french fries, buttered noodles, and corn on the cob. Dessert was tempting, but he had no more room on his tray. He took a large ice tea, unsweetened, at the drink station. He was pretty thirsty.

He joined Daddy, Sascha, and Creighton at the table where they were already plowing through their food. Sascha had taken the sweet route, going for all the desserts he could grab, including an entire Black Forest cake. Creighton had cleaned out the carving station, and had a couple of made-to-order omelets, while Mushroom Daddy, apparently a vegetarian, had about half the salad bar in front of him, as well as a selection of hot vegetables.

"This isn't bad," he said around a mouthful of potato salad, "but mine is better."

"Green Thumb," Sascha said.

No one laughed. Somehow it wasn't as funny as before. Maybe they weren't as stoned, or maybe they were all just concentrating on the food.

"Mmmm," Creighton said, at least acknowledging Daddy's remark.

Ray just kept on eating. The food was indescribably good. Ray wasn't sure why. Sure, he was stoned and Daddy's pot was potent. Powerful yet with a curious mellowing effect, it heightened Ray's senses, intensifying his sense of smell, taste, and touch. He smiled as he popped a piece of steak in his mouth and chewed slowly and thoughtfully. Too bad Angel wasn't here, he thought. He'd like to see her smoke a joint of Daddy's weed. It would really loosen her up.

That was it. He felt really, totally, 100 percent relaxed for the first time in weeks. Probably months. He was back in Branson with few prospects except a return bout with Butcher Dagon and an unknown number of henchmen with unguessable powers and abilities, but that was okay. That was in the future. He would handle it as it came, like he always did. Tonight he was just a guy enjoying a meal. If he wasn't with friends, he was with comrades, and that was just about as good. He never had many friends in his life, but he'd had comrades plenty and he'd never let them down. He hadn't won every fight he'd ever been in, and over the years he'd lost some of the steadfast men who'd stood at his side. But that was life. At least he knew that he always did the best that he could and he never ran from a fight.

He tore off a chicken leg and looked around as he bit a chunk out of it. Mushroom Daddy had just said something, he'd missed exactly what, that had set both Creighton and Sascha laughing. Daddy joined them and then he did, too. He laughed aloud at nothing, though apparently, if you believed Barnett, Armageddon was just around the corner and the fate of the world was hanging in the balance.

"Let it hang," Ray said aloud. The others all looked at him.

"What?" Creighton asked.

Ray shook his head. "Nothing." He looked around the table at the three, shaking his head. "You are three crazy sons of bitches." He picked up his ice-tea glass and tipped it in their directions. "I salute you all."

They laughed, grabbed their glasses, and returned the toast, and Ray laughed with them, the hardest of all.

◆

Somewhere in Kentucky

IT WAS THE CARBURETOR. Fortunately there was a small town at the bottom of the mountain with a service station. It didn't have the right type of carburetor in stock, though the guy knew a guy with a junkyard that probably had a couple of old hippie vans laying around it somewhere. The Angel told them they were in a rush. She flashed the platinum card and the service station attendant managed to take his eyes off her (he barely seemed to notice that John Fortune was glowing) and he took off to find the part. The Angel checked them into the town's single decrepit motel, figuring that some sleep on a real bed would do them some good. She'd told the mechanic where they'd be, and to come and get them as soon as he was finished.

"You know," John Fortune said, after they'd checked in, "I've never shared a motel room with a girl before."

The Angel forestalled a grimace. This, she didn't need. She said the first thing that popped into her mind. "I have to take a shower."

John Fortune nodded, his eyes wide as if he were considering the possibilities. "Sure," he finally said. "I'll just wait for you here."

The Angel went into the bathroom and quietly locked the door. Maybe, she thought, if she drew this out as long as she could, John Fortune would get distracted by the TV or something. It didn't seem likely.

The water came out of the showerhead at a trickle. She took as long as she could, but the mildew and fungus stains on the stall wall did not incline her to linger. The towels were paper-thin and didn't really dry her body as much as blot it kind of fruitlessly. She wrapped a paper-thin towel around her form and stuck her head out of the bathroom, but John Fortune was lying on the room's single bed, sound asleep, a bright aura shining all around him.

The Angel sighed in relief. He'd been very tired, she supposed. She watched him for a few minutes. His face was angelic, if not exactly godlike. He looked like everybody's favorite son.

She dried herself as best she could and shrugged into her jumpsuit again. It was tough to put on while she was still damp. She wished that she'd thought to bring her duffel bag along so she could change into one of her spare suits, but it was still sitting in the Escalade back in New Hampton. She hoped that Ray had remembered to return the SUV to the rental agency before the late charges started to pile up. He probably hadn't, though. He didn't seem particularly dependable, even if he did seem to have some uses.

She tiptoed into the tiny room and sat carefully in the creaky chair next to the bed. Something nagging at the back of her brain made her feel jumpy. It was a sensation that something was breathing on her. Snuffling about her in the dark. She put it down to nervousness about the Allumbrados somehow striking their trail. When someone knocked on their door in the middle of the night, she jumped.

It turned out to be the mechanic. He was finished with the van.

The Angel awoke John Fortune. He seemed groggy and at first was disinclined to get up. She felt his forehead in concern. He was hot, of course. She wondered if he was running a temperature, or if it was his ace metabolism acting up. She knew that it could take some getting used to. When her card had turned ten years ago it took months before she'd gotten used to hers. Her mother never had. She never believed her when she said she was hungry. That she was starving. She just called her a glutton, and said it was a miracle that she wasn't a fat pig because of all the food she ate. It was hard to be hungry all the time.

She finally got John Fortune up. It was about three o'clock in the morning by her watch. She overpaid the mechanic enormously. She felt guilty about it, but as Ray had said, Barnett could afford it and after all she was doing God's work.

They hit the road again in the dark. The Angel, even though she knew it would add a couple of hours to their trip, was more determined than ever to take the detour she'd been considering. Something was driving her. Calling her, really. She wondered if it was old ghosts.

Whatever the source, it could not be denied.

♥

Peaceable Kingdom: The Angels' Bower

IT WAS DARK BY the time Nighthawk and his group arrived at the Peaceable Kingdom. A limo had been waiting for them at the airport and taken them to the suite reserved for them at the Angels' Bower. The hotel was quite crowded.

They went up to their suite. Nighthawk thought it was a little kitschy, but kept quiet because Magda was quite taken with it and Nighthawk saw no need to stir up trouble. Usher was satisfied because it was comfortable. That was all he needed. Nighthawk checked in, and they waited. They didn't have to wait for long.

The doorbell rang within half an hour and Usher answered it. A bellhop and a luggage cart piled high with massive trunks stood in the corridor outside. "Mr. Nighthawk?" the brightly scrubbed young man asked.

"Inside," Usher said, stepping back.

"Special freight delivery," the bellboy said, wheeling the cart into the room.

Nighthawk nodded. He gave the boy a twenty. He knew what it was like to be in his position.

"Thanks," the bellhop said. "Want me to unload the cart?"

"No thanks," Nighthawk said. "We'll handle it."

"Have a nice stay at the Peaceable Kingdom," the boy said at the door. Usher smiled at him, nodded, and closed and locked it.

"Our agent came through," Usher said, taking a heavy trunk off the cart as Nighthawk watched.

"Of course," Nighthawk said. He watched Usher and Magda unload and assemble their equipment for a while, then suddenly stood and stretched. "I'm going to go for a walk. I want to get the feel of this place."

"What are you sensing, John?" Usher asked. Magda looked up from assembling an automatic shotgun.

Nighthawk shook his head. "I don't know yet." He nodded at the weapons they were unshipping from their padded trunks. "But we'll need those before it's all over."

Magda grunted wordlessly and went back to assembling weaponry. There was something of satisfaction on her face. *If it was in her,* Nighthawk thought, *she'd be whistling right now.*

"Go find some food when you're done," Nighthawk said. "Needless to say, room service would not be a good idea."

Usher shook his head sadly. "Grubbs always loved room service."

Magda grunted wordlessly again as Nighthawk went out into the corridor and took the elevator to the lobby below.

It wasn't that late, but the lobby was already quiet. Outside, the night was pleasantly cool. Nighthawk walked around the grounds. He didn't have much company. The patrons of the Peaceable Kingdom seemed to be part of the early-to-bed, early-to-rise crowd, even when on vacation.

He passed by a couple of night walkers like himself, once a knot of twoscore or so women wearing name tags that proclaimed themselves to be members of MAGOG, whatever that was, probably on the way back to their hotel from some function or another that had just ended. They were chatting animatedly, clearly enjoying themselves.

The Peaceable Kingdom was, Nighthawk admitted, a nice, well-groomed place, sanitary and unthreatening, where those who liked their fun safe and predictable could have a good time.

And why not? These people worked hard for their money. If they wanted someplace to come that was a little mysterious, a little exotic, yet catered to what they believed, upheld their view of the world and affirmed their place in it, that was fine by him. One thing that his long life had taught him was that people needed different things from life. The Peaceable Kingdom served the needs of its patrons admirably.

He was a little worried, though, about what might happen here in the next couple of days. Nighthawk hoped that the cardinal and his team would stop the Angel long before she reached the Peaceable Kingdom with her charge. In Nighthawk's experience, high-powered weaponry and tourists didn't mix very well.

He could have skipped all this. He could have faded off into the night or taken the train out of town with Cameo. But two things had held him back, one practical, one theoretical. Practically, he didn't want to cut and run, leaving a pissed-off cardinal wondering what had happened to him. Contarini didn't take desertion lightly, and Nighthawk didn't want to be looking over his shoulder for the rest of what still might be a rather long life. Theoretically, his vision to the contrary, what if the cardinal was right and the boy was the Anti-Christ? Revelations were extraordinarily difficult to interpret, and stranger things had happened in this world. Granted, not many. But the cardinal, for all his demagoguery, was an educated man. He knew things that Nighthawk could not even begin to guess at. What if he were right, and the boy was the Anti-Christ, or at least some kind of tool of the Devil? Nighthawk couldn't walk away from this until he was sure, one way or the other. And his gut told him that it was all coming together. Soon. That all the forces for good and evil were gathering in one place. And that place was not called, this time, the Plains of Megiddo, but rather Branson, Missouri, and that it was his fate to be among their number.

He had already traveled far on this holy road, and had learned much. He had to walk the final few miles and see what waited for him at the end of it, no matter how rocky or dangerous the way.

♠   ♥   ♦   ♣

Chapter Nine

Peaceable Kingdom: Barnett's Office

AS IT TURNED OUT, Barnett was more than happy to see Fortunato and Digger. Fortunato was in fact surprised at how eager he was to see them, as he invited them up to his headquarters after a simple phone call on Digger's part. Barnett's penthouse office was located at the top of the Angels' Bower, at the end of a short corridor guarded by two men in suits and dark glasses. Fortunato didn't need special power to tell him that they were cops. He'd seen plenty of their type before he'd left the world. Since Barnett was an ex-president, that meant Secret Service. He scanned their minds as Downs gave them their names. They were nats. Competent enough, but nothing more. They knew nothing other than the fact that Barnett was expecting them. *Good to know,* Fortunato thought, *that we aren't walking into a trap of some kind.*

He was still surprised, and a little suspicious, at Barnett's eagerness to meet with them.

The antechamber to Barnett's office was like that of many other business offices. The decor lacked the faux Middle East crap that infested the other parts of the Peaceable Kingdom Fortunato had seen. A very decorative blonde sat at the receptionist's desk. She looked at Fortunato with almost predatory interest and flashed an inviting smile.

"Mr. Fortunato. President Barnett is waiting for you in his office. Please go right in."

"Fortunato is fine," he told her. "For future reference."

"Fortunato." Her voice caressed his name. Her look promised more.

"Great," Digger said. "Let's go."

The blonde took on an expression of professional regret. "I'm afraid that President Barnett would like to have a few words with Fortunato in private. I'm sure you understand."

Digger frowned. "Well. Not really. But if I must wait to see the great man, then I must wait." He perched casually on one corner of the receptionist's desk. "Have you ever considered a career in modeling?" he asked as Fortunato knocked on the office door.

Fortunato glanced back to see the blonde regard Digger with polite distaste as Barnett called out, "Come in."

Fortunato entered his office, closing the door behind him. He took a few steps, then stopped, looking all around.

Is everything fake in this place? He was standing in a replica of the White House's Oval Office, down to the insignia woven into the carpet, the desk, and the draped flags behind it. Sitting at the desk was a handsome, well-preserved man, perhaps in his fifties. Fortunato recognized Barnett, though he had been out of the country during both terms of his presidency. Before his career had turned to politics, Barnett had been a popular conservative evangelical preacher. Fortunato had never been politically active, though he knew that Barnett's attitude toward wild carders wasn't exactly benevolent. He could extrapolate further how Barnett felt about mixed-race wild carders who had once pimped women and dealt drugs and were now Buddhist monks.

In the old days Fortunato would have read his mind without a second thought. Now, after the years in the monastery had leached him of his arrogance and taught him something about humility, he thought about it first, then jumped into his mind anyway. His son's life was on the line. It wouldn't have surprised him if Barnett was involved some way in the attempted kidnapping, and this was a sure way to find out. What he read there, though, surprised him.

"Fortunato!" Barnett said, rising from behind his desk and extending his hand. "It's a pleasure, a real pleasure, to finally meet you."

Fortunato came forward and guardedly took Barnett's hand. His handshake was firm and strong. His smile was sincere, as were his words of greeting. Barnett *was* genuinely glad to see him. "Sit down," he said.

Fortunato did.

"Drink?" He indicated the cut glass container in easy reach on his desk. "Oh. Can Buddhist monks drink alcohol?"

"Some more than most men," Fortunato said. "I don't, however."

"Fine, fine." Barnett sat in his own chair and beamed across the desk. "Well. Glad to see that you've turned your life around and become a brother of the cloth. So to speak."

"Forgive me if I seem impatient," Fortunato said. "But there are some questions I'd like answered."

"No doubt." Barnett smiled back. "But couldn't you read my mind to get your answers?"

I could, Fortunato thought, *and I already did, at least partially.* "You know that I turned my back on my powers when I left this country."

"So the story goes," Barnett said. "But I've heard strange things about your recent doings in New York City. People say you came back from the dead and stopped an ace from destroying the Jokertown Clinic. Hell, people are saying you're still in New York doing all kinds of miracles. Healing the sick. Curing the deaf. Turning baking soda into crack, for all I know."

"Careful," Fortunato said. "Your prejudices are showing."

"Hell, man, the only thing I'm prejudiced against is sin. You know that."

Fortunato shook his head, as if unconvinced. "Was that your ace who attacked the Jokertown Clinic?"

Barnett laughed out loud. "Is *that* what you think?"

"I don't know what to think. All I know is that someone with some very powerful underlings wants me dead, Peregrine dead, and our son dead."

"That ain't me," Barnett said. "That's the cardinal's boys."

"The cardinal's boys?" Fortunato asked.

Barnett nodded affably. "Pay attention, now," he said. "The boys after you are the Allumbrados, the Enlightened Ones, as they're so puffed up with pride to call themselves. It's an ancient and secret office of the Catholic Church. Goes way back. Has ties to another Holy Office that still exists officially, but hasn't seen much action lately."

Fortunato frowned. "The Inquisition?"

"That's the one." Barnett nodded. "These papal boys are run by Cardinal Romulus Contarini. Real nasty stuff, actually. They hire all kinds of criminals and scum. Jokers and aces and real people alike—"

"'Real people'?" Barnett was so smooth that Fortunato had to occasionally remind himself not to forget where the evangelist was really coming from.

Barnett shrugged apologetically. "I don't like to use the term 'nats.' It's demeaning."

"Uh-huh."

"All right," Barnett said. "Just between us, let's cut the crap. You know that I've preached against the wild card, but it's the virus I've preached against, not its victims. The virus has turned its prey into things both lesser and greater than human. They get my pity, my help, and whatever solace I can give them. But the virus—the virus has caused unimaginable misery in this world and it must inevitably be eradicated."

"You haven't changed a bit," Fortunato said.

Barnett shook his head. "I haven't. But the world has. There's no doubt in my mind that the End Days are upon us. The signs are all around. Israel. Moral decay. The wild card itself. The downfall of Communism." He paused and looked seriously at Fortunato. "The boy, John Fortune."

Fortunato looked back just as hard at Barnett. "What about him?"

"He is, without a doubt, Jesus Christ reincarnate. The Second Coming is upon us and the battle of the Millennium is about to start." Barnett held out his hand, forestalling Fortunato's incredulous reply. "Now hear me out. I'm not the only one who realizes that John Fortune will play a critical role in the upcoming struggle. Contarini and his Allumbrados believe this as well. Only, wrongheaded as usual, the damned Papists think he's the Anti-Christ. They believe that he must die, while I *know*, I know as well as I know the love of my God, that he must be shielded. He must be sheltered and protected until he realizes his fate and brings about the Kingdom of God on Earth."

Fortunato, who had edged forward on his seat during Barnett's speech, sank back in the chair, flabbergasted at the ex-president's words.

"I know," Barnett said at the stunned look on Fortunato's face. "How can they be so wrong? How can they be that stupid? Well, God has, if you forgive the metaphor, thrown us a curveball on this one. I could hardly suspect myself that He would choose a stained vessel such as Peregrine to be the mother of His Son, but God does work in mysterious ways—"

"Wait a minute," Fortunato interrupted, unable to contain himself any longer. "What about me?"

"Well, what about you?"

"I was there when he was conceived. I can assure you that this was not a case of virgin birth."

Barnett shook his head. "We all have a place in God's plan. Some of us just aren't aware of what that place is."

"And some of us," Fortunato said, "are so certain that they think they can put others in their place."

"Well, just so. Look. I know you want to help the boy. I want to help the boy. I showed you my hole cards. Time for you to show me yours. Go ahead. Read my mind. I'm not faking it."

Fortunato smiled like a wolf. "All right," he admitted. "I already did. That's the only reason why I'm still sitting here, talking to you."

"Outstanding!" Barnett beamed. "You know I'm telling the truth then. You know that I'm sincere." He stood suddenly and went over to a large window overlooking his domain. "C'mere. I want you to see something."

Fortunato levered himself out of the chair and joined Barnett at the window. He towered over the nat. They stood on the opposite side of many fundamental beliefs. But Fortunato had the distinct impression that Barnett was not only fearless in his presence, he was actually glad of Fortunato's prowess and was confident that he could turn it to his service. *If ego was a wild card power,* Fortunato thought, *he'd have it in spades.*

"Look down there," Barnett said, pointing to the square below them, pulsing with activity.

"At what?" Fortunato inquired.

"At all of it. Because all of it can be yours."

Fortunato queried the ex-president with raised eyebrows.

"You want money? It's there for the taking. You want power? Say the word and your word is law. You want entertainment, excitement? It's available in infinite varieties in infinite supply. It'll never run out. You want women?" Barnett winked at him. "We're grown men here. You like that sweet little blonde thing out there at the reception desk? You can have her. You can have damn near everyone in this place and let me tell you, the infinite variety, the gut-grabbing excitement of *that* will never run out, my friend."

Fortunato smiled again. "And in return all you want is my soul?"

Barnett put his hand on Fortunato's shoulder and laughed aloud. "Your *soul*? You think I want your *soul*? Your soul can go to Hell for all I care, and it probably will." Barnett shook his head, chuckling. "No. I want your help. I want you to join with my little group as we stand against those damned Papists."

Fortunato put his hand on Barnett's shoulder, and the smile on Barnett's face slipped a bit as he gripped it hard. The decision came to him, suddenly it seemed, but with all the power of a revelation from God. Once this was over he would return to the monastery and rejoin his brothers on the pathway to enlightenment. But from now on he wouldn't allow himself to be so single-minded. He would welcome messages, even visits, from the outside world, and perhaps he would someday walk in it again himself. But as nothing more than a father, as part of a family, and as a humble monk.

"That's fine, then, because I don't want money. I don't want power. Not even women. I just want to see the boy, and be sure that he's safe."

"Hell, son, that's easy enough. I could have him here in twenty minutes, if that's what you want."

Fortunato frowned. "Why haven't you brought him in earlier then?"

"Jesus Christ, Fortunato, excuse my French, do you have to read my mind again to figure it out? The battle lines are drawn, son. Armageddon is coming as surely as the dawn, and we're in the weak position. The enemy is legion. We are few and though our hearts are pure I've got more faith in guns and big, strong aces than I do in the virtue of our souls.

"He's safer where he is now. Sure, the cardinal has made a couple of lame attempts on him, but my people have done all right so far in thwarting the old Papal ass-kisser. I want John Fortune here only when we're ready to meet them face-to-face and kick their sorry butts back to the Vatican."

"And you think my joining your side will tip the battle?"

Barnett looked at him with a calculating expression. "Once you were the most powerful ace on the face of the Earth. Even that prissy little alien Tachyon thought so. Sure, there were guys around who could twist you into a pretzel. If you'd let them get their hands on you. But there was a time when there was nothing you couldn't do." He paused for a moment. "There was a time."

Fortunato smiled. "I'm back."

"Are you?" Barnett asked him. "I hope so. I truly hope so." He went back to his desk and toggled the intercom. "Sally Lou, sweetie. Get me Bruckner on the phone. Got a job for him. Thanks, honey."

"Who's Bruckner?" Fortunato asked.

Barnett smiled. "He's the man you want when you have a special delivery that just has to make it through on time."

♣

Peaceable Kingdom: The Manger

RAY WOKE UP FEELING great. He had a touch of indigestion, but that was only to be expected considering the amount he'd wolfed down before staggering back to Jerry's hotel suite. They had an extra bedroom since they hadn't called Ackroyd yet, so he hit the sack instead of making his way back to his room in the Angels' Bower and conked out like a baby who'd just crawled a marathon.

He had no dreams, good or bad, and when he awoke it was with a totally clear head. There was no foggy pot-induced brain-cramping residue. He just felt fit and ready for the day. Ready for just about anything, in fact. He stretched lithely, feeling all his muscles glide smoothly in place, pain-free and worry-free for the first time in what felt like a long, long time. He went into the living room.

Mushroom Daddy was still snoring on the couch. He watched him for a moment, regarding him like one would a favored dog, thinking that the hippie wasn't that bad after all. Thinking that somehow this would all work out. Thinking that he'd like to see Angel again, but that would have to wait. He should, he thought, go over to the Bower and see Barnett and find out exactly where she and the kid were.

Behind him, someone cleared their throat. He turned. Jerry and Sascha had come out of their bedroom. Jerry was yawning. Sascha was frowning.

"What," Sascha asked, "does Barnett have to do with all this?"

Yazoo City, Mississippi

THE ANGEL AND JOHN Fortune reached Yazoo City by morning. The land through which they'd driven had changed from mountainous to flat, though the road became older, bumpier, and no easier on the old van. Sometimes the Angel thought it would take a miracle to get them all the way to Branson. Sometimes it seemed that it was only her faith that kept her going on this mad cross-country trip, her faith and the eager innocence of the boy Savior sitting next to her, his eagerness for life radiating like heat.

"What's planted in all those fields?" John Fortune asked as they rolled by mile after mile of flat Mississippi Delta country, the rich brown soil of which nourished rows of waist-high plants.

"Cotton," the Angel answered briefly. Cotton was still king in Yazoo, as it had been for centuries before her time. As it would be, probably, forever. It was a king she had no love for, nor loyalty to.

They broke through the flat landscape and ascended the rolling hills that hemmed in Yazoo City, seat of Mississippi's largest county, home to ten thousand citizens. The rest of Yazoo County's population was scattered in small hamlets and rural enclaves, on farms and plantations, around swamps and along the Yazoo River itself.

"Where're we going now?" John Fortune inquired patiently. "Are we going to get to Branson soon?"

"Soon," the Angel assured him. She hadn't told him about her planned detour. She could barely articulate the reason for it to herself, let alone John Fortune. "I want to stop here first and visit my mother. If that's okay."

"Sure," John Fortune said. He looked out the window, which had been rolled all the way down due to the van's lack of air-conditioning. "Sure is hot."

That it is, the Angel thought.

Heat was the most common sensation she recalled when she thought of her childhood. Wet, sticky heat that plastered her blouse to her back as soon as she put it on in the morning. That squeezed beads of sweat through her pores to trickle between her breasts and down her rib cage if she exerted herself the least little bit. Or even if she sat quietly in church while the fans rotated uselessly overhead.

Although miles from the twisting bends of the Mississippi River as it flowed down to the Gulf of Mexico, Yazoo was moist. Alligators still roared in the night in her acres of swamp, and the catfish raised in her myriad lakes was an important cash crop. There was more than a touch of the primeval about it. The Angel felt they'd turned back the clock to somewhere in the middle of the last century. Or even the century before that.

"Nice houses," John Fortune commented as they passed through a high-toned residential area. "Though some could use a new paint job."

"Old money trying to stretch," the Angel told him. "It doesn't go as far as it used to."

They drove by whitewashed two-story homes and entered a part of the town where the houses were smaller and even more in need of paint. The lawns were wilder than the manicured yards of the affluent district, with cars up on blocks and ancient appliances scattered about as if their owners hadn't enough energy to carry them farther. Some—an old wringer washing machine here, an old sink there, even a toilet or two—had been turned into planters brimming with profusions of flowers of all colors and descriptions, from tiny daisies white, blue, and yellow to columnar hollyhocks thrusting up to Heaven. Other abandoned appliances, especially the ancient refrigerators, were just rusting death traps, waiting for some kid to lock themselves in and suffocate.

The Angel took the narrow, twisting lanes automatically, turning without thinking until on the edge of the poorest part of town she drove through an open wrought-iron gate into a tree-shaded park with a scattering of white stones and gray monuments like candy tossed on a gently rolling field of felt. She parked the van and it gratefully shuddered to a well-deserved rest. John Fortune looked at her from the corner of his eye, without turning his head.

"Your mom's here?" he asked.

"That's right," the Angel said. She got out of the van and after a moment he followed her.

It was quiet in the cemetery, and cool. Her mother's grave was on the side of a hill sheltered by a giant pecan tree that spread its branches above a score of graves like a benediction. The slab was small, and bore only a name and two dates, 1961–2001. The Angel stood before it, then sank to her knees in the cool grass, putting her hands on the earth as if to caress that which lay underneath it.

"Hello, Mama," she said in a low voice. "I've come to see you again." She paused, gathering her thoughts. "I know it's been a long time since I've been able to come by. I know I've been out in the world, which you told me was so evil and so dangerous, but there was just nothing here for me. Nothing for me to do, Mama. No way for me to live. You must understand that."

Her mother had not wanted her to go out into the world. She had told her, over and over again, of its traps and perils. After all, she'd gone out herself and had gotten nothing out of it but a bloated belly and a daughter cursed at a very young age. Probably from the tainted blood of her beastly father, whom she never spoke of. But maybe, just maybe, by the evilness of her own contaminated soul.

"And I've been out in the world doing good. Really, I have. I brought someone to see you." The Angel turned and beckoned to John Fortune, who was standing a respectful half a dozen paces back, watching uncertainly. He came forward as she gestured, and nodded briefly.

"Hello," he said.

"You're in Heaven, Mama, so you must know who he is. You must know something of what is planned for us poor sinners on Earth. You—"

"Must know he is the Devil incarnate," a voice said behind them.

The Angel whirled, instinctively shielding John Fortune with her body. Behind them was an ancient mausoleum. Shimmering upon its cracked stone wall was a circle of darkness, a tear through the fabric of space. Two men and a thing had come through the tear. She recognized the cardinal. The man with him was restraining something with a collar and leash that might have been human but walked like a dog on four limbs. That had an inhuman face with deep-set eyes and slavering jaws, and a long snout whose damp nostrils quivered as it sucked in great lungfuls of air and tried to lunge at the Angel and her charge. A third came though the doorway and laughed. He was big and handsome as an angel with golden hair and large blue eyes and a strong, dimpled jaw. The Angel felt her stomach clench. She couldn't tell if it was with fear, revulsion, or desire.

"I told you Blood would find her eventually," the Witness said.

Contarini nodded. "Start with the girl. The boy is for later."

He let go of Blood's leash and the joker/ace leapt forward on all fours like a hound, drool frothing on his gaping jaws. The Angel tossed a stern, "Stay here," to John Fortune, and stepped to meet him.

Blood sprung into the air screaming. She met him with a grim scowl, catching him with one hand on his throat and one on his crotch, pivoted, and slammed him to the ground with most of her strength. He hit like a bag of cement tossed from the roof of a five-story building, grunted, and got back to his feet. But he wavered as he came toward her, breathing heavily. The Angel could see that his heart was not in this.

She smiled. Even though he was bigger than her, he was no match for her righteous strength. The only thing that had saved him from the full force of the body slam was the thick sward and soft dirt he'd landed on. Nothing, she thought, could save him from her fists.

He leaped at her again, his powerful haunches launching him like a tiger. This time she met him with a hammering uppercut that spun him end over end, sending him flying back in the direction he'd come. Contarini had to dodge his flailing limbs as he flew by.

The cardinal ground his teeth in rage. "Useless creature," he spat at the cowering joker who tried, but couldn't get up. He turned to the Witness. "Take care of her! Teach her a lesson."

The smiling ace stretched like a cat. His knuckles made crackling sounds as he clenched his hands into fists. He approached slowly, smiling confidently. Smugly, really. He had a reason to be smug, the Angel thought. He was still the most handsome man she had ever seen.

"Remember the lesson I taught you before," he said as he approached. "Now it goes further."

The sudden sound of the van's horn startled them both. The Angel whirled to see John Fortune behind the wheel, a determined expression on his face, leaning on the horn and bouncing up and down on the seat as the van rolled over the bumpy sward, bearing down on them.

The Angel leaped away just as Fortune slammed on the brakes and spun the wheel. The van sideswiped the Witness. He didn't even try to get out of the way. There was the thud of metal slamming into flesh and the van flung the Witness twenty feet in the air, where he hit the spreading branches of the pecan tree that were nodding over the nearby graves. Branches cracked and broke and fell along with the Witness.

John Fortune wrestled the van to a stop and shouted out the driver's-side window, "Get in! Get in!"

The Angel responded to the panic in his voice. Her first thought was to check to see if the Witness was still alive, and if he was, to kick his ass as hard as she could. But she realized John Fortune was right. They had to get out of there. Fast.

The sliding door on the driver's side was crumpled inward, but was still holding on the frame. That was good. The van engine's was idling at such a high rate that it was threatening to sputter out at any second. That would be bad. She reached the passenger's-side door and pulled it open. John Fortune floored the gas pedal before her butt hit the seat. The van slewed around crazily for a moment, then the tires gripped the turf and they headed for the unpaved road running through the cemetery.

As the Angel glanced back she saw Cardinal Contarini crouched behind one of the monuments, shaking his fist at them and screeching something in Italian. The joker looked up groggily, a blank expression on his inhuman face. The Witness was still lying under the broken tree limbs on her mother's grave.

That was close, she thought, leaning back in the seat. She looked at the boy who, beyond denial, was her savior. He was concentrating on guiding the van over the winding cemetery lane, but he glanced over at her.

"See," he said. "I told you I could drive."

She smiled at him. His smile glowed back at her like the shining sun. They left the cemetery, hitting the city streets. The van rattled along making alarming sounds as John Fortune cruised at a sedate thirty miles an hour. The Angel realized that there was no way it was going to get them to Branson. They would be lucky if it got them beyond the city limits. She guessed that this situation could be classified as an emergency, and she reached for her cell phone. She hit the Hand's number on the speed dial.

"President Barnett's of—"

"Sally Lou!" the Angel said, trying hard to control her voice so that John Fortune wouldn't get more worried than he already was. "Let me speak with President Barnett—fast!"

"He's in conference now," she said in the snootily superior voice that she liked to use on the Angel.

"I don't care if God the Father Himself is in there planning Armageddon with him," the Angel said in a tone that made John Fortune stare at her in surprise. "Connect me with him. Now."

Pleased when Sally Lou connected them without another word, she barely gave the Hand the chance to say hello before she blurted out their situation. He took it like he took everything else. With calmness and poise.

"Can you hold out for twenty minutes, honey?" he asked sedately.

"Twenty minutes? I don't—"

"You're going to have to," he said just as soothingly. "Twenty minutes. That's all. I promise you."

The Angel took a deep breath. She had the Hand's assurance. Though he was just a man like everyone else and a sinner as well, he had never let her down. In any important sense, anyway. "All right," she said. "Twenty minutes."

"Twenty minutes," Barnett confirmed. "Where are you, exactly?"

She told him.

"Fine. Get to the highway. Wait by the Yazoo City on-ramp. Don't move from that spot. Help is on the way. Gotta go make it happen."

He hung up. The Angel listened to the dial tone, then looked at John Fortune, who was gazing at her with a trusting expression.

"Help is on the way," she told him. Though how in the world it would arrive in such a short time was utterly beyond her.

◆

Peaceable Kingdom: The Angels' Bower

RAY TRIED TO EXPLAIN his position as they took the escalator down to the elevator bank in the lobby, but Jerry wasn't in a forgiving mood. Mushroom Daddy listened with amiable interest while Sascha just listened, as usual.

"It's not like I lied to you," Ray said. "Or even wanted to lie. You and Ackroyd made some unjustified assumptions the first time you saw me, and went right on assuming from then to now."

"And you let us," Jerry pointed out for the fifth or sixth time. "You let us think you and Angel were working for the government."

Ray shrugged. "There's no skin off your nose, is there?"

"No skin off my nose?" Jerry said, just this side of outraged. "It's a lot different thinking that we were going into this with government backing—or at least governmental knowledge and consent—and then discovering that the 'government' in this case was Leo Barnett."

"Hey," Ray said, "he was the president once, wasn't he?"

"*Was*," Jerry said. "That's the operative word."

Ray shrugged. "Look, you're an ace. If you call changing your face an ace—"

"I do more than change my face," Jerry said hotly.

"Yeah, okay, whatever. I'm not saying you're a deuce, exactly. But you know how it is. The life of an ace is complicated. You can't tell me you've never had a secret or two. Especially if your power is changing identities. Hell, your name's probably not even Creighton."

That stopped Jerry cold. Ray was right. Righter than he knew. Jerry's whole existence was based on shifting identities. On lies he constantly told others. And himself. He was never just plain old Jerry Strauss. Most of the time he was someone else. The Projectionist. The Great Ape. Lon Creighton. Jerry Creighton. Alan Ladd. Butcher Dagon. Everybody *but* Jerry Strauss.

If Ray realized that he scored, he kept quiet about it. They eventually made it to the elevator bank, and Ray punched the button for the penthouse. The boys were on guard in the corridor. They must have received word of some kind of possible attack, because they had their handguns out and leveled as the elevator doors swished open.

"Hey, man," Daddy said. "That's so not cool!"

"Relax," Ray said to both Daddy and the Secret Service men. "It's me. You're safe."

One put up his weapon with an audible sigh, the other was more hard-assed about it. "Well, look what the cat dragged in," he said, pointing the barrel of his gun to the floor, but not holstering it. "Billy Ray. A blind guy. A hippie—"

"Don't worry," Ray said. "I'll tell them not to kick your ass."

"We've got to see Barnett," Jerry said. "Is he in?"

"He's already got company," the armed agent said doubtfully, "but . . ."

"I'll vouch for these guys," Ray said.

"Even the hippie?"

"He's undercover CIA," Ray said quietly as he went on by. The others followed him.

Sally Lou was on the phone when they entered the waiting room. She jumped nervously as Ray and the others tramped in.

"Guilty conscious?" Ray asked.

"Why, why ever would I have a guilty conscious?" she asked.

"Just a joke," he said. "Buzz the big guy. Tell him we're coming in."

"He's with someone—"

"So am I," Ray said.

Ray led the way. In the office Barnett was behind his desk, beaming. Sitting before the desk frowning was someone Ray hadn't seen in years. "Fortunato," he said. He stopped. The others piled up behind him.

"Come in," Barnett said affably. "You've brought some friends, I see. Good, good. We're just sitting around here chatting, trying to decide who's gonna go to Yazoo and pick up John Fortune in"—Barnett checked his watch—"just about fifteen minutes from now." Barnett looked at Fortunato. "Billy Ray would be a good choice, don't you think?"

Fortunato didn't look totally convinced, but he nodded nonetheless.

♥

Peaceable Kingdom: The Angels' Bower, Coffee Shop

JOHN NIGHTHAWK AND HIS team sat in the hotel coffee shop, enjoying a late breakfast.

Usher had a plate piled high with scrambled eggs, bacon, ham, hash browns, biscuits and gravy, toast, and a side of pancakes. He was still of an age when he could eat and eat and not put on an ounce. Magda had a cup of grapefruit juice and toast. Dry. She didn't particularly worry about her weight, but was of an age when she took nothing joyful out of life, and always would be. Nighthawk had his coffee and donuts. He was of an age beyond caring about his weight. It helped that he had an ace's metabolism.

He scanned the sports page, noting last night's box scores. He was pleased to see that the Dodgers were doing better. Hanging at about five hundred, Brooklyn still had room to improve, though as a lifelong Dodgers fan he had little room to complain about the last thirty-five years or so. Still, with Gooden joining Strawberry in retirement two years ago, the last tie to Reiser's glory years had been cut and they were casting about for a new leader and new team identity. This Reyes kid looked good. His headlong style of play reminded Nighthawk a little of Honus Wagner.

His cell rang. He flipped it open, listened, and said a few quiet words. He hung up and looked at his team. "Enjoy your breakfast," he said. "It starts soon."

Usher nodded and shoveled half a pancake, loaded with butter and syrup, into his mouth. Magda grinned and started to pray aloud. Nighthawk put the paper down and took a drink of coffee. It was cold. Suddenly, so was he.

♣

Yazoo City, Mississippi: The Highway Interchange

THE VAN'S ENGINE CHUGGED like an asthmatic with a smoker's cough and the door rattled against the frame like a skeleton with rheumatism.

"We'd better stop and switch places," the Angel said.

"Ah," John Fortune said, "I'm doing okay."

"Yeah," the Angel said, "but we're headed for the highway. I'd better take over. Park it and slide over. Better not turn the ignition off. I don't know if we could get it started again."

John Fortune pulled over to the side of the street. He put it in park and slid over on the seat. The Angel lifted herself up to scoot over him, but suddenly she felt his arms around her, pulling her down to his lap. He kissed her, half on the lips and half on the cheek. His skin was warm, as if he were burning with fever, but dry. He wasn't sweating.

"John—" she said, pulling away.

"I know, I know. I just couldn't help myself."

"Help yourself to a seat over there," she said, indicating a spot next to the passenger-side door. "There's a time and a place for everything, and this is neither."

"Will it be time when we get to Branson?" he asked hopefully.

The Angel bit her lip as she pulled away from the curb. He was her Savior, but he was just a boy. A good-looking boy, but a boy. She felt nothing for him but awe coupled with an instinct to guard and protect that was surely maternal in nature. But she couldn't bring herself to disappoint him completely.

"We'll see. Things will be hectic when we get there. You'll be an important figure, with a lot to do."

"I'll always have time for you, Angel," John Fortune said, and she smiled a smile of genuine affection.

They made it back to the highway in minutes. She pulled off to the side of the entrance ramp, turned off the van's engine, and checked her watch.

"What's going to happen now?" John Fortune asked.

The Angel shook her head. She was as mystified as he was. But whatever was going to happen, she knew that it had better happen soon. They waited five or six minutes, and then a dark shadow suddenly appeared on the side of the overpass buttress, though there was nothing to cast it.

"Angel—"

She nodded. "I see it."

The gate had opened again. Blood and his handler came through the hole in the concrete buttress first. The joker-ace lifted his head up to the sky, his snout sniffing. Cardinal Contarini followed, as did the Witness. The Angel's heart sunk further when a squad of well-armed minions a dozen strong followed. They fanned out and slowly approached the van where it sat on the highway verge.

Contarini smiled, but there was nothing of goodwill in it. "I told you that we'd be better prepared this time."

The Angel clenched her teeth and tried the engine. "Don't flood, don't flood, please don't flood," she pleaded as she pumped the gas pedal.

"Take your foot off the gas and your hands off the wheel," Contarini ordered, "or we'll shoot you down right now." He gestured and his Allumbrados took braced firing positions.

The van's engine suddenly caught and purred quietly like a cat. The Angel took her hands off the wheel. She could think of only one plan. It wasn't much of one, but it was the only hope they had.

"John," she said quietly out of the corner of her mouth, her lips unmoving. "I'm going to floor it on the count of three. I want you to open your door and fall to the ground. Roll. Roll hard and far away."

"What are you going to do?" the boy asked. For the first time ever, she heard fear in his voice.

"What I have to," the Angel said quietly.

"You'd better get out of that ridiculous vehicle before I count to five," Contarini shouted.

"Angel—"

"Please." She looked at her Lord. She loved him like she never loved anyone else, with pure, undying affection, and the taste of her failure was bitter in her mouth. "Please, John—"

"One," Contarini said.

"One," the Angel whispered.

"Two!" Contarini shouted.

"Two," the Angel whispered.

John Fortune looked at her, his face fixed with fear, and suddenly his eyes went wide and his arm flew up, pointing back down to the highway.

"Look!" he shouted.

When the Hand had said it would take twenty minutes for help to arrive, it was one of the few times in Angel's experience that he was wrong. It took eighteen.

The southbound lanes of the highway were empty but for a roaring wind and flashing lights that had no apparent origin. Suddenly, as if it had broken through a landscape-painted canvas, an eighteen-wheeler pulling a silver trailer just appeared as if it had been placed there by the hand of God.

Perhaps it had, the Angel thought.

It was highballing maybe a hundred miles an hour and it hardly slowed down as it took the Yazoo City exit. It was upon them like an angry behemoth before they even realized it, flashing past the van in a New York minute. She saw a heavyset man with a cigar clenched between his teeth and a cap on his head behind the wheel, which was on the wrong side of the cab, and she saw Billy Ray grinning like an idiot next to him and then they went by.

Contarini screamed like a woman. Blood pulled away from his handler and was running like a dog from the highway. The Witness stood mute and astonished as it barreled down upon them and Contarini shouted, "Shoot, you fools, shoot!" and automatic gunfire split the morning like continuous rolls of thunder only to whine and ping against the glass and grille of the cab's front.

The Allumbrados scattered at the last moment as the driver downshifted and fought the wheel with consummate skill, throwing the truck into a skid that swung the trailer among the gunmen, tossing bodies like tenpins. Only a few escaped. Before the truck came to a screeching halt in a swirling cloud of dust, the passenger-side door opened and Billy Ray was among them.

The Angel blinked. He moved like a dancer, but his graceful steps brought pain and destruction to his partners in the bloody ballet. He struck with hands and feet, elbows, knees, and head. A single blow to each opponent. That was all it took. Some tried to shoot, but they missed him. Some tried to run, but they weren't fast enough. Contarini was among the first to go down, the Witness the last. He towered over Ray like a giant. He swung his powerful right arm at Ray, but it moved as if in slow motion. Ray dropped to the ground. He put all his weight on one leg, doubled under him, and lashed out with the other. His foot caught the Witness on the right kneecap. The Witness screamed like a horse with a broken leg and went down rolling in the dust, clutching his leg and shrieking.

"It's only a dislocated patella, pussy," the Angel heard Ray sneer.

"Wow . . ." John Fortune said.

The Angel woke from her trance. "Come on!"

She threw open the door and grabbed John Fortune's arm and hauled him after her, half dragging him as she ran toward the waiting truck, passing bodies, groaning and silent, that littered the ground. The Witness watched her go with his face clenched in pain. He mouthed gibberish at her and tried to crawl toward her and John, but suddenly Ray was between them.

"Back off, asshole," he said, and the Witness stopped, groveling in the dust.

Ray looked up at her and she saw his face gleaming like a saint's in an ancient icon.

"Ray—" she said, and before she knew what she was doing, she'd grabbed his shoulders and pulled him to her and covered his mouth with hers. He returned her kiss with equal fervor until the driver shouted out from the cab, "Time enough for that later. We'd best be getting on," and he gunned his engine for emphasis. He had an English accent.

Ray broke the kiss and looked at her with startled eyes. She looked away, blushing at her terrible boldness. She didn't know what had gotten into her, but she did know that she'd savor the memory of that kiss for a long time.

"Come on, come on, I ain't got all night. Manchester United's on the telly in"—the driver checked the wristwatch on his beefy, hairy forearm—"half an hour and I got a ways to travel to get home."

The Angel jumped into the cab after John Fortune, and the wheels started rolling as Ray leaped up and slammed the door shut.

"Scoot over," the trucker said. "There's room for all." He concentrated on negotiating the downhill ramp back to the highway and had his rig going eighty by the time they hit the main road again.

He glanced over at the Angel and John Fortune, grinning around his foul-smelling cigar. "I'm John Bruckner," he said by way of introduction, "Order of the Silver Helix and freelance lorry driver. They call me the Highwayman. I bet you thought we were in for it when those yobbos started shooting?" He patted the dashboard lovingly. "Nah. Not to worry. This is my special rig. All tricked out for those 'difficult' deliveries. Hang on, now," he warned.

The Angel was too dazed to comment as the speedometer crept up to one twenty and then passed it effortlessly.

"Here comes the shortcut," Bruckner called out, and everything shimmered and they were suddenly someplace else.

The landscape through which they passed was bizarre. The color of the ground, the quality of the light, the very angles of the cliff faces and rock formations they flew by were utterly alien. When she saw some of the rocks move as if they were living things, she had to look away. The Angel glanced up at the sky. The sun was green.

"It's kind of freaky," Billy Ray said in a low voice, "but don't worry. Bruckner will get us through." His hand rested lightly on her left thigh. She put her own down on his, not to remove it, but to enjoy its warmth. Ray smiled crookedly. There was blood on his face, possibly his. She touched his cheek, wiping it away. She laughed.

"What?" Ray asked, frowning.

The Angel shook her head. "I—" It was hard to explain. She gestured all around, at the bizarre landscape, at her companions. "I haven't felt so good in a long time," she finally said. "Have I gone crazy?"

Billy Ray grinned. "You think I'm qualified to pass judgment on someone else's sanity? Me?"

"We'll see," she promised.

♠ ♥ ♦ ♣

Chapter Ten

Peaceable Kingdom: The Angels' Bower

"DO ME A FAVOR, Digger?" Fortunato asked. He and Digger had left Barnett's headquarters, Fortunato excusing himself with the explanation that he had to get ready for his son's imminent arrival. But something else was also on his mind.

The reporter looked up from his laptop where he'd been plinking out the latest chapter in the story of Fortunato's return, using only approximately three fingers on each hand, but still making pretty good time. He was sitting at the desk in their suite in the Angels' Bower. Fortunato was reclining on one of the semicomfortable sofas.

"Sure."

"Keep an eye on me. If it looks like my heart has stopped beating, call for help."

Digger frowned. "Okay."

Fortunato went slack as he used almost the last bit of energy stored in his body to go astral. He hovered above his unconscious form for a moment as Downs went quickly to the sofa. The reporter grabbed Fortunato's wrist, frowning as he felt for a pulse. He released it after a moment, seemingly satisfied but still looking a little shaken, and moved the ace into a more comfortable position on the sofa, with his legs straight out, his head on a pillow, and his hands placed loosely in his lap. Though the result looked like a corpse waiting for a coffin, Fortunato was touched by Downs's unexpected solicitousness, and he smiled as he flew through the closed window and out above the Peaceable Kingdom.

Fortunato had never been to a theme park before, so he had no idea how the Kingdom compared to, say, Disneyland. He suspected that they had the same kind of layout. He went a little higher so that the land below him looked like a Monopoly board, the various properties organized to allow for a smooth flow of people from one part of the park to another.

He'd glanced through the Kingdom's brochures to familiarize himself with the lay of the land, so at least he knew what he was looking at. In the front, to his right, was New Jerusalem, Barnett's somewhat sanitary reproduction of a portion of that ancient city, containing all the locales relevant to Christ's life and death—the Via Dolorosa, the Plain of Golgotha, even the rock-hewn Tomb of the Sepulcher—but condensed for the tourist's convenience. There were also plenty of souvenir shops where T-shirts, coffee mugs, bumper stickers, and necklaces of rough-forged nails like those that pinned Christ to the cross could be purchased.

To his left was Rome of the Martyrs, including a scaled-down version of the Coliseum where various amusements were held, though no Christians were thrown to lions. All entertainments, the brochures said, were in good taste with no blood spilt, but one could still get an idea of the decadent and debauched practices of the pagan Romans. The underground catacombs, which were obviously not visible from Fortunato's viewpoint, came complete with grisly scenarios depicting the lives and deaths of the martyrs, and were also quite popular.

Behind him was Medieval Land and the Vault of Heaven, all with attendant stores, restaurants, amenities, shops, and rides, but something drew Fortunato forward, to the Coliseum-dominated Rome of the Martyrs, as if what he needed could be found there.

He flew between the guardian statues of the apostles, three each guarding a quadrant of the Kingdom. Something was calling him. It wasn't the sounds made by the five thousand people attending the revival or seminar or whatever was taking place in the scaled-down Coliseum. It was the promise of energy that saturated the air. As he hovered over the center of the open-roofed structure, he was astonished to see that everyone, all five thousand or so attendees, were women. They ranged from the young to the old. They were all fairly well if not fairly tastefully dressed. They were virtually all white, but Fortunato could remember few Asian faces among the tourists, and even fewer Black. The fact that they were all women seemed somehow appropriate, as if he'd come full circle. Once, he'd derived all his power from women. Now perhaps he would again.

His astral form hovered in the air above the Coliseum. A wooden platform below him bore a podium draped with banners proclaiming MAGOG—Mothers Against Gods or Goddesses—in intricate letters. A woman stood behind the podium, leading them all in song. She was flanked on either side by delegates in folding chairs. He didn't know what the song was, but by its lugubrious tones and solemn, dirgelike beat, he assumed that it was a hymn. After the song ended, the woman standing behind the podium spoke, but Fortunato didn't listen to her. He had other concerns.

He assumed the lotus position above the platform as currents of energy roiled below him like a tsunami starting to build in some far corner of the Pacific. Passion rose up among the five thousand. Their thoughts were chaotic, their need great. They wanted so badly to belong to something all-important and good. They wanted so awfully to give of themselves to something greater, so he let them.

He accepted what they offered.

Energy flowed up to him like manna in reverse. It came in through the pores of his astral body, soaked into his insubstantial capillaries, was gathered into his veins and sucked into his invisible heart. Like a great explosion of terrifying light it burst into his brain and Fortunato was glad that his actual physical brain was safe on the couch in the Angels' Bower, because his material organs could not have withstood the energy that pulsed like miniature bombs to every beat of his insubstantial heart.

It was too much. He couldn't contain it all. He knew he had to give some back, and besides, it was the polite thing to do.

He looked at the woman behind the podium. She gripped the sides of the pulpit with an almost stricken look on her face, her teeth clenched, her hair, once so sensibly coifed, now disheveled in wild disarray, her very posture pleading and yet giving at the same time. Fortunato had seen that pose many times in the past. It required very little to push her over the edge, so he did.

A low, unbelieving moan growled out of her throat. She shook as if in an invisible wind, her eyes screwed tightly shut, her mouth slack and panting.

She wasn't the only one in that condition. They all were. Some screamed, some laughed, some cried. Some fell out of their chairs, some leaped out of their seats. For some the sensation was nothing they'd ever felt before in their lives, for some it was as familiar as Saturday night. Some called on Jesus, some their husbands, some a boy nearly forgotten over the years. Some a girl. Some wanted a cigarette, but this was a nonsmoking facility.

Fortunato shared it all while siphoning the maelstrom of energy that they'd released. The crush of emotion would have killed many men, but his ace-enhanced mind and his Zen training pulled him through, though it was the wildest experience he'd ever had in the course of a wild life. He basked in a glow of warm satisfaction for a moment, but suddenly he burned with his own need to go, to do, to find again his son.

His eyes opened and focused on Digger Downs, who was standing over his body sprawled on the couch, staring down at him with concern.

"It's all right," he told the reporter. "I'm back."

"I guess you are," Downs said. "Where the hell have you been?"

Fortunato shook his head. "No," he said. "I'm not the kind who kisses and tells."

♠

The Short Cut

"WHAT IS THIS PLACE?" John Fortune asked. He was flushed with excitement. Sitting next to him, Ray could feel the heat flowing off him in waves.

"The Short Cut, lad," Bruckner said expansively, as if that explained everything.

It was good enough for Ray. He looked out the windshield. The green sun was moving slowly but perceptibly across the sky. Soon it would set, though "soon" in this place seemed a concept hard to define. The road was flat, straight, and well-maintained, though the plants crowding its verge were like nothing Ray had ever seen. They were like trees, but their branches had no leaves. The trunks were bulbous, fleshy things, in shades of green, violet, and vermilion, shot through with scarlet veins that circulated a fluid that Ray was uncomfortably sure resembled blood. He watched them suspiciously as they whizzed by in Bruckner's lorry, something bothering him. He realized that their branches were moving, though not in a wind. They writhed in several different directions at once, as if at their own volition.

He was about to point this out to Angel when something, suddenly and out of nowhere, hit their windshield with a horrific splat, squashed against it, and spattered like a water balloon tossed out of a ten-story building. A wash of purplish goo instantly covered the windshield. Bruckner clenched his teeth on his cigar as he turned on the windshield wipers.

"This could be a problem," he said, downshifting as the wipers and the windshield glass itself started to smoke.

"This ever happen before?" Ray asked.

"Rarely," Bruckner said. "Sometimes the locals raise a bit of a tussle."

"This place has locals?" Angel asked.

Bruckner grinned without humor. "Oh, yes. Best if we stay clear of them, but sometimes we don't have much of a choice. They used to be real quiet. Never bothered me. But in recent years . . . something's stirred them up. It's like, sometimes, they want my truck." The lorry braked to a halt, and he looked over at Ray, Angel, and John Fortune. "We'd better get that windshield off before the acid eats all the way through. But not to worry. I carry spares."

"And the locals?" Ray asked.

"Figger you and the lady can handle them, me lad. That's why you're here, after all. The boy can help me replace the windshield. You two guard our flanks, front and back."

"Guard them from what?" Angel asked.

Bruckner grinned again. "Anything that looks strange."

Ray and Angel exchanged glances. Ray nodded, and she put her hand on the door handle.

"Oh, one more thing," Bruckner said.

"What?" Ray asked, starting to get annoyed.

"Funny thing, but guns don't work in this place."

Ray shrugged.

Angel said, "I'm covered." She paused for a moment, frowning. "At least, I hope so."

"I carry some stuff in the back you can use."

Ray nodded. "All right. I'll go to the back, with you. Angel, watch the front."

"All right," she said.

"All right," John Fortune said.

They all looked at Bruckner.

"All right," the Brit said. "Let's do it."

The air, like everything else in this place, was strange. It felt odd on Ray's tongue. It had a bite to it, like a summer night after a lightning storm. The quality of light was also odd, probably because of the different-colored sun, now hanging on the horizon.

Bruckner rolled up the trailer's rear door, and for all his size, lightly leaped up into it. A weapon rack was bolted on one of the walls. Swords, spears, bow and arrow.

Too bad Yeoman isn't with us, Ray thought.

"What do you fancy?" Bruckner asked.

Ray decided to keep it simple.

"Those." He nodded at a brace of morning stars.

"Good choice," Bruckner said. "But watch out for splatters of what passes for blood among these boyos. Sometimes it can be corrosive."

Ray nodded, and Bruckner tossed him the weapons. Their handles were black iron, as long as his forearm. Their heads were the size of Texas grapefruit, spiked. The chains attaching handle to head were about two feet long. Ray swung them once or twice to get their feel. He nodded to himself and ran through an extemporaneous kata as John Fortune watched with his mouth open. Like all weapons, they felt like Ray'd been born with them in his hands.

"Right, me lad," Bruckner said, clapping John Fortune on the shoulder. "Ever change a windshield before?"

"No," the boy said.

"Nothing to it," the Brit said cheerfully. "Give me a hand with these suction cups."

Ray turned his back to the truck, scanning the land. It was flat and relatively featureless. If there'd be trouble, it would come from the weird forest a dozen yards from their flank.

Bruckner and John Fortune got the spare windshield from the case where the trucker kept it among a plethora of other spare parts, and part of Ray listened as they went to the front. Bruckner greeted Angel, who answered in a steady voice, and then issued a stream of commands as he and the boy attacked the ruined windshield.

Thoughts of Angel slipped languorously through Ray's mind, though most of it was focused on the odd-moving trees, if that's what they were, bunched by the side of the road, if that's what it was.

Suddenly it became darker, almost without a sense of transition. Ray looked back to the horizon, and saw that the green sun had gone under. The light took on a quality that Ray had once seen while snorkeling in the Bahamas at a depth of thirty feet. It seemed denser, darker, and somehow a lot less friendly. A full moon rose rapidly on the other side of the horizon, splotched and diseased-looking, shining with a greenish, almost phosphorescent light the color of gangrenous flesh.

As if the rising of the leprous moon was a signal, things started coming out of the oddly moving trees.

They were many-legged, spiderlike creatures whose bulbous bodies were held high off the ground by too many skeletal legs. Big spiders were one thing, Ray thought, but these had heads and features that were disturbingly human. Except for their protruding fangs, which dripped ichor that steamed when it spattered on the ground. They scuttled like crabs, moving fast. Their bodies, white and bulging and hairless, were the size of large dogs.

"Angel," Ray called out. "You'd better get over here. Quick."

There were twenty or so in the pack, and they didn't seem to be afraid of Ray.

Ray whirled at a sudden sound at his side, but it was only Angel. She looked as if she were about to make a remark, then saw the spider-things. "My God!" she said.

"Don't blaspheme," Ray reprimanded.

She shook her head. "I wasn't blaspheming. I was praying."

"Pray harder," Ray said, "because here they come."

The arachnids were on them, tittering like high school girls as their fangs clacked together, dripping steaming ichor.

"Save my soul from evil, Lord," Angel said, "and heal this warrior's heart."

Ray caught a burst of light in his peripheral vision, and the arachnids reared back, screaming, as Angel plunged into their midst, her flaming sword held high. She screamed. Ray couldn't tell if it was from anger, fear, or revulsion, as she swung her sword and sheared through the front legs of one of the things. It collapsed, grimacing ferociously. Angel lunged. Her sword speared the thing's body, white and hairless like a dead fish, and it burst like a balloon, spattering her with droplets of ichor that steamed as it ate into her fighting suit.

"Watch out for their blood!" she shouted in warning, pirouetting to cut the legs out from under two others that were trying to circle them.

Ray realized that they were in a bad spot. He danced into the midst of their attackers, swinging right and left with the morning stars. One missed, the other crunched an all-too-human-looking face. The spiders' titters changed to disturbing high-pitched screams, but they still came.

Ray turned and twisted like a dervish. He saw Angel shouting wordlessly as she held off half a dozen of the things with long sweeps of her sword. Thankfully, the spiders seemed more afraid of her, or perhaps it was the light emitted by her weapon, than they were of him. So many gathered about him that he had to shift constantly to avoid their lunging, clacking jaws. Luckily they couldn't spit venom, but it was only a matter of time before they'd both be splattered with enough of the poison to do some serious damage.

The pack was all around them as Ray saw something out of the corner of his eye—a human figure, tall and bulky, dressed in a long leather duster that swept to the ground, standing and watching.

Perhaps, Ray thought, *directing.*

Ray moved in a seemingly random pattern as he attacked the hunters, taking off a leg here, battering a head there, pulping a squishy abdomen, clenching his teeth as venom spattered, clinging to and eating away his fighting suit. It soon looked as if gigantic destructive moths had been at it.

Half a dozen of the things were broken around Ray, screaming like girls with broken arms but still dragging themselves after the pack, their fangs clattering angrily. He hadn't spotted Angel in long moments, but he could still hear her fighting at his back as his seemingly irregular movements took him in a curving path toward the observer watching the hunting pack, maybe ten feet away. One of the spider-things stood at his back, between them.

Another hunter lunged at him from the front. Ray pulped its head like a bug on the bathroom floor, whirled, and dove to the ground. He slid between the legs of the arachnid behind him, who stood there with a look of almost human astonishment on its caricatured features. He raked the bottom of its gut as he went by, twisting desperately to avoid the deluge of steaming fluid that burst from it like a ruptured bladder, and grunted aloud when some splashed on the back of his hand. He turned a complete somersault and came to his feet face-to-face with the observer, morning stars raised high.

And he froze.

The thing had no face. Its head was a featureless white cone that tapered to a wet red tentacle that quivered like an eager tongue.

But that wasn't the worst of it. Something clung to its neck, its mouth fastened onto its dead white flesh, its large eyes regarding Ray with unblinking hatred.

"Ti Malice!" Ray blurted aloud.

Not many knew about the obscene Haitian ace who had wreaked unaccountable havoc before vanishing from human ken over a decade and a half ago, but

Ray was a compulsive reader of secret government files and there wasn't much he didn't know about obscure aces. Especially the bad ones.

The Haitian's tiny arms encircled the thing's thick white neck, and his slug-like body hung down its back. Malice rose up, his mouth coming free from his mount's neck with an audible slurping sound. Malice's mouth was like that of a lamprey: round, ringed with tiny, sharp teeth, and a tubelike tongue that sucked the blood from his host. He hissed at Ray, spitting dark, purplish blood. The thing he rode raised its featureless face to the moon and somehow howled, sending shivers down Ray's back.

It moved. But Ray moved faster.

He blocked the thing's lunge with one of the morning stars and swung the other like it was a baseball bat and Ti Malice's head was the ball.

He hit a home run. Malice's head splattered at the impact. The feeble grip of his arms around the creature's neck broke, and Malice shot backward and hit the ground twenty feet away, bouncing and rolling, leaving a smeared trail on the thick, gray grass, which twitched agitatedly above the tiny body, and finally closed over it like hungry snakes.

The creature slumped to the ground, shuddering all over. Ray stood over it, undecided. It lifted an arm, as if in supplication, and behind him Ray sensed all movement stop. He held his blow as the thing stood. Not quite human-shaped in its long trench coat, it regarded Ray with its featureless face. Ray forced himself to look back. Forced his gorge to stay down. After a moment, without making sound or gesture, it walked backward among the trees.

What was left of the hunting pack followed it, taking a wide berth around Ray as it did so. As they vanished among the eerily moving trees, Ray let out a long breath he didn't realize that he'd been holding. He turned to look at the battlefield, the ground splashed with ichor and littered with smashed and slashed spider bodies and parts.

"Angel!" he called, and realized that she had slumped to her knees, her head down, unmoving.

◆

Peaceable Kingdom: The Angels' Bower

JERRY STARTED TO FEEL a little uncomfortable under Barnett's smiling scrutiny. Ray had departed to go on this mysterious mission to pick up the kid and Fortunato had excused himself as well, leaving only Jerry and Barnett alone in his office. Jerry cleared his throat and spoke, just to break the increasing sense of tension the inscrutable Barnett had been projecting.

"Nice office," he said. "It looks familiar."

Barnett nodded. "It's a copy of the Oval Office in the White House. I felt very comfortable there."

"Uh-huh," Jerry said.

There was another long minute of silence until Barnett seemed to feel that he'd softened Jerry up sufficiently, and spoke again.

"I just like to get to know my friends, Mr. Creighton," Leo Barnett said, "so I can tell them more easily from my enemies. It is Mr. Creighton, isn't it?"

Jerry's guilt for ragging on Billy Ray for lying to him returned, redoubled.

"Well," Jerry said after a moment, "let's say that's my name for the purposes of this discussion."

Barnett nodded after another long moment of silence stretched between them. "I see that in your own way you're a careful man. I can understand that. Even admire it. I'm a careful man as well, and I like to know whom I'm dealing with. I had you checked out by some of my connections, and you don't add up. Your past is shadowy. The history that does exist is rather unusual. By the way—I hope you don't mind my excluding your man Sascha from this little conversation. Though I'm willing to trust you to a point, I don't like the idea of exposing myself to a telepath, even a low-grade one, for any length of time."

"That's all right," Jerry said amiably, even though he detested Barnett's pompous tones. "Why are you leaving Mushroom Daddy out of the discussion?"

Barnett raised his eyebrows. "Because he's a complete flake? Because besides being an unknown goofball, he's also apparently a drug dealer? He positively reeks of the marijuana smell."

"How do you know what marijuana smells like?" Jerry asked him.

Barnett smiled, not prettily. "Enough. We have to lay our cards on the table. I'm afraid that although we've gathered John Fortune to our bosom, he's not entirely safe. The Allumbrados will still come after him, and Cardinal Contarini—who is the head of that detestable organization—has aces working for him. The boy will be in danger when, not if, they discover we've got him here at the Peaceable Kingdom. Since it's your job to protect him, and it is also totally in my interests that he remain safe, I suggest we join forces until we can break the back of the Allumbrados and they no longer pose a threat to the boy's safety."

Jerry was loaded with questions. "That's all well and good," he said. "I agree in principle, but somebody's gotta explain some things to my satisfaction."

"All right," Barnett said.

"All right," Jerry repeated. It occurred to him that he had only Nighthawk's word on the Allumbrados. It would be nice to have another, although clearly not necessarily unbiased, viewpoint. "What exactly is your interest in John Fortune, anyway? And who in the hell are the Allumbrados and what do *they* want with the boy?"

"They are tools of Satan and they want him dead," Barnett said succinctly, "while we want him to stay very much alive."

"But why, for Christ's sake?"

"Because," Barnett explained impatiently, as if this were the dozenth time he had to go over it, "he is Christ."

"Christ?" Jerry asked, nonplussed. "You mean, like Jesus Christ?"

Barnett sighed. "Yes, of course. Are you a believer, Mr. Creighton?"

"A believer?" Jerry asked. "Yeah, I guess so."

"There is no guessing, Mr. Creighton, when it comes to matters of faith. You have either accepted Jesus Christ as your personal savior, or you haven't."

"Well," Jerry said. "I guess I haven't."

"Then I'm not going to bother to explain things that you can't comprehend. No offense, Mr. Creighton."

Jerry wasn't feeling particularly gracious, but he didn't want to argue theology with the ex-president. He grunted.

"I've written a tract that proves beyond a shadow of a doubt," Leo Barnett said, "that John Fortune is Jesus Christ, Our Savior, and that His coming will usher in the Millennium and the Kingdom of God on Earth. If we can keep the Allumbrados from getting their way."

"Wait a minute," Jerry said. "I've spent a lot of time with the boy over the years. He's a nice kid and he might make a decent ace when he grows up, but he's never given any indication that he's divine."

Barnett shrugged. "There are any number of reasons why you believe that. Perhaps you're not particularly perceptive, Mr. Creighton. Or perhaps He's not ready to reveal Himself as yet, as part of His Divine Plan. Perhaps He's testing you, and us all. Or perhaps, just perhaps He Himself is not yet aware of His Divine Nature."

Barnett flipped a hand with each reason. The longer that he knew him, the more glad Jerry was that he'd never voted for the bastard.

But that was then, this was now. Barnett did control some powerful—Would minions be the word?—yes, minions, who would be helpful in protecting the boy, especially if the crazies were still after him. "All right," Jerry said, although reluctantly. "I guess Fortunato seems to think you're okay. I can trust his judgment. For now, I agree that we should combine forces."

"I applaud your wise decision," Barnett said. "Are there any more aces in your organization?"

"Well, there's Peter Pann and Topper and maybe Ezili. And Jay Ackroyd, of course." Jerry thought about it for a moment. "Other than Jay, I don't know if any of them would be particularly useful in a fight with these Allumbrados if they have goons like Butcher Dagon working for them."

"Can you get Ackroyd here?"

Jerry shook his head. "He's got a badly broken ankle. He'd be more of a liability than an asset, as much as he'd like to be here for the denouement."

He was happy to see that he stumped Barnett with that last word.

"All right," Barnett finally said, after puzzling over it for a moment. "Just as well, then. Let's all get together again soon. I'll let you know when John Fortune arrives."

"Branson will certainly be safer if we take him someplace else," Jerry said.

Barnett made a denigrating gesture. "Who cares about Branson? It's John Fortune's future that worries me."

Jerry frowned. "There's a lot of innocent people here. An ace battle of any size could cause a lot of casualties—"

"Not my concern," Barnett interrupted. "We must do whatever will be best for John Fortune."

Jerry stood. He was *really* glad that he'd never voted for this asshole. "All right," he said tonelessly. He nodded and left the office, Barnett watching him with eyes as calculating as a cruising shark's.

"How'd it go?" Sascha asked, standing as Jerry walked out of Barnett's sanctum.

"Yeah, man, what's up?" Mushroom Daddy asked.

"Remind me never to stand between Barnett and something that he wants, no matter how nutty it is," Jerry said.

"He's that bad?" Sascha asked.

"He's worse," Jerry said. "Much, much worse."

♥

The Short Cut

THE ANGEL LOOKED UP at the sound of approaching footsteps. They were so soft that at first she thought it was one of the spiders returning for the kill, but it was only Billy Ray. He dropped down to the ground before her.

"What's wrong?" he asked, a concerned expression on his face.

"Burning—" she said, straightening up on her knees. She could see Ray's concern turn to horror as he realized that the top of her jumpsuit had been slashed open by the snick of a spider's fang, and then stained with the beast's ichor after she'd gutted it.

"Shit," Ray said. "Hang on."

She watched him with a strange detachment. It was partly the pain from the acidic fluid soaking the front of her clothes, partly, she supposed, the effect of the venomous vapor as it stunned its victim.

Ray grabbed her jumpsuit at the waist and ripped it at the seam. It flew apart at the force of Ray's strength. He yanked her top away before she knew what he was doing. Underneath the jumpsuit, the front of her sports bra had been snipped in two by the creature's fangs. One breast was still covered by the fabric of the cup, the other had slipped free.

She felt his hands on her stomach and rib cage. Oddly, it didn't bother her. It took her a moment to realize that he was using a rag torn from his own fighting suit to carefully blot away the ichor that had eaten through her jumpsuit. Fortunately, it had taken most of the venom's corrosive strength to work through the leather, though her skin was burned in several spots as if touched by a lighted match. Her mind began to clear as Ray ministered to her, and she realized for the first time that she was half-naked before him.

"Think we got most of it," Ray said, his head bowed before her, concentrating on his task. "This is some strong shit—Jesus Christ!"

The realization that Ray glimpsed her breast flashed through the Angel's mind, but somehow it didn't bother her as much as she thought it might. But when she looked at him she saw that he was still concentrating on her stomach, and self-revulsion grabbed her as she realized that he'd seen the scar.

"What happened here?" Ray asked, looking up into her eyes for the first time.

She was caught by his gaze. She couldn't look away. She knew the scar was hideous. It started at the top of the hidden patch of thick dark hair that grew at the juncture of her thighs and crawled like a pink meandering snake for eight inches up and across her flat, white abdomen.

"My mother did it," the Angel heard herself saying. Her voice came as if from a great distance.

"Your mother?" Ray asked incredulously.

She nodded. "I came to her the first time I bled. I had no idea what was happening to me. I thought I was sick. That I was going to die. She told me to stop crying. To be calm. That it was the curse that came to all women, but she would save me from it. From that curse and all the curses that came from it. She took me into the kitchen and took a knife out of the drawer and tried to cut out my uterus."

"Good God," Ray said.

The Angel was so lost in memory that she didn't even reprimand him. "I would have died on the kitchen floor if my ace hadn't turned right then. Somehow I survived the wound, though I'll never have children. Which is a blessing. They'll never have to worry about the curse of the wild card."

Ray grabbed her upper arms so hard his fingers bit into muscle and flesh. "Listen," he said in an insistent voice, "the wild card virus has killed hundreds of thousands of people. It's destroyed a lot of lives. Maybe millions. It is a curse, but so's the goddamned flu. You lived through it. You lived and became something, I don't know, bigger than human. Stronger. Wilder. More vital and more goddamned beautiful than any frigging angel. For you the wild card wasn't a curse. It was a damned blessing. Millions of women would kill to be you. Don't waste your life worrying about some crazy fears your whacked mother had. She was her. You're you. You're one in ten million, babe. Never forget it."

A dam broke in the Angel's mind. "Do you really think so, Billy?"

"Of course I do, and jeez, don't cry—"

She threw herself upon him, bearing him down on the ground, her arms going around him and her lips seeking his. They hit his chin, then slipped up and covered his mouth just as he was saying, "Hey!" and she silenced him with her tongue. She saw a startled look in his eyes and then they caught fire and one hand was tangled in her hair and the other was seeking her breast that was swinging free. She shifted her hips giving him more room and his hand found and cupped it, his thumb running over her suddenly hard nipple and she sucked on his tongue in a sudden stab of delight.

She had never felt anything like this. Never. The ecstasy of prayer. Of fasting. Of privation. They all paled beside the sensations that were running like fire on her nerves. Her pelvis pushed against him and she could feel the sudden hardness between his legs even through the fabric of their clothes. She wanted him. She wanted him more than she wanted her God, more than she wanted Heaven.

"Angel," he panted in her mouth.

"Angel," John Fortune said, coming around to the back of the truck, "we're finished. Bruckner says—"

She looked back wildly over her shoulder as John Fortune stared at her, stricken. "Angel?"

"John—"

He turned and ran back to the front of the truck without a word.

Stricken, she turned to look at Ray. "He has a crush on me."

It sounded so lame as she said it, but Ray only shrugged. "Not a surprise." Ray closed his eyes for a moment, then stood and helped her up. "We'll talk to him later. Explain things. In the meantime, it's probably a good thing he interrupted us." Ray looked around. "This is not exactly the place to lose our heads. We might have really lost them."

"Is it just an interruption?" the Angel asked, half afraid of his answer, whatever it would be.

"It better be," Ray growled.

Bruckner's voice came from the front seat of the lorry. "Get a move on, will you? It's getting late. I don't like to be on the road when the moon's up."

The Angel took a step away. Ray caught her hand.

"Here," he said gruffly. "Can't have you running around like that." He stripped off the top of his fighting suit. His body was wired with cabled muscle. The Angel wanted to feel it pressed tightly against her, to run her hands over it all. He smelled of the sweat of battle. He put his shirt around her shoulders, brushing the remaining bra cup off her other breast. He palmed it for a moment, and she shivered as her nipple stiffened. She shrugged into the shirt and buttoned it, almost groaning at the unexpected pleasure of the material kissing the tips of her naked breasts.

He kissed her lightly on the lips, unexpectedly gentle. "Go on up to the truck," Ray said. "I better recover Bruckner's morning stars."

She nodded and ran up to the front of the truck. Bruckner gunned the engine, grinning.

"Climb up, lass. Let's hit the road."

John Fortune held the cab door open. He wouldn't look her in the eyes.

"John," she said softly, "we'll talk later."

He said nothing. She brushed by him, feeling the heat of him.

"You too, lad, let's get rolling."

John Fortune swung up onto the seat next to her. Bruckner engaged the gears and the truck started to roll.

"Hey!" Ray shouted from the rear. "Don't forget me."

The Angel could see him in the rearview mirror. He smiled, bent down to pick up the morning stars, straightened, and started to run toward the truck. *He looks like an animal,* she thought. *A wild, untamed animal.* The sudden thought worried her, but she knew that she had gone so far that she couldn't go back. Not this time.

The truck was rolling, but not fast. Ray caught up quickly, running easily. He had both morning stars in one hand and held out the other for John Fortune to give him a boost up through the open door. The boy reached out, their hands touched, and Ray started to pull himself up into the seat. Suddenly, terribly, he screamed.

The stench of burned flesh speared the air.

♣

Peaceable Kingdom: The Angels' Bower

BARNETT HAD CONCEDED THAT Fortunato should have a chance to greet his son in relative privacy, so Fortunato was waiting alone for the truck when it rumbled to a halt by the Bower's rear service entrance. It disgorged three passengers from the front seat, and took off again with a farewell blast of its air horn. The driver seemed to be in a hurry.

Fortunato recognized all three. Billy Ray, of course. The woman who called herself the Midnight Angel. And his son. His eagerness at finally seeing the boy for the first time face-to-face was tempered by the realization that something had gone terribly wrong during the last moment of the rescue. He couldn't bear, for the moment, to delve into their minds.

"He didn't mean it," the Angel said.

Ray's teeth were clenched against the pain shooting through his hand. He gripped it by the wrist with his other hand.

"I'm sorry," John Fortune said worriedly. "I don't know what happened. I couldn't control it for a moment—"

"It's okay," Ray said in a strained voice. "I'll be all right in a little bit."

He held the fingers of his hand apart from each other as they curled in pain. They were burned so badly that their skin was black and flaky. Fortunato could smell the stink of seared flesh.

"Ray," he said, "are you all right?"

"Yeah, fine," Ray said shortly. "I should go get some salve for this burn."

"What happened?" Fortunato asked.

"An accident," Ray said. "I'll be all right."

Ray was sincere in his attempt to ease the boy's obviously troubled mind, but Fortunato could detect uncertainty in his voice and manner. Not for his own ultimate recovery, but at what really lay behind his injury. Fortunato only nodded.

"Thank you for bringing my son back safe," he said. He turned to the Angel and nodded at her as well.

"My pleasure," Ray said.

"Take care of your hand," Fortunato told them. "We'll talk more later."

"I'll go with Billy," the Angel said, glancing back at John Fortune, who was holding back with a worried expression on his face. "We'll talk soon, John," she said, but the boy only nodded.

As they went by him, Fortunato could sense something growing between the two of them, and he refrained from looking any deeper into their minds. He felt only gratitude for what they'd done for him. He felt as if he would be in their debt forever.

He looked at the boy, and John Fortune looked uncertainly at him. He wondered what he should say. "Hello," Fortunato finally said.

"Hello," his son replied.

Fortunato could see himself in the boy's features, in the golden tan color of his skin. But Peregrine was there, too, and it made him sorry for what he had missed over the years. Of what could have been his. But those years were over and done with. There were more to come, and those were the years that concerned him.

"Do you know who I am?" he asked.

His son nodded. "Mom showed me pictures. She said you were the most powerful ace ever, but you gave it up."

"Did she say why?" Fortunato asked.

Fortune looked thoughtful, as if Fortunato's question had put aside the fear and doubt that had been foremost in his mind. At least for a moment, anyway. "She said that you couldn't pay the price of being an ace anymore. That the world weighed heavy on you, and you had to leave it behind."

"Your mother," Fortunato said, "is perceptive. And most kind."

It struck Fortunato for the first time exactly why Peregrine had been so protective, perhaps overly so. She wasn't afraid so much of crazies out to kidnap him for gain or harm him for thrills. She was afraid of his very nature, afraid that the dynamite he carried in his genes might explode at any second.

Looking at him you saw a handsome, easygoing boy on the verge of manhood. But if you knew his background, if you lived with it every second of every minute of every hour of your life, you knew that someday he was going to explode and most likely die. His genes were infected with the wild card. There was no doubt about it. Both his parents had it, so it was certain that he did. It awaited only expression, in many cases caused by some surprise or shock that would turn his card; then it would kill him.

But he had beaten that, hadn't he? His son had a chance for glory. He'd grabbed the one in a hundred chance to be an ace. But even so, turning an ace could be almost as great a curse as turning a joker, or drawing the black queen. The names of ace victims were legion, from the earliest days of the wild card on. Brain Trust. Black Eagle. Kid Dinosaur. The Howler. Hiram Worchester. Desperado. The list went on and on. Fortunato couldn't remember all the aces who'd suffered because society eventually turned on them.

That was why Peregrine had protected their son so fiercely. Fortunato saw it now. Seeing his son in the flesh for the first time, he knew why she did it. And he knew that, ultimately, she was doomed to fail.

"I'd like to call Mom," John Fortune said. "Tell her that I'm safe."

"That's a good idea," Fortunato said. "Do you want anything else?"

Fortunato could tell that he held back something. Something he was afraid to or was unwilling to discuss with this stranger who was his father. Finally, he said, "I'm awfully hungry."

"Let's get you some food, then. I have a suite in the hotel. We can order room service. Talk and get to know each other a little."

"Cool." John Fortune smiled.

Ah, Fortunato thought, *the resilience of the young.*

"Mom told me about you," John Fortune said, "as soon as I was able to understand why I had a different name from my dad. But now that you're here and all, what should I call you?"

"Call me Fortunato, if you want. And I'll call you John."

"Sweet," John Fortune said. "Fortunato." He tried it out, and smiled. He seemed to like the sound of it.

Fortunato put out his hand. John Fortune reached to take it, then hesitated. It was clear that he was afraid, but not for himself. He was afraid that his touch would burn Fortunato, like it had burned Ray.

Fortunato took his son's hand. He was prepared. His relaxed, smiling face didn't change expression. But he was glad that he'd just taken on a load of energy. He built a wall, a buffer, between his flesh and his son's. Otherwise, caught in the trap of the boy's hand, his own hand would have cooked, would have burned worse than Ray's. He released John Fortune's hand, and together they turned and went through the hotel's service entrance.

"Are you going to stay in America for a while?" John Fortune asked. He seemed to be totally unaware of the heat his body was generating. His skin looked normal, except of course for the glowing halo. It wasn't flushed or even sweating.

"Yes," Fortunato said, the fear again biting his insides like a great viper. "Yes, I am."

He suddenly realized that his son might not have drawn an ace, after all.

♠

Peaceable Kingdom: The Manger

USHER WENT TO THE suite's door, peeked through the peephole, and turned back to Nighthawk.

"The gang's all here," he said, and opened the door. Contarini came in. His faultless suit had recently been faulted. He had grass stains on his knees. His white shoes were scuffed with dark Mississippi dirt. There was a bad tear in his jacket's breast, and one sleeve had been partially torn free of its shoulder. His silk shirt was wrinkled, soiled, and sweat-stained. He didn't look happy. "It didn't go well?" Nighthawk asked.

Contarini shook his head wordlessly and collapsed into the nearest chair. He scowled at the vinyl upholstery. "They have the luck of the Devil riding with them," the cardinal said.

Usher and Nighthawk exchanged glances. "Naturally," Nighthawk said. "What happened?"

Magda fluttered helplessly about the cardinal as if she couldn't decide whether to shine his shoes, sew his clothes, or wash and iron his shirt, as he told him in minute and surprisingly profane detail what had happened, pausing to shoo Magda away when she'd finally annoyed him too much.

Nighthawk sighed. "I guess they've beaten us now, for the moment. We'll continue to keep an eye on them. The boy will be easy to spot. Perhaps you should return to New York, to rest and consider the next move."

Dagon and the Witness nodded in agreement. "That would be smart," Dagon said.

"No." They all turned to Contarini, whose voice had taken on the chill of doom. "I want this farce ended. Now."

"Now?" Dagon repeated. "I don't—"

The cardinal fixed him with a stare that quailed archbishops. "Not 'now,' literally. But as soon as possible. I want this ended. I want this Devil's spawn in our hands. I want to return him to the Holy See, or, if that is not possible, I want him dead."

"Do you think that's wise?" Nighthawk asked. This was the first time that the cardinal had actually called for the boy's death. The pressure, Nighthawk thought, was finally getting to him. "In this place? After all, Las Vegas is one thing—"

"This place is no different!" the cardinal blazed at him. "It's a low-class tourist trap for fat, comic-book-reading Americans. They have no clue as to the strength and tenacity of the Allumbrados!" He turned his bleak gaze onto Nighthawk. "Blood is not far from this . . . this disgusting fairyland. I want you to supervise him as he brings in all the *obsequentes* that we have. All armed. We'll take the Devil's spawn as soon as they're all in place."

"If you drive Blood too hard," Nighthawk said, "you'll kill him."

"Let him die and be damned," the cardinal said. "His only chance at salvation is to die in Christ's service, anyway. He should welcome the opportunity."

We'll see about that, Nighthawk thought. He suppressed a sigh as he stood.

"I guess this means we'll have to skip supper at Loaves and Fishes," Usher said. Nighthawk nodded.

"Pity," Usher said. "They have great grits." He looked at the Witness, who scowled back at him. "You can't really get them outside the South," he said seriously.

◆

Peaceable Kingdom: The Manger

RAY WAS TIRED, BUT he could not sleep.

His hand hurt, but it was bandaged and healing, as were all his numerous other wounds. He was jazzed as he always was after a fight, though it hadn't been much of one. The Witness might have provided some real competition, but he'd been a disappointment. It kind of disturbed Ray when he'd screamed like a little girl. The trip through what the Brit had called "the Short Cut" had been disturbing as well. Sure, he'd got to put a period to the career of Ti Malice, and that counted for something, but fighting spider-things wasn't exactly his cup of tea. And although he'd suddenly gotten to know Angel a lot better than he had before, he couldn't find her. She'd vanished after he'd gotten his hand bandaged, and the Peaceable Kingdom was one damn big place when you were trying to find a single angel in it.

He paced his room. It was usually like this. The adrenaline took forever to leave his system, making him edgy and keeping him awake no matter how much he wanted sleep. He looked out the window of his room. Night had come to the Peaceable Kingdom, and he was back to wishing that he was just about anywhere else in the world.

He started, uncharacteristically, at the tentative tap at his door, a single knock, unrepeated.

"Who is it?" Ray asked.

"The Angel," she said quietly, barely audible through the door.

He was before it in a moment, and opened it. She stood in the hallway, blinking, her hair mussed, her leathers dirty and sweaty, scuffed and torn, still wearing his shirt. She was beautiful.

"Come in," he said, and she did.

She stood awkwardly in the middle of the room. "John Fortune is asleep," she said. "Fortunato is with him."

"Good," Ray said. "He okay?"

Angel shook her head. "We don't know. He's frightened, exhausted. The Hand—"

"What's with all this 'Hand' sh—stuff?" he asked.

"That's his title," Angel said. "The Hand of God."

"Jeez," Ray said. "And to think I knew him when he was only the president of the United States."

Angel closed her eyes, and Ray could see that suddenly she was on the verge of tears.

"Hey, what's the matter?" he asked. "I didn't mean anything. You can call him the Spleen of God for all I care. What's wrong?"

She took a deep, shuddering breath, controlling herself. "Nothing. Nothing. I'm just tired. The job is done. We've saved him from the Allumbrados. But . . ."

"Yeah," Ray said. "The job is done, but life goes on, doesn't it?"

Angel looked down at the floor. "I don't want to be alone," she said in a small voice. "I can't be alone anymore."

"You don't have to be," Ray said. He came close, but didn't touch her. He felt an odd sensation. For a moment he couldn't identify it, then he realized that it was fear. He was afraid to touch her, he realized. Afraid of how she would react.

"I meant to take a shower, to clean up, but I don't have any other clothes—"

Ray laid a finger softly against her lips. At the touch of his flesh on hers, his fear was suddenly gone. He smiled, but suppressed a relieved sigh. "You don't have to apologize."

She finally looked at him. She had the darkest, largest eyes he had ever seen. They were two sad bruises in the alabaster of her face. "My mother never let me listen to music," she said, seemingly irreverently, "except in church. She thought that music was the tool of Satan. But sometimes she'd drink, like that night she cut me, and listen to records she had from when she was young. She'd listen to them over and over again. They were all scratched and hissing so you could barely make out the words. One of them had a song on it that said something like, 'I'm afraid of the Devil, but I'm drawn to them that ain't.' I didn't understand the words then, but I think I understand now why she listened to that song. I think I know what it means. I think I'm the same way as my mother."

She looked seriously at him.

"I think you think too much sometimes," Ray said, bending his head to hers.

Unlike their first kiss, this one began soft, but didn't stay that way for long. It grew in hunger and passion. Her mouth tasted so good that he wasn't sure how she got out of her clothes or even whether she or he had taken them off.

She was magnificent. That was all he could think. Her breasts were heavy and dark-tipped. Her nipples were already erect. She moaned when he caressed them. Her breath hissed inward when he took one in his mouth. Her hips were wide, her waist narrow and ribbed with muscle. Her thighs were lean and sinewy, the juncture at them dark and inviting. He put a hand there and she shuddered against his body. He trailed his fingers across her flat abdomen, tracing the path of the scar as it twisted upon her stomach.

"It's so ugly," she said.

"Nothing about you is ugly, Angel."

"You're not just saying that?" she asked in a whisper.

He bit her neck gently where it curved into the ivory strength of her shoulder. "Have I ever lied to you?"

"I don't know," she said, shivering as his kisses went up the column of her throat, "but you'd better not now."

They fell on the bed. She was already ready. It seemed like she had been for quite a while now. She closed her eyes. "Thy will be done," she said, and gasped when he took her.

It was a wild ride. Ray had never experienced anything like it before. She was strong and eager and he didn't last as long as he wanted to. He did have the pleasure of bringing her to at least one screaming orgasm before he succumbed himself and shuddered against her in what seemed like an endless stream of pleasure. They lay together, panting, and Ray shook his head.

"I've never screwed like that before. You're so strong. So hungry."

"I've never screwed before. Period."

"Well," Ray said, "that was one hell of a first try." He leaned back on one elbow, but couldn't keep his hands from the silken skin of her breasts. Their nipples puckered again at his first touch. "Did you like it?"

She closed her eyes. "It was glorious." She opened them and looked seriously at Ray. "When can we do it again?"

He laughed. "With any other guy, it might take awhile. But, lucky you."

"What do you mean?" she asked.

"Don't you know that one of my powers is regeneration?" he asked.

Her laughter turned to groans of delight as his mouth closed over hers.

Chapter Eleven

Peaceable Kingdom: The Angels' Bower

THE CORRIDOR LEADING FROM the elevator to Barnett's sanctum was lousy with Secret Service agents, and the second string—Mushroom Daddy, Digger Downs, and that kid Secret Service agent whose name Jerry kept forgetting—were in the reception room with Sally Lou. She looked as cool and desirable as ever.

Only Barnett and Fortunato were inside. Barnett looked up sourly as Jerry knocked and entered. He was not, Jerry realized, in a good mood. He turned to Fortunato. "You were saying about the boy?"

He must be really worried about something, Jerry thought. *It's actually showing on his face.*

Fortunato shook his head. "He finally fell asleep. I didn't want to wake him." Fortunato looked bleakly at Jerry. "He should be dead. I'm afraid that he didn't draw an ace after all, but a Black Queen."

Jerry felt Fortunato's words like a hammer blow to his guts. "That can't be," he said. "He was fine—"

"Was fine," Fortunato said with grim finality. "It seems that his Black Queen is an odd bitch. Slow acting, but progressing geometrically. His body temperature rose well over fifty degrees during the night. I can't even begin to guess what it is now. I'm not a doctor, but I can recognize death when I see it coming. How high can his temperature go before his body just burns up?"

"Maybe it's part of his ace metabolism," Jerry said hopefully. "Maybe his body won't burn."

Barnett nodded eagerly. "Yes, of course. He *is* divine—"

They looked at him and frowned. Fortunato spoke. "Maybe he is," he said, though his tone indicated his dubiousness, "but his surroundings aren't. How long until he's a danger to everything around him?"

"You can't know for sure that he will be," Barnett said. He looked like a man who was fighting hard to maintain an unlikely viewpoint.

"He burned Billy Ray by just touching him," Fortunato said in a leaden voice that lacked all hope. "He would have burned me if I hadn't shielded myself. And the process seems to be speeding up. He's getting hotter, faster. If it keeps going at this pace, by evening he'll consume everything around him. He won't be able to control it at all."

A depressed silence settled over Barnett's office.

"There's one possibility left," Jerry said. He and Fortunato looked at each other, and nodded. "The Trump," they said together.

Years ago, Dr. Tachyon had managed to concoct a cure for the wild card virus, but it was so dangerous in itself that it was only administered when a patient was facing inescapable death.

Barnett frowned. "Isn't the Trump pretty unsafe?"

"Fifty percent fatality rate," Fortunato said, looking at no one.

"You can't . . ." Barnett began, but his voice ran down to silence.

"We must," Jerry said, "if we're sure the kid is going to die. Or pose a danger to his surroundings." He looked at the ace sitting next to him. "Sorry, Fortunato."

"No," Fortunato said heavily. "You're right. But we have to be sure."

Jerry nodded. "The Jokertown Clinic has the only supply of the Trump." He sighed deeply. "I'll fly back to the city and get a dose. By the time I get back we should know for sure if we'll have to use it. One way or the other."

It was hard for Jerry to volunteer to fetch the Trump. Very hard. Over the years John Fortune had become something like the son he'd never had. He'd seen him grow up to be a nice kid. He'd seen him apparently beat all the odds and become an ace. Now death was again panting over his shoulder. *It would have been easier,* Jerry thought, *if he'd just drawn a Black Queen that day in Vegas. But the kid deserved better than that. . . .*

"Hang on," Jerry said, looking at Fortunato. "He almost beat the odds when the virus struck him. He has an even better chance with the Trump."

Fortunato nodded. He looked at Barnett. "If you believe in the power of prayer," he told the ex-president, "get down on your knees for the sake of my boy."

To his vast surprise, Barnett came around his desk, sank down on his knees, and bowed his head. "Let us pray," Barnett said.

Peaceable Kingdom: The Angels' Bower

"WE DON'T KNOW EXACTLY where the boy is," Nighthawk told the cardinal, "but we will soon." He frowned. "There may be something wrong with him, though," he said.

The cardinal interrupted angrily. "If we injured him somehow, all the better. The assault teams are in place. Start the attack."

Nighthawk nodded equitably. "As you say."

Peaceable Kingdom: The Angels' Bower

THE ANGEL DIDN'T QUITE know where she was when she woke up. It was still morning by the bedside clock. She'd slept deeply, almost as if she'd been drugged. As she lay drowsing she realized suddenly that her bone-deep weariness was gone. She felt refreshed. Somehow replete. She turned and looked at the rumpled bed beside her, and Billy Ray was gone. She sat up, holding the sheets around her breasts, feeling the touch of the fabric everywhere on her naked skin. The room was quiet and empty. Billy Ray was gone.

She felt so . . . ashamed. They did things last night she could scarcely imagine, let alone believe. And she had reveled in it all. She had lain in his arms panting with lust like an animal. She had kissed him willingly. She had joined with him willingly. She had laughed with him between bouts of lovemaking. She . . .

Wasn't ashamed, actually. It surprised her to realize that. She wasn't ashamed of what she'd done. It had been a wonderful night, wonderful and glorious in a way she'd never experienced before. She wanted to have other nights like that with him.

But Billy Ray was gone.

Maybe her mother had been right. Men used you to sate their lusts, then cast you aside, leaving you with the consequences of your actions. A swollen belly and a child to burden you for years. Well, the Angel thought, at least that last part couldn't happen to her.

The song her mother had played obsessively said that love is touching souls. The Angel was sure that more than their bodies had touched last night. She was sure their souls had as well. At least hers had. That was the only way to explain the complete and utter ecstasy she'd found, coupled with a sense of peace and rightness that she'd never felt before in her life. She'd found that. But there was no telling about Ray.

And now he was gone.

"Just like a man," she said aloud, and suddenly the door opened and Billy Ray came into the room with an armful of packages.

"Hi, babe," he said, grappling with the packages and the door, finally managing to close it without dropping the boxes he carried. "You're finally awake." He paused. "What's the matter?" he asked.

The Angel realized she was glaring at him. She sank down into the bed and pulled the sheet up to her chin. "Nothing," she said in a small voice.

He spilled the packages on the bed and sat down next to her. "Okay. I had to get something to eat after last night's workout." He grinned wickedly at her, and put his hand on the sheet over her upper right thigh and squeezed. "I don't sleep much anyway. You looked like you needed your rest, so I didn't want to disturb you by ordering room service. Also, I knew you didn't have any clothes so I picked up a few things for you. You can do a proper shopping trip later."

The Angel was almost overwhelmed by his casual thoughtfulness. "I—I can't accept these things from you—"

"Why not?" Ray frowned. "Besides, I found Barnett's charge card among the remains of your jumpsuit, and put everything on it. The jumpsuit was a total loss, so I tossed it. Hope you don't mind."

The Angel shook her head, barely holding back her laughter. She had climbed again from the pits of despair to the very heights. "Of course you did," she said.

"Huh?"

"Never mind. How's your hand?"

Ray frowned and held it up. He looked at it as if it were an alien object someone had grafted to the end of his arm without him realizing it. He stripped the tape away, and the bandage underneath. The skin covering his once-burnt flesh was smooth and pink as a baby's bottom. He grinned and wriggled his fingers.

"All right," Ray said, as if surprised. "It healed pretty fast. Maybe that's why I've been so hungry. Grab a shower and get dressed and let's go get something to eat. I'm hungry again and I'll bet you're famished."

He was right. She was ravenous. She started to slip out of the other side of the bed, the sheet still drawn around her, and Ray grabbed it and pulled it away. Her first reaction was to cover her breasts and loins with her hands, but that was ridiculous. She blushed, but leaned close to him.

"I could drink a case of you," she said, "and still be on my feet."

"What?" Ray said, frowning.

"It's our song," she told him, and laughed at his befuddled look. She grabbed him and kissed him hard, then let him go and, still blushing, walked self-consciously to the bathroom, his eyes following her every step.

♠

Peaceable Kingdom: The Angels' Bower

THE ANTEROOM WAS EVEN more crowded after they piled out of Barnett's office when the meeting ended. Barnett stayed behind to continue his prayer vigil.

Digger Downs had been chatting up Sally Lou, and Mushroom Daddy was watching the kid Secret Service agent, Alejandro something or other, who was ostensibly on guard duty, make Sally Lou's pens and pencils wriggle around on her desk as if they were snakes.

"Very cool, man," Daddy said. "Animation. That's a power I could dig. Kind of like Mickey in 'The Sorcerer's Apprentice.' Ever watch that movie stoned, man? The dancing mushrooms are just hilarious."

Sascha was gone. Barnett had intercommed Sally Lou to get Jerry a reservation on the next available flight to New York. Sascha had gone ahead to the airport to make sure there weren't any screwups. Downs looked intently at Jerry and Fortunato as they exited Barnett's office, dropping his try at charming Sally Lou. "Something's going on," he said. "I can tell."

Fortunato grimaced. "I suppose I owe you the whole story. The boy's down in our suite, still sleeping. Come along, and I'll tell you."

They left the office together, and Sally Lou turned to the phone bank.

"What's up, man?" Mushroom Daddy asked Jerry, breaking off his conversation with the Secret Service kid, who looked somewhat relieved.

"Heading back to New York," Jerry said. "I've got to pick up something at the Jokertown Clinic."

He figured there was no sense in spreading the real story around. Mushroom Daddy nodded.

"Might as well go with you, man," Daddy said. He looked very sad. "I was planning on driving my van back, but it doesn't look like that's gonna happen. It's gone, man. I only had three hundred thousand miles on it."

Jerry felt sympathetic. To a point. "Shit happens, man," he said.

Mushroom Daddy nodded philosophically. "Ain't that the truth."

Sally Lou looked up from the phone she'd just answered, blank-eyed.

"Uh," she said, "Uh—"

"What is it, man?" Daddy asked.

"Armed men are attacking the Bower," she said in an oddly calm voice, as if stunned by the news. "They're trying to reach the penthouse."

"Shit," Jerry said. "The Allumbrados! Get Barnett on the horn." She nodded rapidly. "Tell him what's happening," Jerry said. "Tell him to freeze the elevator banks. With any luck we can catch a bunch of those assholes between floors if they're dumb enough to try to come on up on the lifts. Call Fortunato's suite. Call Ray. Try to find Angel. Let them know what the hell is happening. We'll go downstairs and check things out."

"I'm coming with you," Alejandro said.

"Your duty's with Barnett—" Jerry began.

"My duty is to stop anyone coming after him. He's safe here with the other agents guarding the corridor, at least for a while. Besides, you'll need me downstairs."

"All right," Jerry said. "No sense wasting time arguing over who belongs where. Come on."

They went to the north stairwell at a run, stopping only briefly to tell the agents on duty in the corridor what was happening, and headed downstairs. They went down half a dozen flights before Alejandro, leading the way, suddenly pulled up short.

"What's the matter?" Jerry asked. "You okay?"

Alejandro nodded silently and drew an automatic from his shoulder holster. "I am," he said. "Unfortunately, I'm afraid that I can't say the same for you two."

"Hey, man," Mushroom Daddy said, "that's so not cool."

"I don't want to do this," Alejandro said, "but blood must sometimes be spilled in the service of the Lord."

"What are you talking about?" Jerry asked. "You're a Secret Service agent!"

Alejandro nodded. "I am. I am also a *perfecti* in the service of Our Lord, a somewhat higher master whom I am even more tightly bound to serve."

Shit, Jerry thought. *What—*

Mushroom Daddy moved. He swiveled on one foot, lashing out with the other, catching the turncoat Secret Service agent on his gun hand. The agent lost his grip on the automatic, and it went clattering down the stairs. Alejandro went after it like a cat after a fleeing mouse.

"Run!" Daddy said, and for once the hippie made sense.

He and Jerry turned and fled back up the staircase. Jerry hit the steel fire door just as a bullet ricocheted off it near his head, reverberations from the gunshot pounding his eardrums like tiny hammers. He and Mushroom Daddy pushed through the door, then closed it behind them, leaning against it and breathing deeply.

"Where'd you learn how to do that?" Jerry panted.

"Bruce Lee movies, man," Mushroom Daddy said. "He's the king."

"Well, thanks," Jerry said.

"No problemo, man," Daddy said. "Even a pacifist has to kick ass sometimes." He paused to take a deep breath. "What do we do now?"

Jerry shook his head. It was clear that the plan to go back to the city to get a dose of the Trump was no longer feasible. There was nothing much they could do, now, that seemed remotely helpful.

Peaceable Kingdom: The Angels' Bower

ANGEL WAS STILL SUFFICIENTLY self-conscious to dress in the bathroom.

Pity, Ray thought. He loved watching beautiful women get into clothes. And out of them, for that matter. He was particularly interested in seeing her in the underwear he'd picked up. Though he was sufficiently realistic to get her a plain, boring sports bra to wear under her new jumpsuit, he'd also picked up a few rather more lacy numbers for casual wear. He stuck with thong panties all around, though. You couldn't beat those for looks and all-around wearability.

Angel came out of the bathroom, a concerned look on her face.

"Don't you think this is a little low-cut?" she asked, gesturing at the front of the new outfit.

Ray shook his head in admiration. "No," he said. "I'd say that it's just about right."

"And a little too bright?" she asked.

He shook his head again. "Nope. It's about time you got out of black, babe. It has its place in a wardrobe, but it can get depressing if you wear it all the time. Red suits you."

"If you say so," Angel said uncertainly.

Ray nodded enthusiastically. "I do. Now let's eat. I'm starved."

She smiled. "Me too."

Ray's room was on the first floor above the lobby and shop level. When possible he always took rooms on the first floor. He didn't like to deal with elevators in either emergencies or on an everyday basis. They went down a flight of stairs that led from the room block to the hotel lobby, and Ray immediately knew that something was wrong. He could smell it even before he saw it. It was an odor he knew well, a mixture of blood and gunpowder residue.

"What in the bleeding hell?" he asked aloud.

He and Angel stared at each other, then gazed around the lobby. It was deserted, except for a couple of bodies lying in pools of blood. Some were moving feebly or groaning, most were not.

"We've got to help them," Angel said.

Ray grabbed her arm as she started forward. "First we have to find out what the hell is happening," he said. "Split up. Look around outside. I'll check the lobby. Don't go far, and if you see anything that might explain this, for Christ's sake, come and get me."

Angel nodded. "Don't blaspheme," she told him.

"Right." He grabbed her by the upper arm. "And whatever you do, be careful."

She smiled briefly, dazzling him, and was gone. He turned and headed for the shops lining the lobby.

The only person in the first one he went into was a gray-uniformed security guard who was bravely defending the deserted store from nonexistent looters. The guard was a badly shaken youngster with badly shaking hands. Ray was glad he didn't have a gun or else he would have shot someone, probably himself, out of fear-induced ineptitude. He flinched when Ray marched up to him and tried to duck under the counter by the cash register, but Ray hauled him up.

"Get a grip, Howard," he said, reading the kid's name off his tag above the fancy badge pinned to his shirt pocket. He reached for his own identification wallet, flipped it open, and shoved it into the kid's face. "My name is Billy Ray. I'm a federal agent. You got that, Howard?"

The kid stuttered a frightened, "Y-y-y-yes, s-s-s-sir," that Ray almost interrupted three or four times out of sheer impatience.

"What's going on out there, Howard?"

"I don't know, sir," the kid said. "But there's dead men out there in the lobby. Some of them are *security guards.*" He said that as if it were the most shocking thing imaginable, and started to cry. Ray shook him by the collar until his teeth rattled.

"Snap out of it, goddamn it," he said. The Allumbrados had come after them. Again. It had to be them. The persistent bastards. But no one would believe the story if he told it the way it really was. He let go of Howard's collar, took out a pen and scribbled a name and a phone number on the back of a card from his wallet. "I want you to call this number," he said in clear and precise tones. "Tell them Billy Ray told you to report to Nephi Callendar. Tell him that a gang of aces are trying to assassinate ex-President Leo Barnett under the guise of robbing the hotel. Tell him to get help out here, pronto, or else the Secret Service will have a dead ex-president on their hands. You got all that, Howard?"

The security guard nodded.

"What's my name, Howard?"

"Uh. Leo Barnett?"

Ray slapped him once across the face, fairly hard, then grabbed his shirt before he could fall down. "Wrong, Howard. My name is Billy Ray. It's on the other side of the card. The man I want you to call is named Nephi Callendar. I've written his name on this side of the card. Now, what's the story?"

"Uh, Leo Barnett is, uh, robbing the hotel, and—"

Ray sighed. "Just tell them Billy Ray said to get their asses down here or else there'll be a dead ex-president on the five o'clock news. You get that right, and there'll be a promotion for you. You fuck up, Howard, and I'll hunt you down myself and kill you. You got that?"

"Yessir," Howard managed.

Ray sighed. It was the best he could do. If he made the call himself they'd only want him to stay on the other end of the line and answer useless fucking questions. The odds were, anyway, that help wouldn't arrive in time. Whatever was going down here was going down fast. But there was always the slim chance that the Feds could show up in time to be useful.

Now, Ray thought, to collect Angel and get up to Barnett's office, fast. That was where the bad guys would be headed, after the kid who was ensconced in Fortunato's suite on the floor below Barnett's HQ. If Barnett, or Fortunato, or somebody was on the ball, they'd have already stopped the elevators, maybe catching some of the bad guys in frozen steel cages. He couldn't count on that, though. He could count on the fact that the cardinal probably sent a shitload of bad guys on this little adventure. He was probably really pissed by now.

Ray cut through the lobby at high speed, closing his ears to the cries of the wounded civilians he passed. *No time for you now,* he thought. *Just hang on, hang on and we'll get to you ASAP. If we can.*

He spotted Angel just outside the tall glass doors leading up to the lobby's main entrance at the top of the set of marble stairs. She was looking out into the courtyard in front of the hotel and the surrounding parking lot.

"Angel—"

She turned to him, and silently gestured outward. In the courtyard were the Witness and Butcher Dagon, both. They were surrounded by armed goons. Alejandro Jesús y Maria C de Baca stood on the lowest step of the marble stairs, looking up at Angel.

Ray grinned his crazy grin. "Alejandro," he called. "Now's your chance, kid. Let's see your stuff."

Alejandro nodded slowly. Behind him, the Witness and Butcher Dagon approached, though the gunmen kept their distance. Alejandro did and said nothing until the two aces joined him. He looked at them and nodded, then he looked up at Ray.

"It'd be best if you just gave up, Billy. I don't want to see either you or Angel get hurt, and I'm afraid you're pretty well outnumbered."

Ray frowned. His pulse beat with sudden anger. "Why you little bastard," he said. "I always thought that you were too polite."

Alejandro shrugged. "I'm sorry to hear that. I am a great admirer of yours."

"Yeah, well, I never liked you."

"He gave you good advice," Witness said. "You'd better take it. We have to join the party inside. If you let us pass, we'll just let you go. If you try to slow us down, we'll kill you."

"How's your knee, you prick?" Ray asked. "Still walking with a limp?"

Witness scowled, but Dagon grabbed his arm and shook his head.

Alejandro shrugged again. "As you will, Billy."

"Call me 'Mr. Ray,' you traitorous shit."

Alejandro turned and looked over his right shoulder, a frown of concentration on his youthful features.

Angel lifted her arms to the Heavens. "Save my soul from evil, Lord," she intoned, "and heal this warrior's heart." Her sword appeared as always, a roaring flame in her hands. She smiled at him. He was happy to see that her smile was without the taint of fear. "Stand with me, Billy," she said. "'One sword at least thy right shall guard,'" she semi-quoted.

Ray grinned crazily. "'One faithful heart shall praise thee,'" he responded in the same spirit. "With all due respect to Thomas Moore."

Her eyes widened in surprise. "Why, Billy. I'd never guess you went in for poetry."

"Stick around, babe. I'm full of surprises."

"I believe I will," she said, nodding.

From the parking lot came the sound of ancient stone groaning.

"Oh, crap," Ray said.

The statues of the three apostles that stood in front of the Angels' Bower climbed down creakily from their daises and approached the lobby entrance like arthritic giants.

♥

Peaceable Kingdom: The Angels' Bower

JOHN FORTUNE COULD NO longer sit on the bed without the sheets smoldering. The glow of his halo was so bright that it made Fortunato's eyes ache. Downs, at his side, stared at the boy with a gaping mouth. The reporter was so stunned by the unexpected turn of events that he didn't even ask Fortunato any questions.

John Fortune wore his sneakers to insulate the bottom of his feet so that he wouldn't leave burn marks on the carpet. A wet towel was wrapped around his waist. Fortunato was afraid that anything else would burn. He had to get a new one every few minutes and exchange it with the one his son was wearing. There was no sign as to how high his temperature would eventually go.

"Maybe," Fortunato said, "you'd be more comfortable in the bathroom. You could lie down in the tub for a while. Rest some."

"I'm okay," John Fortune said, "but, yeah, you might be right."

He seemed to realize what Fortunato didn't want to say. That he was becoming a fire hazard in a hotel room that had so many flammable objects in it.

"I'll go with you. We can talk for a while."

"That'd be nice," the boy said.

As they headed for the bathroom, the doorbell suddenly rang. Fortunato stopped and looked at Downs. "Digger," he said. "Go with John. I'll be with you in a moment."

Downs nodded. "Jeez," he asked the boy, "does it hurt?"

John Fortune looked more bewildered than frightened. "No. Not really. It's just . . . strange. I feel warm, but it's not uncomfortable. The heat feels soothing. I am hungry, though."

Fortunato watched them go off together, then went to the door and peered out through the spy hole. He quickly unlocked the door when he realized who was outside. The ace who called himself Creighton came in, accompanied by the enigmatic Mushroom Daddy.

"What happened?" Fortunato asked, then realized there was no time for niceties. He read the story from Creighton's mind. He glanced at Mushroom Daddy, who looked back innocently at him. Fortunato took a stab at his mind, but could not gain access to it. The man clearly was a mystery, a puzzle that would be interesting to solve, but Fortunato had no time for idle pasttimes. "All right," he said. "I get it. Alejandro is out of our hands, for now, and there's no time to retrieve the Trump, anyway. It's no longer an alternative."

"Right," Jerry said.

Fortunato nodded. The only question was what to do now, and Fortunato had no answer for it.

Peaceable Kingdom: The Angels' Bower, Lobby

"INSIDE," RAY SHOUTED, AND the Angel followed him unhesitatingly.

They went back into the lobby through the tall glass doors, the statues following them ponderously, like twenty-foot-tall golems.

"How is this possible?" Angel asked.

"It's that frigging kid," Ray said. "His power is animation. He can make inanimate objects obey his will. And apparently his will is for them to squash us."

Glass shattered as the first statue hunkered down and smashed through the doors, showering shards all over the lobby's interior. To her shame, the Angel was unsure which of the apostles this statue represented, so she thought of it as Peter. Even though it was a holy figure, she screamed an inarticulate battle cry and hurled herself at it, swinging her sword as hard as she could.

"Hamstring the bastard!" Ray shouted.

It was a good idea, but the Angel decided to aim even lower. The bastard couldn't walk if it didn't have any feet, she thought, and immediately wondered if Ray was being too great of an influence on her. Her sword skimmed the floor and chopped at Peter's ankle. It clanged against stone, shivering in her hands. Her arms went numb almost up to her elbows, but she felt her blade bite deep. A sizeable chip flaked off Peter's ankle, running up into his calf. The force of her blow caused the statue to sway like an oak in a storm. She suddenly wished that she had John Bruckner's morning stars. With those she could reduce the statue to rubble in a matter of minutes.

One of the other statues, *Call him John,* the Angel thought, was crowding past Peter. John took a ponderous swipe at the Angel as Ray called out a warning. She ducked and the very tips of John's fingers brushed against the back of her shoulders, hurling her backward on the floor. She slid a dozen feet, broken glass scraping her leather jumpsuit, but it held.

Ray darted forward, grimacing in anger. He leaped at Peter, planting one foot on the statue's injured leg, and swarmed up his chest like a monkey climbing a cliff. He rammed his shoulder under Peter's chin and heaved. The ponderous sculpture tipped over backward and fell hard to the lobby floor with all the grace of a drunken sailor.

The Angel levered herself to her feet and bounded after Ray. As Peter reached for Ray with his left hand, the Angel swung her sword and sheared through his wrist. His hand flew off and shattered on the lobby floor.

Ray kept going. He slid between John's immense, widely braced thighs. The statue bent forward slowly at the waist and tried to catch him as he went by. He missed and the back of his exposed neck presented a tempting target. The Angel braced herself and brought her sword down like a headsman's ax. Her first blow bit deeply. Using all her strength, she yanked the blade free desperately, then wound up and swung again as the apostle turned his head and looked at her disapprovingly. She said an apologetic prayer under her breath as her second blow caught him in the side of the throat and John's head sprang from his neck. *Thank God,* the Angel thought, *that it's not bleeding.* She dodged around the statue's blindly groping arms, following Ray, whose slide took him against the legs of the third statue. *James*, the Angel christened him.

Ray's hands dragged on the floor, and a smear of blood followed him as glass shards sliced into his palms, but that was the least of his worries. James caught him in his marble hands, and lifted him high. He squeezed, and Ray screamed. *Oh, God!* the Angel thought.

The statue lifted Ray high over his head and the ace spasmed. The Angel thought that Ray was trying to jerk himself away from the giant's crushing grip, but there was no way he could escape from the statue's cruel hands.

But he wasn't, the Angel suddenly realized, trying to pull himself free. He was throwing something. Something clear and sharp that he'd grabbed off the floor as he slid by.

A nine-inch-long, razor-sharp glass shard glimmered in the sun as it flew to its target and buried two-thirds of itself in Alejandro's stomach. The Allumbrado cried out and gripped it, cutting his palms deeply as he tried to pull it out of his gut, and failed. He looked at Ray with a stricken, unbelieving expression. The Angel saw their eyes meet for a moment, and then Alejandro slumped to the ground. The statue, holding Ray above his head like a fond father might playfully hold his infant son, kept leaning back, back, back, until it fell backward against the steps leading into the lobby, shattering into several hundred chunks of rock.

Ray hit the ground behind it, rolled, and came to his feet. He twisted briefly, as if trying to put a sore back back into place, and the Angel could see the crazy grin on his face. "Never send a boy to do a man's job," he said to Dagon and the Witness, who were standing ten feet away, and suddenly, like that, he was on them.

♠

Peaceable Kingdom: The Angels' Bower

JOHN NIGHTHAWK STOOD BEFORE the door to Fortunato's suite. Usher and Magda were pressed against the wall out of sight on one side of the door. Blood and his handler were on the other. He looked at Usher, nodded, and raised his hand to knock when the thunderbolt of revelation struck him.

Danger was in that room. Danger for the entire world. Nighthawk saw fire consume everything. The land was blackened, the oceans boiled away. Even the very air was aflame. And the boy was the center of all, surrounded by flame but not devoured. *Perhaps Contarini was right after all.* Perhaps the boy was the Anti-Christ. The warning in Revelations regarding false prophets ran through his mind along with the images of all-devouring flame. He had to think about this, but now was not the time. His hand wavered, then came down on the door to Fortunato's suite, knocking politely.

After a moment, it opened a crack. A small, neatly dressed man peered out. He cleared his throat. "Yes?" he asked.

"We're here for the boy," Nighthawk said.

"Boy?"

Nighthawk smiled. "John Fortune. There's no sense standing behind the door. We can take it down in an instant, if we have to."

The man seemed to think for a moment, then opened it all the way. "I'm Digger Downs," he said as Nighthawk came in. "Reporter for *Aces!* You're?"

"Anonymous," Nighthawk said as he entered the suite.

Downs started to close the door, but Usher, followed by Magda and then Blood and his handler, pushed by. "Hey—" Downs began, then fell silent when he saw the weapons Usher and Magda carried, and the look on Magda's face. Nighthawk knew that Downs really wanted to say something when he caught sight of Blood, but he kept his mouth shut.

Nighthawk looked around the room. "Where's the boy?" he asked.

"He was here—"

Nighthawk looked Downs in the eye. "It's better you bring the boy out than we go looking for him."

Magda jacked a round into her automatic shotgun for emphasis.

"Hey," Downs said, "if it was up to me—ah, Fortunato."

Nighthawk recognized him as he came out of one of the bedrooms. He was tall, thin, and light-skinned. Energy shimmered the air around him like heat waves in a desert. Blood, who had strange senses of his own, whimpered at the sight of him and cowered behind his handler's legs. *If I drained him,* Nighthawk thought, *I could keep going for another century. At least.*

"You can't have him," Fortunato said flatly. "Unless you go through me."

Magda brought her shotgun up with a cry of pure rage. Fortunato glanced at her, and she froze, literally, in mid-scream, her mouth open, face contorted, shotgun almost leveled.

"Impressive," Nighthawk said. "How many minds can you handle at once?"

Nighthawk nodded at Usher.

"Dad—it's all right." John Fortune came from the same bedroom Fortunato had. He looked a little disheveled, a little frightened, but basically all right. "I don't want anyone else to get hurt because of me. I'll go with them."

Nighthawk smiled at him. "Good boy."

♦

Peaceable Kingdom: The Angels' Bower, Courtyard

RAY KNEW THAT THE only thing that kept him from immediately being blown to shit and back by the Allumbrado gunmen was the fact that they'd blow Witness and Butcher Dagon along with him. He decided to stay nice and close to them.

Ray got in one lick on Dagon before the British ace could transform, an openhanded slap that split his lip and knocked him on his ass. Dagon transformed as he lay on the ground glaring at Ray, but was too wary to attack immediately. He and Witness circled Ray carefully. Out of the corner of his eye Ray could also see the gunmen creeping up and around him, also trying to encircle him. He realized that if they got close enough to aim carefully, he'd be in trouble.

Something the size and general shape of a softball whizzed by and struck one of the gunmen between the shoulder blades, knocking him flat. He didn't get up. Almost immediately another chunk of stone from the shattered statue struck a second gunman in the chest. Instead of rebounding, it stuck there, squishily.

Ray laughed. "Good girl, Angel," he said.

Some of the Allumbrados fired at her, but she crouched low behind some of the bigger statue chunks, then popped up a moment later in another spot and let fly with another stone, taking most of another gunman's head off.

The Witness suddenly turned and ran, heading for the lobby. Angel leaped up. A storm of gunfire knocked her off her feet. She was hit, Ray was sure, at least once.

"Angel!" he shouted.

"I'm okay! I'm going after him!" Ray watched her start to crawl back toward the lobby, carefully keeping to cover.

"Remember, Angel," he called after her. "He's afraid. He's afraid of pain." He looked at Dagon, grinning. "But I'm not."

Dagon's animallike jaw slavered stringlike lengths of drool.

Ray stood still, stretched like a cat, and grinned. He watched Angel slip into the lobby, get to her feet, and run after the Witness, who had vanished up the staircase. He felt something—pride, awe, and lust—rush through his system. He suddenly realized that he was in love.

"Well," he said to Dagon. "Looks like it's just us boys."

Dagon gibbered something unintelligible.

"Let the fun begin," Ray said.

♥

Peaceable Kingdom: The Angels' Bower, Fortunato's Suite

FORTUNATO LOOKED AT THE boy, frowning. John Fortune nodded almost imperceptibly as he went by him. Fortunato opened his mouth as if to speak, but held his peace.

"Let's go," John Fortune said.

Nighthawk looked at him. "You're not glowing," he said.

John Fortune shrugged. "I stopped doing that a while ago."

Nighthawk removed the glove from his left hand, and put his fingers out, almost on John Fortune's face. Fortunato darted into the old man's mind. He almost rebounded in surprise at what he saw there. Ancient power, tempered by wisdom and grace. He realized that Nighthawk meant them no harm.

Nighthawk's hand dropped down and he smiled. "Nice try."

"What?" John Fortune asked, bewildered.

"It's no good, Jerry," Fortunato said. "He knows."

"What?" John Fortune said.

"That you're the bodyguard," Nighthawk said.

Jerry Strauss slumped. "It was worth a shot," he said.

Nighthawk nodded. "I suppose." He put his glove back on his left hand. "Now where's the boy?"

"He's in the bathroom," Fortunato said with sudden hope that somehow Nighthawk, with all his strange powers, might be able to help his son.

Nighthawk looked at his troop. "Wait here," he said. He paused, looking at Magda. "Take her gun away," he told Usher. "I don't want her to come to pissed and armed with an automatic shotgun."

Usher nodded. "You'll be all right?"

Nighthawk looked at Fortunato. Fortunato nodded.

"For now," Nighthawk said.

They headed for the bedroom, the disguised Jerry Strauss following. Fortunato stopped him with a hand on his arm. "Thank you for trying to save my son."

"It didn't work," Jerry said.

"This wasn't the only time you tried. And succeeded."

"It's my job," Jerry said. "But it was always a pleasure, as well."

"This way," Fortunato told Nighthawk, leading the way to the bathroom. The hippie was still with his son. He looked worriedly at Fortunato and the others.

"He's getting hotter, man. I tried to help him, but there's nothing I can do."

Fortunato nodded. Nighthawk stared at John Fortune as he stood naked in the shower stall. His halo was an angry aura, flickering like rays from a tiny sun.

"John, are you okay?" Fortunato asked.

The boy shook his head. "I don't know. I'm hotter. Now I can't touch anything cloth without burning it."

Fortunato swallowed hard.

"We need the Trump," Jerry said. "But there's no damn time."

Nighthawk looked hard at the boy. John Fortune looked back at him. He seemed more puzzled than frightened, but Fortunato knew that he was putting the best face he could on his fear. He suddenly was very proud of his son. Very proud, and very frightened for him.

Nighthawk suddenly seemed to come to a decision. "Yes, there is," he said.

♣

Peaceable Kingdom: The Angels' Bower, Courtyard

THE ANGEL RACED UP the stairs, taking them as quickly as she could. At first that wasn't too quick, as she smarted from the ricocheting slug that had bounced off her back and knocked her down and, she was sure, bruised her badly. But she couldn't let a little thing like that stop her. By the time she reached the third floor she was taking the steps two at a time as she headed for Barnett's office. She was sure that the Witness was after Barnett, and she wanted to head him off before he could harm the Hand.

She was breathing hard when she reached the upper floor, and went through the secret panel in the service corridor that allowed direct access to Barnett's office, bypassing Sally Lou's domain. She burst into Barnett's office, and paused. Barnett was on his knees in front of his desk, praying aloud. There was no Witness.

Barnett fell silent when she came into the room and rose up.

"Angel!" he exclaimed when he realized that it was her and not some form of sudden death. "I knew you would come to me in the time of my need!"

"You're safe," she breathed.

"Of course," he said. "Now that you're here."

She looked around the room. "Where's John Fortune?" she asked. "Fortunato, the others?"

Barnett's eyes looked wild. "Burning in Hell with that demon child, I suppose."

"What?" the Angel asked. She realized that something had gone very wrong.

Barnett came up to her. He was sweating and disheveled. She had never seen him like this before. "I was in error," he said. "I confess my sin to you, before God. The boy is not Christ, but a demon burning with hellfire—"

"What are you saying?" the Angel asked, aghast.

"It's true. Even Fortunato admits that the boy is out of control. That he burns not with the Grace of Our Lord, but with the flames of the Pit. Unless he is stopped he will turn the Earth into an inferno."

"You're crazy," the Angel blurted, and was immediately appalled at the words that had slipped out of her mouth.

"No, no I'm not," Barnett said. "The revelation has come unto me. He is a child of the Pit. You must go to him," he said, suddenly sly, "and slay him." He looked at her, nodding approvingly. He put his arms around her and tried to pull her to him. "Then come to me, and comfort me in my hour of need, for I am in sore need of succor."

"You fucking idiot," the Angel said, shocking herself again, but at least avoiding blasphemy. She pushed him away, and he fell onto the carpet. "I was with him for a long time. There's no evil in him. He may—" Her world took another lurch, but it had been doing a lot of that lately. "*You* may have been wrong. He may not be our Savior. But he's not a demon. That's just stupid."

Barnett looked as if he was in shock. "Foolish woman—"

He never finished his thought. The door to his sanctum's secret entrance suddenly burst open, showering bits and pieces into the room. The Angel threw up an arm to deflect fragments of flying door and blinked when she saw the Witness limp into the office.

He smiled. "My prayers," he said, "have been answered."

The Angel stood silently, staring at him.

"I saw you enter the stairwell," the Witness said, "and decided to follow you. I waited outside the door to hear the revelations of this pathetic fool whom you've wasted your time following. It was good to hear him finally admit his error. To acknowledge that we Allumbrados have been right all along—"

"I say," the Angel said, suddenly utterly sure that she was right, "that you're both wrong. John Fortune is an innocent child, nothing more. Neither savior nor demon."

The Witness laughed contemptuously. "Stupid woman. What do you know? First, I shall beat you senseless to save you for later. Then"—he looked at Barnett, cowering on the carpet—"I will slay this false prophet, this supposed man of God."

"Ambitious," the Angel said. "But deeds, not words, are what count in this world."

"Remember that when I throw you on that desk and make you beg for your life, slut, in the costume of a Devil," the Witness sneered.

The Angel shouted in righteous wrath and sprung like an unforgiving fury at the Witness. He grabbed her, catching her around the waist, but leaving her arms free. That was a mistake. Her first blow cracked his left cheekbone, her second knocked out two teeth. The third smashed his right eye socket, the fourth glanced off his forehead. Already she could feel his grip around her waist slacken.

"Ray was right!" she hissed into his face. "You're a weakling who's afraid of pain. But I'm not!"

She headbutted him, smashing his nose flat, and the Witness groaned and let her go. She dropped to the floor, pivoted on her right foot, spun to gain momentum, and kicked him through the wall. He hit the wall of the corridor beyond, bounced, and fell flat on his face.

♠

New York City: The Jokertown Clinic

HOWEVER THIS ALL WORKED out, Nighthawk decided that he had to try to save the boy, and perhaps the world. "Come with me," he said to the bodyguard.

Jerry looked at Fortunato, who nodded, and then followed Nighthawk back into the suite's living room.

"Blood," Nighthawk said.

Jerry groaned. "Not this again?" he asked.

Nighthawk nodded, then turned to the joker-ace. "You've been to the Jokertown Clinic?" he asked.

"He's been a patient there," his handler confirmed.

Nighthawk took his leash. "Let's go," he said.

"Finn's office," Jerry said helpfully.

Blood turned to the nearest wall, and after a moment a black circle appeared in it. When they passed through Blood's tunnel through space, nausea hit Nighthawk like the mother of all hangovers. Somehow he managed not to throw up as they walked out of the hole in the wall in Finn's office, right before the astonished doctor who was standing behind his desk trying to catch up on some paperwork.

"John Fortune?" Finn asked in an unbelieving voice.

Jerry shook his head. "Nope. Jerry Strauss."

"This is John Nighthawk," Jerry said. "I believe you know Blood."

Finn nodded dazedly. "He's been a patient."

"Thank God for that," Jerry said. "Otherwise he couldn't find his way here so quickly. Listen, Dr. Finn, we're on the clock. We need a dose of the Trump virus. And we need it fast."

Finn nodded. "Of course," he said.

♦

Peaceable Kingdom: The Angels' Bower

FORTUNATO WENT BACK INTO the living room, pacing impatiently, almost unable to bear the thought of what he was about to do to his son. He only had to wait a few minutes. Nighthawk came back through the hole in the wall, leading Blood. He gave him to his handler, and both he and Jerry followed Fortunato back into the bathroom, where the boy was burning so hot that no one could approach him. Jerry put a syringe, already loaded with the Trump, on the side of the tub.

"Okay, John," he said, "you'll have to inject yourself, but that's no big deal. You can do it."

The boy looked at them. Fortunato could read the fear in his eyes. "I know it's scary," he said, "but it's your best hope." *Am I condemning him to a terrible death,* Fortunato thought, *or saving him from one?* He could barely breathe. He couldn't imagine how the boy felt.

"Hey," John Fortune said, his voice cracking only a little, "I've beat worse odds before."

"That's right," Jerry said. "You can do it, kid, I know you can."

John Fortune reached for the syringe. His hand trembled only a little. He took it in his hand, and the glass melted like snowflakes on a griddle. Fortunato felt something like death pass through him as everyone groaned in anger and frustration.

"There's only one thing left," Nighthawk said. He took the glove off his left hand and stepped forward.

♥

Peaceable Kingdom: The Angels' Bower, Courtyard

DAGON GROWLED LIKE A beast. He took a step backward, and was suddenly among the Allumbrados, claws and teeth flashing. Screams etched stricken expressions on the gunmen's faces as the Butcher moved through them.

"Dagon!" Ray shouted.

He must have heard, but he paid Ray no attention. The Allumbrados were dead in moments, all of them, and suddenly Dagon turned back into a naked tubby man.

"What the hell are you doing?" Ray asked.

Dagon smiled. "Turning coats, right?"

"We've got to fight this out," Ray said.

"Do we?" Dagon asked with raised eyebrows. "We tried that once before, and neither of us liked it very much."

"I liked it enough to try it again."

"Ah, but I didn't, dear boy."

"I should kick your ass."

"Don't be a dolt," Dagon chided him. "Don't you have more important fish to fry? You shouldn't even be wasting time talking to me."

Ray ground his teeth in frustration. The bastard was right. "This isn't over between us," Ray flung over his shoulder as he rushed back into the Bower's lobby.

"For now," Dagon said, smiling, "it is."

♣

Peaceable Kingdom: The Angels' Bower

"NO!"

Fortunato stepped in front of Nighthawk, blocking his path to the boy. The old man looked at him with sorrowful eyes.

"You know how dangerous he is," Nighthawk said in a soft voice. "He'll burn hotter and hotter, but he won't die. He'll eat up the world, maybe even ignite the atmosphere. He has to be stopped."

A noise came from John Fortune, a squeak of fear that he couldn't control.

"I know," Fortunato said in equally low tones. "But you can't do it."

"I only have to touch him for a moment—"

"He's too hot already. You'll die before you can touch him. Your flesh will shrivel and burn."

Nighthawk smiled. His eyes crinkled and Fortunato could see something of the true age that was in them. "I've had a long life," he said. "Maybe it was my fate to live it this long so I'd be here today to stop him." He paused and looked at Fortunato pityingly. "It's quite painless, you know."

"You'll throw your life away for nothing. But maybe I can do something," Fortunato said. "Besides. I'm his father."

Nighthawk looked at him steadily for a long moment. Then he nodded.

Fortunato nodded back, then he looked at Jerry Strauss and Mushroom Daddy. "I want to be alone with my son."

"You sure about this?" Jerry asked him.

Fortunato nodded again.

"Good luck, then," Jerry said. He and Nighthawk exchanged glances, and Fortunato was aware of the surprise they felt about being on the same side of this conflict.

"Luck, John," Jerry said.

"Luck, boy," Nighthawk said.

"Thanks," John Fortune said in a small voice that could barely be heard as they went out of the bathroom.

Mushroom Daddy paused on the threshold, turned, and said, "God bless us, every one," and closed the door as he left the room.

Fortunato turned to his son and smiled. "Are you frightened?"

John Fortune nodded. His halo danced like the rays of an agitated sun. "Yes."

"I am too. That was why I went to Japan, you know."

"You were afraid?" John Fortune asked, as if surprised at Fortunato's admission.

"Yeah." Fortunato sighed. "Afraid of losing more pieces of myself. More of the people around me. Afraid of being the most powerful ace in the world, yet in the end being alone."

"You're not alone now."

"Neither are you." He held out his arms. "Come to me, son."

"I'll hurt you."

Fortunato shook his head. "I'm Fortunato. Nothing can stand before me. Not the Astronomer. Not the Swarm. Not even the wild card virus."

John Fortune got out of the bathtub. Fortunato could feel his eyebrows curl and singe as his son stepped closer, but he didn't flinch. There was a nanosecond of horrible pain as they almost touched. Then Fortunato stopped time.

His astral form fled his body, but maintained a thin thread, a tenuous link to draw energy through, for it would take tremendous amounts of energy to implement his plan. Fortunately, size was a meaningless concept on the astral plane. Fortunato went down into his son's body. He propelled his consciousness through his son's bloodstream, flashing like a corpuscle through his veins.

Searching, he found the changes wrought by the virus in John Fortune's brain, nervous system, and all the cells throughout him. Fortunato wasn't an expert, but he knew that it didn't look good. The cells were twisted abnormally, blasted and sickened. *This will be rough,* he thought. The enemy was almost numberless, and he was only one man.

He broke himself into a million fragments and ordered them into battle against John's body. He fought it cell by cell, shifting, rearranging, and cleansing, but never harming. He burned energy at a prodigious rate as he willed John Fortune's cells to repair the damage the wild card virus had done. Thankfully, he didn't have to guide them in the process, to tell them exactly what to do. They knew themselves, wired deep in the mysteries of their DNA, how to correct themselves. He just had to supply them with the energy they needed, and the time. He gave freely of both. He hoped he had enough.

He settled in for the longest, most difficult battle in his life.

♠

Peaceable Kingdom: The Angels' Bower

RAY KNEW WHERE HE would find the Angel. He went to Barnett's headquarters as quickly as he could. The corridor leading to Barnett's office sanctum was empty. Ray rushed into the reception area to see Sally Lou sitting behind her desk and the two Secret Service agents crowded around the door leading into Barnett's office, looking in but afraid to enter.

Ray brushed by them as if they were children, and they didn't even protest. He took in the room with a single glance. Barnett was on his knees, praying loudly. Angel was standing by him with her hands on her hips and a frown on her face. He also noted that a hole had been punched through one of the sanctum's walls. The Witness lay in the corridor beyond. He didn't look too good.

Ray rushed up to Angel. "You had me worried there—" he began.

"Sometimes," Angel said, "you think too much. Kiss me."

He did, with enthusiasm. He could have kept it up for a long time, but he realized that things weren't finished, by any means.

"John Fortune—" he said somewhat breathlessly as he pulled away from her.

She nodded. "He's in Fortunato's suite. There—something's wrong with him," she said with a concerned expression. "His temperature is rising. The Hand—Barnett said that it was out of control."

Ray glanced at Barnett, who was loudly praying for guidance and forgiveness. He nodded. "Let's go."

♦

Peaceable Kingdom: The Angels' Bower

TIME WAS MEANINGLESS ON the astral plane. Fortunato couldn't tell how long he'd been fighting. It seemed like forever. He gave of himself with every single battle with every single recalcitrant cell of his son's body. He knew that he didn't have much left. He needed help, but there was no one to give it. If he'd had a physical body, he'd be exhausted. Even without one, he was still exhausted. That was a sign of the desperate state he was in.

But all throughout a hard life, Fortunato had never given up. Never once. Not even when he'd gone to Japan, he finally realized. It had been a step in his evolution that he'd had to take. A time to rest, reflect, and learn. It had not been a wasted sixteen years if it had enabled him to do this.

♥

Peaceable Kingdom: The Angels' Bower

RAY AND ANGEL BARGED into Fortunato's suite. Inside it looked like the Jokertown Clinic's emergency room on Saturday night, crowded with patients and worried onlookers. Some of them seemed to be members of the other team, Ray realized, but nobody seemed to care, so he didn't.

"John?" Angel asked, staring at a worried-looking figure standing near the doorway to one of the bedrooms.

He shook his head. "No. It's me."

"Creighton," Ray said.

"My name's not Creighton. It's Strauss. Jerry Strauss. I just wanted you to know that."

Ray nodded.

"John's in the bathroom, with Fortunato," Jerry said.

"They've been in there a long time," Mushroom Daddy said.

"What's going on?" Ray asked.

A little old Black man standing next to a big young Black man armed with an automatic weapon said, "He's trying to heal him."

Ray shook his head. Time enough later to sort out who was who. "Well—has someone checked on them lately?"

No one said anything.

"Someone should," Ray said.

Still no one said anything. He looked at Angel, who nodded. He went quietly through the bedroom, Angel at his side. He listened at the closed bathroom door, but heard nothing.

"Should I open it?" he asked quietly.

Angel nodded again.

He hesitated, took her hand, then quickly opened the door. Fortunato was lying on the bathroom floor, his son in his arms. As they watched, John Fortune's golden aura flickered and went out. Ray and Angel stared at each other for a moment, then rushed into the bathroom, vaguely aware of the crowd that had gathered at the door behind them.

Ray gently lifted Fortunato off his son and felt his wrist. He looked at Angel, then at the others crowded around the bathroom door. "There's no pulse," Ray said flatly, as if he could hardly believe it himself. "Fortunato's dead."

"The boy?" Angel asked in a shaky voice.

"He's all right," Fortunato said. He lifted his head and opened his eyes and gripped Ray's arm hard. It was the only thing that prevented the stunned ace from dropping him. "He's all right. Tell Peregrine not to worry. He'll just be a normal boy now. Tell her I took the virus . . . away . . ."

"God," Ray said. "My God. You have no pulse. You're dead."

Fortunato smiled. "That's right," he said, and he kept smiling as his body slumped in Ray's arms.

John Fortune opened his eyes, looked around the room, looked at everybody crowding around the doorway, looked at Fortunato's limp body in Ray's arms. He asked in a quiet voice, "What happened?"

The Angel went to him and put her arms around him. She said nothing, but held him as he cried, until he stopped shaking.

Apocalypse

THE FEDS ARRIVED ON the scene, as usual, half an hour too late. Agents from half a dozen bureaus wandered about the lobby of the Angels' Bower in a daze, watching as EMTs helped the last of the wounded civilians.

Ray and the Angel sat in the lobby's wreckage with John Fortune. The Angel held the boy's hand while he stared numbly into space. Jerry Strauss, who wore his real face, Sascha, back from his fruitless trip to the airport, and Mushroom Daddy stood around them. Barnett was up in his penthouse, praying and refusing to come down. The Witness was still unconscious in the hallway. Magda was still frozen in Fortunato's suite. Ray figured it would be better to leave them up there for now. Couple less things to worry about.

"Man," Ray said. "I don't even want to think about trying to explain all this." He looked at the old Black man who had just joined them, and the young big Black man at his side. "Like where in the hell you fit into it."

"Us?" John Nighthawk said. "We were never here." He and the big guy strolled away.

Jerry looked at Ray expectantly.

"Go ahead, take off," Ray told him. "I'll save a ton of the paperwork for you."

"Thanks a lot," Jerry said sourly, turning to go.

"And Jerry—" Ray added.

"Yeah?"

"It was fun."

Jerry paused. "It was. In an odd sort of hallucinogenic kind of way. Come on," he added to Sascha and Mushroom Daddy.

"I wonder if I can find another van," Daddy said wistfully. "Hey! We could drive back together!"

Digger Downs came by, his tape recorder in his hand. "Hey, guys," he said.

Ray looked at him unenthusiastically. He still hadn't forgiven Downs for once dripping blood on his fighting suit, sixteen years ago. "What do you want?" Ray asked.

"The story," Digger said. "What happened between John Fortune and his father during those last moments?"

"Can't you leave the kid alone?" Ray asked.

"No," John Fortune said quietly. "I'll tell him. I'll tell him about the most powerful ace in the world, and the final gift he gave me."

The Angel nodded. "Your father would want the story to come from you."

Downs had his tape recorder out and was listening with a wide grin—*Visions of a Pulitzer probably dancing in his head,* Ray thought—as Billy Ray and the Angel strolled away.

"Well," Ray said, gesturing at the devastated lobby and the squads of cops and federal agents wandering around it in a daze, "alone at last. Got any plans for this evening?"

The Angel shook her head. "Do you?"

"I was thinking of a good meal, a hot shower, a romp in the sack, and then about twenty hours of sleep. How's that sound?"

"Billy—" She stopped, started again. "I've got a lot of thinking to do."

"We can always find some time for that. I guess."

"Do you really believe that you and I can make it?"

Ray shrugged. "I don't know. I believe we'd be crazy not to try, though. Besides, I could drink a case of you. Whatever that means."

"You remember our song!"

"Remember it? Hell, I've never even heard it."

The Angel smiled and put her head on his shoulder as they stepped through the debris littering the lobby floor.

"By the way," Ray said. "You look bitchin' in red."

♣

CARDINAL ROMULUS CONTARINI SAT alone in Nighthawk's suite. He jumped when Nighthawk opened the door and came in on silent feet.

"Well?" he asked.

Nighthawk sighed. "Well, you were wrong, as usual."

"Wrong?" Contarini said angrily. "I was not wrong! I am righteous in my faith and in my wrath! We will begin again," he said, a cunning look in his eyes. "The diabolists cannot match the might of Mother Church—"

"But you were right about one thing," Nighthawk said thoughtfully as he approached the cardinal. "There is a false prophet in this story." He removed the glove from his left hand. "It was you," he said, reaching for the cowering churchman.

♠

HE HAD BARELY SAID hello, when suddenly it was time to say goodbye. But life, and death, are like that, Fortunato thought. He remembered the last great Zen lesson.

Enlightenment comes to you only when you stop looking for it.

He stood some where, on some thing, the universe open before him.

Death Draws Five Starred:

Billy Ray — created by John Jos. Miller
Fortunato — created by Lewis Shiner
John Nighthawk — created by John Jos. Miller
Jerry "Mr. Nobody" Strauss — created by Bud Simons
The Midnight Angel — created by John Jos. Miller

COSTARRED:

John Fortune — created by Gail Gerstner-Miller
Ellen "Cameo" Allworth — created by Kevin Andrew Murphy
Leo Barnett — created by Arthur Byron Cover
Peregrine — created by Gail Gerstner-Miller
Digger Downs — created by Steve Perrin
Mushroom Daddy — created by John Jos. Miller
The Witness (The Bigger Asshole) — created by John Jos. Miller
Butcher Dagon — created by John Jos. Miller
Cardinal Romulus Contarini — created by John Jos. Miller
Dr. Bradley Finn — created by Melinda Snodgrass

FEATURED:

Jay "Poppinjay" Ackroyd — created by George R. R. Martin
John "The Highwayman" Bruckner — created by George R. R. Martin
Father Squid — created by John Jos. Miller
Daniel "Yeoman" Brennan — created by John Jos. Miller
The Living Gods — created by Gail Gerstner-Miller
Usher, Magda, and Curtis Grubbs — created by John Jos. Miller
The Witness (The Asshole) — created by John Jos. Miller
Alejandro Jesus y Maria C de Baca — created by John Jos. Miller
The Jokka Bruddas — created by John Jos. Miller
Sascha Starfin — created by John Jos. Miller
Blood and Buck — created by John Jos. Miller

WITH:

Josh McCoy — created by Gail Gerstner-Miller
Peter Pann — created by George R. R. Martin
Jennifer "Wraith" Maloy-Brennan — created by John Jos. Miller
Elmo Schaeffer — created by John Jos. Miller

SPECIAL GUEST APPEARANCE:

Cole Porter